Enjoy the book!

Storms

of

Firе

by Joseph Guerrero

BOOK ONE OF THE LIGHT BRIGADE SAGA

www.thelightbrigadesaga.com

Printed in the United States of America
First Printing: July 2014
ISBN-13: 978-0615858852
ISBN-10: 0615858856

TABLE OF CONTENTS

SPECIAL THANKS

The journey to write a book can be a tough one...and a long one. I have been working on and off on this tale for over 20 years. Of course, there is very little interest in the book business for a science fiction series from a novice author. So in the end, I wrote what I wanted to read. This is the story I wanted to tell with no limitations or restrictions. It's as dark, violent and strangely romantic as originally envisioned. Needless to say, the creation of this book challenged the patience of my family and friends. Thanks to my long suffering wife, Becky Lam. Thanks to my test readers: Marc Lopez, Diana Guerrero and Cathy Chan. Special thanks to Clare Bornstein for finally making the book safe for human consumption.

Storms of Fire

PROLOGUE

Boy falls in love with girl. The end of the world has come.

Children should be warned that love is no fairy tale. That love can begin and end lives. Truth is – real princes are cruel. Beautiful princesses are ugly inside. And the wicked witches are admired. As for the brave knights, they fight and die for nothing.

Somehow, people still find hope in this broken world. Even in the absence of light, good still exists; love still grows – hidden.

So with war and death, this story begins…

Storms of Fire

PURE NATION

The vicious sound of bending metal, the sputter of dying engines and vague screams all pierce the usual silence of the night. Against plumes of smoke in the fire-lit sky above Seattle, two titanic ships sit off shore as if suspended on invisible strings.

Slowly rotating around, the air ship, Arlington, focuses its five massive deck guns on its opponent, an enemy frigate. Firing a full broadside, the night is briefly blinded. Already injured and bleeding fumes, the enemy ship bursts with flames and streams down toward a grave at the bottom of the Pacific Ocean in a heap of swirling debris.

The victorious Battleship Arlington slowly rears up on its massive hind engines and pushes skyward out of the battle's polluted lower air, it's short, but wide wings easily cutting through the clouds.

The Arlington is a floating platform of hell fire, a merciless tool. It is the essence of a weapon of war – an object of focused destruction. No weapon though, fierce or deadly as it may be, is anything more than those who control it.

Admiral Samuel Grant knows this well. Under his command, the Arlington has become more than hate set in motion. The ship has taken on the soul of its commander. No matter the nefarious intentions of faraway bureaucrats, Grant reigns over the Arlington as a benign ruler. And with that, the beast has become a guard.

"Helm, steady as she goes," the Admiral orders as he looks over the damaged bridge. A body is laying over one of the stations unattended. No one has had the time to deal with it. "Have all ships in the battle group report in," he commands.

Rising above a thin cloud layer, the ship settles into a slow forward cruise. The massive thruster array under the hull keeps it aloft and straight. From this high vantage point, the war below is reduced to smoldering pots of flame and sudden streaks of red and blue discharges.

As he sits down at the command post, he looks out over the horizon. For all their effort, the battle tonight has not gone well. Losses have been devastating and the city has not been spared any wounds. His superiors have insisted on a bloody course of action to bring the "Pure Nation Rebellion" to a close. And what a rebellion! A bunch of zealot generals pushing their ultra-radical social ideas on the nation, advocating the mass destruction of the entire, supposedly inferior *human* population. Humans and the genetically engineered Nuhu (New Humans) are not that different in his opinion, but his opinion doesn't amount to much. Victory, in the minds of those who do matter, is worth the loss of a limb, be it a human or Nuhu limb. The limb, in this case, is the whole population Seattle.

A tired Admiral Grant reviews the various stations of the "U" shaped bridge and begins to pace around them, checking the condition of his surviving crew.

The bridge of an Air Corps battleship is arranged with the tactical-radar station and helm in the middle along the curve of the front window, with the navigation and communications stations along the right bulk head and the engineering and security posts to the left. His station sits at the center rear of the "U" with the 1st officer's post located at his right. A 3D holographic battle environment generator is directly in front and a flat tactical ground map display is to his left. All stations have views of the main window and the five screens directly above displaying ship status, weapon status, and electronic views of the port, stern, and starboard of the ship.

Having finished off this last remaining rebel frigate, Grant considers his options to bring aid to the broken city. But as calls for help begin to flood in, he realizes the city will long be in recovery no matter his efforts. He finds no solace in the fact that the battle will be considered not only an ample victory, but a great victory. At least, that's how the government will undoubtedly play it.

Reports are coming in non-stop; death is all over the city — hundreds of thousands dead from SAW bomb drops (sonic/acoustic weapons with the destruction ability of 1/10 of a low yield nuclear device), crushing entire neighborhoods. Tomorrow though, the media will proclaim otherwise, conveniently neglecting to show any of the widespread devastation. President Eaves will smile and announce the trouncing of the rebellion. Lies and little lies are the new truth. Such is the operating procedure of this government and this nation, the great North American Union (NAU). But Grant is no liar, he longs for a time when he would no longer take orders from those without honor.

"Sir! Several new targets are emerging from the forest floor," a woman calls out.

Admiral Grant quickly steps up to the tactical station. A young, intense Asian woman, Lieutenant Amy Zhu sits scanning the various object-detection display screens. Her eyes are laser-focused on a grouping of lines and numbers crossing her main, center screen. These masses of algebra-skinned snakes are gliding quickly in the wrong direction. Every so often the screen scrambles, prompting a series of quiet swears under her breath as she tries to identify the intruders. Not giving up, she soon makes a frightful determination.

"Two Harpy fighters and three Bear bombers running heavy," she says in a restrained, but obviously fearful voice. She quickly runs a scan. Amy turns to face the Admiral as her lips quiver, "Scan shows ID positive for a radioactive warhead. They are heading northwest, straight for the refugee centers. It's a suicide mission isn't it, Sir? We can't get those people out in time. Can we?"

The Admiral's mind quickly flashes to his boy, Jordan. Jordan is the closest thing he has to a son, a human orphan he raised. But under the law, Jordan could never be his true son. He is out there, in the battle, somewhere...

"Admiral Grant. Your orders please," Lt. Zhu pleads.

Grant notices that Lt. Zhu is clutching a photograph. He knows she also has family out in the battle, her sister on the Battleship Antietam.

"Check for aviation near-by, anything that can intercept," the Admiral orders. "I don't care if it's a biplane. Put up the revised scenario on the 3D."

"Aye Sir," she says and quickly scrolls through several screens on her side terminal. A distorted projection of the air battle and the involved forces flickers to life in the center of the bridge, nearly indiscernible due to enemy jamming.

Another voice clocks in, shouting over the din, this is the communications officer, Lt. John Colony.

"Light Carrier Alaska reports they're also tracking the nuclear loaded heavy," the man says holding a headset to his ear.

"Lt. Colony. Request the Alaska to respond," the Admiral answers as he looks over the 3D image before him. The Alaska is only a mile from the enemy. His second in command, Captain Wallace, comes over and exams the map as well.

"Alaska took a lot of damage, unlikely they can do anything," Wallace says, typing a command on the 3D control console. The Alaska is highlighted. It is shaped like three sticks holding a big box — the flight deck. It is the smaller of the two carriers in the NAU fleet. The larger one being the heavy carriers with their two separate flight decks.

"Negative. Alaska reports their launch bay is damaged. They are rushing repairs and estimate clearing the tube in 15 minutes." Colony pauses. "Sir, I'm getting new reports of new engagements to the south. Two frigates have turned colors and are engaging the Light Carrier Texas."

In his thoughts, the Admiral knows he has been tricked. In a last ditched effort to seek revenge, the rebels have sent bombers deep into the city while the turncoat frigates pull his forces away.

In seconds, the city will be crushed into rubble by undeterred SAW bombs and a nuclear weapon of unknown yield. How could he have been so blind? These rebels are ideological zealots, mad with murder, not caring what it costs to impose their beliefs.

"Colony, where is the Carrier Grindstone?" the Admiral asks, scanning the limited 3D aerial map. He doesn't see it. "They were making way to join us. Where the hell are they?"

"Long range radar has gone down," Amy advises. "Atmospheric clutter interfering with all our scans. I can't even find our satellite feed."

"That's suspicious. I think we've been compromised," Colony replies looking concerned at the Admiral. "I might be able to tap into one of the Russian positioning satellites."

"Do it," Admiral Grant agrees, suspiciously eyeing a stone faced Captain Jim Wallace.

Colony quickly walks over to the blood covered navigation station and moves over the dead body. He adjusts the nav's controls, illegally taping into the Russian GPS network. Soon the large main screen soon comes to life showing the entire western region. "Got it. They are over Oregon. Still too far to help us. Zhu, sector 2, there is some activity there. Check your instruments again."

"Aye," Amy answers. "Nice work Colony."

"Damn those slow heavy carriers," the Admiral barks at Captain Wallace. "Get someone to take Ensign Loughton's body out of here."

"The lifts are locked," Wallace replies flatly.

"Have them use the damn stairs," Grant growls.

Lt. Zhu, yells excitedly, "Admiral, on tactical, there are two Malone MA-17 Sharkhunters escorting a damaged medical cruiser ten miles from here! Obtaining their status now."

Suddenly flush with hope, Admiral Grant looks over to Colony. "Comm. Get me a hold of those two war birds now."

"Already on it Sir. I have…I have…" Colony stutters and then says with reluctance, "Lt. Commander Grant, sir, on vox."

"Admiral," Lt. Zhu quickly chimes in, "Those two fighters are reading near exhausted ammo and fuel."

The bridge goes silent. All eyes lock on the Admiral. The Admiral ignores this newfound attention and picks up a headset. He is about to order the boy he raised to go on a suicide mission.

"Lt. Commander. This is the Admiral. We have five aircraft preparing to attack the civilian refugee centers with weapons of mass destruction. You…you two are the only ones able to engage."

***

Ten miles away, Lt. Commander Jordan Grant stares at his Heads Up Display (HUD). He is almost out of ammunition and fuel. They must know this. The situation must be utterly desperate for the Admiral to even consider sending them. His cockpit canopy is cracked in several places, already having seen intense combat—even a big bug would crush it, but he remains silent about his ship's condition.

"Admiral, mission understood. Shark 1, Shark 2 responding." Jordan answers.

The two fighters break off from escorting the damaged ship and race across the night landscape barely scraping over treetops in their haste.

***

A secretly furious Admiral Grant watches as seven lines gently come closer together on the 3D tactical imager. The true battle for Seattle is about to begin.

"Sir. I must warn you," Captain Wallace says quietly into his ear, "Two ancient Sharkhunters piloted by humans are no match for trained Nuhu. The Harpy is the finest fighter in the world. We should prepare for the worst. We should evacuate the outlaying Nuhu population away from any nuclear fallout." He dispassionately moves back to his desk, never looking at the "liberal" Admiral. "Perhaps the Pure Nation rebels will have their day after all. They may have done this the wrong way, but nobody up high really disagrees with their beliefs," he says this indifferently, even though the death of thousands, including Nuhu, is imminent. "Genetic superiority is reality. This will be a lesson that humans should have been culled long ago. There never would have been any war to begin with."

With both humans and Nuhu on his ship, Grant looks at his second in command with disgust. The government assigned this fool to his ship and he can't just throw him off into the ocean. He still can sting back.

"Well Wallace," the Admiral announces loudly, "we often disagree. Seattle is full of people of all kinds, none of which deserve to die for the warped dream of a few. If a monkey threw a rock and knocked down those planes, I would promote the damn beast. Lives matter, not genes."

SHARK OF THE SKIES

Jordan begins to sweat. He has seen bad odds before, but always in a fresh, undamaged fighter. Looking over to the side, his rookie wingman Steward "Watcher" Stoneriver is flying erratically.

"Watcher, even out your movement. Keep that thing low and steady," Jordan warns.

"Ghost, I've got a problem," he yells back. "Flight controls are sluggish."

Jordan dips his fighter to exam Watcher's plane. The right wing is vibrating. "Back off thrust and pull away now. You've taken damage to your right wing."

"Negative Ghost, I'm with you."

"Not a request, turn that wreck around," Jordan presses. Watcher slows, but does not break off.

Jordan's own ship is not much healthier. Warning lights slowly blink on about an engine overheat. He overrides them. A solemn whisper repeats in his head, "No turning back this time." Noticing that Watcher is still on his radar, he is about to order him back again when, as the horizon gives way from forest to a sea of city light, alarms blare. They have been targeted.

"Missiles! Two," Watcher yells, "Approaching from the…" he says as his plane, unable to maneuver, bursts into flames.

"Damn rook!" Jordan yells as he pulls his Sharkhunter fast down into the cityscape, narrowly avoiding Watcher's wreckage. He told him to go back. A second missile barely misses and impacts on a building behind him sending debris hurtling earthward. However, Jordan is not concerned with objects behind him. What's that? A light post? He turns aggressively, barely missing the post as the fighter barrels far too close to street level. The amount of air passing under his wings is limited here and their ability to create lift is diminished. He thrusts the engines up to a dangerous level to compensate. It becomes a second by second operation to keep from hitting parked vehicles and other ground level obstacles. One mismatched push of the flight controls and he's going to be gum on the sidewalk.

A Harpy fighter takes sight of his aircraft and recklessly enters the canyon of buildings after him. A huge burst of energy explodes around him as the Harpy fires and misses, hitting a glass building.

Jordan screams with mad intent and pushes the throttle to full. As the engines light up, the plane goes supersonic within the city. The sonic boom shatters the glass faces of skyscrapers as he passes mere inches from them. Glass falls everywhere; a deadly crystalline rain upon an already crumbling city.

Having no choice, Jordan pulls the plane out from the city and turns tightly trying to burn off speed. He is out in the open sky— vulnerable. His heart is racing painfully as he pulls massive G's, blurring his vision. As the forces of gravity pound on him, his mind kicks into overdrive and exerts control over his body. The beat of his heart slows inhumanly, defying the play of the G-force on him. Relaxing, his vision sharpens and he sights the three Bear bombers in the distance.

They are breaking off in different directions, but he is too late to react; one of the Bears drops its first bomb. A huge sonic wave bursts from the ground and several city blocks instantaneously crumble into dirt and rubble. There is no time for grief.

Jordan quickly accesses the situation, looks around and spots the agile Harpy fighters coming around below him. He's got the drop on one and engages with focused rage.

To the enemy pilot's astonishment, her far superior Harpy is struggling to shake the larger, slower Sharkhunter off its back. Jordan is pushing his fighter past the breaking point. The canopy cracks are becoming pronounced, pieces of plastic splinter off into the dark night. Metal screams in revolt as he follows the more nimble plane turn by turn.

Jordan's got a speed advantage; the acidic smell of his enemy's spent ammo overwhelms him as he draws dangerously close to the Harpy. Soon a sound, a good sound rings, Jordan has missile lock. He releases the missile and the first Harpy bursts apart in an orange flower of flame. That's it for missiles though; he is out.

Pressing on, Jordan comes up on the first Bear.

This heavy unmaneuverable behemoth is all armor and bomb racks.

He takes a shot with his cannons and hits, but only small metal flakes come off the Bear's very thick skin. But Jordan is a master of gunnery, undeterred he continues to follow the metal beast relentlessly, always hitting near the same mark. The Bear's skin cannot take it anymore. Finally, a lethal burst of blue energy releases from the Sharkhunter's dual cannons and rips the Bear apart.

No time to relax, his mind burns with a question, "Can't the Admiral send more help?" he wonders. His dual cannon's battery is running on empty. In order to evade the Harpies, he cannot tap his engines larger battery reserve without losing valuable speed. Both Sharkhunters and Harpies have limited power, too small to carry a reactor like capitol ships, they instead depend on rechargeable energy cells. Speed is everything. Speed is keeping him alive. He would give anything for a full energy cell.

Soon Jordan sees the evil glow of the second Harpy on his HUD. He dives back down into the city to hunt it down.

There is a new unpleasant noise in the cabin. Looking over to his right engine, Jordan sees a plume of smoke exiting. Damn thing is overheating. The engine uses the batteries to run small fluid cooled turbines. A small solid fuel block is burned to increase top speed performance. Either the solid fuel is burning or the coolant system is failing, he can't tell. He doesn't need the solid fuel to keep flying. If he shuts the engine down, he slows, handing an advantage over to the Harpy. If he leaves it on and the coolant system fails, it could burn out suddenly. All he needs now is for his left ear to fall off too.

Disengaging the engine, the plane lurches and he hastily adjusts for the lack of power and lift. As the smoke clears behind him, the second Harpy becomes visible. It has swung around. His radar has failed! Jordan lurches his flight stick to one side. His breathing becomes intense as G-forces press him into the seat. Once again, he forces his body to overcome the strain. His vision narrows and just before he blacks out, the plane comes out of the turn. The maneuver has bought him time as the Harpy is forced to fly high and wide. Snap snap. Cracks appear on his wing, Jordan notices. This is not his day. Then again, no day is ever his day.

The second Harpy re-engages and fires. Jordan knows he must push the Sharkhunter harder. This is no longer military flying. This is a flying circus. He talks to himself in his head, "Where's that tunnel?" "This is crazy!" and "Last ditch."

Red bolts fire past him. The Harpy is gaining. Jordan slams the damaged engine back on. A bolt steams by his canopy. A second blast burns a hole through the right wing and it cracks some more. He spins the plane to avoid another blast making the Sharkhunter shudder terribly. The airframe makes sickening, clacking sounds, struggling to hold together. Worse, the damaged engine emits a loud whine. Ahead, he spots the traffic tunnel, but he has to wait a second more. Now is the time. Just before he over flies it, he pushes down hard on the yoke.

The plane sinks. His stomach walks up his throat, but this is no time to throw up. His head fells a little dizzy and his hand wants to slip. He has to fight the desire to sleep. The ground is a blur — just a streak of rushing concrete. On pure instinct, he pulls up. There is a terrible gnashing metal sound as his plane scrapes the ground before bouncing into the tunnel as if someone kicked it in there for a goal.

Struggling to steady the lurching plane, Jordan misses kissing the ceiling of the tunnel by barely a foot and heads again for the barren floor. Except the floor is not barren, several thousand people have taken refuge in the tunnel. There is a huge unilateral scream as the plane barely avoids shaving off a few heads. Fortunately, the Harpy pilot is no fool and did not follow.

With tremendous effort, Jordan stabilizes his flying metal bucket. In the near distance, he sees the tunnel exit coming fast…and the Harpy coming over. Jordan throttles up and bursts from the tunnel. The Harpy's thin armor is no match for the surprise attack. Jordan's precision hits are devastating and the Harpy is soon separated from two of its four wings, sending it spiraling to its death.

The odds are getting better. It is now only two to one. He thinks, "How's the ammo level?" Jordan's heart sinks. How can he drop two Bears with almost no ammo? No choice. Deal with one then the other. He tracks the first Bear.

The ugly bulbous craft is not hard to find. Jordan can see its bombs shinning against the city lights. Pushing hard, the damaged engine makes angry grinding noises. "Just a little longer," Jordan pleads. The plane starts to vibrate hard. "Son of a bit…" he starts to swear when things get worse fast.

The engine expires and parts burst out from it. A hot steel shard hits the canopy, partially collapsing it. Wind rushes in. The flight controls fight back at Jordan, but he regains level flight. The cockpit panel sparks. All his instruments go dark. He loses his electronic targeting. His battery and ammo levels flicker away. But, the Bear is still in front of him.

Eye balling his target, like the aces of old, Jordan lays down a firestorm. It lands randomly on the Bear's back. Soon, he notices a wobbling armor plate on the Bear's right.

Jordan's guns sputter. The ammo is almost exhausted. He knows he only has one last attack with them.

Fighting his own plane, Jordan works to get the perfect line of sight. He remembers the track of the last burst of fire. In his mind, a visualization of the firing path required forms. The two planes form in his imagination. His finger itches about the trigger, but he has to wait for the right alignment. His mind is calculating faster than any computer, moving the imaginary planes as if real life. Suddenly, everything moves as he anticipated. The two planes dance across each other. This is *the* opportunity. He takes a breath, steadies his hand. The last burst of fire is released. A hit! The Bear tumbles into a spin and slams into the surface.

With only one more target, Jordan scans the horizon for the final kill, but what will he kill it with…spit? There must be help coming. He has no way to tell. His communications system is fried. As it stands, the world only consists of him and the final Bear. And then, there it is, the bomber emerges from behind a plume of flame and smoke.

No ammo, no missiles, he is still faster than the lumbering Bear. Speed, that's it. No other choice. He still has one weapon — the body of the plane itself.

Arcing about, he lines up the Sharkhunter behind the Bear. There is unusual shaped bomb on its rack. Jordan's teeth shudder with a terrible realization. The rebels are truly mad. Where they found one, he doesn't know. They had all been destroyed. Jordan prays that the nuclear bomb will not explode on impact.

The Bear takes evasive maneuvers. He'd never ram it this way. They enter a hilly valley. Jordan diverts and shadows the Bear from an adjoining canyon. He would have to guess on its position. His mind flares back on, creating a virtual environment again. He can see the Bear clearly in his head. All Bears have a speed restriction. The way the thing is crawling across the sky, Jordan assumes the pilot is not skilled enough to override his computer. Jordan throttles up, guessing his speed against the Bear's. The Sharkhunter shakes and the wind noise became unbearably. He could, from time to time, see the Bear across the ridgeline, but in the hills the Bear's radar is useless. Each view of his enemy giving him new info, small fragments of data to add to his brain's real-time simulation, all helping him perfect his suicidal attack.

Making final adjustments to his path, he settles for a route and takes a last deep breath. He aims for a break in the ridgeline. A vision of a girl comes into his head — Jennifer.

This is it. The Bear appears as he planned! It is merely inches in front of him. He slams the engines. There is a tremendous crash, a mangling of metal bodies.

Cold. The feel of the air around him is cold. He is tumbling, falling through the sky. There is a hard pull. The ground rises up to meet him. It is rising up awfully slow.

Winded, Jordan looks above him. A torn and partially burned parachute is holding him to this life. On the ridge, the smoldering remains of both the Bear and his Sharkhunter litter the steep slope. The nuke, thankfully, is resting in one piece near the wreckage.

Hitting the ground hard, Jordan is pulled across a road until his chute catches on a light pole. He is exhausted. Unable to remember how he got out of the parachute rigging, he stumbles around in nearly intolerable pain. At the minimum, he busted up a few ribs. Still, he shouldn't be alive at all.

From the look of his surrounding, he figures he has landed in a suburb. There are soldiers sweeping down around him, looking at him in awe. A wall is to his right. He slides down against it. The wall is nice and cool — solid. He passes out.

THE TEMPLE OF SWORDS

High upon the Battleship Arlington's conning tower, the Captain's quarters are tiny, especially when compared to any of the new air carriers, but they didn't have the view.

The expansive sight of both heaven and earth is nothing short of breath taking. How could it not be? His office has floor to ceiling windows on all four sides and fortunately, gale force air conditioning to deal with September's still scorching sun. He looks at his watch. Jordan should be arriving shortly. Several months have now passed since the end of the "Pure Nation" rebellion and life has moved on.

Peach colored clouds float by outside as the afternoon sun casts a golden color upon his worn face, the result of the 30 years in the Air Corp. Now over fifty, he feels tired. The Admiral worries that he does not have the energy for the dark days he fears are ahead.

At 15,000 feet, the clouds are always cotton ball puffy and sadness does not linger long in their midst. Anyways, there is no better time, he thinks, then today for a little bit of family ceremony.

Admiral Grant releases an uneasy breath as he paces around his desk. This is a very proud day for him, but a nervous one as well. He taps a long wooden box situated on his desk.

Thoughts still trouble him; people talk of a prophecy in private. Religious zealots are multiplying across the world. Admiral Grant though, does not believe in such things. Still when he acquired the sword in the box this past summer, the maker made many chilling remarks.

***

Admiral Grant is meandering about the narrow medieval streets of Toledo, Spain looking for a store. Shopping in any form or function is foreign to him, too many years of military provisions. Here the buildings are dense, almost unbroken walls of stone and concrete making the search overwhelming. He is showing a bit of sweat on his forehead as he heads up yet another hilly street.

His friends in the service told him the best place to buy a truly unique sword is the shop of Lopez & Sons...by anyone's definition, the

21

only real *Exitor* masters still in existence. However, he did not expect it to be in the old district. None of the buildings are clearly marked. Plus, he doesn't speak a lick of Spanish. His GPS is useless. According to the satellite, his destination is the middle of the Tagus River. Where is this damn place? Without thinking, the Admiral steps blindly onto the cobblestone roadway.

A frail looking vehicle zooms by nearly taking off the Admiral's nose. Grant yells at the vehicle as its driver simply waves hello. Unnerved, he wipes his brow. It is the middle of July and the streets are simply simmering.

Obviously, this part of Toledo has not implemented magnetic streets. The whizzing of uncontrolled solar powered jalopies is a bit much for his nerves. Unlike the Union with its computer controlled avoidance systems, these lightweight "cars" are purely human managed and a menace.

Finally managing to get across the street, Grant sees a small door attached to a big stone building. A simple wood sign reads, as best as he can tell since it's in Spanish, "Lopez & Sons Exitor Sword Works." This must be the place. Grant enters and is soon overwhelmed by the sight.

Inside the building, a cathedral has been built to house these special weapons. The swords are presented individually upon displays of beautifully carved wood. The swords themselves, which are gently glowing under lights, are the only hard surfaces amongst the curved natural setting. Grant walks slowly from masterwork to masterwork. Some seem to lighten as he approaches...others darken. One sword in particular glitters as he passes, he touches it gently and then it speaks...

"A fine instrument for a novice. Light and agile, but brittle," an ancient white-haired, grey-bearded Spaniard says in clear English, coming out from the shadows. His manner is intense and his movement slow and deliberate as he approaches the old warrior. The Spaniard's eyes are sharp and silver, quickly discerning Grant as a North American. As he stops, he bears his weight upon a gnarled wooden cane. "They say the warrior picks the sword. No. These swords cannot be forced to a master."

The Admiral backs away from the glittering sword, amused at such a marketing ploy. He readies himself for an avalanche of mumbo-jumbo about the "living" metal, but he wants the best for his boy and will do whatever it takes. "I've heard such fanciful stories before," Grant sniffs. "I don't believe in magic or that metal can live."

"So be it," answers the Spaniard with a bored look to him. "Walk around and choose the one you find pretty."

Flustered by the sheer variety of swords, Grant looks around in an awkward, absent manner, unsure about what to choose. He begins to say, "It's a gift for my...um...ward." Son would be a better description, but he is not allowed to officially use such an endorsement. He quickly regrets using the term. "I am getting older, and being a military man, it is time to select someone to carry the honor of my family crest. He will be a knight of the NAU just like I have been. I want him to carry your steel."

The man says barely holding back his disgust, "Your knights are no more than over privileged children."

"He is the *son* of a Nuhu Admiral. He is not a child," the Admiral makes a point not to say the word "ward" again. The government calls Jordan his ward...not him. He looks at the Spaniard bitterly, wanting to speak up and defend himself, but chooses not to do so. The Spaniard's hard feelings are typical of most people outside the influence of the NAU. Truthfully, the NAU has never been a good world citizen.

"Makes no difference," laughs the Spaniard incredulously, folding his scarred hands tightly. "Buy him some pocket knife elsewhere. The Crested used to be the law keepers, now they use their swords to coerce and terrorize." But the Spaniard then stops and reconsiders; he looks at the proud man standing before him. The Admiral is clearly disheartened. Why the Spaniard wonders? What kind of boy could bring a Nuhu Admiral to his shop...a human's shop? "If this boy is not your son why would you honor him so highly...especially you...a Nuhu Admiral? Blood is everything in the NAU."

"My son is a human," Admiral Grant says with reluctance.

"I see. A human sword for a human son!" the Spaniard howls with no hidden malice as he approaches the Admiral. "Such filth of ideas is spreading...damn your genetic ideology."

"And it must end," the Admiral replies having expected the fierce reaction. "How can I say this? I am well aware that none of us are perfect."

Looking at the Admiral's deformed arm, the Spaniard relaxes as his curiosity grows. "This human, you give him the honor of your name? That is not the act of a guardian. That is the act of a proud father."

"I cannot give him my blood, but I can give him my title and all will know my beliefs by the blade he carries. A title that will make him equal under the law," Grant professes proudly. "He will be an example that all people are equal by nature regardless of class. He needs a fine sword, a sword of unquestionable quality. Human or Nuhu, you are the best."

"I now understand why you are here," the Spaniard grins. "A sword given in honor is a bound greater than blood in this room. If that is your true intention, you have indeed come to the right place." The Spaniard circles about the room looking at the swords and then peers back at the Admiral. "You are a military officer of high rank. Is the man to carry your crest a military man like you?"

Answering like a slapped child, Grant mumbles, "Jordan. Yes"

"Jordan Grant? The young hero?" the Spaniard says with spiked interest. His hands tremble and he must put them down against the counter to stop them. "You are Admiral Samuel Grant? I have heard of you too."

"How is that possible?"

"You have fought alongside an *angel of steel*. Haven't you?"

"Angel of steel? I have...many times," Admiral Grant says stunned again. "Though many would not call her an angel."

"True, but I do. I crafted her swords, her mask," the old man confesses and then ponders, "Stories that are told to small children are seldom true but you and I know that monsters do exist. You must also know of certain prophecies of the future."

"She told me many things," Grant begins, "but my son is not the one they fear."

"Prophecies are hard to interpret. Hard to know what is their real purpose and it is good you are not easily influenced," the Spaniard says, apparently deep in his own thoughts. "We all struggle to find that single day when we know what kind of person we truly are...or decide to be. Today is my day," the man says to himself and turns to the Admiral, "So be it. So be it. I will play my part."

24

"You've heard of him?" Admiral Grant responds with some surprise. "My son?"

"One who risked so much for so many will be called to service again...but what service? We are fools of fate except the few who rise above their birth; the few who reach a clarity of purpose." He walks over to a case and pulls out a set of keys. The Spaniard's face takes on an unnatural expression as he asks, "Do you believe in fate, Sir?"

Admiral Grant says with a nervous laugh, "Fate is for people who fear life."

The Spaniard nods in agreement as all the swords in the room go dark. "Be it science or religion, there is truth and lies in both. As for fate, what really is it? In both science and religion there are beliefs in the absolute. Fate is an absolute belief."

"In my service, I have come across many who thought themselves special...chosen," Admiral Grant says with great heartache. "Most soldiers' fate is to die. The luckier few die poor old men." The Admiral looks around at the darkened swords wondering if this is magic or the best sales pitch ever. "Our world is barbaric and unjust. There is no control, only the flawed thinking of the power mad few who impose their will on the many."

"Those who pretend to understand the great steel say that a sword's color reflects the good or evil within a person. We are defined only by our character in a crisis. Your son is great because of his actions. Do not listen to those who would condemn a child for just a name. Quintero and your son have nothing in common."

"You know of Quintero?" the Admiral says, appearing concerned. Is this a man or a mind reader? Or worse, a spy? He knows secrets, deep secrets and this makes him fearful.

"Exitor speaks and it remembers. It is of the very Earth," the Spaniard says coldly. "Rest your concerns. I pick no sides for I know fear, but I do harbor hope. Hope that I can push the balance."

The Admiral remains silent.

"Come with me. Let us see what is stronger, the love of a father or the pull of fate," the Spaniard laughs greatly and puts his arm around Grant. He pulls him toward a giant metal door and opens it with a key. "These trinkets out here will not do."

Admiral Grant looks stunned as the swords on display cost thousands of dollars. The sword smith had just called his own, rather expensive, swords "trinkets." What on earth is he going to show him? The Crown Jewels of England?

They both exit the wooden chamber and enter into a tunnel. As the tunnel opens to a large expanse, Grant is floored by what he sees. It is a factory the likes he has never seen…more a medieval fever dream. Visibly hot, smoke and dirt rise up into the air and then carried away by huge ceiling vents. Abnormally giant workers, wearing jointed metal suits, tend to their craft in hives of fire and molten steel. The large earthen pits seem raw wounds in the red dust floor of the workshop. In fact, the whole factory glows a gentle red.

Moving in careful harmony, the workers move glowing vats of molten Exitor to various molds. Others endlessly pounded metal shafts into their respective shapes. Grant notice the workers wear huge metal masks with a single, red darkened glass eye slot. They appear to him as relatives of the mythical Cyclops.

All movement stops and the workers stare in a single gaze as the old man leads Grant to a plot of land that resembles a graveyard. Several large chests are bolted to the ground here with large heavy chains.

"What do you have in those chests?" Grant inquires, somewhat overwhelmed.

"Exitor swords are not a new invention as some would have you believe. Some are old and have histories of their own, lives of their own. My father used to call these 'the Ancients.' I will tell them of your son."

Grant begins to feel very odd in this environment. The old man wants to *talk* to the swords. For a second, he thinks about bailing out. Something deep inside him, a feeling he cannot quite explain, implores him to stay. Always a curious man, he settles down and decides to let things play out.

The Spaniard walks over to the graveyard of swords and sits on a small wooden stool. He cannot be heard as he describes something to the boxes. His hands move in motions as if describing a plane. Suddenly, two boxes become brighter than the others. The old man turns to Grant.

"Come here," the Spaniard commands the Admiral.

Grant approaches, a little put back about being given an order.

"Interesting that it would be these two, each with opposite histories," the Spaniard says never looking up at the Admiral. The old man then laughs and gazes up with one eye, "One is a symbol of hope and laughs at fate. The other is fate itself and serves only butchers."

"How do I tell the difference?"

"I have never seen two swords summoned. It has always been…pre-ordained," he says. The Spaniard looks at one box with distaste. "I am servant of God and I know my place. I make the tools as I am instructed. The wind is not evil or good. It can cool your face or destroy your home. You alone must choose."

The Admiral takes a hard look at the old man. The Spaniard is near tears.

The old man warbles. "Kindness can make a weapon something more that it was ever meant to be." The Spaniard waves the Admiral to come closer to the boxes.

Grant's hand hovers. A feeling of dread fills him.

"My father just ordered mine from a catalog," Grant laughs nervously. "Not that I could use it anyways with this clipped arm." He notices that the whole of the factory has walked over and is watching them. "Why are they so curious?" he asks.

"My people are not curious," the Spaniard says and smiles, "They have faith. Day after day they work the gifts of the earth out from the ground. They have faith the world is good."

But Grant is not really listening anymore, he has become interested in the beautifully decorated boxes before him — they seem to call out to him. Made from marble, no expense has been spared housing one weapon. It has gold symbols all over. The other is a sturdy wooden box of oak with silver lines. Though he is strongly drawn to the beautiful gold one, he hesitates. Thinking about Jordan, he looks over to the plain box with the lack of gilding on it. It reminds of him of his son, strong and understated. The other box fades back to darkness. Grant backs away as the old man approaches the simple, but beautiful oak box.

"Why this one Admiral Grant?" the Spaniard asks. "I guarantee you the other is far more beautiful, an unmatched creation; intricate and etched by the finest artisans, truly the sword of an emperor."

"That is not the sword for my son," Grant says softly. "If I have chosen poorly, I am sorry."

The Spaniard quickly grabs the Admiral's hand and breathes deeply, "These times are dark." The Spaniard is trembling with joy. "Long has this sword sat unwanted. Now comes the time of change."

There is a relaxed murmur from the workers as factory returns to life. It is as if they feared the opening of the dark box.

Drawing the keys again from his coat, the Spaniard opens the locked case. There is a splendid tapestry inside which he moves to reveal a slender silver sword of unquestionable beauty. The slightest ray of light hitting the sword makes it shimmer brighter than any cut diamond. "I present to you Novo. Though, it has had many names. This is the true weapon of a knight."

Overwhelmed, Grant stares at it amazed. "It's magnificent. But I cannot afford such a thing."

The old man smiles widely, "The sword is priceless. I cannot sell it. I can only give it to you. But acceptance bears consequence, this item has a life of its own. It has an agenda."

Grant looks shocked, still amazed by the stunning sword. "A gift?" he says.

Taking the sword in his hands, the old man walks over to a wall with beautifully carved wooden boxes. He places the sword in one. "Generation after generation, as so many in the past, want nothing more than wealth and power. But some are different, they dream of home and family. Tell your son this is not the sword of a warrior. It is not a sword at all. One day he will understand." The Spaniard hands the smaller box to Grant.

The Spaniard turns and faces the dark box again. It has mysteriously opened and the sword vanished. His face becomes nervous and concerned. "Two swords; one light, one dark. Never have these two faced each other. If one is destroyed, there will only be light or darkness. Today, I have started the end of the world."

THE CREST

A chime sounds and the Admiral awakes from his memory.

His son walks in and salutes, crossing both his arms across his chest. The Admiral stands and returns the salute. Jordan's khaki colored fatigues are in sharp contrast to the Admiral's stately blue uniform.

"Lt. Commander where in hell have you been?" the Admiral inquires. The standard Air Corp ship uniform is a light blue shirt with black pants.

"Baking," Jordan says sternly.

The formal demeanor is soon dropped and the two men embrace warmly.

"Jordan. You feeling better?" asks Admiral Grant with sincere concern. He leans against the front of his desk. "I heard your injuries are taking some time to heal."

"These broken ribs are slow to mend, but I don't really need to breathe," Jordan jokes, but he is as fit as ever. He notices a big wooden box on the desk, but decides not to mention the white elephant in the room.

"Your military service, hard for me to believe, is finally coming to a close." The Admiral's smile mimics a cat as he presents the young man with a letter.

"This could cut either way," Jordan says looking a bit worried. "I've been in a holding pattern this whole summer. They sent me to the Academy in New Mexico to train rookies."

"I've heard you're a natural instructor, but I think I have a better place for you."

Taking the letter, Jordan is puzzled by his guardian's bemused answer. So he does as any other battle harden soldier would do, Jordan raises his eyebrows in total confusion.

"Your application to Pacific Technical University has been accepted. You are to be given an early release so that you can begin with the fall session," the old man grins. "That is your letter of acceptance."

Delighted, Jordan paces around the office hoping not to bounce off the walls. He finally cracks a smile, "Finally something goes my way."

"It's amazing what saving a few hundred thousand Nuhu civilians can do, suddenly impossible things become possible. Yet it will remain up to you to make grades and stay there. Many will want to see you fail."

"They can curse me all they want. It hasn't stopped me all these years," Jordan says with the confidence of someone has broken the odds over and over. With a bit of shaky hand, he folds the letter and tucks it into his pocket.

The Admiral smiles, "You do remember Jennifer?" The old man then sniffs, "I would like to say your sister, but..."

"Why would I remember her?" Jordan interrupts, looking immediately glum. Jennifer and he have a long, long history.

"She's been at Pac-Tech for years and I fear you are closer to graduation than she is at this point. After what happened with her mandatory service, I hope this will end better."

Rubbing his eyebrow, Jordan recalls, "Well. She got herself *out* of mandatory service."

"It is very embarrassing when your own daughter is dishonorably discharged," the Admiral begrudgingly admits, his voice hinting at long hidden anger.

"At least she didn't cut the General's leg entirely off," Jordan sighs. "I mean...she was a *medic* of all things."

"I think she meant to cut it off," the Admiral says, now a bit flush in the face. He wishes to have spent more time with her, but his life has never been free of complications.

"They let her off easy at least," Jordan points out well aware of the double standard of military punishments. "Some of us are just born lucky." By some, he means Nuhu.

In a sudden shift, Admiral Grant grows more introspective. "Jordan. Supposedly, I am a superior being. You know I have never treated you any differently."

Without trying, Jordan inadvertently stares at the man's deformed arm. He knows the Admiral did not come by his rank and position easily. The man once known as "One Shot Grant" is now the most feared commander in the fleet.

"You have many gifts, but most valuable is that mind of yours — logical and cunning," the Admiral continues. "But be careful of such skills. I was never able to call you son, but I was able to give you my name…and my beliefs. Don't disappoint me as well."

"I won't Sir."

"You have made me very proud these last ten years. You came up through ranks by your actions and not because of my connections. Not once did you ask me for help. You have done better than any son could have. Therefore, as an officer and gentleman of the North American Union, and as your trustee and guardian, I place upon you the responsibility of my family name and our honor. This sword represents the crest of the family Grant." He taps on the box. "You now have the responsibility of caring for the citizenry of the land and upholding the values of the nation. Of course, it is only honorary and complete bullshit," the Admiral says with a smile before becoming a bit misty, "You are the first and only human to be allowed the honor of becoming an Officer of the State. After your duty to this country, the genetics committee could not decline my request to pass my title onto you." Admiral Grant opens the box and reveals the magnificent sword and its matching silver scabbard.

A twice stunned Jordan gently lets his hand hover over it and sparkles. "A Spanish blade," he says with the studied eye of a good student. "This is no toy. It's lethal in its simplicity." The silvery sword suddenly pulses warmly as Jordan's hand comes closer. "I think it likes me." He picks it up and the sword literally glows. It is beautiful, light, and feels perfectly balanced in his hand, but also solid and wickedly sharp. Unlike any sword he has ever seen before, the sword and scabbard form a single, seamless piece when joined, though this makes it look like a big metal stick. Who designed such an ugly scabbard for such a beautiful sword?

As he pulls the sword back out, two hand guards extend out from the handle and lock into place. That's very different and the mechanics of it are invisible to the eye. There is an engraved circle with an "N" on the outside of the scabbard. The Admiral picks up on his odd quizzical look.

"The letter is for Novo. Apparently the Spanish like to name their finest swords. It's an antique. As you know, Exitor is black like the rock it comes from," the Admiral says. "I've never seen one this bright, even more so than your Master Kenji's."

31

Mesmerized, Jordan peers at the sword. Its mirrored finish reflects the world around it, especially his face. "Master Kenji often talked about swords like this as if they were ghosts from another time."

"Don't put to much thought into superstitions. I'd be more concerned about the reactions of your fellow Officers of the State," the Admiral warns.

"Not going to think about them either," Jordan gripes. "Who is the maker?"

"Lopez...one of his last before he died."

"Lopez? That made waves throughout the martial art guilds and schools," Jordan relays as he examines the sword even closer. "There are no burr marks on this sword. The finish is remarkable, impossible. How much did you pay for this? Did you put up the Arlington as a down payment?"

"Truth is Lopez gave it to you."

Jordan says nothing, instead intrigued why a stranger would give him such a thing.

"Some nonsense about fate and choice."

Intrigued by the blade more than his father's story, Jordan continues his study of the sword in a ray of daylight. He grabs a piece of paper from the Admiral's desk and tosses it into the air. It slowly floats down over the blade and is immediately cut with no effort. "I'm going to poke my eye out with this thing," Jordan jokes in an effort to suppress his amazement.

"The Exitor won't let you get hurt. It knows its master...so they say, but I have never tested the theory," the Admiral says tapping the metal wall. "I like things that are solid and unquestionable. Putting my hand across a sharp blade, not going to happen."

"You never once practiced. Did you sir?"

"Frankly, I don't even know where the damn thing is."

"Math and science are mostly reliable, but not always," Jordan states glumly as if talking from experience.

"I'm sure your friend Mark Whatley would disagree."

Jordan chuckles, "I'm sure he would and that's his right, but not everything can be explained, that's my feeling. I might be good at rationalizing things, but..."

"That day, long ago, in the canyon," the Admiral mentions, "Forget it. There was no angel, no voice. You survived because you did not give up."

"There are things that happened that day I cannot explain," Jordan remembers. He then passes the sword over the cusp of his hand.

"Stop!" the Admiral warns with sudden fatherly alarm.

Opening his hand, it is clearly free of blood or injury. There is a pained silence between the men.

"How did you do that?" the Admiral asks, not believing what he sees.

"A better question is how does the sword know not to hurt me?" Jordan remarks as the Admiral shakes his head.

"Let's put aside the hocus pocus," Admiral Grant says, "I want you to be aware that you are heading into a war zone. Pac-Tech is a divided school."

"I'll deal with it."

"Listen son, when a group of Nuhu supremacists like the Pure nation, who wanted to overthrow the government to impose absolute genetic rule, gain so much support, I worry. Discontent is growing out there, on both sides."

"Are you trying to scare me Admiral?" Jordan says with a wry smile. "I know my place in society. I'll work the system as I always have."

"That is not the kind of loyalty I expect from you," the Admiral says gravely. "Be loyal to all the people. That is your true duty."

"True duty?" Jordan repeats. "A soldier serves a nation."

"Nations fall but the people last. But when nations fall, the people suffer. Who will protect them then?"

"Sir, what exactly are you getting me ready for?" Jordan questions as this family meeting turns into a briefing.

The Admiral hesitates. He thinks about his own wife, a now radicalized Nuhu, but she wasn't always. With a hint of resentment, he says in a cold, hard manner, "There is something about the Pure Nation Rebellion that was not right. Something sinister."

"I'll keep an open mind then," Jordan responds.

"When you see Jennifer again, remember that in the extreme. She has always been a selfish little girl. Don't be fooled into following her on some wild quest…again."

"She is a good person," the young Grant says with a smile, "I know that much. Deep inside, there is good in her."

"Trust me son," the Admiral sighs and looks distant, "people change all the time, not the way we expect, and never the way we want. You and I, we are like oak trees, bent by time, but still unchanged, still standing in the wind."

He and Admiral Grant firmly shake hands. Glancing into the older man's eyes, Jordan sees his own reflection looking back at him.

***

Outside the captain's quarters, Jordan looks out over the clouds as Lt. John Colony comes around the corner. He is a tall man with broad shoulders and even a broader smile. His tightly cropped blonde hair is bristling under his cap.

"Hey Ghost!" Colony laughs broadly. "Good job you did in SeaTac. All those beautiful Seattle ladies were asking for you, especially the Nuhu ones."

"Don't let Wallace hear you," Jordan says. "He doesn't approve of mingling of the species."

"Fuck him, the Admiral has that snake under a microscope," Colony mentions. "Interesting that our radar systems starting going nuts at the most inconvenient time."

Jordan nods in agreement, but looks around cautiously none-the-less. You never know when a secret police officer might be listening.

"Word is Wallace is getting a new commission," Colony says, "that old tugboat, the heavy carrier Grindstone world's ugliest flying X."

"A fleet carrier?" Jordan says with some surprise. "Those dual bay carriers may be tin cans, but they are the future."

"Hunks of junk."

"Funny you should say that, I was assigned to the Carrier Anvil once, could never sleep. The hull was paper thin."

"This reeks of a government of appointment," Colony says and looks around for any bystanders. "I think this whole rebellion was a fraud. Our hands were tied since day one on how to handle those guys. Hell, we were all the way up by the Aleutian Islands when the battle started. Yet the Grindstone couldn't find its way from Oregon?"

"Cool it John," Jordan says quietly.

"We can't hide our feelings forever," Colony states loudly with a sly smile. "Wouldn't that be something to fight for...free speech?"

"My fighting days are over."

"The world is always spinning," Colony says with a wink. "Your old man is recommending me for the 1st officer post on that next gen battleship, the Shiloh, Admiral Kline's new ship."

"Might be the last of her kind," Jordan points out.

"Never," Colony says with a frown.

"Here's hoping," Jordan says with sincerity.

Colony and Jordan exchange a salute before Colony leaves for his meeting.

A sullen Jordan moves over toward a window and studies his new gift...the sword Novo. It reflects the sky on its shiny skin. Though Admiral meant only the highest praise by giving him his crest, this is going to make him a target of much anger and distrust. Something he can handle, but rather not.

He feels a cold sensation on the back of his neck. The same dark feeling he has before every battle. Shrugging it off, he looks out across the sky. It's beautiful and calm. Maybe, the future is not as dark as the Admiral fears.

All his life, he has only wanted to blend into the crowd. Now like his new sword, he will stand out...something shiny and out of place amongst the clouds.

ONCE AND FUTURE

Gazing out of a six-foot circular portal, Jordan yawns as he wakes up. The Pacific Ocean is zooming by below at a brisk pace and it has a lulling effect.

He leans back on his chair and stretches. This glittery white civilian liner is not remotely similar to the gunmetal surrounds of a military ship, not at all. He particularly likes the big comfy "strattocruzer-seat" he is currently occupying. The seat is the size of small car, a small very cozy, soft car. Hopefully, no one will take offense to a dirty human sitting on it. Then again, he didn't look the part, especially with his new sword resting in the empty chair next to him. Officers of the State have the right to carry their "honor" weapons at all time. They also have the right to duel whoever offends them. This has the bonus effect of keeping the riff raff away and adjacent seats unoccupied.

There is a slight shudder along the floor as the liner moves down to a lower altitude and encounters some choppy air. A few passengers yelp, uncomfortable with the sudden change, but Jordan doesn't flinch.

People should expect as much from a flying box, The Smartfort TR-800 liner forces most of the passengers to sit in the middle of the plane for a reason. With supersonic cruising speeds to worry about, the designers went for safety and hid the outside as much as possible, because a TR-800 cannot glide without power. Much like most of today's large craft, the 800 is dependent on a vertical thruster array for low altitude flight. Lose power…it drops. Fortunately, it has four engines plus the array. The array, just like it sounds, is made up of hundreds of thrust points and not all need to work for it to function safely.

Jordan, looking back outside, sees a large fog bank coming up around them. They must be nearing San Francisco and its ubiquitous eternal grey blanket, guaranteed both morning and evening.

The Western Capitol soon peers out from behind the grey. The out dated Golden Gate Bridge still guards the bay. There has been lots of talk lately of tearing it down and replacing it with a wider, more modern structure. People of the NAU have no love of the old.

Personally though, Jordan is always glad to see it every time he comes home. The past, after all, shouldn't be forgotten. It reminds you about whom you are.

The liner slows and Jordan feels a subtle bump as the vertical thrusters kick in for the descent in. This makes for a fanciful moment as the gleaming white and glass towers of the city slowly rise around them as if fingers of a closing hand.

Of the modern cities, San Francisco is still the jewel of them all, a beautiful mix of architecture from a century ago with the new majestic, monolithic structures of modern day.

The main transportation hub is now coming into view as the transport curves around the Marina district and then beelines for the old Presidio grounds. A circular structure with a beehive's worth of activity is the main attraction. Vessels of all sizes are darting in and out from its many open levels. From here, Jordan will transfer to a tiny Sky Skiff and take a ten-minute flight across the bay to Pac-Tech in Marin County. The University sits in the shadow of the redwood-covered giant, Mount Tamalpais.

As the liner circles awaiting landing pad clearance, he catches a glimpse of the conical mountain in the distance.

Admiral Grant's home is very near the school in Mill Valley, walking distance actually. Although he dreads staying there again, Jordan has little spare money and that's a big motivator to save on costs, savings that could go toward his own apartment. Plus as a human, he would not have an easy time finding a job.

The dread has a name. The Admiral's wife, Samantha, is an ardent Nuhu supremacist and a vocal supporter of the limitation of human rights. She made life miserable for him during his childhood and there is no reason to expect better treatment now.

Though never overtly hostile toward him, she has always been cold and indifferent. The Admiral figures, and probably correctly so, that radical elements will not dare go after him with her on the property. In an odd way, she provides him with a shield.

Jordan frowns as he remembers the pleasure it gave her to stick him in the pool house when he grew old enough.

On the other hand, the pool house suits him. Not only does it separate him from Samantha Grant, it also keeps him far enough away from someone far more insidious and dangerous; the nefarious Jennifer…blonde perfect Jennifer, who lead him down one too many dangerous trails, quite literally too.

Finally soft-touching on its assigned pad on the second floor, the liner opens up its entire front end to provide every row an easy exit.

The day is a bit chilly, as most days are in the Bay Area, with cold winds blowing from the ocean and around the landing pad. He pulls on his thick, dark blue, military coat, and fastens it tightly.

Once passing the security checkpoint and picking up his duffel, he makes his way up to the highest level of the Hub. Here rows of Sky Skiffs wait to take passengers to all places near and close.

The robotic attendant, riding a rail on the ground, escorts Jordan to a four seat Skiff headed across the bay. Entering, he immediately notices the sparse, rickety design compared to the large, comfy Starfort. He hopes the robotic pilot isn't as flimsy as the skiff itself. After all, the robotics industry has never been able to get these things to think. They can only followed pre-defined routes that are supposedly "secure." Jordan prays that they won't run into a stray flock of seagulls. With no other passenger, the door locks by itself and the skiff gently rises into the sky. Concerned, Jordan gulps as several birds fly by a little too closely.

The flight across the bay is short and mostly free of any frights, except for some modest bobbing over the city of Tiburon. Slowing down with a lurch, the skiff follows Blithedale Avenue into Mill Valley. Safely arriving at Pac-Tech, Jordan feels a little worn out. He rubs his weary eyes as he looks around the school's Trans-Hub. People are arriving for the new session in droves. They all look like they know what they are doing, unlike him. He has to find the school's registration office and turn in his financial voucher by the end of the day or else face losing his government funding. He dares not to ask any other of these stuck-up students for help. They might think he is a valet.

Deserving or not, the school is populated by upper class kids who only want a prestigious college on their resume. If a family has enough cash, they magically meet the schools tough entrance requirements. Not very fair, but that's the way it is.

With a little work, Jordan finds an old school interactive map on a kiosk since his wireless devices are unfortunately not working. The map goes on and on. Pacific Technical University is a huge complex, an overreaching array of low-rise buildings spread out over a large wooded area. These organically styled buildings emerge out from groves or hillsides; a very stunning effect. Some of the bigger buildings actually go deep underground to hide their true sizes. After scrolling around a time, he finds the location of admissions just as he hears a cacophony of yelling voices behind him.

Walking around a large arching steel and glass building, named Diana Hall, he sees the cause of the commotion. A demonstration is raging in the middle of a large grassy expanse down below him, known simply as the Quad. The brouhaha has something to do with human and Nuhu unity. Jordan chuckles at hopelessness of that cause, but it does explain the wireless disruption. Each University has a security detail of secret police called "regents." The regents limit communications at the drop of hat usually any time there are activities they don't want broadcast around the globe.

Not remotely interested in getting involved any protests, Jordan bypasses the Quad and heads toward a set of five buildings on a hill. There is a shuttle, but that isn't Jordan's style. He decides to walk by taking an impressive glass enclosed stairway.

Jordan soon exits into the ornate, colonnaded Union Courtyard, which is surrounded by the three frumpy, original buildings of the University built sometime in thirties. A large monument dominates the court here with a tall flagpole at the center. To his left, he finally finds the Administration building. It has a sign across the entrance, which reads, "Welcome Class of 2004!"

The regal looking lobby of black marble is off putting to him as he enters. A robotic attendant, built into a wall, speaks up.

"Greetings comrade, where may I direct you?"

"Financial Aid," Jordan replies.

"Present your See-Glass for info transfer," the robot states coldly.

Fishing through his things, Jordan pulls out a small glass-looking panel about the size of a sheet of paper. The transparent panel lights up briefly as it receives the data from the bot.

Using its delicate looking arm, the robot then points him toward the right direction. Jordan navigates the labyrinth of a building with disgusted dismay. Every now and then, he the pulls the See-Glass up to eye level and a superimposition of a digital map appears over the hallway showing him where to go. After avoiding a few other similarly bewildered students, he finds the right office. There is no line and Jordan goes directly to an open window.

"Hello Sir," a pretty, vaguely Latin, brunette lady answers. She is obviously a Nuhu. Coming from the same general mold, they all have the same cookie-cutter good looks, albeit a bit skewed between models. Never too fat or too skinny, they have the same general body shape as if the original genetic planners took their inspiration from fashion dolls. Bored to death, she doesn't bother looking at him.

Jordan remembers an ex-girlfriend who worked at a Nuhu clinic. She showed him the ropes of ordering a baby. A new mommy and daddy could pick the hair, skin and eye color of their choice, regardless of ethnicity. The better technicians could predict the appearance of the baby by adulthood by about eighty-percent. Understandably, most parents wanted their children to look like them in some way, plus the law required at certain degree of genetic traceability. After all, the government wants to be able to tell who is who…and who is responsible for who.

This particular Nuhu woman is staring blankly into a glass panel and toying with an empty coffee cup. "What can I do for you?" she sighs as she taps on the screen bringing up a password prompt.

"I have to turn in this voucher for my tuition," Jordan says and hands her his papers as she finally looks up. With a sigh, she proceeds to pick up his forms. She passes a wand over them and they appear on her screen instantly. "Grant. That's a good family name, especially in these parts. Any relation to the Admiral and Samantha Grant?" she says with some interest now. She measures him up and smiles coyly.

"Maybe," Jordan smirks, noticing her peaking attention.

"You're obviously military," she states and begins to bite the tip of a stylus.

"It's the haircut? Right?"

The woman laughs, "You look handsome actually. Military voucher remember." She finishes validating his papers on her computer. "Here's your receipt. You're fortunate to have a family name that has some clout. You won't be a sad little Nuhu stuck in a human level job."

"Could be worse, you could be in the cafeteria," Jordan jokes as he turns around to leave wanting to avoid any "human" related discussions. With his sword slung across his back, it is hard to miss.

"No way!" the woman says with deep curiosity. "Oh my god, you're crested too?"

"…and potty trained," Jordan replies, trying to tuck the sword behind his head.

She laughs, "You're not a typical prince."

Jordan leans over the desk and says quietly, "In fact, a crest in Europe represented a knighthood, not royalty."

"Here you are royalty. You can do whatever you want and get away with it. Money and power are all corrupting. Isn't that what they say?" the clerk states as she stares at his massive biceps.

"All I have is the stupid sword," he states flatly. "Wouldn't need a voucher otherwise."

"Hey," the woman then says hopefully. "My friends and I are meeting up at the Student Union later," she offers with a big smile. "I'll buy you an espresso and you can tell me about the war."

"I need to settle in first. Thanks though," Jordan answers with all the politeness he can muster. As soon as she finds out he's a dog, she'll be the one barking. Then again, all Nuhu have the same eyes, different color, but the same glossy, glass look. He'd rather not look at a set of marbles for the rest of his life. Truth is, he really doesn't want to deal with the eventual rejection.

"Well, you know where to find me…here. I'm always here. My name is Carmen," she waves bye, looking disappointed.

Perhaps, Jordan thinks as he leaves, he should have told her he is a natural human and made a case for himself, but he is not in any mood for a debate.

Outside, a group of seven athletic dolts in military formation march out from the near-by humanities building. These yahoos are wearing pseudo-military uniforms, obviously Officers of the State with too much pride and money. Their leader, a tall, buzzed cut blonde man of about twenty-five, stops and looks at Jordan. Jordan immediately tries to walk away, but unclips his sword just in case the shit hits the fan.

"Let me see your credentials," the handsome, blonde man says stepping in front of him. He puts his hand out for the card.

Sizing him up, Jordan mentions, "Those are nifty costumes. Sale somewhere?" Of all the Nuhu models, he really dislikes the blondes, especially having grown up with one. They all seem to think they are beyond reproach.

"Watch your tone, these are Home Front uniforms. We, because of our status, have been allowed to fulfill our mandatory service here in the NAU," the blonde states proudly. "With the rebellion only recently put down, we have to make sure we know who our friends are."

Jordan says, intentionally rude, "I wish I could have spent the last few years playing pretend. How fun."

"Play?" the guy repeats, looking pissed.

Jordan looks pleased.

Blondie speaks up, "I have certain chartered powers. In fact, all of us here are Officers of the State. We need to keep our nation guarded, especially, from an unknown man carrying an Exitor sword. Like I said, with the rebellion just over, we can't be too careful," the Officer states. "I.D. Card...*now*."

"No, I use this thing to shave," Jordan snickers and then reluctantly hands over his identity card, which the man places on a fancy See-Glass with a gold border. With a quick move, Jordan moves hand up, taking hold of his sword holster as if it is bothering him. In fact, this leaves his hand inches from it. "I fought against the rebels. They were never in the Bay Area. I think we're all safe," Jordan informs the group as he notices that these fake soldiers are getting edgy. Some have their hands on their swords. They are all taking their "title" a little too seriously! At least, they don't have guns...or so he hopes. Jordan then asks, "Are you satisfied now?"

The Officer smiles as he reads off his display, "Jordan Grant, an Officer of the State? What's with the games? You are honor bound to protect and enforce the policies of the State and are expected to serve the Nuhu community."

"I'm just here to study," Jordan grumbles, becoming annoyed. He tries to walk away again but the man puts a hand on him. The others partially extend their swords.

"Why are you so reluctant to talk to us?" Blondie asks, beginning to wonder about Jordan's intentions. "Many here in this county want to give humans equal rights. A human would not know what to do with them." He continues in a more hostile tone, "You shouldn't joke about your sword. Swords are our symbol of power…and of our leadership over the inferior. A leadership position that is under threat."

Several people are beginning to take notice of the altercation. They stand at a distance and watch, including a red-haired woman in a gray uniform. No one interferes as no one wants to get in the middle of disagreement between Officers of the State; people with the unwritten right to kill.

A now fuming Jordan stares at the man a long time. The annoying blonde is caring an obnoxious set of dual black Exitor swords, but they are latched down into his leather carrier. He might be a sword master, but he is no soldier. Jordan then says in all seriousness, "I do not alter my morals for the likes of you or any other person." Jordan tries to move again. He gets a firm hand on his chest. "Don't," Jordan warns and locks his eyes on the man.

"A liberal," Blondie says, foolishly flashing a gun tucked in his belt and then threatens, "Liberals are only good dead." He doesn't notice Jordan's hand moving ever so slightly. Blondie then howls, announcing to the whole courtyard, "We are the only real power."

"I disagree." In the blink of an eye, Blondie finds Jordan's sword on his temple. The blonde man moves to counter, but Jordan pushes in closer. The poor Officer of the State begins to tremble as a puddle appears under him. The others circle around Jordan and he yells out so that all can hear, "If any of you move, my sword will see the inside of his head." He then looks at the others with a battle hardened face and orders them, "Back off. Now!" He has a commanding presence and they all move away. "Check your See-Glass carefully again, Blondie. Do it slowly."

The blonde man stumbles back, swallows hard, and checks the record on his card scanner. He stares at the screen in utter disbelief. Several cops arrive, but the red-haired woman waves them off.

"A human Officer of the State? How dare someone give you such an honor," the man says with a blank expression, maybe hoping the screen would magically change. "I will file a protest with the government. This is a disgrace."

"So it is," Jordan growls and pops the card out of the reader. He walks off, never losing eye contact with his new enemies.

The blonde man yells angrily after him, "I demand a duel!"

"Go fuck yourself," Jordan says, turning away and not taking the demand seriously.

"This is not over," Blondie yells and turns back to his friends, "far from over."

Ignoring him, Jordan shakes his head. Maybe it would have been easier to join Blondie's little horde of monkeys and play pretend, but the damage is done. At least, Blondie will have to wash his shorts and that gives Jordan some satisfaction.

***

The estate of Admiral Grant is only a short walk from the University. Old growth trees loom over this neighborhood with their leafy canopies providing eternal shade and their deep roots buckling the sidewalk in places. The little afternoon sun that passes through the leaves creates a false pleasant atmosphere. As he walks on, the sun dips down over the mountains and an orange cast overtakes the landscape.

This neighborhood is made up of many large homes. But from the street, they are practically invisible. Most are hidden behind walls of tall hedgerows. A few of the smaller houses are visible, but they are still set back far from the street, defended by large green expanses of grass.

Alert as always, Jordan notices several cars parked outside the Admiral's house. Samantha Grant is probably having a party — again.

Familiar with avoiding her friends, Jordan ducks in through the bushes, avoids a couple of low lying tree branches and carefully sidesteps several thorny roses to emerge in the garden. There is a large square Olympic-size pool here and a redwood gazebo that could hold a full orchestra. The house itself is a nondescript mansion, as if mansions could be nondescript. It is big, pale white, overinflated and has two massive columns in front. In fact, he could say the same about Samantha.

44

The pool house is right across from the manor and partially hidden amidst a grove of young redwoods. He hopes Samantha has not taken it upon herself to change the access key. Typing in his old code, the door unlatches and Jordan enters his tiny home, only to be greeted by a nasty musty smell. He quickly cranks open a couple of windows.

Taking off his shoes, he notices the floor is ice cold. Oh yes, he forgot. There is no carpet, only tiles and a drain in the center of the floor hinting at the original purpose of the building. Maybe, he should put on a swimsuit.

The pool house is one big room with a low wall that doesn't reach the ceiling. This wall forms an "L" shape. Behind the wall is a restroom for ten. Tucked around the bend of the "L" is a small kitchenette, which is out of place in such an ornate, overgrown toilet. The good thing is that there is always an empty stall, or two.

Greenhouse style floor to ceiling windows make up three of the four walls. These windows can be electronically darkened, thankfully, but Samantha installed an override switch inside the manor so she could put him on display at her whim.

For Samantha, this is the only benefit of having him: bragging rights. She loves any opportunity to give the impression of generosity. Flip a switch and there appears the orphan human boy for all guests to see.

Fortunately in his teen years, he got smart enough to disable it.

Jordan decides not to turn on the lights; there is no reason to announce his presence. Even as the sun goes down, there is ample light filtering in from the brilliantly lit manor.

As he sits down on his old twin bed, he notices a thin layer of dust covering all his old things. This makes him seriously want to rent a room somewhere, but the only place he can afford is in the not so safe Canal District in San Rafael. He could always stay with his buddy, Mark, but it won't be right to room with one of the university's professors. They say home is what you make of it, but this place holds little fond memories for him. He wonders why God gave him no family. This bothers him for a second before he sees a box by the door.

Great, someone has been using his stuff as a doorstop. Jordan moves the box away from the glass door and opens it. There is mishmash of junk inside including a plastic sword stand. He takes the stand and places his new blade on it. It makes for an awkward pairing.

A few shards of glass are littered across the bottom of the box. He carefully pushes the fragments aside and finds a broken picture frame. It is of him as a boy with a smiling woman. She is in her early twenties and has her arm around him. Jordan has to hold back some tears. For a time, Sophia was like a mom to him, now she is just another unwanted memory. He puts the picture back into the box to be discarded later.

A second picture, just a torn up, ratty magazine image of a house by the sea with a family of four standing in front, is also in there, but this gets better treatment. Jordan takes it out and places it on his desk carefully. He looks at it for a few seconds, but his rumbling stomach breaks his thoughts.

Obviously no effort has been made to prepare for his arrival, not that he expected any, though he expects Admiral Grant asked. The room looks like it has been used for storage and only recently cleared out. Dirt imprints of boxes cover the floor in places. Samantha probably made promises to clean the room, but did the minimal. How the Admiral and her ended up together, he'll never understand. The Admiral did say to him once that she was a different person in her youth. People change; she is a prime example of that.

With a sigh, Jordan looks around the room and studies his various fading sketches of planes. Some of them are drawn with child-like simplicity; others are very detailed. There is a big poster of Henry Malone, the first man to make a sustained, powered flight. Henry was also a black man and broke more barriers then just gravity.

His eyes keep wandering until they settle on upon a glass chess set. It is half finished. One day he and the Admiral will finish it.

Something smells. It's a good smell this time: food. Noticing a draped object on his dresser drawer, Jordan walks over and removes a napkin placed over a tray. A small, but nice diner has been left for him.

Plus, there is a note. It reads, "Welcome home you idiot. Why didn't you call! I've been worried sick. I don't know who is worse. You or dad! By the way, Sam is aware of the crest thing. Hide the sword. - Jen."

Even though the staff prepared the dinner, Jordan appreciates the small gesture. When Jen acts like his sister, their relationship is good.

The problem is they are not often brother and sister. Their relationship is more…complicated.

He looks over at the house and sees people in the mansion windows. To his disgust, he notices the blonde moron from the University.

Spinning an old-fashioned world globe, Jordan watches the laughing partiers across the yard. He wonders if Jennifer is in there. The door suddenly slamming open disturbs his thoughts.

"You set off an alert, but I knew it was you." an older, dark blonde woman says. Still very attractive, Samantha stands in the doorway dressed to kill. He hopes he is not the intended target.

"Didn't mean to bother you," Jordan remarks without ever looking at her.

"As a national hero, it doesn't suit you to hide," she says with a crooked smile. "Lots of people want to meet the savior of Seattle, but I won't force you. One question though, where's Jennifer? Where's my daughter?" she inquires, her tone harsh.

"I haven't seen the ape face."

"Hmm," she says almost accusingly. "I *thought* you two were close, but I guess things change."

"Things do."

"My daughter has gotten herself involved in this whole human and Nuhu unity movement at the University," Samantha points out, stepping uncomfortably close to him. "If you care for her, please dissuade her. It could be damaging to her marriage prospects."

"I don't think I can convince her to do anything," Jordan turns away. He begins to eat his dinner.

"Don't you want her to be happy? I think you do," Samantha insists. "You've kept her from disgracing herself from time to time." The Admiral's wife then puts an icy hand on his shoulder. He cringes. "She does listen to you. As you know, Jen has no skills or value except for her beauty. Please try."

"Will do," Jordan says with a blank look in his eyes.

"Oh and give me that sword the Admiral gave you," she says suddenly. "I'm afraid it was a bad idea. The man you threatened today is here and he cannot stop talking about it. Christian is the national

Exitor champion and he could have injured you. The Admiral would have been horrified."

"That man has never seen a real fight," Jordan insists and looks over at the sword stand. He doesn't need a sword to protect him or make him stand out. "It's right next to you. Don't touch the blade. Use a…"

She doesn't listen. But before Jordan can react, she touches it and jolts back. Stunned, Samantha holds out her bitten hand. One of her fingers is bleeding profusely. "I forgot. It's an Exitor sword. I feel dizzy," she says as a stream of blood gaps across her fingers and she sways falling down toward the floor.

"Hold on," Jordan exclaims, catching her. He then rapidly guides her into the bathroom. Samantha looks pale. He disinfects the wound and skillfully wraps it up, stopping the bleeding. "It's nothing. You'll be fine."

"You are used to seeing blood. Aren't you?"

"Often."

"Thank you. Keep the sword," she says, her voice cracking, struggling to be polite. Samantha then leaves immediately.

A tired Jordan closes the door behind her. He then picks up the sword off the floor. "You're a lot of trouble," he says to it.

There is a sparkle of blue light across the metal. He looks closely at the sword. Words flash across the blade:

She deserved it.

Unnerved, Jordan quickly drops it back in its box. "It's been a long day," he groans and closes the lid with a loud thud. He looks across the yard at the party; people are smiling and having fun. There are several couples hugging and kissing. Turning away, he falls onto his bed, refusing to look anymore.

SWORD MASTER

Any school would not be a school if the first day didn't try to break one's spirit. Jordan is late. He fell asleep without setting the alarm and just got up about twenty minutes ago. This is obvious from his uncombed hair and un-tucked shirt.

Messing with his sword every five minutes slows him down as he races toward the university. It bounces awkwardly on his back with every step. Every now and then, it smacks him on the back of the head as if to remind him of its presence.

He seriously thinks about leaving it at home next time, but his first class is Martial Disciplines. This is a class he didn't need to take. However, he knows the sword master well and Jordan doesn't want to offend Master Kenji by not taking one of his classes. Though, offending him by being late is not much better.

Quickly changing into his combat uniform, he joins the class, already deep into warm ups. The combat uniform resembles a mix between a fencing suit and a judo "gi" except they have a polymer blended into the material to protect the wearer from accidental cuts. The itchy things are also stiff and smell of rubbing alcohol.

Sneaking behind the back row students, Jordan begins to follow the lead student, the "Sempai" up front. Fortunately, the Sempai has not noticed him. She quietly takes them through some very standard stretches. His attention waning, Jordan's focus goes over to the sword master, who is seated on a mat. The Master is a quiet looking Japanese man, built like a stone wall, who is watching everything intently. His eyes cross with Jordan's and they exchanged a pleasant nod.

With the initial warm up complete, the Sempai yells out, "Seiza" and the students form into a tight square around the perimeter of the practice mat. They place their swords out before them and sit rigidly and unmoving. Though there are some exquisite Exitor swords, a great many more look like rebar. Needless to say, a great deal of eyes fall upon Jordan's sparkling blade.

Too busy trying to sink into the woodwork; Jordan doesn't notice the Master standing in front of him.

"This is truly a rare sword. You should all take a look. Purest of the pure. Forged by skilled, noble hands for only those with the…." the master stops and turns to a sulking Jordan. "Hello young Mister Grant. Welcome home. I followed your exploits with great enjoyment."

"Thank you Master Kenji."

The Master kneels before Jordan's sword and places his hand over the blade. The blade sparkles brightly. "Onegaishimasu, may I pick up your sword?"

Jordan responds, "Hai Sensei."

"Domo arigato," the Master says as he gingerly picks up the sword. He examines it for a long time as a sorrowful look falls upon him. But then as if seeing something within the blade, he smiles. "Subarashiiyo," Master Kenji says and places the sword back in front of Jordan. "A very talkative soul your sword has, Jordan. Though Exitor blades come in many colors, usually grey, often changing, this one cannot be anything else but silver. It is unique. This sword knows no master. This sword is its own master." He stands up and looks at the class, "Students, an Exitor sword is a dangerous object, not to be taken lightly. Some would say that a gun is better. But can a gun penetrate today's armor? No. There is no metal stronger than Exitor. Isn't that so Jordan Grant?"

"Yes Sensei. That would be true," Jordan agrees. "I've seen swords used in ways that are hard to describe.

"Class. Jordan grew up in this area. He would spy on my practices at home. Later he began to mimic me, a mischievous shadow. So I trained him, he grew a little too confident and how can I say...borrowed my sword. It is a day the local police still remember."

Jordan face turns red, "I didn't think it would cut through those cars like that."

"You were wrong. Were you not? However, Jordan has come a long way from using a sword as a can opener. He is very good. Jordan please stand up at the ready and lead the class in 'oji-waza', the common defense drills."

Jordan stands front and center in the class. He is handed a safety helmet that looks like a mesh of metal wires. A couple of girls are laughing at him. This catches the attention of Master Kenji.

"Jennifer. You are the Sempai, the head student. This is unacceptable behavior." Kenji snaps.

"He's not that good. I'd say he requires a few more lessons, especially in charm."

"Do not dishonor your fellow students," the Master huffs.

But Jennifer just keeps going, "He's not my fellow student. Jordan is a forgetful, ungrateful, uncaring fool."

Jordan winces, "Hey Jen, missed you at the house last night."

"Sempai," the Master says in a commanding voice at Jennifer. "It is your right to call out your fellow students in this class. Do you wish to challenge?"

"I challenge Jordan. *He* can prove he is not a fool."

A flustered Jordan puts down his Exitor sword and heads over to a wall. He reaches for a practice blade made of a graphite composite.

"You still play with toys?" Jennifer says in an insulting tone. "Pick up the real one or sit back down. After all, the Admiral gave you his title. I think that sword belongs to me."

"Jennifer. That is enough. Prepare for your fight," Kenji says annoyed.

Grinding his teeth, Jordan picks up his Exitor sword again. He looks over at Master Kenji for approval. Kenji, who is standing next to him, nods. He slaps Jordan on the back and whispers, "Defend your privates. She is dishonorable when angry."

The students remove their swords from the floor and place them behind themselves. Jennifer picks up her gray, unremarkable Exitor sword and spins it in her hand. She dons a helmet.

"Kakari-geiko...Hajime!" the Master yells and sits down.

Cocky Jennifer pulls her sword up high to the "jodan-no-kamae" position and mocks, "You know I had to buy my own sword Jordan. My parents considered me too irresponsible to own one, but I'm sure my steel is as hard as yours."

Without warning, she charges and swings at his head. He has no time to strap down his own helmet. It goes flying as Jordan hits the deck. Spinning about, he jumps to a stand and brings up his sword in defense. Jennifer is very quick and is already on the attack. The two swords hit hard.

Obviously mad, she pushes him back with a several quick lunges at his gut. Jordan responds well, but is not ready to fight this hard.

Noticing an opportunity, Jordan flips his sword around his back on her attack. Jennifer's sword makes no contact and instead cuts a huge rift in the practice mat. Unbalanced, she over steps and Jordan laughs.

Switching hands, Jordan comes back fast upon her with a strike aimed at her unprotected legs, but she dances away. "Damn she is quick," he thinks. Easily parrying against his secondary attack, she smiles like naughty girl who just got away with something.

Increasing the speed of her blows, the sound of metal-to-metal impacts becomes almost rhythmic. In the background, Jordan can hear Master Kenji describing the fight,

"Exitor fights are different than dueling of the past. Though resembling broadswords, their light weight makes the fighting mechanics similar to traditional fencing, but their greater strength allows for harder blows like in Kendo, the Samurai way."

Just at that moment, Jennifer moves her sword high above the back of her head and slams down on Jordan. He blocks but missteps. Her sword's tip flies by his stomach.

With an eye on the fight, Kenji continues, "These modern swords are not just piercing weapons. They can easily remove a great deal of flesh from an opponent as Jordan almost found out."

Lovely, Jordan thinks. He has had one square meal since he got home and now Jennifer is being praised for trying to remove it. Ok, enough of this. Time to give her a little warning shot across the bow.

Switching tactics, Jordan goes on the attack. He varies his blows to make her movements slower. She is faster than him, but he could always pull a trick or two on her. He pretends to grow tired and misses a contact. Immediately, Jennifer goes for another powerful overhead blow, but he quickly grabs her wrist, holding her sword up high. He then wallops her on the butt with the broadside of his sword. She yelps embarrassingly.

Unfortunately, this move has the wrong effect. A shocked gasp rings up from the class. Jennifer turns and looked at him, seething. She is now in a complete rage, her eyes tearing up, her lips quivering. He knows this face. This is when she losses it.

Belatedly, Jordan gets the idea that perhaps he should have let her win a long time ago. He looks over at Master Kenji who simply shakes his head and covers his eyes.

Yelling, Jennifer attacks him with a fierceness he has not seen before. Well, there was that a time when he shot her favorite doll into orbit with a model rocket, but that was years ago.

Her blows sting and the vibrations from the blades are so hard he feels his fingers going numb. He has had it. Jordan unleashes a heavy counter attack of combination moves. The din is massive. Slightly put off balance, Jennifer stutter steps and quickly backs off. She looks at her sword. There are several massive, deep gouges.

Trembling with the defacement of her prized sword, Jennifer is out for blood. But, he is annoyed now too and doesn't want to let her win.

They are both exhausted though. Their blows grow sloppy. Jennifer makes one more full-hearted attempt before tripping on the mat and falling on him. They both hit the floor hard.

She straddles him with a smile. "I'm on top. I win," she says between heavy breaths.

Distracted, Jordan is more interested in her breasts. When did she get so…

She notices what he is looking at and covers up. "I'm not a girl anymore Jordan!" Quickly getting up, she bows to Jordan and then to master Kenji. She then grabs her things and makes to leave.

The class, noticing that they have not killed each other, applauds happily.

Steamed, Jennifer looks back at Jordan oddly and heads for the lockers quickly. She turns around at the last moment. "You owe me a new sword," she demands and walks out, throwing her broken sword on the ground.

"No honor. All emotion," Kenji says picking up her sword. "Jordan, you'd better go after her. Calm her down before she murders someone."

Barely changed, Jordan pops out of the gymnasium. He sees her straight, long blonde hair swinging, pendulum like, as she hastily steams away. Talking to her right now would not do much good, but he catches up with her anyways.

"Jen," he says, "what's eating you?"

"You didn't like the way I said hello?" She walks even faster.

"I'm sorry about the sword," he says, rushing after her. "Will you stop walking so fast?"

"I have to be somewhere," she huffs. "And this is not about the damn sword."

"Sis!" he yells, knowing it would get her full attention.

Clenching her hands, Jennifer stops dead in her tracks. She looks at him with her icy blue eyes. The anger is almost a third party between them. "We have never been brother and sister. You know that."

"Your father asked…"

"My father is not your father. How many times do you need to hear that?"

Jordan argues back, "Fine, so we are not brother and sister. We're not a couple either."

"And whose fault is that?" Jennifer says and pushes him away. She then storms off. Jordan can say nothing. Frustrated, he sits on the ground where he was standing. He should have stayed in the military. Then again, some mistakes can never be undone.

WILD MAN OF MARIN

A voice is now yelling at him. Who could it be now? Couldn't they see he has just been run over by an angry woman? Is he providing an obstacle to aerial navigation?

"Did somebody drop you here?" a man asks, his voice slithery and downright evil.

"I ejected," Jordan growls with annoyance though full well knowing who it is. Then with a relaxed laugh, he turns around and asks, "What's up with the voice Mark?"

"Gotta be cool," Mark growls. The dark man then rattles off in his best monotone, "Get up loser."

Possibly the best engineer in the world and definitely one of the most intelligent individuals, Mark Whatley is an oddity for many reasons. He's standing there with his hands in his black leather jacket, in eighty-degree heat, smiling through scruffy "kung-fu master" whiskers. Mark is also otherwise clad in all black, with black boots and criminal intent black sunglasses. He looks more like a rock star than a professor. And, he has metal chains dangling everywhere in case the other elements went unnoticed.

"I don't suppose you could expel Jennifer?" Jordan groans as Whatley gives him a hand up. Whatley's ethnicity is hard to place. He looks a tad Asian, a bit Hispanic. The truth is he is half Filipino and half German.

"I saw the whole ugly thing," Mark mentions in his gravelly voice, "You probably shouldn't have slept with her."

"Why don't you tell the whole world my sex life?" Jordan asks, looking around nervously. "I thought we were going to die."

"Classic. Does that line really work for you?" he sniffs. "Hard for anyone to love Jen lately. She's always been a rich shit, but now she's just a shit."

"I wouldn't know," Jordan responds with a dose of fake shock.

"Right," Mark grins and as he strokes his whiskers. "You decided to have a relationship with her and then u-turned after resisting all those years. Yet you wonder why she's mad?"

"Thanks buddy. I needed another verbal whipping right about now," Jordan replies. "Do we have to talk about my failing love life?"

"Are you're living at the estate? That's not going to help with her across the yard."

"Everything is expensive here. Even the dorm is expensive. You want to rent me a room?" he retorts.

"My girl wouldn't like it, but I will ask around for a job," Mark promises. "Just hold out for a while."

"I appreciate that. What girl?"

"All in good time. For now, come with me." Mark waves and walks quickly away. "I have something of vast interest to show you. A perfect cure for your genetic woes that won't cost you a dime."

"It better not."

Whatley leads him to the faculty parking lot. Jordan has to do a double take. He sees something that looks the offspring of a Lamborghini and a UFO; a freaking amazing car, a car that is probably worth more than most houses. It is a platinum color and looks as if it could sprout wings and fly away. Beefy 25-inch rear wheels and a large spoiler ring out the exotic, toy car design.

"Maybe a drive in this will get your mind off things," Mark chides.

"Do they pay you in gold bars here?" Jordan says stunned, "Italian?"

"Hmm…Japanese," Mark groans and then explains, "You know who Martin Malone is?"

"Henry Malone's son? Of course I know him, he designed the Sharkhunter I used to pilot. Hell, his father and Carlton Brummer designed my father's battleship."

"He needed some help with a new fighter navigational system that didn't know north from south. You know, EchoTech's intentionally buggy crap," Mark says with a swagger, "I figured it out in a day and 48 hours later this shows up at my door. And to put the record straight, Brummer was more an engine guy and Henry Malone, well, he could just about do anything."

"EchoTech is going to be after you if you keep talking dirt about them," Jordan warns as he runs his hand across the sleek car's rounded fenders.

"You don't have to tell me," Whatley howls. "Damn that evil witch Emily Wu."

"Are these panels some kind of aluminum?" Jordan interrupts. "They're translucent."

"A nifty new aluminum and plastic composite called Al-plas," Mark clarifies. "It's an Onzo G850...prototype."

"And they trust you with it?" Jordan says as he exams a somewhat odd protrusion from the roofline. "What's with the giant ice cream scoop?" He circles his hand along the inside of the abnormally large air intake.

"Never ask a magician about his tricks. After you're done petting it, how about you get in?" Mark suggests.

"This beast had better have some fantastical computerized nannies," Jordan quips. "You're nearly blind."

"Thirteen surgeries," Mark grins. "Still can't see clearly more than twenty feet."

Mark is well known for his terrible eyesight. So the idea of going for a ride with him is fairly unnerving. Jordan then decides...the hell with life. Who wants to live forever? Swordfight for breakfast, why not a 250 miles per hour flaming wreck for lunch? He doesn't need his head anyways. Jennifer is going to cut it off sooner or later.

"Don't be afraid," Mark coolly conveys to his skittish passenger. "Trust in technology."

With a swish, Jordan pops open the gull wing door with a tap of his hand. It gently swings open with a mechanical hiss.

The inside of the vehicle is covered in cozy light brown leather with the occasional aluminum highlight. Unlike the fighter jets he is used to, the Onzo's seats are pure butter, butter that slowly contours to his shape, probably some kind of dense memory foam. The dash is unusually high, he thinks, creating terrible visibility. But when Mark hits the engine on button, the car rears up on its back wheels and the road becomes clearly visible.

"Semi-robotic, self-adjusting suspension. It'll change our riding position and body angle as the rate of speed demands," Whatley proudly states. "First of its kind."

"Robotic? So it's partially independent from your inputs?" Jordan questions. "The car thinks?"

"Computers have been monitoring and varying operations on cars for some time now. The difference is the suspension arms are fully articulated with mechanical biceps and wrists. The car is actually aware of the road and has the flexibility to compensate for changes quickly. Kind of like the way our brain keeps us level subconsciously when we walk, yet we instruct the body where to go consciously."

"The Japanese and their fascination with robots. I love it," Jordan says, barely hiding his growing excitement. "Set this thing loose."

Glad to abide, Mark brings the engine to life with quick push of the accelerator pedal. A fierce mechanical whine prevails in the cabin from the electric motors. The G850 then speaks up in a stern female voice, "Prepare for travel. I will secure the cabin."

Seat belts on rolling roof-mounted arms run across them and lock into place. The cabin is purged and purified air begins to circulate from on-board tanks. Rubber seals can be heard inflating around the windows as the doors lock.

"Just how fast are we going?" Jordan asks, wondering about the need for an artificial environment.

Smiling, Mark quickly hits an override switch into the manual position and pulls away.

The voice chimes in, "Manual travel mode selected. Warning, manual travel is illegal on North American MagWays."

"Shut-up nag" barks Mark as he approaches an immense elevated roadway. A large ramp leads up to it.

Automated signs blink a warning, "Approaching MagWay. Prepare for Magnetic Travel." Several vehicles cruise by at about 120 miles per hour, in the slow lanes. Mark opens a makeshift panel and reveals a small touch screen. Jordan clutches his armrests.

"Uh, you modified the car?" Jordan swallows.

"Just a little," Mark says very seriously.

The car flies up the entrance ramp and accelerates with a monstrous roar. It immediately throws the occupants back against their seats. Increasing in speed, there is a slap as the magnetic striped tires snap to the metal-enriched asphalt. Jordan tries to breathe normally.

Racing up over 200 in less than three seconds, they are soon approaching 275. The window shield distorts in front of the driver.

"What's that?" Jordan asks nervously. "Looks like a terrain generator on a commercial liner. You expect bad weather?"

"Similar. This creates a 3D radar projection of the road ahead. It uses satellite maps to generate the terrain in real time and the radar adds the moving objects. It allows me to judge the road better at this speed, considering I'm almost blind without my contacts. The prediction AI on commercial software is too slow. I had to come with my own algorithms and calculations." He squints at the screen. "You would think some doc would come up with a good eye fix after all these years."

Darting from side to side, the car passes other vehicles as if they're bugs pinned on a board.

"You're not allowed to go this fast," Jordan says as the speed reaches 300.

"I reprogrammed the speed limiter. I traded some tech specs with the Onzo programmer. I also added some new software of my own devious design," Mark says with pride.

Unsure, Jordan stares back at him. "Reprogrammed the limiter? That's a felony."

The computer barks loudly, "You have exceeded the safe speed restrictions for this section of the MagWay. Prepare for auto shut down and await arrest."

"The Onzo guy didn't give me the codes to shut her up though. Bastard!"

Increasing speed, the car reaches 350. Towns are buzzing by them with little more detail than a smeared paint drawing.

"Relax. She ain't gonna shut nothing down," Mark says and fiddles with his homemade panel.

A turbo-copter is soon zooming above the Onzo. Red and blue lights appear behind them as several police cruisers struggle to catch up.

"Damn it," said Mark. "The fuzz."

"This is going to be an expensive ticket," Jordan says. "Maybe a day in jail for you. A decade for me."

Mark smiles, "They are probably trying to scan the car's hardwired I.D. so that they can find and use the factory shut down code. Even a common crook would know how to rip that mother-fucker out. I've got a scrambler that gives them a different I.D. with each scan. Ha. Ha." Tapping the open panel, Mark makes an adjustment and the car shudders. "The fuzz can only go 350, that copter at best 450. Not nearly fast enough," Mark settles into his seat. "Get ready to sizzle."

A screen in the middle of the car projects an overhead map with several moving dots on it. The female computer then says, "Traffic prediction complete. Engage auto mode when ready."

Switching the car back into auto mode, Mark puts his arms behind his head and smiles a devilish ear-to-ear grin.

Two magnetic skids come down from the bottom of the car and snap to the MagWay. On the sides of the G850, two small wings protrude out of from the rear fenders and Jordan can feel the down force increasing dramatically on the car.

The Onzo feels glued to the roadway. A third giant wing extends out from the trunk as the rear of the car opens to reveal two small thrusters.

Whaazump. A popping sound rings and the car screams down the roadway. The vehicle has become an electric bolt sparking between two points. Jordan feels like he is flying on a tethered jet. He cracks a smile. The turbo-copter and chasing police cars are left far behind. The 400 mph dial is off the map. Soon there is a shrill howl as the wings retreat back into the body, the car returns back to a slow, but legal 150 mph. The world comes back into focus and Jordan finally lets go of the armrests.

"Holly shit," Jordan says with glee.

"I thought you might like it," Mark laughs as he slows and ducks behind a convoy of trucks.

"What speed did we hit?"

"Upwards of 600 mph," he points out. "Any faster and our supersonic wake would have blasted cars off their magnetic tires. And by the way, welcome to Lake Tahoe."

Stunned, Jordan peers out the window and sees the rush of snow covered alpine trees spitting by.

"Aren't you worried that their going to photo ID you?"

"Photo of what…a blur? I got a static discharger keyed to the government highway signal," Mark says with little concern, "Anyways, I got a friend who can access the MagWay database for a price. All cops are crooks."

"You're a modern day pirate."

"I'm getting a skull and cross bones painted on the hood later," Mark jests as he exits the MagWay and turns the car around.

After an equally blurry ride back to the Bay Area, the car pulls back into the Pac-Tech parking lot. The two buddies exit. Jordan restrains a giggle. He loves technology, especially in the demented hands of someone like Mark.

"How did you ever get a thruster system attached to a hybrid motor? There's not enough power." Jordan asks. "Did you stick a military charge pack in there? But then again, that was visible thrust, not forced air. That requires a fuel and not just electricity."

"Nope, no batteries and no fuel. I can run this puppy at full speed all day and all night with zero cost and no environmental impact. Oh, it's good tech and it has nothing to do with hydrogen or fission," Mark says happily. "It's my new secret. I'll tell you about it later."

DUPONT: SECRET POLICE

As a month of classes comes and goes, Jordan is walking through campus and heading for the library. He passes by the small forest reserve on the edge of the University and soon walks by the Henry Malone Science Building. Continuing on his winding path that takes him between several buildings and the odd-looking student union, he finally reaches his destination. There must be some major exams going on. The library is packed to capacity and he can't imagine going in there. He makes a beeline to the open space of the Quad instead and stops dead in his tracks outside of the Lucas Creative Arts Building.

Blondie is out here. The idiot and his buddies are roughing up some humans. Jordan turns away from them and heads up hill toward the vast Diana Hall. Hopefully, there are no more familiar faces to run into, in particular, one angry blonde woman.

Fortunately, Jordan has only seen passing glimpses of Jennifer since the first day of class. Master Kenji took the initiative and moved Jennifer to a different session. This allows them to beat other students into submission instead of each other.

Mark's classes have also been as good as expected. Somehow Jordan always mysteriously manages to get all the quiz questions in advance, a nice perk, but not everything is great though. As he sits down, a group of students comes running through the Quad. They are being chased by the police. The students throw cans of spray paint at the police. Jordan ignores this and opens a book.

There is obviously a lot of discontent at the Pac-Tech with demonstrations on the school grounds nearly every day. The increase in police presence is notable, but this is not too bad except that he has to show his I.D. about five times a day.

One positive consequence, the OverForce regents, the secret police division who patrol all educational campuses, have banned all weapons from the University including ceremonial ones. Jordan doesn't have to carry his bulky sword anymore. At least for the time being, the other Officers of the State have filed a complaint that this violates their indelible rights, but he doesn't care.

As far as he is concerned, he doesn't like the stares the sword causes anyways. Usually there are human and Nuhu lines. With the sword, he always has to use the Nuhu line as the other humans would scatter in his presence. Now, he can go back to being just another invisible human and that suits him better.

His phone beeps. There is a message from Mark reminding him of their plans for the evening.

Tonight, finally some fun. The man in black has something important to announce. Whatever the hell it is, he hopes it does not go supersonic.

***

Ill-tempered Mrs. Grant does not like Jordan's questionable friends picking him up at her house. So instead, Jordan is relegated to waiting at the school's SF-MAG terminal until Mark shows up.

The SF-MAG is a three section; double decker train on wheels and it is a great public transit system. Several of these "buses" come and go while he waits. They are still driven by people as some things are still better controlled by "soft logic." Soft logic is the name coined by engineers for a human brain versus the hard logic of a computer. A few years ago, the SF-MAG's went digital and ran over a few dozen people. Turns out, computers have little regard for wayward life forms that cross streets illegally.

A half an hour goes by, Mark is always late as it takes him forever to dress. Jordan's butt is getting sore, so he decides to get up and stretch.

His movement catches the attention of a near-by Nuqla Cola vending machine. It bubbles over to him and speaks up loudly.

"Hello sir! You look parched," it says cheerfully.

The machine is an ugly array of sickeningly happy faces that are slowly moving around the flex-display covered cabinet. He guesses that they are supposed to be grinning, but people have banged on the sides so much that they are all distorted. In an even more jolly voice this time, the machine nearly yells, "Sir, you look tired and need a pick me up. Nuqla makes any Nuhu feel like a new you!"

Jordan has had enough.

Looking right into the machines electronic blue eye, he kicks the cabinet so hard he swears the faces squint in agony. The vending machine shuts-up and pretends to be out of service, slowly rolling away.

Finally, Mark's G850 pulls up with a roar. A stunning red head is with him who is as hot as the sun. This couldn't be his girlfriend? Could it? No way. This supposed girlfriend of his has been a no show for a month. And, his last girlfriend was a giraffe with glasses. Maybe this is his big news. He can finally afford an escort.

As the gull wing door opens, the stunner smiles at Jordan and jumps out of the passenger seat. Automatically, the rear cowl glides back and the front seat tilts forward to allow Jordan entry into the tiny back seat. Once both are in, Mark pulls away, driving in a very civilized fashion.

"Jordan. I'd like you to meet my fiancée — Rina," Mark says happily.

"Fiancée? Jesus Christ! You couldn't send me a text about this?" Jordan snaps. "This is no simple announcement; the spawn of Satan is actually getting hitched."

"I think that's taking it a little far," Rina says, turning around to offer him her slim hand. "Wish we could have meet sooner, but I was away."

Used to being put down, Jordan is surprised by her willingness to shake hands. Usually, there is always an acknowledgement of class before any undesired contact.

"I'm a human, miss," Jordan states, holding his hand back as if stricken with the plague. He dares not even make eye contact, but that may have to do more with her chest than her class.

"I know," she replies and keeps her hand out. With no response coming, she moves his head to face her. Offering her hand again, he shakes it carefully as few Nuhu are this nice at first. "Don't worry, I'm not going to pull genetic rank. We've met before actually," she smiles broadly. "I was an observer on the ground during the Battle of Seattle. My team saw you eject."

"You're the ones that recovered me," Jordan says and gratefully thanks her, "I'm sorry. I don't remember much after I punched out. I owe you guys."

"We owe you a lot more," she says, flashing a brilliant smile. "I wouldn't be here otherwise."

Confused on what exactly to say, Jordan answers with an awkward nod.

Fortunately, Mark chimes in at that moment, "Rina here is with the OverForce. She is here to protect me from my bad self."

Jordan thinks, did he just say OverForce? She's a freaking secret police officer?

A coy Rina laughs, "He has a reputation for exceeding his mandate and needs to be baby sat."

Mortified at this news, Jordan suddenly feels uncomfortable. The Over Force is the secret police of the government, not the kind of people to associate with for a light dinner. They are also notorious for their dislike; some would say outright hatred, of humans. Their agency was originally formed to deal with the anti-genetics movement back in the 1950's. What is an O.F. doing in the car with him? Wait...they are engaged? Mark's half human! His head is going to explode.

"My friend you look nervous," she says, looking herself over in the passenger side's mirror. "Mark and I have grown very close. I was on a six-month rotation to protect him, now permanent. That brain of his is priceless."

"Let's put my head in a jar and get rid of the rest," Mark mocks. "She is also now one of the OverForce's regents at the University. You'll be seeing a lot of Officer Dupont, scourge of Pac-Tech."

"Relax Jordan, not everyone is so closed minded," she says, tapping him on the knee. "Don't judge a book by its cover. Read a little."

"An O.F. shouldn't be seen with me. I know Mark can get away at being a Nuhu because everyone wants to pick his mind, but me, I still have to stand in the long line for the bathroom," Jordan points out.

"Need I remind you that you are an Officer of State and just about above in class and rank to everyone. You earned it, not like the others," Rina says with a frown. "I think your father put you in that position to break barriers, not hide behind them."

A fiendish Mark conveniently adds, "Stand in the girl's line if you want, no one can say a thing."

Ill-looking, Jordan nods silently in agreement. His gut feeling is telling him to bail out on the evening. On the other hand, she is saying things that would get most OverForce agents sent overseas. Either she is crazy or she is trying to bait him into saying something treasonous. Or, maybe he is acting as closed-minded as most Nuhu. Jordan decides to keep an open mind and see where things go.

Finally after an uneasy ride, they reach the restaurant — an Italian / Chinese fusion place called Mama Bacons in the seaside town of Sausalito. There is a whole chain of them across the NAU and are well known for their slogan "We're good...because we're good." So much for creative advertising, but the food is truly good.

This particular location is housed in a light brown building with neon trim and huge round, aquarium windows. They enter through an impressive spinning water tunnel and are quickly seated at a semi-circular table with changing images of food projected on a holographic mist. As they sit down, the table turns to face the aquarium window, effectively becoming its own little room...a great feature for conversation, especially discrete conversation.

A panel electronically slides opens and a waitress looks in, "These are our specials today. Tap on anything you like." She waves her hand over the table and visual menus appear before each diner. Rina taps on the images of a few items. Jordan and Mark agree with the selections and the waitress leaves.

"Nice touch," Rina says, "having a live person. You go to fast food and all you do is key in your order and then a machine pukes out same half-ass looking crap. I hate machine made food as much as machine made people."

"Hey," Mark says in a more serious tone, "have you heard about that new law they are going to pass?"

"Pass?" Rina guffaws. "It's nearly a done deal."

A distracted Jordan is more interested in watching Mark stroke the nylons on Rina's remarkably long legs. She is pornographic in proportions and is the focus of much unwanted attention. However, Rina seems completely unaware...or unconcerned. "I'm a little out of touch. Samantha cut the service to the pool house."

"Are they blocking the news feeds at the University again, Rina?" Mark asks.

She stabs at the table with a chopstick and then answers, "What do you think? With all the demonstrations going on, no news is the norm.

However, I think Mr. Grant here could find a work-around if he wanted."

Looking sheepish, Jordan admits, "You're good at your job Rina. I don't look at the news. I want to be out of the loop."

"You need to know this stuff," Mark says annoyed. "President Eaves wants to reduce the rights of humans even more. They're arguing that if humans are less capable then they should have less rights, less pay, less everything." Mark then tells him, "I think a pure-breed dog might be a step above a human soon."

"So what?" Jordan concedes as the waitress returns with drinks. "Air Corps rations tastes like dog food. Nothing new."

"This is no joke," Rina says, picking up the story. "They are really trying to do it. But you really got to think why. I think they need more bodies for that quagmire in France. A law this strict will be easy to break."

"I was born the way I was born," Jordan says, reluctant to speak his mind. "I don't break laws and they don't break me."

A chime sounds. The table turns back to the public space as the waitress returns with their order. It is being carried on a small-motorized table. It is the most basic kind of modern robot.

The food is soon served, but this dinner is not going easy on Jordan. He looks down at his hot and sour fettuccine and wonders if next time they'd turn him away at the door unless he's accompanied by a cocker spaniel.

Things get worse as the table spins. That's when he catches a glimpse of Jennifer. She is seated at a table across the room with Blondie from the first day! What gives? Immediately getting red, Jordan goes dead quiet. Why is he feeling like this? He has to shut down his emotions.

Sensing a shift in Jordan's mood, Mark looks at him puzzled. He catches sight of the blonde, beautiful pair just as the table finishes its rotation. "Ah, I see the problem," he says.

"That's just Jordan's sister isn't it?" Rina states the obvious. "Bad taste in men though," she adds with a frown. "That guy is mental. I had him jailed for a week for nearly killing his fencing teacher. He even offered me money to put the heat on someone."

"Who?" Mark asks, looking concerned. "Hope it's not me. I gave him a bad grade last year. Guy can't put two wires together."

"No someone named Grant," she answers, but Jordan doesn't react. "Did you hear me?" she says. He is still starring at the wall. "What is it with you and her?"

The boys respond at the same time, "It's complicated."

"So your evasions have nothing to do with me being OverForce?" she asks.

Finally waking up, Jordan follows up and states, "Historical baggage." He immediately looks down at the table and tries to burn a hole into it with his gaze.

"What gives here?" Rina states puzzled. "Admiral Grant is listed as the legal guardian for both of you, one standard delivery birth and one human adoption." She turns to Jordan. "Historical baggage?"

"You know an awful lot about me," Jordan snaps at her out of character, finally looking at her in the eyes with a deadly seriousness.

"It's my job. Can't help it," she smiles somewhat embarrassed. "I can tell you the in's and out's of that guy she is with though. Parents are rich. They own the local beer distributor. He's that national champion of…"

"I don't care," Jordan says calming down as he starts to eat again.

Mark leans over to Rina and states, "Most men fall in love with the first girl who opens her legs. Jordan's no different." Snickering, he then wryly re-tells, "They had a thing. Him and Jen. They broke up after dummy here re-enlisted."

Embarrassed, Jordan chokes up, "It's not that simple." He breaks his metal chopstick in half with just his fingers. "Jerk."

"I'm not the sick fuck who slept with his sister," Mark laughs hard. "What's even worse is that you both pretend so hard not to want each other. Walk over and snap Christian in half like that chopstick."

"What the hell?" Rina says angrily looking like she is getting ready to pull Jordan's heart out. She probably could too. Her nails are long and pointed enough. "You had sex with your sister?" She then looks at Mark. "And you, you are telling him it's alright?"

"Rina," Jordan scrambles to explain. "Samantha tried to make damn sure Jen knew she and I were not related. That strategy…kind of back fired."

"Understatement of the century," Mark says in an overly caring voice, "They're in love."

"That's not true," Jordan growls, turning red.

It is true.

Catching on, Rina laughs hard, "Mark you are so right. That's so wrong, but kind of sweet. There's no biological relation, so I guess there's no harm."

"Ok enough fun with my past," Jordan exclaims exasperated. "I can't believe I'm talking this way with an OverForce officer."

"You can trust me," Mark says. "You can trust her. Rina had a tough up bringing too. She understands you more than you think."

"So Miss Know-it-all, tell me more about Blondie," Jordan suggests to Rina as he tries in vain to put the chopstick back together.

"Christian Palin is a perfect example of Nuhu factory breeding," Rina proclaims proudly sitting up straight. "He's dumb as a post and as strong as an ox. He has a history of violent mood swings which, conveniently, are purged from his official records, but not our records."

On hearing this, Jordan suddenly becomes concerned, "The guy sounds dangerous."

"Just like Mark?" Rina jokes, her hand making the motion of snake and factiously bites Mark.

"Jen is getting in over her head again," Jordan remarks, looking at Mark. "I should have gone to M.I.T."

"Cheer up," Mark points out, finishing his drink. "Jen is just playing him."

Jordan and Rina both stare back at the Professor in disbelief.

"What?" Mark gets defensive. "All three of us grew up together. We're close. She tells me things." With quick grace, Mark immediately grabs the bill as it spits out from the center of the table. He looks over at Jordan. "Do you think they can break a gold bar?"

TO PROTEST OR NOT

Dark grey clouds hang ominously overhead, then again, this is the Bay Area and dark ominous clouds are commonplace.

October has come quickly with low temperatures following in step. With these days of uncomfortable cold, Jordan is reminded of a few miserable nights he spent in the Himalayas. Stubborn, he insists on studying upon an icy bench even as his ass freezes. He has come to like this particular bench. Situated on a hill, it gives him a nice view of the Quad stretching out below him, though the occasional leafless tree gets in the way, but no students do.

Though fearless in combat, Jordan is not compatible with crowds. So much so, he refuses to sit inside the warm library, instead insisting on using the great outdoors as an alternative study room. At least, some other idiots are outside as well. A large demonstration, again, is going on. This has become an annoying daily occurrence. These hooligans are out by the school memorial; two giant statues situated toward the back of the Quad.

The word has spread around campus that several protestors had been roughed up by the police the day before, hence the new barrage of demonstrations. Jordan thinks they are wasting their time. Police are easily bribed. Somebody else paid them to do it.

In the mist of the protest, Jordan spots a familiar ponytail. Jennifer is in the middle of it all, screaming her head off to an interested crowd. They begin to march up toward the administration buildings.

Looking around, Jordan sees their target. A large contingent of police, in full riot gear, is gathered in front of the buildings. Jordan worries that things are getting a bit dicey.

Not for himself, but for Jen. Too bad her beliefs, like the weather, have a habit of changing unpredictably. As he thinks about her, Jordan feels the wind picking up and shivers noticeably.

"Watching the show?" Rina announces loudly, causing Jordan to flinch, as she sits down next to him. "This is a nice view. I could sniper one of those kids easily from here." She is decked out in full OverForce regalia along with a hat that dwarfs her head. The hat has a large brim with a puffy center and a not-so-subtle brass emblem of the NAU flag with a dagger across it. "I usually watch them from the grove over there by Rodgers Hall, it's less obvious than this perch."

"Love the hat," Jordan grunts and looks back down at his books, occasionally passing his See-Glass over sections of them. He pretends to be busy scanning, but isn't. His true attention is on her every move. "If you want a proper sniper position, the roofs are ideal. No obstructions."

"Aren't you cold?" she mutters and as she buttons up her long, light-grey wool coat, her breath floating away before her. "I have to be out here daily monitoring these yahoos. You don't."

"Are you monitoring me as well?" Jordan asks pointedly, though he shouldn't be pushing his luck with the secret police, even a seemingly friendly one. "You seem to have a particular interest in me." He feels a rush of anger flow through him which he must hold in check. Though he won't be intimidated, he doesn't want any necessary heat either.

"I'm curious," she says straight up, moving closer next to him. "There're not a lot of people who would stand up to Christian Palin," Rina states, her eyes locked on his.

"Ever since I got beat up as a kid, I've never been able tolerate bullies," Jordan says through gritted teeth as he zips up his coat as well. What is this? The inquisition? Why is Mark seeing this person?

Rina has a faraway look to her as if in two different places at once, thinking about many things. "So why are you letting Christian make you out to be the bad guy? Do something."

As the police break up the protestors, Jordan decides to answer her question with no ambiguity for better or worse, "Guys like him feed off attention. I'm not going to give him what he wants."

"Too bad," Rina sighs and adjusts her side-arm.

"A lot of people died fighting the rebellion. People who couldn't get out of their service like Palin. Let him hate me."

"People hate me too," she says quietly as a few leaves drop behind them. She pulls out her gone and aims it at the protestors. "How many of those kids do you think I could hit from here."

Jordan doesn't react. He simply says, "None. You're sights are off."

She puts the gun away and smiles. "How did you know that?

"You just moved them before pulling your gun out," he notes as he looks down the hill and sees that several of the protestors are watching them. The last thing he needs is to be seen as collaborator. "Why are you testing me?"

"If I'm making you uncomfortable, I can leave," Rina suggests taking note of the protestor's growing attention, especially from their leader, Adrian. "Just because you're Mark's friend, I shouldn't have assumed I was too. I don't blame you. I really don't." She rushes to gather her things and stands to leave. A disheveled teddy bear falls from her pocket and onto the bench. It's a mangy little thing that is probably several years old. With delicate care, Jordan picks of the fragile memento of the past and hands it back to her. "My mom gave me this the last time I saw her. She didn't want my dad to let me go, but we were too poor." Rina puts her hand to her face and turns away, not wanting Jordan to see her pain. "It's hard for people to trust me. My intentions are not always clear. To be my friend, you have to read between the lines. Not many people can do that."

"If a friend is all you are looking for," Jordan tells her, after all she is as at much at risk for being ostracized as him, "then go ahead and keep your seat." He reaches up to her and tugs at her arm. "My dad told me after I got beat up; be polite to those who are polite to you. Be polite to those who you do not know, but be fierce to those who harm you. You have been polite and I have not. I'm sorry."

"Really?"

"I mean it," Jordan says sincerely. "You're sense of humor could use some help though."

"You're probably right," she says. Smiling stupidly, Rina pulls out a bag of some small cookies. "Try one of these my fellow outcast," she offers him.

Unsure, Jordan cocks his head to one side, making sure they are not being watched. They are. "If someone sees you…feeding a human…might make for some strange stories."

"Come on Grant," Rina says as she waves the bag around. "If you're trying not to hate, I'm trying even harder. But as far as the uniform is concerned, they don't let you take it off. You're expected to die in it. So go ahead and take the damn cookie."

He takes a cookie and bites it. She's right. It's good.

A happy Rina gets up. "Got to go and pull the police's chain before they do something stupid." She stands up and pulls down her long coat. "Don't worry about pissing off the bullies; I've got your back."

"Thanks for checking up on me," Jordan says with difficulty. "It does get lonely here."

Rina nods slightly, "I know it does."

As the gray-clad lady walks away, Jordan spots the new number one on his avoid list, Christian. He and his associates, no...punks, march by the remaining protestors and stop suddenly. Christian turns a deep red.

Embarrassed, Christian confronts Jennifer and tries to pull her away from a group of protestors surrounding the memorial. They argue and after a while she looks off into space ignoring him.

Tired of being disrespected, Christian tries to grab her but she just steps away angrily. After making some interesting hand gestures, she turns and storms off.

Shaking his head, Jordan wishes he could have heard that conversation. It might have been entertaining, but he has somewhere to be. He packs up his things and heads for the university's server farm.

Buried in the bowels of the main engineering building, Jordan must descend several levels underground by a variety of elevators. There is a multitude of security scanners to pass through here. With a School of Engineering pass, he manages to get in with little trouble as it falls on the freshman students to service and monitor the equipment banks down here.

He comes to massive blast door that looks like it was designed to withstand an air strike—most likely it was. The door opens slowly as it is several feet thick.

The server farm resembles more a forest of flat black trees with little glowing bugs scrambling all over them. This installation stretches at least a half-mile back and a number of students have been known to get lost for hours down here as personal digital devices are not allowed. As is the case with most engineering students, few dare call for help for fear of looking stupid.

With excellent navigation skills, Jordan noticed on his first day down here that the server banks are laid out in color coded grid. He takes a beat-up looking See-Glass from a shelf and begins his service routine.

The back of his ear begins to itch and he looks around. He feels someone is down here with him, but sees no one down any of the long aisles.

He hears a rustling noise and shivers. Listening, all he can hear are the distinct hum of the cooling fans.

As the first bank of servers go through its diagnosis program, Jordan becomes bored and pulls out a text book. There it is again, he thinks. He looks around trying to find the source of the rustling noise. Instead, Jordan picks up on a distinctive scent and relaxes.

Focusing back on his quantum physics textbook, Jordan scratches his head. He is never going to need this crap. Suddenly all goes dark.

"Not funny Jen," he complains as he pulls the red protest flag off his head. A fiery Jennifer is now standing in front of him. He can tell by her posture that her feelings are hurt. "How did you get down here?"

Ignoring his question, she waves a finger in his face. "What's up with you?" she says between gritted teeth. "I'm out there protesting for human equality and what do I see? You dining with the OverForce."

"Judge not, that thy not be judged," Jordan says looking back down at his book.

"You stole my bible. Didn't you?" Jen insinuates.

"Found it in the trash," Jordan corrects, wondering in his head what a manufactured being needs with a bible anyways. Then again that's the same kind of closed-minded thinking that he abhors. With a sigh, he takes a seat on a squat server that passes for a decent bench.

"If I put it there, that's where it belongs," Jen snaps back, wrapping her protest flag tightly around her hand as if getting ready to punch him. "Why would you want that dull book anyways? It's illegal for you to have. Tell that detail to your grey suited friend."

"OverForce agents are often recruited young," Jordan says, moving on. He's having a hard time not staring at her beautiful eyes. They are a hypnotic ice blue. Then looking down at her butt, he also notices an EchoTech security badge stuffed in her pocket which explains her mysterious entrance. A better question though is how did she get it? "Sometimes they grow up and no longer fit into their gray suits," he then adds.

Unyielding in her disgust of Rina, Jen caustically exclaims, "Good people don't associate with *their* kind."

"Jen," Jordan says, still trying not to look at her. "We've all done awful things."

For a few seconds, she seems to settle down. "I'll never forget what you've done for me," she admits and sighs hard. Trembling, Jen is having a hard time being humble. "The world may burn, but I'll never forget."

These sudden truthful outburst are why he likes her so much. Jen can be a complete bitch, but there is always a nugget of good in her.

With a bewitching smile, Jennifer then steps right in front of him and kneels down, forcing him to face her. "I want you to join in the protests and stand up for your people," she insists, taking hold of his hands.

He has to be honest and speaks from his gut, "This country is rotten to its core. It won't change."

She lets her face hover over his. He can feel her warm breath as she says, "If the flame of change is never lit, no one will ever see the fire."

Struggling to focus, he reminds her, "I know you stole from General Kroll. How does that make you morally superior?"

With her smile eroding, Jen sighs and looks bewildered. She spins her hair around her pinky as she thinks. "I wanted to show him for the pig he was. But honestly, it was a way to get of the service…away from all the killing," she concedes and sits down next to him, "Do you really prefer being alone just so that you don't have to face anyone?"

Confronted with the truth, Jordan answers reluctantly, "I don't belong anywhere. You know that. The sole human Officer of the State." He thinks about the protestor bravely waving their flags wildly at the campus police. This makes him feel a bit ashamed.

"I was mad when you stayed in the Air Corps," Jennifer admits as a small service bot shuffles past them. "Why did you throw me away?" She leans her head on his shoulder and for a second they sit in silence.

"After what you said, I had no reason to come home." Unable to get any work done, Jordan shuts down his tablet. "What do you *really* want with me Jen?" He says and kicks the bottom of server with his shoe. The last thing he wants to be is a poster boy for any cause.

"You said it. You're a human Officer of the State," Jen replies plainly, reaffirming his fear. She does want a poster of him.

Expecting such an answer, Jordan simply takes a deep breath and folds his arms as if trying to protect his heart from being ripped to pieces. She only wants to use him.

"You have always been by my side and now I really need you," she says, playing with his feelings. "You can belong. Help us."

"You're just a walking contradiction. You were mad at me for staying in the military and now you want to start a revolution?" Though a little revolution might not hurt, he thinks. Jen is not the person to lead it.

"This is not the same," she insists.

"Fighting, yelling, begging, doesn't change this world, nothing does, especially not knives and bullets. Don't you get it?"

"Come on, stop with the negativity. Don't act like I don't know the real you. You've always been a rebel," she says with a cool confident demeanor. Her hand casually strokes his leg to his utter discomfort. "We can be together again…in a way."

Getting a bit mad, he strongly states, "A few years ago you wanted to be my wife, then you suddenly got genetic cold feet. If you are involved in the civil rights movement, it's not for me and it's not because you believe."

"I could never fool you Jordan," she laughs and nuzzles up to his face. "I am the top of the social cream here. There is power to be had. Power is freedom. If I have power, you will be free in essence."

He begins to pull her close, longing for a time long since passed. "We don't need this. We don't need anything but ourselves."

"Oh please," Jen says with a veiled disgust. She pushes him away. "Aren't you tired of being nothing? Of being told what to do? You only have title, but no money, no assets. What kind of life what that be?"

Waking up, Jordan sighs, nearly having fallen for her charms again.

"Unlike you, I could use Daddy's crest," Jen admits looking blue. "He always finds a way to make me feel insignificant. You, on the other hand, he pushes up and up and…"

"I never wanted it." Jordan then offers, "I'll give it you."

With her mood darkening, Jen exclaims loudly, "I wanted it from *him*."

Finally tired of Jen's nagging, Jordan warns. "I stayed in the service because I wanted to fly. With one dream dead, I went for second best."

"Always dreams with you. Those things are fun when we were young, but what about the future?"

"And you think wealth and power fixes everything?" Jordan growls as he remembers his experiences in the war. "I've seen good people do bad things because they wanted too much. Jen, you don't want to make choices you'll regret. Power is not freedom. Power enslaves."

"You're afraid. Afraid to step above the average…to be superior. Do you really think that power will turn you into someone like Palin? Come on, have a little faith in yourself," Jen states and looks away from him. He is so short sighted, she thinks. They both could tower above everyone else, symbols of ambition used correctly. "I know what you want in life: a family and a little house out by the sea." She leans over and kisses him on the cheek. "One thing I like about you Jordan, at least you're consistent, but I'll never be domesticated."

Speaking about Christian, Jordan reminds her, "Your new boyfriend looked pissed earlier. If you need me, I swear to you, I'll be there in a second."

Jen then interrupts with a big smile, "You still love me." She then strokes his heart with her hand. "One day I'll have this back."

He doesn't answer, only starring back at the beauty that was once his friend and lover. She is so tantalizingly close again, but she might as well be in another universe. They are walking separate paths. She is on the way to delusion and he is just plain lost.

"Don't worry about him," Jennifer says getting up. "He wants to marry me. Frankly, his family has the money to finance my ambitions."

Completely disheartened, Jordan's hopes collapse. "So he's what you want."

"He's what I need. And for god's sakes, learn to be social before you become a bitter old man." She then bounds away with a wink and a grin, disappearing into the electronic forest. Her voice rings out over the server hum, "Your heart will always be mine!"

THE DARK HALF

Jordan is now seated at a packed table in the library with a small coffee by his side. Despite the crowd, he seems to be in a surprisingly good mood for once. He is scrolling through a selection of songs on his phone before settling on neo-classical. Maybe this social thing isn't so bad. And maybe, there is still hope for to repair the relationship with Jen. Though he would never admit it to Mark, he still deeply wants her back.

Looking beyond the sea of heads, he sees that it has gotten late and night has fallen. His stomach is starting to growl, but he still has a lot to study. Fortunately, he's got a brick of history notes from another student which should get him ahead. He taps on the tabletop it and the school emblem appears; a shield resting on a wreath. Jordan puts his See-Glass over the emblem. Through a wireless connection, Jordan's notes are displayed on the table. With his fingers, he quickly sizes the page to his comfort.

A fist falls on the table and his coffee nearly topples. The other students all look up immediately as rather angry looking OverForce officer stands at the head of the table. She drums her fingers on the surface. Very quickly, the other students pick up and leave, save one. Jordan goes back to his studies.

A grinning Rina slides over next to him. She has a flyer in her hand, but keeps it at her side.

"Hi," she says.

"Was that necessary?" he asks as he watches the scurrying students flee. So much for his foray into being social.

"You don't like crowds," she says while madly chewing on a bagel.

"Glad you remembered," he says, trying to hide a smile. "Are you always packing?"

"I don't really have time to eat, so I just pick stuff up all day. It's the nature of the job," Rina answers truthfully and hands him half.

Still focused, Jordan is now skimming over an electronic copy of an aerospace magazine for Mark's class, displayed on his palm computer and concurrently on the electronic tabletop as well.

"Homework?" she frowns.

"It's an article on the effects of heating as an object increases into extreme velocity. Very pertinent to next generation fighter aircraft design," Jordan says and notices her hand is squeezing his knee. He looks over at her crookedly.

"Sorry, force of habit," she says. Rina suddenly gulps, moving her hand away and quickly changes subjects. "This is a news release from HQ back east," Rina says and hands him the notice. "Thought you should know."

A curious Jordan reads out loud, "Addendum to National Racial Code, Article 88: A common human or any being of questionable lineage can be conscripted into the armed forces as retribution for illegal acts. NRC Article 88 will be enforced at the discretion of the local judiciary." Putting the paper down, Jordan rubs his eyes.

"Don't worry too much," she says.

"Trying to thin out the herd?" he asks, though not really expecting an answer. He crumbles the paper up with a restrained fury. How many wars does one nation need to live through before realizing they accomplish little?

"Trying to thin out their potential enemies, it's not just humans going to that so-called police action in France," she says very seriously. "France seems to be a popular destination for anyone the government doesn't like."

"Maybe I should just buy a ticket to Europe," Jordan coldly laughs. "I always wanted to see the remains of Paris."

"I thought you didn't care," Rina reminds him and elbows him gently.

He doesn't answer. There is only so much he can tolerate. Whether big or small, he hates bullies of all sizes. He just didn't expect to fight the whole fucking NAU.

"Try to keep your nose clean and everything will be fine," Rina says and pinches his cheek. "And keep away from Jen. I'm sure this edict will light her fire. Last thing I need is for her to gather a mob here. Happened before…ever heard of Rain Malone?"

"Sounds familiar," Jordan says though distracted.

"Started a movement back east. They go suppressed and so did the news. I don't want to see that again…ever." Rina seems like she is going to cry, but forces herself to stop. Jordan, focused on the flyer still, doesn't notice.

"Jen is harmless," he states protectively. "Spray paint and spit are her weapons."

"Let's hope it stay that way," Rina warns as she looks at her phone. It shows several video feeds from across the campus as well as the police feed. "Anyways, you got powerful friends watching over you." Catching herself, Rina flinches knowing she shouldn't have said that.

"Who?" he states both intrigued and worried.

"Forget that I said it," Rina states mysteriously.

Suddenly it dawns on Jordan, now he understands how he really got into Pac-Tech.

"Figures," Jordan says depressed. "My father pulled strings. Didn't he?"

Noticing his change in mood, Rina bluntly informs him, "Sometimes grades are not enough. You needed a little help." She says, "I know Malone. He's not as bad as people say he is."

"Martin Malone?" Jordan repeats with audible surprise. Martin Malone, the famous industrial baron and aircraft tycoon, bought his admission. Malone's father's name is on the freaking lab building. Plus, he probably owes Mark several favors. "Rain Malone...makes sense now. That's your connection to him."

"Best not to talk about it," Rina says sorrowfully. "Like I said, forget it."

Having lost his appetite, a frequent occurrence lately, Jordan stays at the library way into the late night. Rina has long gone and her bagel only partially nibbled on.

A projected mural on the wall shows a Galleon sailing on the high seas. The seas morph into a vast field of stars. From the stars, a circular constellation forms and this becomes a clock face. It reads five minutes till midnight and he has had enough of studying for today. Closing his books and shutting down his display, he exits the library. There is almost no one around. He still sees a few dim shapes in some of the buildings —late night classes, but otherwise emptiness. There is a scream by the Student Union and he turns to see.

A woman lurches in front of him. She is soon tackled by a pair of campus cops as a bunch of Officers of the State circle around. They begin to heckle the woman.

Christian Palin and his gang are having a good time watching as two police brutes harass the young woman. She struggles and they pin her to the ground. The woman is dressed in overalls and apparently works in the school cafeteria, most definitely a human.

"I didn't take anything!" the young woman cries as the female cop pushes her head down against the pavement.

"Human, you've been accused of stealing," the female cop says angrily.

"She's the one that took my purse," a stuck-up looking peacock of a lady says. "I'm almost certain of it."

"Almost?" Jordan says loudly, coming into view, instantly regretting speaking up.

"Back off," the male cop says, raising his nightstick.

Not easily intimidated, Jordan then observes, "Where's the purse then?"

"Nuhu witness. End of story," the male cop yells and threatens to strike Jordan. "Last warning!"

Jordan does not budge, but instead feels a burning frustration building in his gut that this is no kind of justice. He then boldly states, "The word of a Nuhu is not enough."

Pissed off, the male cop moves bash Jordan across the face, but finds an iron fist in his abdomen instead. The crooked cop falls hard to one knee. The other cop attempts to pull her service weapon, a low powered, high repeater, the Hammer PD-2, but Jordan quickly disarms her of the small gun before she can charge it up.

The Officers of the State shuffle, but Christian Palin motions for them to back off as he sees that Rina is lurking in the background.

"You're going to pay for this..." the male cop screams as Jordan turns tables and pushes him into the ground. With a gun pointed at her, the other cop simply stands in silence.

A cool Jordan looks over at the terrified cafeteria worker. "Did you take the purse?"

"No sir," she warbles. "My shift was over and I was walking home. That's it."

"You," Jordan yells over to the old lady with the bad hair. "Where were you coming from?" He hovers over her like an ominous specter.

The woman seems to be a foot shorter now. "I was attending a lecture…in Lam Hall," she says, stymied by Jordan's insist tone.

"Lam Hall? That's clear over on the other side of campus," Jordan asserts and points off into the distance. The cafeteria is just around the corner.

The peacock continues to insist, "She's the only human around. Obviously, she needs the money."

"Unless she can teleport, there is no way this happened," Jordan faces the Nuhu lady and then says angrily, "You just picked the first person you saw."

"What gives you the authority to tell me what I did or didn't see?" the now embarrassed peacock yells back with fury.

"Is this really worth it?" Jordan asks as he turns her to face the cafeteria worker. "Look at her. She's terrified. This will cost her everything."

The peacock doesn't answer. She simply looks away.

"Did this women steal from you?" Jordan insists.

"No," the peacock finally answers.

Having heard enough, Jordan says to the worker, "Go home." She gets up slowly and looks at the cops. The cafeteria worker then takes off running.

"You have no right," the female cop yells at Jordan.

"He's an Officer of the State," Christian Palin states angrily. "He has every right."

"An Officer?" The two cops look at each other concerned. "Sorry sir, we're didn't know," the woman says. "Please don't report this to our superiors. We could lose our jobs."

Annoyed, Jordan then carefully disarms the PD-2 handgun by removing its charge clip and returns it to the cop.

"Now he wants to be an Officer," Christian growls to his cronies.

Christian and Jordan share a harsh stare as the group of people disbands. So much for the low profile, he stuck his head way out on this one.

Starting back home, Jordan decides he needs to cool off with a longer walk. He takes a path in through a heavily wooded area, which serves as the ecological studies area. He likes this so called "Maria's Nature Trail" for the fun way the street lights shine through the trees, brandishing cheetah spots on everything. He doesn't know who Maria was or why her nature trail is paved. Regardless, it leads to the main road, Blithedale Avenue, and is usually devoid of people, but not this time. Unknown to him, a greeting party has been arranged in his honor and they are waiting for him. By the time Jordan rounds a blind corner he is surrounded.

"You insulted a Nuhu. Questioned her moral authority," Christian sneers as three of his comrades start to encircle Jordan. "We call you out human!"

"An honor fight? With one against four?" Jordan says, almost thinking it's a joke. They move in closer. Unfortunately, it's no joke.

"An insult to one Nuhu is an insult to all," Christian conveniently replies.

The motley group looks upon Jordan with wolf eyes and prepare to strike. He begins to move counter to them, trying to keep all four within his sight lines. There is a tinge of fear within him, but he forces it away. Instead, he allows rage to build. He tells himself — make them regret this.

As his mind takes over, the entire surroundings begin to fade into blackness. His enemies become uniform shapes in his eye. His brain is a tactical computer, sharpened for battle, easily sizing up the threats around him.

Quickly arranging the four by strength and skill, Jordan plans his attack. Information streams into his eyes and is tabulated into usable data.

Jordan observes the brute to the right is straying from the others, he's scared. He also notices that Christian is holding his hands too high, a sign of inexperience. The scene becomes a drawing on a board. A drawing he can read and use.

Christian signals his cronies to attack. But Jordan is at the ready; he counters the attack by engaging the man who is straggling. Not expecting this, the man hesitates. Jordan has judged correctly. He is the weakest of the three. He easily grabs the scaredy-cat by the face and rams him into a tree. The man's head makes a popping sound. His brain rattled, the man drops out cold, but not dead.

Two others are coming for him. Jordan knows he can't take them both. He has to separate them. Otherwise, they might pin him down so that Christian can beat on him. One of them, he notices, is hobbling a bit. He is wearing a jersey of some kind. It is probably a bad knee or another kind of sport's injury.

Rolling onto the ground, Jordan snaps a kick right into the man's damaged knee, buckling it. There is a horrendous sound of cracking, snapping bones. The man flips onto his back. He screams in agony as Jordan flash kicks him in the stomach. The scream becomes a gasp.

Jordan hears footsteps. Feeling the wind brushing by his ear on the right, he can sense someone is reaching for his neck. He quickly ducks and rolls.

The attacker grabs nothing but air. Then with a quick two-footed bounce, Jordan stands up frighteningly fast and thrusts his elbow into the man's Adam's apple. Stumbling back, the man is gurgling and unable to scream as Jordan's fist hits his face. The man's nose is crushed in three places, raining blood across Jordan's shirt. This cowardly man has had enough and tries to hide.

Mad and disoriented, Christian backs off. Jordan is not even warmed up.

The vile Christian charges like a mad animal. Jordan realizes that he has read Christian right. He has no skill at hand-to-hand combat. He is merely going on brute strength.

Trained in the martial arts, Jordan lays into him with an array of punishing hits. Jordan treats him no kinder than an oversized piece of tough meat. Years of frustration against every racist Nuhu pour out of him with every blow, he strikes and strikes again, every punch making a more and more audible, wet landing.

Bloodied and pained, Christian tries to run away.

A horrible, unmasked ferocity consumes Jordan's soul. Jordan is a punishment machine. He pulls Christian back toward him. Slamming his fists into him again and again in rapid combinations, Christian's face is reduced to a red pie. Jordan's hands have become raw at the knuckles as Christian's skin begins to sag. He is his to execute at will.

"Stop it!" cries Rina. "You're gonna kill him."

"So what!" Jordan yells, "What's one more piece of shit?"

Grabbing his arms, Rina attempts to use her Nuhu strength advantage to pull him away. To her surprise, she can't even budge him. Jordan is far stronger, stronger than any Nuhu she has ever fought.

"Jordan," Rina pleads. "I know what it is to be a murderer. You're better than this."

Her words hit him harder than any punch. Jordan drops the nearly unconscious Christian to the ground. Suddenly ashamed, Jordan doesn't know what to do with himself. He's lost control. He's allowed his anger to consume him, awaking a terrible strength.

"I saw the whole thing Jordan. They started it, but I think you better leave, now," Rina orders and begins to examine Christian who is breathing through blood bubbles. "My god you did a job on him," she says and pulls out her phone to call for an ambulance.

Disgusted at himself, Jordan takes off running as fast as he can, darting deep into the ecological reserve. Tree branches smack him as he races by. Tripping and falling all the way, he ends up by a natural amphitheater. Here, he finally drops down next to a couple of dumpsters and amongst decomposing bits of lettuce and pools of dark liquids, he takes count of himself. A stench of staleness and rot permeates the air here. Jordan finds it comforting as he feels foul himself.

He doesn't want to cry and show any weakness, not to a Nuhu or anyone. His eyes betray his feeling of guilt and swell with angry tears. Looking at his beat up hands, he still feels the hate running through them. It is long to dissipate.

Though he wants to be left alone in peace, he knows that a vengeful beast lives within him, waiting to come out. The beast wants revenge for being born into an evil society, revenge for the death of his parents, revenge for all injustice. The tears come out and with them the rage is washed away. He hides amidst the muck for what seems hours without end.

Around 3 AM, he starts to walk home.

A heavy air stirs around him all the way. The sky is darker than it has ever been. The streets feel empty and alone. Anger, hate, and vengeance are his only companions. As he steps out of the darkness and heads home, he leaves the vile trio behind. He doesn't want them.

KOBORN

Fidgeting, Rina is not comfortable as she thinks about the night's events. The time is five in the morning, but their boss Koborn insists on an early meeting. They drive up a long narrow, winding road through the hills of the city of Larkspur. At the top of one such hill, a giant mansion sits with commanding views of the cities to the east and the forests to the west. As the gates to this mansion open, Rina worries about the coming conversation. The guards wave her to pass. Mark, who is with her, yawns with disinterest.

"What's up with all this fuss?" Mark asks her as they pull into the massive driveway. "I would have done the same."

"They would have killed you," Rina says, completely honestly. "I've never seen anyone so strong." Her mind soon begins to accept an idea, a theory that she fears even considering. "What have you guys been hiding from me?"

A nervous Mark, as if reading her thoughts, forces a laugh, "Those girls probably don't know what hit them."

"You're not funny," she scolds and exits the car.

Mark argues, looking sleepy, as he follow her out, "If Christian doesn't show up to class tomorrow, nobody would care."

"Forget it," Rina says and hits the doorbell. "You know what I'm thinking. It's nothing to joke about."

A stiff ancient butler greets them and shows them up to Koborn's office. It is a cavernous, cold space. A distinguished older gentleman is waiting for them here seated behind a beautifully sculpted desk. He is dressed in warm coat and does not look as if he'd been asleep. Rather, he seems to have been already awake.

"I got your message Miss Dupont," he says in a regal British accent. He then turns to face the pair. "Remarkable, he beat four strapping Nuhu lads without any show of fatigue."

"We all know how to fight," Mark interjects, the sliver chains on his biker jacket rattling. "I think we should just forget about this incident. It's no big deal."

"The standard military training you all receive? Hardly," Koborn replies as he raises an eyebrow. "Admiral Grant is right. Jordan has shown unusual tolerances and abilities recently. They analyzed his flight over Seattle. The Air Corps engineers had a hissy fit over it. They say no Nuhu could have withstood the G-forces his body took. So you know what they did? They threw the data out."

"That's a good thing," Mark says relaxing. "We don't want any detailed blood tests ordered."

"So what is he?" Rina asks concerned. "In the OverForce, we hear a lot of strange tales. Tales of genetic experiments that have resulted in human monsters."

"Jordan is not one of Dr. Magen's experiments. Still I appreciate your analysis. I will let Malone know he did right to recruit you to our cause," Koborn says and studies a cup of tea. "However, the topic is concluded."

"If he's not an experiment, he must be a human aberration," Rina states, looking furious. "There is a reason aberrations are terminated upon birth."

"Don't over think," Koborn scoffs loudly as the tension in the room rises. He looks over at Mark with disappointment.

"Aberrations are mentally unstable. They are prone to delusions, aggressive behavior...violent behavior. Some even hear voices and go psychotic," Rina states alarmed, pacing around agitated. "His outburst tonight could be a warning sign. It's unthinkable to let him go on with no knowledge of his condition."

"The decisions on how to handle Jordan are not within the scope of your mission."

"I get it," Rina declares, trying to hold back her resentment. "Don't trust the double agent."

"Malone trusts you and that is enough for me, but knowledge that does not travel is safer kept," Koborn states this loud and clear as a young, beautiful woman enters. She contrasts sharply with the plastic looking Rina. This woman has a natural, real woman's beauty: not too thin and definitely not built like a boy with breasts. She hands Koborn a metal briefcase.

"Your dispatch is here from General Harrison, Grandfather. His envoy just dropped them off and I thought you should see them right away," she says.

"Gabrielle, you are dedicated, but you should not be up at this hour," Koborn says, briefly opening the case. "Harrison is very efficient." There are several tubes of blood inside.

The stately woman notices the two others in the office and smiles, "Hello Professor Whatley. Late night for all rebels?"

"I assume you know the Professor," Koborn says as he examines a tube of blood under a light. "This tall attractive woman is Rina Dupont, an officer of the OverForce and one of Malone's best agents. The arrival of this package is fortuitous timing."

"I've seen you at campus Miss Dupont," Gabrielle says and carefully studies Rina's face. "You have…a very interesting past."

"Some of us are born without choices," Rina pronounces clearly for all to hear. "If you think being sold to the OverForce at eight is interesting, good for you."

"Rich or poor, you can still be born without choices," Gabrielle grins, but her dislike of Rina is obvious.

"Officer Dupont," Koborn cuts in. "Make sure this case is sent off to the lady known as the Silver Mask. I suspect you know of her already. She is currently at Malone's testing facility in the Mojave. Tell her to let me know the results of the analysis as soon as she has them."

"Are those the rebel blood samples from the Seattle?" Mark asks worried. "Did they find traces again?"

"You already know the answer, Professor Whatley," Koborn states coldly and moves the case over toward Rina."

"Fine," Rina snaps, taking the package and storming away.

"I'd better go after her," Mark suggests, looking concerned.

"Mr. Whatley," Koborn says quickly, pulling gently at Whatley's sleeve. "No one told you to fall in love with her. She has wounds that run deep. Wounds that will never heal."

"Who doesn't?" Mark replies and comes up to the desk. "Ever since the war, I can't sleep. Things keep replaying in my dreams, terrible things." Mark reveals and then says, "There was this lady I knew when I was as a kid-- her name was Sophia. She used tell Jordan and me all this nonsense, but now I understand what she was trying to say."

Koborn sits up at the utterance of this particular name.

A bitter Mark continues, "She used to say, 'in the absence of light, we must become the light.'" His stoic mask breaks a bit as Mark thinks about his rough childhood, but none of them had it as bad Rina. "We are all trying to do right. We are all trying to find our way out of the dark. Cut her some slack."

"Your prerogative Professor Whatley. However do not let Rina look too deeply into Jordan's history," Koborn orders as Gabrielle silently watches the proceedings.

"She knows they flush babies that aren't to code. She also knows that if Jordan keeps showing new talents, other OverForce officers might take notice," Mark explains. "I tried to talk it down, but you went on and on. Rina likes Jordan. He's been kind to her."

"Understood," Koborn sighs. "Malone is a believer in Cotillard. Does Rina believe in that French prophet as well?"

Gabrielle coughs loudly upon hearing this bit of news.

"Not a chance," Mark sneers, but he has his own fears about Rina. "Jordan is a lot of great things, but he is not some mythical bringer of doom."

Nodding his head, Koborn concurs. "Nevertheless, best to keep the zealots under our supervision. If Rina and Jordan develop a close friendship, that may be useful as she reports to Malone. Malone has his suspicions, religious suspicions, about Jordan. If he is dissuaded, that could be useful."

"I'm more worried about the Government. Bribes will only get you so far," Mark warns as he notices Gabrielle's unusual interest in the subject.

"That is why we have brought him here. Make the offer to join the rebellion," Koborn instructs.

"How much do I tell him?" Mark asks looking back at the door. "Everything?"

"Only enough to get him to join," Koborn clarifies.

After Mark leaves, Koborn turns to his granddaughter. "Gabrielle," Koborn says cautiously. "Do me a tremendous favor. Could you watch Jordan Grant for me? See what kind of man he is."

"I'm not comfortable with that suggestion," Gabrielle complains. "That would make it inconvenient for me to keep a low profile...especially if I'm giving someone an eyeful all day."

"You misunderstand me." Koborn warns, "Watch, but do not contact, remain distant…be a phantom."

Feeling put upon, Gabrielle rebuffs, "This man is a hero. People who risk their lives to save others usually do not warrant such suspension. So what if he is an aberration? Martin's father, Henry Malone, was one too, though they didn't know it back then."

"And *that* knowledge remains here," Koborn reaffirms. "I know you are a good judge of character and not easily clouded by dubious outside ideas like our friends."

"I thought Malone was an intelligent man of science."

"Don't be so insulting. Whatley is right about one thing, we have all been pulled together to fight this growing darkness," Koborn sighs hard and looks at his hands. They are old and worn, much like his soul. "No fight is ever won alone and he knows that."

"England will always stand," she says proudly. "Alone if need be."

"Will it? After the fall of France, a woman began making certain predictions that came to pass. They call her the Saint of Leon," Koborn recalls. "Will we soon have a fake saint to soothe our fears?"

"I know all about that nun Emilie Cotillard," Gabrielle huffs in disbelief. "Anyways most of her predications concern the end of the world, not specific people."

"Not all," Koborn says. "I have no reason to doubt Malone's sincerity even if I do not agree. Whether he wants to keep Jordan close or just be helpful is irrelevant. Either way, Jordan is safe and that keeps the Admiral happy. If you do as I ask, then I will be happy too."

"Very well," Gabrielle reluctantly agrees.

Koborn takes a long sip of his tea and quietly states, "Jordan's a very handsome young man."

"Don't be silly," she says looking out at the rising sun. "I'm not looking for love. Love does not last. You and I both know that too well."

"He is also noble and honest. Rare qualities."

Gabrielle replies, "Rare indeed."

THE FUSE

There is something inherently wrong with knowing the feel of tearing flesh, the sound of crunching bone beneath hardened knuckles and the warmth of newly spilled blood. He sees the gore covered face of Christian falling away from him. Shivering, Jordan wakes up with a start, his shirt drenched in sweat. There is an animalistic side to him, a vicious side that he can use. It is a dark place he fears, but it is a place of power. A place he hopes to keep well under control.

A familiar ceiling is above him and that is a good sign as the fight has been only replaying in his dreams. Even though he didn't start it, he feels dirty as if a foul creature had been set free. He almost became a murderer. What does that say about his true nature? Jordan doesn't even want to think about it.

9 A.M. and time to get up, his hands are still bruised from the previous night. Not wanting to attract unwanted attention, he struggles to find some gloves to cover his cut-up looking knuckles. He hopes that Rina succeeded in keeping the fight under wraps as the last thing he wants is every Nuhu jock trying to match fists with him. Checking his slender card phone, he relaxes. No message of impending doom.

A heavy fog has rolled in this morning spreading its melancholy magic. Feather wisps of mist circle about every building as he enters the school grounds. But this is okay; Jordan feels grey himself.

He is wearing a hand-me-down brown leather jacket from Mark that has seen better days, much better days. The jacket is still warm enough though for the Bay Area fall.

That's why he becomes instantly annoyed when someone starts tugging on it. Turning around, Jordan sees a lanky man with messy long hair and wild eyes. "Hey, we humans must stick together."

Jordan then puts his arm around the man. "I like you too."

"This is no game," the longhaired man sighs, pulling away. "Why do you hang with an O.F.?" The man then becomes even more insistent. "Do you know what the OverForce has done to our people? You're a crested human and an example that we are just as good as they are. Fight with us!"

"I've done my fighting," Jordan states, his mind flashing back to the night before.

"Good fights are never done," the man nearly yells. "Show no fear in the shadow of oppression. Stand and be seen as unafraid. Stand and feel victory!"

"Rina's a friend. Deal with it," Jordan says flatly and takes a step, before turning back. "Anyways, what do you guys hope to achieve? Jen sounds like she wants to go to war."

"I'm not talking about physical fights. Our movement is not about violence," the man implores. "Come to our meetings and see. I'll never agree to the use of violence. The instant we do, the NAU will break us. I know that. It happens all the time."

"Things are just very complicated for me right now," Jordan admits, remembering what Rina said about Rain Malone.

"Man, one day you'll have to take a side. Then again, maybe neither side will want you by then," the man says scorn and finally walks away. Jordan doesn't know when he became the focus of so much attention, but he wishes he could go back in time and change things.

Making his way through the tide of students, Jordan is walking up a gentle slope to reach the Astronomy Lab when Rina catches up with him.

He turns suddenly on her, "What?"

A blindsided Rina looks blankly at him, "Whoa. Having a bad day?"

"Some goof with long hair confronted me a second ago and got under my skin," Jordan tells her and leans up against the building. "I see the seeds of civil war everywhere. God, I don't want to see any more bloodshed, not here, especially not here."

Rina leans up next to him, "I know. We'll make sure it doesn't happen."

A fearful Jordan looks as the students walk past them oblivious to the storm of destruction that seems to be right off shore. "I feel the breath of battle against my back."

"He's just one guy," she says with a yawn. She only got about forty minutes of sleep. "Adrian Simmons is stated pacifist. We think he might have been involved with some vandalism to Nuhu property. Smart enough to not push his luck...and definitely smart enough not to start a war, unlike your ex."

"What about last night?" he asks. "I'm sure that's going to sting me in some way."

"I don't think Christian Palin realized how close he came to being recycled. But Jordan, he's not going to forget what happened. His face will not forget what happened. He will be after you," Rina then takes a long pause to think before speaking. "Jordan you almost killed those men. Frankly, I almost wanted to let you do it. The only reason I stopped you was to save you from yourself."

"I appreciate it," Jordan says earnestly. "You look like you need a nap."

"Class is starting," Rina reminds him as she tries to hold in a yawn. "I'll load up on Nuqla Cola later." She pats him on the shoulder.

"Want to meet for lunch at the Student Union?"

"Can't. I have a meeting. Might be my only chance to catch some winks," she states with a grin. "Mark and I are going for a jog in the afternoon. You want to come? Might help blow off some steam."

"Maybe."

"I'll take that as a conditional yes," Rina replies. She then in exhaustion accidentally drops something. It is a rosary.

"This yours?" Jordan asks as he picks it up and hands it back. "We need to get you a purse considering the way you lose things." He notices that the rosary has some sort of addition around the cross; two circles.

"No, found it this morning," Rina quickly says and faster than light puts it away. "Purse? Not me. Not ever." She grins sheepishly and takes off quickly. "See ya."

The Astronomy Lab is a large domed room. He sits down on one of the many reclining chairs in the room. Class starts and gentle red LED lights illuminate a digital pad on the side of his chair. Taking out a memory card, he plugs it into the pad. He whips out his favorite stylus—a silver one that Jennifer had given him for his birthday, and is ready. He chuckles to himself quietly. His only friend at school is a secret police officer. With his luck, she'd probably turn on him one day. They are all just hard wired that way.

Looking up at the dark dome, his thoughts shift to Jennifer. Admiral Grant once told him Samantha had once been open minded and a little wild, much like Jennifer now. But as she got older, stature and family became more important, especially when it came to her own daughter's future. He does have some vague memories of Samantha being caring when he was just a tot. Her change was not subtle, but came abrupt and overnight.

How long would it be before Jennifer decides to takes her place in the Nuhu world? How long before her not subtle and abrupt change?

As for him, he feels that he should not be a part of her life anymore. Imagine telling the Admiral that he and Jennifer are lovers! No way. There is no way he is doing that. He'd rather move into a cave.

Soon, the class begins with a three-dimensional model of the universe appearing within the dome, not on it. This is accomplished by using three projectors and a special translucent screen. The screen stretches across the dome and is impossible to see in the dark. Though, anyone looking from above the dome would see a flat image.

When he was a boy, he used to dream about traveling into space and to the planets. But space is the domain of robots as no people have ever been there. The government, against all science, claims that humans and Nuhu cannot survive in space, banning any manned expeditions. Space has only been seen remotely through robotic eyes. Jordan wishes those eyes could be his instead.

But now he is older and those fantastic dreams have faded, he is lucky to have been at least a pilot. The upper atmospheres are as close to space, he tells himself, that anyone is going get. Especially since like the rest of his life in the NAU, those decisions are in someone else's hands.

The lights soon come back on in the classroom and Jordan quickly makes his way outside. At the same time, he reaches into this pocket. All he has is about ten bucks and he's hungry.

Although only early November, money is already starting to be a big problem. Jordan has underestimated the amount of money he needs for supplies and transportation. Of course, he will have to cut corners...probably in food. Ready-to-eat-noodle cups are going to be the order of the day soon. Well at least, he will not have to worry about gaining weight. Starvation is a great diet. As a last resort, he can always raid the manor house and risk being shot at by the staff.

The Admiral had given him some money early on, but he has already used most on school supplies and the school year isn't even half over, in any case asking for more is not his style. He does get a small stipend from his military grant, but that isn't much either. As for finding a job, that has become a tricky ordeal too.

His father, ah, the Admiral kind of put him in a bad position. If he wants to get a part time job at the University, he will be mocked. The only jobs readily available are janitors, but as an Officer of the State, he would be expected to be in high position. A janitor carrying a sword on his back would surely be a joke. Though if it came to it, Jordan decides, he will do anything to stay at Pac-Tech.

This brings him to the pizza dilemma. As he passes through the Student Union, a little past noon, the smell of the fresh pizza is circling through the air, enticing him. They make awesome pizza here. Humans are fantastic cooks. The hell with money he thinks, life sucks anyways, time to spend a little cash. He pulls out his ten bucks.

After obtaining his costly, but delectable morsels, Jordan searches for a place to hide, hoping to consume his two thick-crust pepperoni slices and large Nuqla Cola in harmony.

He really should have fought the urge to go with the Nuqla Cola. The government banned caffeine several years ago. In response, the cola companies came up with the stimulant Uberphine. Uberphine keeps you awake for hours and makes you pee like an open water hose. He knows he is going to be doing the hula in his seat during English class.

The Student Union building is an interesting place — it kind of looks like a sideways shipwreck. The outside design may not be for everyone, but on the inside it is full of nooks and crannies to disappear into. Most of these nooks and crannies are equipped with their own table and window. These places are nice and often full, but today, luckily, he quickly finds a spot, deeply hidden away in within the recesses of the Union.

Of course, Jennifer tracks him down as if he is a big black spot on a white wall.

"I've been calling and calling," Jennifer screeches and pulls over a chair. "You're not just anti-social. You're a god-damn ghost."

"It's lunch time," Jordan says without looking up. "I didn't want to be found."

"You're always thinking about food. What's that? Pizza again?" she says. "Don't you ever eat healthy? Where's the chocolate milk?"

"What did you have for lunch?" he asks with reluctance, casually tucking his chocolate milk deeper into this backpack.

"Pills," Jen replies, looking hungrily at his food. "Mom says I'm getting round. She has me taking all kinds of supplements. You know my mom, her dad was a doctor so everything has a cure. Pill this, pill that."

"You don't need a diet. When are you going to grow up and stop listening to her?"

This question seems to stump her as she seems to blank out for a few seconds.

Sucking in his lips, Jordan knows one thing well enough about women. No matter how bad the food is you are eating, they would always have room for a taste. After the bite, they take the whole thing. "Would you like some pizza?" Jordan asks already knowing the answer. He would soon be reduced to one slice and a half empty cup of cola. At least, the soda is refillable.

"Ok. Just one bite," she says grinning.

"I thought you would be livid about the fight between Christian and me."

"That's between you two," Jen mumbles, finishing her bite and proceeding to pick up the whole slice. Jennifer then reaches for the soda. "Can I have sip?" she asks sweetly.

"Go ahead," Jordan agrees. Why do women play these games? They are always hungry but never eat. He didn't even like super skinny, and likely unhealthy, women. A good example of such is seated across from him.

She finishes up drinking half his soda and her expression grows serious. "I want to talk about us, really talk about us."

There are few more dreaded words a woman could utter then I want to talk. She wants to talk? Is she going to change? No. Is she going to ask him to change? Yes.

"No," he answers resoundingly.

"What do you mean? No?" Her mouth is hanging open, full of food, a lovely picture.

Jordan rapidly spits out, "I'm not interested in being a male concubine. How many times do we have to go over this?" He really wishes they could go back to the way they were, but that is unlikely to ever happen. Feeling both insulted and saddened, he wears his pain on his face. Of course, Jen doesn't notice.

"I see. Didn't know this was a negotiation," Jennifer huffs. "Does love really mean so little to you?"

"Stop it. We should just stop talking before we fight," Jordan replies and looks away. His heart yearning to accept her conditions, but his mind objecting. "You made promises and then broke them. What else is there to talk about?"

"No, not end of story." Jennifer tears up. "This can work. Trust me."

"You really want to talk about this again? Prove it," Jordan says and decides to challenge her resolve…and his. "If you can find me at four o'clock, we'll talk. Otherwise, done."

"That's such a woman thing to do Jordan. I found you once today. I can find you again."

"Then do it again," he says. "Bye Jen."

"Thanks for lunch," the puzzled woman says and leaves.

A starving Jordan looks down at his lonely single piece. Better than nothing.

His relationship with her is risking his future. The time has come to make some hard decisions. The time has come to stick her in the past and lock the door. He has to stand up for himself and move on.

So taking up his slice, he feels that a load is being taken off his shoulders. He bites down and it is the best tasting pizza ever. It's glorious. Everything tastes better with a clear mind.

But then again, is this what he really wants? Or, is he just afraid of the consequences?

Rina suddenly appears on the other side of the oddly shaped room, her red hair visible from a mile away. She has no lunch bag or tray in her hand. So much for her meeting, Jordan thinks. But before she can eat his last slice, Jordan vanishes into thin air.

LOST GIRL

Thinking she is losing Jordan, Jennifer is upset, though a little voice within her tells her to let it go. She does not like playing these games with him. Just who does he think he is? Stupid human, he should be happy to be her lover. After all, he will never amount to much with his limited ambitions.

This statement makes her stop and think. Where did that idea come from? She's always believed in him. After all, she's seen him do the impossible. Maybe Jordan is right, maybe she is hanging around her mom too much.

A young Asian girl brushes by her. She quickly drops a memory stick in her hand. The exchange is practically invisible and it's supposed to be that way. Jennifer drops into her purse and continues on her way as if nothing had happened.

Entering into her afternoon history class, Jennifer feels her anger brimming to a boil. Her anger is always quick to rise and long to subside. She detests herself for it, but that only makes her madder.

Deciding that if she pays attention, her frustration with Jordan might magically go away, she focuses on the instructor. All she hears is mutterings about the founding of the North American Union. This reminds her of a day long ago with Jordan, down in the canyon. She stares at her hands. One of her hands starts to shake, forcing her to sit on it.

Her bad memory is interrupted by someone asking about how the current French uprising started. But, her mind soon returns to festering about Jordan.

Doesn't he realize that he is her only friend? He listens to her. People always told her that her only asset is her beauty, but he knows there is more to her inside. He knows she has something to offer the world. Why can't he help her become someone great?

Worse, why does he have to hide his feelings? Unfortunately, Jennifer knows the answer and she doesn't like it. Like always, Jordan is probably protecting her. Society would not tolerate an open relationship between them and that's what he wants. She still thinks her solution is the best. An open relationship? She laughs…impossible. A plaything for a rich girl? Possible.

The class goes on and on. Yawn. She does not care for it. It is a joke anyways. They spend the whole period arguing that the fight in France is about freedom. What a joke. The French don't want the NAU there. The NAU needs to be there. Oh yes, she knows, it's all about the control of a rare mineral, Boxrite. Boxrite is needed to make all those fancy Pentam engines purr on the big ships.

With class mercifully over, Jennifer walks outside. Her long, sleek legs give her a sexy stride. Guys stare at her as she passes. They can't help it. She has spent years fashioning herself to attract the best and the wealthiest. What a blessing in a way, she thinks. To have such power over men…wait…this is her Mom talking again. It's like she controls her thoughts lately.

Her Mom believes she should not be involved in politics and should be keeping out of such troubles. With her perfect looks, all she needs is to marry well and then she can have all the power any women of substance can want, but she doesn't want second hand power. Jennifer doesn't just want power and wealth. She also wants love. She wants her own prominence. She wants it all. Most of all, she wants to prove to the world she is something special.

Her stomach is kind of in knots. She is nervous about talking to Jordan. It is not every day she must say words that can change the course of her life, but today is that day. What will she say to him? Worse, how do you convince someone to love you again? How do you convince someone into taking a subservient position in a relationship?

Maybe her stomach hurts from stealing Jordan's food. She shouldn't have done that. Jordan is tight on money and she knows it. He shouldn't be paying for her, but she likes it when he does. Plus, he always lets her eat everything she wants, something that does not happen at home.

Briskly, Jennifer walks down a circular flight of stairs and heads toward the basement level of the Student Union. Here all student organizations are piled one on top of each other. Behind an unmarked door, the Society for Change is hidden away. Several students are seated in front of the door. Recognizing Jennifer, they open the door and allow her to pass. An armed student, albeit with a baseball bat, stands on the inside, looking out of a one-way window.

This secret space is bustling with activity. Locating Adrian Simmons, the man with whom she shares leadership, she walks up to him. She doesn't need him, but he's easy to control. Jen doesn't care if someone is Nuhu or human. She knows she's better then all of them.

Busy, Adrian is standing by a map with red dots.

Jennifer hands him a memory card and says, "Here are the names of few more pricks and princesses. Make sure they get some unwanted attention."

Gruff Adrian smiles as he looks over the names. His clothes are rumpled and slept in. If not for his young age, his attire would be more appropriate for a retired hobo.

Around them, several others are busy at work on portable computers and making calls. These are both Nuhu and humans, but the coziness does not extend beyond the office door. However to Adrian's credit, his little office is a prime example that both races get along just fine when social expectations are put aside.

"Sure helps having your mom being involved with all the local bigwigs. What kind of list is this anyways?" Adrian asks.

"A fund raising list for President Eaves," Jen laughs loudly at her own cleverness. Though she thinks Adrian is ineffectual smuck, he can sure pack a crowd. He is well liked and well respected amongst the liberal set at the school…meaning almost everyone. This is the Bay Area after all.

"I think your mom would die if she found out you are a leader in the Unity Movement," Adrian chuckles at the irony. He squeezes Jennifer's arm and she cowers away as if touched by a leper.

"If we win, she'll approve," Jennifer groans and walks over to a map with the red dots, anything to get away from Adrian's touch. "How is your vandalism campaign going?" she asks with a yawn. "Still think your child's play is going to pay off?"

"What do you want to do? Bomb buses? Blow up classrooms?" Adrian asks, looking a bit hurt. "My way is getting us attention without any blood."

Indifferent, Jennifer only sighs. She needs an inch of political clout. If this so-called movement is ever going to get noticed, it needs to ratchet up to the next level. A threat commands attention. An irritant gets ignored.

"I do have something bigger in mind. Ever heard of a Doctor Magen?" Adrian asks, expecting her disapproval. "Some kind of big wig in the government, a friend of President Eaves. I think if I harass him we might get some media exposure."

"He's a family friend," Jen says. "Come on, I think you should leave the senior citizens alone."

"That's rather convenient," Adrian says as he point to Magen's house. It is a large estate covering a few acres. "What a win it would be to get the President's attention."

"Oh do whatever makes you happy," Jen whines and opens her purse. She takes a small bag, looks around to see if anyone is watching, and hands the bag to Adrian. "Here's our budget for the next month."

A curious Adrian quickly looks into the bag. "I don't know how you do it. This is Koburn kind of cash." There is a wad of bills inside held tight by a rubber band. "Been doing a little dancing on the side?"

"I don't appreciate the sass," Jennifer says with a sniff. In fact, she did sell her body. The memory of which causes her to shiver. Then in an instant, her mind tells her to move on and not focus on the negative.

"Hopefully, whatever you're doing won't stir up any OverForce curiosity," Adrian says as he puts the money away. He looks at her with some reservation over what he is about to say, "Your brother Jordan..."

"I told you to leave him alone," Jen says with little care as she takes a few pills out and starts to chew them. "He's a little lost right now."

"No, he's indifferent. That's worse than anything," Adrian states and starts counting the money. "Actually no, hanging with Dupont is worse."

"God Adrian. Dupont doesn't seem to be interested in us. She only seems interested in fucking Professor Whatley."

"But she's interested in your brother? Why?"

Shaking her head, Jennifer smiles and waves Adrian off. "He's not plotting with her. End of story," Jen informs him, though she doesn't like Dupont's interest in Jordan either. "I'm still trying to find out what Dupont's angle is. Not even my father can get info on the OverForce, but a friend did get me some details," Jen walks over to a terminal and puts in a memory stick.

101

"You're a bunch of surprise today," Adrian points out.

"Check this out. Its a file on the Pac-Tech security regents," she says and pulls up Rina's folder, printing out her dossier. "We're going to have to move our operation deeper underground soon. That is the only way we can really do what needs to be done, especially as we start the protests against the conscription law. That won't sit well with the school governors or the regents."

"Did you get that from Whatley?" Adrian asks agitated. "Please tell me you did."

"No," she says. "Mark hates the Unity Movement. Thinks it's a waste of time."

"As far as I can tell, he might as well be an O.F.," Adrian insists. "The OverForce are brainwashed train wrecks. These people know no love except the NAU. Anyone in with Dupont must be a loyalist."

Finally having heard enough, Jennifer snorts annoyed, "My god, everyone is your enemy. Have you seen Dupont? Maybe Mark is using her!"

"Whatley is a toy maker. Toys used to oppress the masses," Adrian snarls and hurls a soda can against a wall. He quickly forces himself to calm down and takes a few deep breathes.

After letting Adrian have his fit, Jennifer rebuts, "Trust me, I know Jordan and Mark. All they want to do is fly and explore. Out of the three, I'm only curious about Dupont."

"Maybe," he says, "but anyone who supports the government is an enemy in my book."

"Now you got it. The government is the real enemy and they're not listening. How much louder do you think you can shout?"

"As loud as I can. We must show that humans are not animals," Adrian says. "That's the point of the whole thing is to show we are just as good as anyone else."

"Violence is great drama," Jennifer says as she pages through her file on Rina. She stops on an image of a young black woman. "After all, it works for the OverForce." The picture is marked and she reads it out loud, "Target Rain Malone acquired and terminated by Trainee Dupont. Passing grade." Jen looks down the page. "She killed Martin Malone's daughter," she says with surprise. "Interesting coincidence." She looks up at Adrian and excitedly states, "I'd bet Dupont befriended her and then murdered her. That's what I would have done. Jordan and Mark are in way over their heads."

"You should warn them," Adrian huffs and looks over the file himself. "Dupont is like a poisoned drink, she doesn't kill you until you already had a taste."

"I will…when it's in my interest," she says obliquely. Then to Adrian's dismay, Jennifer pulls an ugly, block shaped energy pistol from a plastic bag and tosses it on the table, "I think her interest in Jordan is starting to make sense. The O.F. is trying to pressure Malone for some reason. That's why they killed his daughter. It was a message. I think they might be interested in using Jordan and Mark to get info on Malone. Mark must be working on something for him."

"This is all making me a little nervous," Adrian chuckles with suppressed fear. "I don't want to go this deep." Then his mood changes, he thinks about what he just said. "Just how did you get the money and information?"

Jen says with disgust, "Let's just say it involves a lot of horse trading with some distasteful individuals."

"They wouldn't be Chinese individuals?"

Offended, Jen frowns and warns, "Don't be so curious. We needed the money so I got it."

"Be careful with Thomas Wu. I've read about that guy on the free-net. He doesn't do anyone favors. Jen, I love this movement. It's my life! But you have to stay away from him," Adrian pleads honestly. He then pushes the gun around with a pencil. "Remember that activist from Berkley? Bill Dunken was split open by one of these Bentz guns. I saw the pics. Take it back. No guns."

"Christian gave it to me," she tells, rolling her eyes at his revulsion of the weapon. "His stuff is never registered. He has dozens. His buddies and him blow up dogs with them."

"That's my point," Adrian says horrified. "That's inhuman."

"Who care about dogs," Jen says and leaves.

Tempted to pick it up for a fraction of second, Adrian then looks at the gun for a long time. He takes a deep breath and looks over to another student. "Hey Carl," he says. "Take this thing and get rid of it."

"How can you trust that woman?" Carl asks taking the gun. "I'm a Nuhu too, but I think this is just a big game for her."

Rubbing his forehead, Adrian sighs hard, "There would be no movement without her."

***

Having finished her official duties as an insurgent, Jennifer steps out into the Student Union. She walks into a restroom. Other women are there and they stare at her. Do they know her secret? Do they see the wolf in a sheep's disguise? Looking into a full length mirror, she sees her own reflection: a young woman of 26, innocent looking with big blue eyes and snowy skin wrapped in a tight white dress. She is athletically slim and no push over. This is the face of the underground —the new social rebel.

For a second, Jennifer doesn't recognize herself. She steps back and is afraid of the image in the mirror. When did she become such a slut? Fighting with herself, she tries to keep focused, but can't. Washing her face over and over again, a terror takes over and she feels like she is going to lose her lunch. Why is she doing this stuff? She hates politics.

Now alone, a wicked expression falls across her perfect face. With tremendous force, she kicks the glass and cracks it. Her image distorts and becomes hideous. Pulling out a hand-sized tube of spray paint, she writes "Death to Eaves" in very large letters and leaves.

Outside the Student Union, security ignores her, blind to her actions. A Nuhu? Do a crime? No. Must have been some foul human.

And speaking of foul, she finds Mark…and of course with him is…his filth, his treacherous government provided prostitute, Rina.

Casually walking up the grassy path toward them, Jen puts on a fake smile. Pity poor Mark falling for Rina's wicked charms and blow up doll proportions. He is so weak minded.

"Hey guys!" Jennifer shouts and hugs Mark. "What's going on?" She gives him a peck on the cheek.

"Taking a break," Mark hums and squeezes Rina's hand. "You look nice today Jen."

"Thanks," Jen says and brushes her hand through her hair. "I always try my best."

104

There is a commotion as someone bursts from a grove of trees screaming her lungs out. "Beware the end of us all is coming," the hysterical woman yells, running up to them. She is wearing a strange emblem on a chain: two vertical silver circles with crosses inside them. "Emilie has seen the future. We must all repent! Do it now while you still can. Everyone repent your ways! Only God's forgiveness can save us! I have read the prophecy. There is no hope. Fear the revenant! The revenant is coming!"

Security shows up and the woman takes off running toward the busy trans-hub, quickly running into traffic.

"What a scary witch!" Rina exclaims, but actually looking concerned. She starts looking at her phone and types something on the screen. "I have to make a call," she says and steps away.

Speaking of witches, Jen studies Rina closely for a second. She looks as if she hasn't slept in days with blood shot eyes and dark patches underneath them. Always scheming, Jen then asks as Rina gets off the phone, "Hey Dupont, one of my girlfriends is having her First Delivery next week. You want to come?" Jennifer bumps Rina in fake friendliness. "Must be hard to make friends considering your type of work."

"It is. I'd really like to meet some new people," Rina says with a hopeful expression and then looks at Mark. He nods his head in reluctant approval. "What time?" Rina asks with a gulp.

"Five. I'll pick you up." Jennifer says, faking excitement at her answer.

"I love First Deliveries. They're so much fun," Rina admits, smiling at Mark. "I haven't been to one since I was a kid."

"Good. I'll see you then. Bye guys." Jennifer then says nervously to the professor, "Mark. You have any idea where Jordan is?"

"You shouldn't push him," Mark suggests. "Let him get used to being home, maybe he'll come around on his own. You guys really need to stop bickering and listen to each other, compromise."

"It'll be fine. I promise," Jennifer smiles and walks away, but soon stops. "By any change did Jordan borrow your car?"

"More like stole, but yeah, why?" Mark says.

"Nothing," she says and walks quickly away. Now she knows where Jordan is.

***

Despite the uncertain nature of the trip, Jennifer always finds the drive to the headlands pleasant. Large billowy clouds are defusing the sunlight, covering the coastline in a golden glow.

Before reaching the Golden Gate, she turns right and heads up into some hills. The road is steep and then suddenly drops off down following the cliff side. She knows exactly where Jordan is.

As she drives past some old abandoned concrete structures, a huge out cropping of rock comes into view. This rock looks like a launching pad right into the sea. It probably could be used as such.

Getting out of her elegant red convertible, she spots Jordan. He is standing at a steep angle and apparently defying gravity. The winds are so strong here a person could lie into them and have the illusion of flying. Maybe, she wonders, this is where he learned to love the sky.

Arrogantly, Jen also leans into the wind. She pushes her luck and moves all the way to the edge where she hangs to life by only a thread. If the wind suddenly stops, she will certainly fall.

Then, as she expects, Jordan's strong hands pull her back from the brink. "Always pushing your luck," he says, holding her tight.

"I know you'll always be there to catch me," Jen exhales.

Walking away from the cliff, the couple sits down in a grassy field surrounded by a spat of coastal redwoods.

"So," Jennifer starts, her flawless blonde hair sparkling in the low afternoon sunlight. She is a vision of beauty perfected.

Not really wanting to have this conversation, Jordan takes a deep breath and looks away from her as if she were toxic. A flock of birds is flying by in a pyramid formation. He suddenly wishes to be in the sky with them.

"Jordan," she speaks up. "My feelings haven't changed in all this time. This thing with Christian is just a necessary evil. He means nothing to me."

"Please Jen, don't talk that way. When we were younger, we used to talk about traveling the world. Anything to be away from here," Jordan tries to touch her hand, but she pulls it away quickly. "I'm still willing to leave with you."

She counters unapologetically, "It's a reasonable solution for us...for you to be my second. People of my status are allowed their divergences."

"They are," he says, "but the answer is still no. I don't like being demoted from husband to servant."

"Damn it Jordan. Servant? I love you," Jen angrily yells. "Life is not about ideals, it's about acceptance."

"I don't compromise on love," he scoffs and wishes he would turn to stone. "Either go 100 percent or fuck it."

"Your ego is just getting in the way."

"Life is just series of disasters. I need someone who will be there when things are bad," Jordan tries to explain. "God knows I'll never have any money. If you really want to be with me, let's just face the future together no matter what."

As if kicked in the head, Jennifer looks at him in complete confusion. "You'd rather we live like beggars? Is that what you are suggesting?"

Frustrated, Jordan just shakes his head.

"We can't live without an income," Jennifer exclaims. "This is not how the world works. My mom is a harpy, but she is right about the NAU. I've absorbed a lot from being around her, going to all these boring political parties. There is no happiness when you're the chair others sit on."

"I'll make my own chair," Jordan sighs. "I won't share you."

"Do you think I want to live this way? No, but we have to accept that we live in a culture that is ruled by class," Jen says sincerely. "Remember back when we were kids on that bus, going to Madrone Canyon of all places. You had that picture of the house even back then. Back then, it was easy to dream," Jen recalls. "That's why I believe in you so much. You overcame that impossible day."

"That day might have been about love for you, but not for me," he stutters, his concentration broken. "What I did..."

"I know what you did," Jen says looking into his light brown eyes. "How can I forget?"

THE CANYON

Halloween morning arrives and the day is already spoiled.

A young Jennifer shuffles uneasily on the sofa as her mom watches the news on a door-sized viewing screen. Another girl has gone missing. So far this month, a girl a week has disappeared. And this has gone on for over two months.

"I don't think I want you going out tonight," Samantha Grant says.

"What about Jordan?" Jen asks.

"That is your father's decision."

Horrible news abounds as the newscaster goes on to talk about the assassination of the Queen of England by the French resistance. A video of the royal family is shown. She has three little girls' ages five, seven, and fourteen. The fat middle child, who looks utterly lost, catches Jen's attention. Her expression of fear and abandonment translates even through the numbing filter of the television screen.

"That girl looks really sad, Mom," Jen points out as Samantha's phone rings with a musical chord.

"Hi Rose," Samantha answers. "I don't think Jenny will be going out...what's that? No...my god," Samantha says and gets up quickly, leaving Jen behind.

A puzzled Jen watches as her mom talks nervously in the kitchen. A maid walks by and her view is obscured. Getting up, Jen walks toward the kitchen as her mom hangs up the phone.

"Jenny," Samantha says with a scared tone. "That was Judy's mom. Judy is missing."

"No!" Jen cries from the doorway. Upset by the news, Jen runs off to her room and slams the door. Samantha knocks on the door, but there is no answer.

"It'll be alright, Jenny," Samantha says calmly. "They'll find her."

A maid rushes up to Samantha and asks, "Is everything alright, Ma'am?"

"Her little human friend is lost," Samantha says in then almost in a whisper remarks, "Better she find a different kind of friend anyways." She turns to face the maid and orders, "Please let the staff know that kids are not allowed off property today."

Crying, Jen walks to the window and looks out toward the pool house. She catches her reflection in a mirror.

Young Jennifer is a somewhat odd looking child. Most Nuhu children see her as a weirdo. They say she has a fish face and the skinny legs of a crow. Jen often hears her mom tell others that maybe she was the product of a dirty gene mix — a mistake.

Never trusting Nuhu children after being teased so often, Jennifer has found two good friends, both human; Judy at school, who has always accepted her…and that funny orphan boy.

That night, her father who is home for once in his life, tries to console her. He tells her that the bad people who did these crimes will be caught. True, the police are everywhere, but they have no leads.

Later in her bed, Jen decides it is up to her to find her friend.

As the morning breaks, Jen sneaks through the house, avoiding the help. She passes her mom who is working out in the house gym. Jen is way overdressed.

Samantha, in order to hide Jen's ugliness, always bought her daughter the frilliest, fluffiest dresses, hence her attire today. Here she is about to go on a hike and she looks like a little princess decked out in bridal white. But the dress be damned, nothing is stopping her from doing right by her lost friend, even if it means getting dirty.

The yard is a huge piece of green real estate. Running across it, she is reminded just how uncomfortable her long dress is and that her stiff shoes are certainly not made for sprinting. She does manage to get to the pool house OK and throws the door wide open.

Jumping around in his underwear, a 13-year-old Jordan is playing with a model of a jet. He is making engine noises, which ended abruptly when he sees her standing there. Immediately, he hides the jet model behind his back.

"You're so immature," Jen says though she is actually two years younger.

Already tall for his age, Jordan is also becoming very muscular. This is a good change for him since he had been a very weak, small child. Jennifer always thought he might make a good boyfriend for Judy someday, but for now the stupid boy is still playing with toys. Who is she kidding though? She likes him too. At school, he protects her from the bullies who tease her.

Shirtless Jordan, on the other hand, is mad. "You act like the whole house is a playpen. You just ruined my flight simulation, pea brain!"

"Put some clothes on!" Jen growls and throw some socks at him.

"Listen ape head, clothes create wind resistance," Jordan explains and puts the jet away. He quickly pulls on some sweat pants.

Breathlessly, Jennifer then goes into a rant, "This is my house. Mom says this is not your house. So that means I don't have to listen to you." Why did that come out of her mouth? She always has to be so defensive.

"What does your father say?" he answers back.

"He disagrees. He always disagrees with me, but that's not important right now. So…sorry, but look," Jennifer runs to a big panel on the wall and bangs on it until it lights up. After an annoying splash screen, the main browser page comes up. Quickly, she brings up a satellite map, which covers the whole gigantic panel. Looking for an area in particular, she uses her tiny fingers to scroll around furiously. Just when she is about to find what she is looking for, Jordan clicks the screen off.

"Go back to your house!" Jordan yells. "No stupid adventures." Sitting down, he picks up a book on modern jets, puts on an intense look, and pretends to be reading. He hates when she gets like this. She never gets blamed for anything. Everything is always his fault.

"I haven't even showed you my plan!" she bellows, unable to believe he is behaving this way. "If you cared about me, you would never say no."

"You're right. The answer is still NO. Last time I helped you, Mrs. Grant got really mad and threw all my clothes in the pool," Jordan howls and points at the extremely large Olympic pool. "That thing is deep!"

"They dried didn't they?"

"Yeah, but that's not the point you snot!" Jordan snipes as he tries to find his backpack.

Jen feels like crying. She wants him to help her like those heroes in the movies. "We have to find Judy. Nobody is doing anything. Nobody cares!" She turns the screen back on.

"Judy is missing?" Jordan asks as he finds a raggedy t-shirt to put on. "When did that happen?"

"Look here," Jen yowls, finally finding what she is looking for on the map. "See this line. This trail is where Judy and I used to go walking with her dad. When her allergies got bad, her father didn't take us anymore, but she loved it. She asked me to go with her the other day. Maybe she went on her own and got in trouble."

"Call the cops with your idea," Jordan mutters angrily. "What the hell is she doing out there anyways?"

Ignoring him, Jennifer keeps talking, "What do the cops care about people like you?"

"They don't."

"So are you going to help me or what? You know I'm right. I'm always right," Jennifer's voice is now desperate. "Judy is human like you. That's why they don't care. They won't look for her. You know it."

Jordan is quiet. After all, it is just going to be a worthless hike and he likes the outdoors. Looking at Jen's homely face, he feels something weird, maybe she isn't so ugly. Actually, the rest of her isn't so bad anymore. What the heck is he thinking? On second thought, maybe the hike would do him good. He needs some mountain air, lots of mountain air.

"OK. I'll go. Let me pack my stuff. You better go and change out of that curtain you're wearing," he tells her.

"I'm going like this," Jen protests.

"No you're not," Jordan counter protests. "Put some boots and jeans on. Now!" he orders.

"All my clothes are like this. I don't have any of that," she says as Jordan makes a face. "Don't roll your eyes, Jordan. It's gross."

After raiding his piggy bank and gathering supplies in a backpack, Jordan motions to Jen to start heading out. There is a secret path to the street behind the pool house. They sneak out quietly and head for the bus stop.

The area Jennifer needs to go to is called Madrone canyon. Fortunately, the number 80 SFMAG bus to Kentfield will get them pretty close. They sit in the back of the bus as to not get any questions. Jordan takes out a book.

"Are you really going to study?" Jen asks as Jordan opens his thick history book. "Why don't you have a digital copy?"

"Your mom took my palm computer away. She said a needy Nuhu deserves it more. Anyways, I like books. You can hit people with them," Jordan says angrily and pretends to swat Jen. "I thought all Nuhu were rich anyways."

"I guess," Jen states and pulls out a fruit snack.

"You should save those for the hike," Jordan suggests.

"I'm not the one who has to carry that paper brick," Jen says, her teeth covered in red, dehydrated fruit. "You got any water?"

He hands her a bottle.

"So what subject is that? Math? I know you love math."

"NAU history. I'm reading about the foundation right now," Jordan says while looking at a chart.

"History is boring. Why do we have to know about all these old dead people? They're boring. Everything you like is boring," Jen says with a frown. She then points at the chart. "Look! Guess what! So boring."

"Not for me," Jordan answers. "I'm starting to understand why people treat me different."

Jen looks over his shoulder. She struggles to read a list named "Significant Dates in NAU History" which reads something like this:

1880 - Foundation of NAU. Also known as the "Quiet Revolution." The previous nation is dismantled by popular vote after ten years of economic turmoil. Founders promise recovery through science and the creation of "thinking machines."

1887 - First recorded sustained, powered flight by Henry Malone of the NAU National Army.

1895 – First Technological Revolution. Economy recovery begins with the introduction of the first computers.

1903 – High capacity battery invented.

1904 – A new metal is found and added to the Periodic Table. Once called "great steel," by ancient cultures, it is renamed Exitor by a committee of world scientists.

1906 – The Great World War (1906-1916) begins with England and France against Germany and Russia.

1907 – Second Technological Revolution. Silicon chip perfected. Nuclear science matures.

1910 – NAU joins war on the side of Germany and Russia.

1912 – Personal computers become common.

1916 - The Great World War ends with the surrender of France to NAU. France becomes a reluctant NAU protectorate prone to violent uprisings which continue to this date. French territories are split amongst Russia and Germany. Britain signs non-aggression treaty with Germany, Russia and the NAU.

1918 – First genetically produced animal is born.

1920 – Third Technological Revolution. Science of genetics soars as human genome is mapped.

1925 – First genetically enhanced human is born from a purified embryo injected into human mother. "Nuhu," short for New Human is coined.

1928 – Engineered embryo perfected. 1st true-engineered human births take place from purified sperm and embryos. Children show greater levels of intelligence and physical aptitude.

1935 – Natural birth is considered inferior. Nuhu is established as a superior breed as most people move to artificial insemination. Subjects provide egg and sperm samples, which are then cloned and removed of impurities. However, several of these early children are born with deformities.

1942 – Calls for human natural birth to be banned due to high cost of procedure. Government establishes "tube farms" to reduce cost of genetic processing.

1948 – 1st Laws of Genetic Exclusion established to control undesirable human births. Genetic birth (via engineered embryos) becomes a right available to all through government clinics.

1952 – OverForce established to control "Anti-Genetics" riots by human activists. Right to live natural birth appeal succeeds in court.

1954 – Electric cars introduced. First clean emissions combustion engine announced.

1956 – First safe fission generators are introduced with the introduction of artificial element Hexium. Hexium is derived from Boxrite.

1958 – Russia invades NAU territory of the Philippines to secure Boxrite deposits. NAU declares war on Russia. Britain and Germany ally with NAU.

1960 – Fourth Technological Revolution. Limited "thinking" computers are introduced. First robots appear on market. Safe fission generations perfected.

1961 – British Uprising of 1961. Failed attempt by a royal prince to overthrow king.

1963 – Russians driven out of Philippines. Unofficial state of war between NAU and Russia remains.

1965 – Annexation of Canada and Mexico into the NAU due to fear of invasion from Russia. Central America invaded by Russia. South American nations vote to become protectorates of the NAU.

1968 – Social Revolution. Sex, color and race discrimination are deemed illegal. Genetics is established as the only measure of superiority.

1973 – Live birth is banned for all Nuhu. Nuhu children are defined as children born in lab conditions from purified embryo and sperm, which are raised from inception to nine months in a controlled, artificial environment. New babies are delivered to parents by special courier trucks. People complain that the system is too cold and impersonal. Many insist on being fertilized. These children are called, "The Half Baked Generation."

1974 - Pentam Fission Engine invented by Carlton Brummer.

1976 – 1st Air Battleship, the Independent Pacific (Indipac), takes flight using Pentam engines. Designed by Carlton Brummer with help from a dying Henry Malone. Over 100 years old, Henry does not live to see it fly.

1978 – Hydrogen becomes common fuel.

1980 – First Air Carrier, The Arizona, takes flight. She could only hold five aircraft.

1981 – Nuhu delivery system called the Phoenix is created to answer complaints. Babies are now delivered to home by a custom air ship. People fall in love with new system seeing it as a "virtual" stork.

1982 – First Russian and British Air ships take flight based on allegedly stolen NAU technology. NAU places embargo on British trade.

1983 – French government grants exclusive mining rights to NAU corporations. French population rise up against so called "destructive" mining operations and declare independence from NAU.

1984 – Russians driven out of Central America by combined NAU and South American forces. Central American nations become protectorates of the NAU. French revolution is put down by NAU. NAU establishes new French government, however a state of war still exists.
1985 – Petroleum banned as fuel source. British controlled Middle East is sent into financial turmoil. Russian signs treaties with Iran, Iraq and Saudi Arabia breaking British control of the region.
1986 – Britain signs alliance with NAU. NAU provides Britain with hydrogen technology.
1988 ...

She slams the book shut on him. "It's making me dizzy," she complains as a magazine picture falls out of the book. It's a picture of house on a beach with a family standing in front of it.

"What's this?" she asks.

He picks up the picture, folds it and sticks it in his pocket without saying a word.

"Your dream house?" Jen laughs. "Biggie dream you have. A house on the beach so you can watch all the bikini girls."

"No," he says. "I only want one girl."

"Kids too?" she giggles loudly.

"Come on. Kids?" Jordan growls. "I'm not some weirdo."

As they approach their stop, Jordan puts away the book. "We're here. Jen, hit the stop bar," he says.

THE CANYON – Part 2

Having arrived at the city of Kentfield, they head up a long road, all uphill, to the trailhead. It is tough going for some. The comfortably dressed Jordan leaves Jen several steps behind.

Jen thinks — some future boyfriend. He's not even waiting. Every now and then, at least, he does look back. Probably just to make sure she hasn't turned back. Someday, she promises herself, she will be every bit his equal.

Finally reaching the trailhead, Jen decides to throw off her shoes and begins to whimper, assuming Jordan could magically make them better.

"What are you doing?" he asks.

"They hurt. I don't have the right shoes. Slow down alright!"

Jordan huffs, "Keep moving. Just walk barefoot."

"With them off it hurts even more you dork!" She throws one at him. He catches it.

Peeved, Jordan peers back at her. He ponders, in a deep way, how could she be so ungrateful and bratty? She is complaining about her feet? Jennifer didn't even have the bus fare! But, he knows exactly what to say to her…

"Arrghhh," Jordan bellows, tossing the shoe back at Jen. It topples in front of her in a little puff of dust. "Put them back on." He then ignores her further whimpering and begins walking down the hard packed dirt trail alone. Having no choice, she hobbles along a few steps behind him.

Trying to pretend she is not there, Jordan looks down at the deep green, tree engulfed gorge that is Madrone Canyon. Vast and huge, this canyon is a place people, especially little ones, could easily get lost in. More troubling, the canyon could also be a great place to *hide in*. There is tinge of concern ebbing at him, a cold feeling on the back of his neck.

As they walk further in, Jennifer starts to feel uncomfortable too, but she says nothing. Even the constant buzzing of bugs seems somehow menacing. For now, she handles the uneasiness. She still sees several houses along the hills around them and this gives her a sense of comfort.

But what is that sound? It's not bugs.

They hear a great deal of voices coming from a bend up ahead. Not the type to wait and see, Jordan runs back and grabs Jen. They dive into a field of tall grass and hunker down. Pollen flies up around them, but this goes unnoticed as five soldiers pass by them, heading down the trail. They are armed to the teeth.

"Jordan. We're going the opposite way than they are." Jennifer whispers happily. "We should be okay."

"What are soldiers doing out here?" Jordan whispers back, his fears starting to materialize. "Something is not right. I'm taking us back home."

"Come on coward," Jen needles him. "They're just training or having a picnic."

"Whatever," Jordan says, giving in.

The pair walks quickly ahead, reaching a split in the fire road. A large drainage pipe rises up from the valley bellow and marks the beginning of a new trail. A rough dirt stairway, cut right into the mountain, leads to a series of switchbacks and then down deep into the dense forest.

With a growing uneasiness, Jordan takes a few tentative steps. Immediately, he feels as if the trail has engulfed him. There are so many trees here that everything further than five feet away becomes a blur. Ferns cover the damp ground making footing treacherous. It is even hard to see the sky the canopy is so intertwined.

"You sure this is where she would go?" he asks. "This place is scary as hell."

Having second thoughts herself, Jennifer nods, yes. "No other trail has the pipe. That's how her dad always found the way."

A still reluctant Jordan asks, "Why would she come out here alone? I wouldn't."

"She said she saw an angel down there," Jen explains pointing down into the trees. "She wants to come and pray."

"Humans aren't allowed to have religion. We're not smart enough to understand. That's what they say," Jordan mentions and then says with disbelief. "An angel? Ha. Bull crap. What did she want to pray for anyways?"

"She wants, um, she wants to become a Nuhu," Jen admits with reluctance.

"Oh," Jordan replies, looking blankly out into the wilderness.

"It's okay though," Jen says. "No one knows that she prays except me."

As they began moving again, Jordan thinks he hears running water. After looking around, he spots a stream tumbling down the canyon side. Hard to believe, Jordan thinks that this beautiful place could hold anything to fear, but his anxiety grows with every step. There is evil here. He can feel it.

The trees become more immense deeper in the canyon. Ferns grow at pre-historic sizes and make the two children look more like insects. An emerald glow infuses the area as if spirits, spirits with the power to control children, beasts and the weather, inhabits the forest. The temperature becomes downright chilly.

Jordan looks over at Jennifer. He could see that she is cold already, holding her arms tightly around herself. In his pack, he has a light jacket, but he decides to let the brat squirm awhile.

Jen slips. "Jordan!" she yelps.

But with little effort, Jordan captures her in his arms. They both laugh and hold tight to each other. There is certain warmth to being so close to Jen. Uncomfortable, Jordan lets go of her. He doesn't mention the squirrely feeling to her.

As he walks, Jordan thinks about some dreams that he has been having…about Jen. He feels odd during these dreams and especially the aftermath. He doesn't know what they mean and why Jennifer is always in them.

"Jennifer. You ever have any dreams…about me?" he asks innocently.

"No. Why?" she asks with puzzlement that quickly turns into curiosity. She starts to grin and giggle, "You've been dreaming about me?" she asks loudly, barely able to control her laughter. "What kind of dreams?"

Embarrassed, Jordan doesn't answer, but turns a bright red. He turns away almost looking to cry.

Realizing her girlish reaction was out of line, Jen sighs and decides to be forthcoming. "I think they mean we are growing up, those dreams. I know boys don't like to talk about stuff like that," she says, pulling the water out of his pack.

"Do they make you feel funny?" Jordan asks, unable to look up at her.

"What?" Jen says with renewed horror. "What do you feel?"

"Wet," he says reluctantly.

"You pee when you dream about me!" Jennifer yells with mock anger and walks ahead. "Jordan. You are such a baby. I don't wet myself anymore."

"I shouldn't have told you anything," he says and coils up.

In fact, Jennifer actually isn't too grossed out. She has been having a similar problem. Unlike Jordan though, she knows her body is changing. She isn't a girl; she isn't a woman. Her mind is somewhere in between. But Jennifer is ready and excited to grow up. She wants him so bad to hold her again…and admit that they both feel something special.

After what seems a very long, very quiet time, they reach the canyon floor. Jordan looks at his watch. They have taken most of the day to get down here. In a few hours, the sun would go drop and they would still be trying to get home. This is going to be trouble for him...again. The things he does for Jennifer.

The canyon floor is muddy and they have to walk carefully. Jennifer looks down at her feet and sighs. Her white stockings are splattered with mud. Every time she takes a step, mud seeps in and out of her shoes. She feels the mud is trying to eat her alive.

A perplexed Jordan spots the stream again. It is running through the middle of the canyon down here. He looks up and down both ways.

"Jennifer? Do we go downstream?" he says, pointing to a path that leads to some welcome sunshine.

"She saw the angel by the waterfall. Do you hear it? I think we should go toward the noise," Jen answers.

Listening carefully, Jordan hears water against rocks far off in the distance. He starts to walk upstream and toward the noise. Jennifer clutches his arm.

The canyon is oppressively grim in this area. Large roots stick out of the ground, exposed from years of run off. There is no green vegetation, save some moss, just mostly a lot of rocks, brown dirt and dark chocolate mud.

A concerned Jennifer wonders how long he would let her hold him. She really is scared. He doesn't seem to mind too much maybe he likes it. Soon, he pulls her hand off and proceeds to hold it. They looked at each other strangely.

Coy, Jordan manages a weak smile. He says, "For safety."

Coming around a corner, they go down a separate, darker branch of the canyon. Here the canyon walls are very high. At the end, the waterfall comes into sight. Not that it is much of a sight. It is made up of grey stones and black water.

"No wonder nobody ever comes down this way," Jordan grimaces. "I've seen water faucets that are more impressive."

"I like it," she lies.

"Great," Jordan growls, "you can have it."

Not paying attention to where she is walking, Jennifer trips. Trying to use Jordan for leverage, she only makes the hapless boy lose his balance too. They both fall into the stream. Having fallen on top of him, face to face, Jen stays dry. Jordan is of course drenched.

She can't help looking into his deep, light brown eyes. An urge hits her and she doesn't know how to handle it, she wants to kiss him. Despite all his complaints, here he is again, right by her side. She moves her lips toward him. He pushes her away.

"Get off. I'm getting soaked," he barks.

Jennifer gets up quickly and hurries away. It is then she notices the tip of a shoe sticking out from the mud and it's not hers.

"Look…at…look at that Jordan," she says with a stutter and a gulp.

"So what? You just lost your shoe," he says and grabs it, but the shoe doesn't budge. He pulls hard and nothing. The shoe is unusually heavy and not coming out easily. Strong for his age, he puts his weight into it. The shoe comes lurching out with the rest of the leg still attached to it. The rest of the body is not attached to the leg.

Horrified, Jordan freaks out and drops the severed limb.

Jennifer gasps and tries to step away, but falls down on her butt.

Pulling himself back together, Jordan grabs Jennifer and starts to pull her back out the way they came in.

"Give me your phone. I'm calling for help," he gulps.

With her hand shaking violently, Jennifer reaches around her neck and pulls out a golden butterfly.

"You girls and your fancy phones," He snarls and taps on the cover. The butterfly makes a sad noise. "No signal down here!"

Putting the phone away, Jen is soon trembling. She sees something. "Why is that rock moving?" she asks, not really wanting to know the answer.

Quickly, Jordan looks back toward the waterfall. A lumpy rock eerily stands up and seems to be stretching into the shape of man. The rock is actually an unnaturally built man. He looks back at them with miss-aligned eyes and bloody mouth. The remains of Judy are on the ground next to him.

Horrified, Jen is about to scream, but Jordan cups her mouth.

Jordan's mind fires up. He quickly judges the sub-human to be seven feet tall, about 300 pounds and ugly beyond compare. The man's right arm is partially fused to his body. The left arm is stubby and shorter than normal, but beefy and oversized. A web of flesh connects his fingers like he some sort of fish man. Worse, his skin seems to be melted and lumpy. The awful skin looks as though it had put it through a meat grinder. But the muscles, they are huge. So large, they seemed to restrict his movement.

"It's some sort of mutant," Jordan sputters.

"Boy. Don't call me that," the creature says with a slur and sniffs the air. "I can smell you, human. I am a Nuhu. Unlike you, I am worthy of respect," the sub-human hisses. "I must eat. But boys are too tough for my teeth, so I'll bury you to soften your flesh. Let the girl come forward. I'll kill you both quickly if you don't struggle."

A worried Jennifer looks at Jordan. Is she really going to be eaten like her friend?

"Run," Jordan says strongly, but neither can move, frozen with fear.

"Suit yourself boy. I will make you suffer," the sub-human promises.

Without warning, the sub-human charges them with unbelievable speed.

"Run Jen!" Jordan pushes her from him as he picks up a large branch. Amazingly, Jordan is every bit as fast as the creature. He slams the branch into the mutant's legs, but the branch snaps with no effect.

The sub-human turns to face Jordan. With one sweep of his stubby arm, he brushes Jordan aside like a feather. Jordan tumbles across the rocky ground and stops only upon hitting the canyon wall.

A helpless Jennifer screams as the walking pile of ground beef approaches her. In her mind, she realizes that being scared is not helping. Stirring her courage, she tries to fight, but her efforts are useless. He takes her by a leg and violently slams her against some tire-sized rocks. There is a crunch, a sickening crack, like a holiday wishbone snapping, coming from inside her leg.

As the sub-human bends down to bite her throat and finish her, Jennifer quickly jabs her fingers into his eyes. He moans angrily and slaps her across the face.

A stressed Jordan has to react. By her cries, Jordan knows Jennifer is hurt bad. He looks at the sub-human and feels his body shake in terror. He cannot beat this thing. But he didn't need to beat it to get it away from Jen.

Without hesitation, Jordan jumps off a rock and onto the sub-human's massive back. Using his belt, Jordan strangles the cannibal as best he can.

The sub-human is shocked by Jordan's unusual strength. He cannot pull him off. He is forced to drop the girl. Violently coughing for air, the man manages to finally smash Jordan into a dead tree trunk.

As Jordan hits, the wind comes bellowing out from him. With his strength gone, Jordan can no longer maintain his grip and falls down into the stream. Desperate, he tries to get up, but Jordan cannot get his footing on the slippery creek bed and stumbles back down. He can see the sub-human moving around him. Too late to escape, the man's huge deformed hand grabs him by the throat.

Panicked, Jordan's mind is fluttering. His vision is blurring and he cannot get free. The tables are now turned. He is now the one being choked. But what to do? This man is all muscle. Jordan has to think his way out. He has to outsmart it. Quickly, he calms his mind. Then the answer hits him he has to die.

Pretending to suffocate, he rolls his eyes back and goes rigid. He lets out a gasp, suddenly, than goes totally silent. Holding his breath, he hopes the sub-human would think he is dead.

Releasing his grip on Jordan's throat, the man slaps him hard across the face. Even though he is desperate for air, Jordan struggles through the pain and keeps his act together. The sub-human smiles and pushes Jordan's face deep into the mud. His attention then turns to the soft, tasty girl.

Convinced Jordan is dead, Jennifer shrieks. As the man approaches to finish her, she tries throwing stones and twigs, but nothing stops him. Her leg broken, she cannot run.

The sub-human licks his lips and reaches for her. She knows the end is coming, but she does not give up. Trying to get away, Jennifer tries to crawl, but only claws herself deeper into the mud.

Holding his bruised throat, Jordan tries to recover. Mud oozes from his mouth, but he has to breathe quietly even though he wants just to suck air in like a vacuum. How could he beat this thing? The only thing to equal the man's strength would be a bus. There are no weapons here. But what could he use instead? Then, he sees his backpack. An idea forms and he looks back at the waterfall. There is a deep pool at its base. The idea is desperate, but he can think of nothing else. Stepping on his backpack, Jordan rips out one of the straps. Wrapping it around his fist, he steels himself for another fight. He throws a rock and hits the creature squarely in the back of the head.

The sub-human turns around and looks absolutely shocked. But Jordan is already off running, heading toward the waterfall. He moves under the plume of falling water. The weight of water hurts, but it is dark, obscuring, which plays to his advantage. Once again, he finds himself wishing for air. He pulls the strap taut between his hands and waits.

Even though furious, the sub-human still hesitates to follow. The murky water hides the child well. He decides there is no choice but to go fish the boy out. This time he will make sure the boy stays dead. He'll twist the kid's head clean off, smash it on a rock and watch the brains pour out.

The creature darts into the water blindly. He feels around, but cannot find the boy. Something is tugging around his legs. He can't see what is doing the tugging, but decides to step and crush it. His legs don't work though! Something is binding them together, tightly together.

Jordan has managed to tie the backpack strap around the creature's legs. He can sense the sub-human is losing his balance, but there is no time to move as the beast falls on top of him. They are both in the pool…drowning.

With Jordan's legs pinned beneath his foe, there is no escape this time, no trick to use. The picture of his dream house floats past him and grows distant. His vision blacks out. The corneas of his eyes flare with a pulsating white noise. He is ready to give up and allow himself to be swallowed by the water. All his fight has been spent.

"You must not fall," a voice tells him from inside his head, but it is not his own voice. Silence returns again as the cold breath of death fills his lungs. Numb, he wants to let go of life. He starts to feel a beautiful warmth and a desire to sleep. But the voice is relentless, filling his every cell. "Stand up!" The voice pushes at him. "Stand!" Every word feeds energy into his tired limbs. He struggles to make his hand move and it does.

Jordan's fingers can feel a tree root. He grabs and then pulls. His legs begin to slide out. He pulls harder. Suddenly, his face is above water. Air rushes into his lungs. He pulls again and his legs are free. Trembling and weak, Jordan stands up.

Looking at the sub-human trying to reach for the strap, Jordan feels pity, but he must finish what he started. Moving fast, Jordan puts all his weight down on the sub-human's arm.

The creature struggles fiercely. His deformed arm cannot help him. His mighty legs cannot help him. Nothing can as the tables are turned. Violently shaking, the sub-human finally drowns, struggling till the end to reach the small ribbon around his legs.

Exhausted and beat, Jordan releases the man's rigid arm. He then notices the tattered shirt the sub-human is wearing, upon it, a military emblem. It is too muddy and old to make out.

There, stuck in the muck, he finds his soiled picture. He picks it up gently and carefully puts it back in his pocket.

Jordan trudges away from the waterfall and falls to his knees. He hears birds singing in the distance…the sound of wind in the trees. The realization hits him. Somehow, he survived, yet not entirely on his own. Jordan wonders if the voice was only raw instinct. For a second, he believes that's all it was, but the fact is, the voice came from everywhere and nowhere. But God has been far from kind to him, why would God finally show up? Why would God care so randomly?

Looking back at the waterfall, the body of the sub-human sits still, dead, half submerged. Unable to hold his emotions, he begins to cry. He covers his face, but starts to shake so bad he has to move his hands away. He's taken a life and it doesn't feel good. No matter the justification, the act of killing is primal and damaging. This unclean feeling will never leave him, always reminding him of the value... and the fragility of life.

"You're alive!" Jen yells, seeing him.

Quickly rubbing the tears away, Jordan stands and moves over toward her. He drops down in a heap by Jennifer...so, so very tired. This time, at least, no one is trying to stop him from breathing anymore.

"Is it dead?" she says emphatically. "Please tell me its dead."

With reluctance, Jordan shakes his head, yes. He looks over at her and sees that Jennifer is holding her leg. He soon forgets about the awful act he's done and moves over to help her. The leg looks bad, but at least no bones are sticking out.

"Jordan. What was that...thing?" she asks.

"It was some kind of man," he says. "What? Did you think all you Nuhu turned out right? Looks like they screwed him up real good," Jordan says not really thinking clearly. "Maybe someone coughed on his test tube."

"I was made like him?" she asks.

Stumped, Jordan doesn't reply.

Looking at her body, Jennifer is obviously scared by the idea. She warbles out, "He's like me? Someone made me in a tube? Will that happen to me?"

"Of course you're not like him," Jordan says unsure. "You turned out perfect so don't worry."

Confused, Jennifer though is not convinced and doubts invade her. Would she too someday become a monster? Is this the fate of all Nuhu children?

125

A busy Jordan is making a lot of noise and distracts her. He is thrashing around some dead trees. Finally, he finds what he is looking for: thin branches.

"What are you doing?" she asks.

"I saw Master Kenji do this when one of his students got hurt on a field trip. It's so that you don't make it any worse. Keeps you from moving." Ripping some straps from the bottom of her dress, Jordan straps the sticks around her leg. She squirms, but puts up with the procedure.

"I'm going to get help. I'll be back," he tells her, pulling his jacket from the remains of his backpack.

"Don't leave me here!" Jennifer pleads.

"If I carry you, it'll take all night and it'll hurt, a lot," he warns.

"I can't stay down here, not with that thing over there. What if it comes back alive in the night," she cries.

"There is nothing down here anymore that can hurt you. But, I'll try to carry you if that's what you want."

She nods enthusiastically yes.

Not looking forward to the walk, Jordan sits down next to her drained. He looks up at the canyon walls. This is going to be a long cold night. He puts the jacket on her and zips it closed. There is a funny look in her eyes. Thinking it is just the pain; Jordan begins to gathers some bigger branches to make a sled.

Night falls and they are nowhere near the top of the hill. Jordan pulls and pulls the sled up the increasingly muddy trail.

Halfway up, his hands rubbed sore by his makeshift wood sled, Jordan stops for a break. Jen is asleep, but OK. He checks to make sure she is warm enough. Snap-crack! There is something in the woods close by.

He ducks behind a tree and stays still. There is the sound of frogs and crickets, but nothing else. A flash of light comes from across the canyon. Jordan, scared, forces himself to look. He peeks from around the tree.

For a second, Jordan sees a woman. Her face is a sliver mask, reflecting the moonlight. Her dress is pure white and floating around her in the breeze. She bows at him and vanishes back into the darkness.

Beyond tired, Jordan brushes the vision aside. If it had been an angel, she would have helped him carry Jen out. He starts to climb again.

Hours later, after a night of wrong turns, branches and thorns, Jordan finally reaches the top of the canyon as the sun starts to come over the horizon. He places Jen down gently. She is very pale and cold, but still breathing. Taking her phone, she slowly opens her eyes and smiles. He hopes there is a signal now. There is.

"It works!" Jordan exclaims.

"Jordan," Jen whispers meekly and waves for him to come closer.

"I want to tell you something. You're not the only one to have those weird dreams. Mom told me I can't always be a child and that it's part of changing into a grown up," she says honestly. "You can't stop it. It just happens. One day you're a kid. The next day you're not."

"Thanks," he says, fully aware his innocent days are now behind him.

"I love you," Jen blurts out.

Moving down over her face, he looks into her blue eyes. "Are you sure?" he says with a crooked smile.

"I'm sure," she says and kisses him on the lips. The kiss is so awkward that they both start laughing. He then puts his arm around her and calls for help.

***

The sun is setting as Jennifer finishes recalling the story. She leans over and kisses Jordan on the lips. He doesn't have the will power to stop her. There would be no more talk of endings today, but an empty feeling still lingers.

"We are fated for each other. I think, no matter what, in the end we'll be together...somehow," Jen mentions. "All that history, it would be a shame to just leave it all behind. I don't think you want to."

"No."

"Then tomorrow will sort itself out. Don't ever believe that I don't love you. It's a part of me, built into me," Jen says. She then leaves him to his thoughts. He watches her red car swirl away in cloud of dust and disappear.

With his mind in turmoil, Jordan walks and walks. He stares as the Golden Gate Bridge's lights turn on for the evening. There is a sad purple glow to the sky as he thinks about his dream girl. For years, he struggled to be with her, hiding their growing relationship, risking his future. Now it's all falling apart and it hurts like hell. That's the problems with dreams, even when they come true, they can just as quickly turn into nightmares. The truth is that life doesn't stop at the high points. It just keeps rolling along until you fall off.

THE PHOENIX

Boney and statuesque, Samantha Grant is an image of beauty slowly fading. She gracefully struts into Dr. Magen's office with a degree familiarity. There is little to see here except for a chair and a translucent barrier opposite it. The walls are neutral taupe color and the art has been picked to be seen and not remembered. She waits patiently as a figure of an elderly man sits behind the screen.

"Come and have a seat," Dr. Magen says in a sweet, rustic voice.

Smiling, Samantha quickly sits down and leans forward toward the silk screen. "I'm glad you could see me again. I know that you often don't take visitors anymore."

"Age has taken its toll on me and I am a vain, vain old man," Magen replies from behind his barrier. "I remember you father, he was a great doctor too. I so miss being young and our work together."

"He always spoke so highly of you," Samantha recalls.

"However, I must be quick as my energy is not what it used to be," he says and points to a table by the chair. There is a container of pills placed on it. "Tell Jennifer to continue to take those with her other supplements."

"I don't think they are strong enough. She is still acting out," Samantha says with alarm.

"Those are as strong a dose as I can dare give you. I promise my fair lady, they will make her listen to you. In time, she will be the ideal daughter of the North American Union."

Getting up, Samantha goes to the table and picks up the pills. She looks back to thank Dr. Magen, but he is gone. A young black woman quickly appears from around a corner. She beckons Samantha to follow and quickly escorts the older lady to the front door.

Once Samantha is out of sight, a second black woman appears that is an identical twin of the other. She closes the door and begins to examine a check-list.

"Fourteen," the dominant twin says with an air of authority. "Track and follow the target, Jennifer Grant. The code word is 'autonomous' and is to be relayed immediately. Monitor the results."

"Yes Fifteen," the other model replies. "Consider it done."

***

Nervously, Rina strums her fingers on a concrete barrier and tries not thinking negative thoughts. She frowns, but quickly forces a smile as a familiar red Italian convertible pulls into the Trans Hub. The passenger door opens automatically and Rina jumps into the comfy leather seat.

"Great day don't you think?" Jennifer says with an overtly chipper tone as she takes a pill and sips some water. She offers one to Rina, "They help you slim down."

"No thanks, I do enough walking every day. Should be a pretty nice day to see the Phoenix come down," Rina says and notices Jen is dressed like a fashion model. She starts fidgeting.

"That's a sexy dress," Jennifer says in joking manner, but isn't really. Rina looks like a slut with her breasts nearly hanging out. "Very appropriate attire for the occasion," Jen politely mentions, laughing inside.

Not comfortable being stared at, Rina squirms around as if sitting on Jell-O. This gets an odd, scornful look from Jennifer. Trying to be friendly, Rina forces herself to say, "Mark helped me pick it out, but I think its cut too low." She pats her chest as if trying to hide it. "The O.F. was a bit sadistic when I was a teen. I think they over-designed my breasts."

Disgusted, Jen ignores her comments. "That Mark, he is such a girl when it comes to clothes," Jennifer laughs and heads for the MagWay. They are soon making way to the hilly city of Fairfax. "When Mark was in high school," Jen recalls as she drives way too fast. "He would never take off his stupid black leather jacket. 100 degrees be damned." She continues her tale as the car pulls out to a surface road, passing the downtown area of San Rafael, "Well the Exitor team thought Mark was gay and chained him to a locker—naked. And, you know how Jordan is. He quit. Our team lost the I.C.E. (International Competition of Exitor) championship that year."

"Jordan is a good guy. One of the few that I know," Rina says innocently.

"You think you know Jordan?" Jennifer giggles insincerely. "You've known him what…a few hours at best?"

An agitated Rina holds her anger as the car travels up into a hilly neighborhood. The houses are getting big with views of expansive golf course below. "I haven't known him that long," she finally admits, "but Mark tells me great stories about him. Unusual for a Nuhu and a human to be that close, but it makes sense the more I'm with them. The only things that really separates all of us are those stupid labels."

"You're very observant," Jen states and glares at her. "I guess all O.F.'s are observant to a fault."

"Did you and Jordan have a fight again?" Rina inquires. "He's been tight lipped and moody. Hope everything is fine."

Steamed, Jennifer forces a smirk, "He's mad?"

"Well your brother had a run in with…" Rina blurts out.

Finally showing her aggressive nature, Jennifer comes to hard stop in the middle of the street. Quickly, the autopilot kicks in and moves the car off to the shoulder. Like a demon released from hell, Jen snarls, "That man was born like an animal and came out of a hole like some rodent. He's not my brother. Got it?"

"Sorry, it was a misunderstanding," Rina says. Jen is baiting her. Pissed, Rina claws at the leather as if a caged tiger. She could slice Jen's throat in a half second, but that wouldn't help matters in the long run.

Sliding back into character, Jen says as she takes control of the car again, "I don't have a brother."

"Your loss," Rina says under her breath, but Jen doesn't hear. Rina thinks that this invitation reeks of a set-up. The whole thing has been a huge mistake. Mark warned her that Jennifer is a whirlpool for trouble. He's right. The idea of jumping out of the car is starting to sound reasonable. She toys with the door handle but there is a sharp drop. Still, Rina finds the choice tempting.

Taking a deep sigh, Rina sulks. She really doesn't have anything better to do anyways. The truth is she likes being included in normal life activities. Whatever Jennifer's real motivations are not that important. She's just happy to be doing something out of her gray uniform for once.

Pulling down the visor, she glimpses her reflection in the vanity mirror. A gaudy red haired woman stares back…a manufactured goddess better suited for men's magazines. For a genetic product, she had not born beautiful, not even remotely pretty. The OverForce made her this way over the years and it hurt like hell each time. Her face was re-sculpted. Her legs were broken and lengthened. Her self-worth was shattered and remade.

In her mind she is still that scared, average little girl, so Rina knows well enough that her beauty is a tool for seduction, a tool to allow her to gain confidence and finally betray. To her, this role comes naturally and effortlessly and she despises that fact. The idea of sleeping with strange men and women is not at all objectionable. Just like being punched in the face a million times, your body just gets used to it. In her field, suffering is simply an everyday fact of life.

There is no room, in the OverForce, for independent thought or identity. Her identity is as sexual bait. She didn't know any other way to act.

But the OverForce ultimately failed in their training, Rina's conditioning is majorly flawed. They made her betray her best friend. They made her kill her. And instead of making her hard and heartless, which was the intention, she became wracked with guilt. Now, Malone, a man she hurt beyond all, has given her the opportunity to right her ways.

"You're quiet. A penny for your thoughts," Jennifer asks with the hopes of sparking small talk again.

"Thinking of an old friend," Rina says her voice cracking.

"Anyone I would know?"

"Rain Malone," Rina says and snaps back into her controlled composure. "She was a lot like you. Thought she could change things."

Surprised by her candor, Jen gulps. Rain Malone is dead. She remembers that Rain Malone was identified in Rina's file as a confirmed kill. "Well, hopefully, you and I can be just as close. Maybe one day you'll treat me just like her," Jennifer suggest with an audible distaste. "Wouldn't that be nice?"

"I wouldn't mind giving you the same level of treatment," Rina answers causing Jen to shiver. "She took things too far. I hear things about you…about what you want to do with the movement. It's a dangerous game to be playing."

"Is that a threat?" Jen howls.

"Friendly advice," Rina states coldly. But as they turn a corner and enter a driveway, her eyes almost bulge out. This is no house; this is a palace. It covers the whole hilltop.

Suddenly, she finds herself starring at her outfit again. Not much, just a simple dress bought at a mall store. She looks fine, she tells herself, but it doesn't help. Inside, feelings of inadequacy eat at her. Rina's mind flashes to childhood, a penniless childhood. She remembers the day her parents sold her into the OverForce. Quickly, she blocks out the memory. Standing up straight, her face goes rigid; her training digs in and she prepares for another social test.

They park the car along the estate's long circular driveway. Several servants come out to greet them and proceed to point them in the direction of the giant, two-story mansion.

Overwhelmed, Rina gulps hard. The house's foyer is bigger than her whole apartment. Giant paintings of the family line the walls. Hell, the servants are even dressed more fashionably than she is.

Toward the back of the property, the pair exits into a formal European garden. A beautiful floral archway has been built on the edge of a huge green lawn with the whole of Bay Area serving as a backdrop. Under some vast white tents, several tables have been set up loaded with fancy food of all kinds. As an army of flawlessly groomed ladies and gentlemen loiter about, dandy waiters hand out pricey sparkling wine.

Under stress, instinct takes over Rina; she suddenly changes character, assuming the confident and stern persona of an O.F. officer. Her performance is honed to perfection. Jennifer notices this and narrows her eyes in disgust.

One young lady is wearing an elaborate flower crown. She is radiant and glowing, overflowing with happiness. Rina cannot understand her joy. Such happiness is beyond her comprehension.

"Jen!" Leticia shouts overjoyed. "You made it!" She hugs Jennifer.

"I'm so happy for you today Leticia," Jen says and kisses her friend on the cheek. "Remember when we used to talk about our first baby back in high school! Now, it's happening."

A beaming Leticia turns and sees the stern Rina and does a double take, even the upper classes fear the OverForce. "You must be Officer Dupont," she says, offering her hand.

"Pleased to meet you. The NAU government shares your happiness today. May God bless you on this glorious day and my God also bless our great Union." Rina spits out in an icy monotone.

"I'm pleased," Leticia says nervously.

"She's off duty," Jen assures. "I think."

With a stiff smile, Rina replies slyly, "The O.F. is never off duty, but you can relax. I am here only socially. No uniform. No badge."

An apprehensive Leticia forces a grin and waves at them to follow her to the food. Icy stares from the other guests follow Rina as she pokes around the hors d'oeures and beverages.

"Nice Rina," Jen growls, "could you be a little less robotic?"

"I thought I was being polite," Rina replies, confused, chomping down on a finger sandwich.

"You need to turn off that O.F. charm. No wonder everyone avoids you people," Jen growls and throws down a glass of bubbly. "Wipe off that lioness' smile and have a drink...or two." She hands her a glass.

"I'm sorry," Rina says and turns red for the first time in her life. "I'm not used to this being myself stuff." She gulps down the sparkling wine and takes another one.

"Then who are you today?" Jen asks puzzled.

The crowd starts to holler and scream as strange music starts to play from the estate's wireless sound system. Someone yells, "Look. The Phoenix is coming!"

A big, round vehicle soon emerges out from some fluffy clouds. The ship has long balloon shape with little exaggerated winglets on both sides.

Leticia jumps in joy and hugs her husband. She starts to cry uncontrollably. She is so happy.

In her own little world, Rina remembers an encounter while on a mission for Malone in France. She met the nun Emilie Cotillard. Cotillard taught her about the connections between humanity and nature. Now, like Malone, she is a believer. What would Cotillard think about this sight? A contrived, artificial event totally removed from nature.

The vehicle lands softly on the green lawn, right next to the arch. A round door opens up and a young man and woman exit. They are dressed impeccable in shockingly white outfits. The whole scene is sickly cute — almost like a puppet show.

They move in toward Leticia, in a well-rehearsed performance, and quickly stop and look at her. They both smile, very broad, very fake smiles. Leticia shakes she is so nervous with excitement. At this point, the man steps back toward the ship.

The crowd yells with joy, "It's a girl!"

With that, the young man goes to the side of vehicle. Several babies emerge from a holding unit and he checks the toe tags to make sure he has the right one. He scans the toe tag with a small tablet device and lifts the baby into his hands.

He walks up and hands the baby over to his female companion.

"There is no greater joy," the young woman attendant says approaching the new mom, "then the start of a new life. Here in my hands is the future of our world, of our hopes. She is yours to love and raise. Congratulations, your baby is a perfect girl, made just for you."

Giving the tearful mom her child, the woman attendant retreats. The crowd applauds; a new Nuhu has been born…sort of.

As the mommy introduces the baby to the gathered crowd, the male attendant pulls the father aside. The father happily signs the delivery receipt and tips both attendants. He is handed a thick manual.

A puzzled Rina is given the baby to hold. She doesn't know how to feel. Here is another example of the absolute perfection of genetic science, just like her; made from the best genes, just like her. She is to be loved…not like her. Rina cries uncontrollably. To all gathered, the tears seem to be of happiness.

Rina thinks, what a great lie this all is. Mass produced babies delivered on time to oblivious clients. Rich or poor, they are all still brought into this world in the belly of a machine. She couldn't shake the idea that perhaps the machine is their true mother, that they have no place in the natural world.

An emotional wreck, Rina looks over at the Phoenix with fake hope. She wishes the machine would take her back, take back all the unwanted babies…like her.

TOOLS OF THE TRADE

With whirls of steam circling around them, long and graceful beams reach out from the walls and up toward the ceiling. The smell of oil and machinery is rich in the air.

This is the belly of a huge metallic whale, but to Jordan it is a cathedral to engineering. Unlike certain people who have many faces, machines have only three: working, not working, and busted. There is nothing more to understand, nothing threatening. He finds the machine world one of order and harmony. The young Jordan likes that. That's a world he can live in.

Captain Grant struggles with the seven-year-old boy on his shoulders. It is hard to balance him since he keeps moving, looking all around. The Captain excitedly shows the boy around the mighty engines of his new command, the Destroyer Axe. It's an older model full of electro-mechanical parts and not much digital, but it's as tough as they come.

Jordan stares with delight as the machines work diligently with their mighty steel claws dipping and surfacing from decks bellow. Occasionally, there is a resounding breath that bursts forth from vents as the generators pull cooling, flowing liquids in.

Several crew members work quietly in the distance, but seem to be happy to give the new Captain and his young recruit a wide berth.

Before this, Jordan had only seen car engines, but these monstrous engines are not anything like those. A car engine's purpose is simple, rotate four wheels. They did not make you fly. Now, he is flying and in love, though he is too young to understand all the details.

The powerful arms he's watching spin tremendous gears, which in turn move the massive flight surfaces outside. None of this matter to him, the ship is alive. It is a great mystical beast and his dad is its master.

**

Waking up from his memory, Jordan tries to focus on Mark's lesson, but the pretty curly haired woman seated next to him is hard to avoid. Rubbing his eyes, he forces her to disappear as several diagrams are being projected above the leather-clad man.

Mark, pointing at them with schoolboy glee, describes the evolution from gear and lever flight controls to the newer magnetic, digitally, actuated ones. Even though he is talking about a subject dear to his heart, Jordan's mind wanders over to a disreputable subject — Jennifer. As much as he would like to move on, she is always haunting some part of his conscious.

Convinced that Jen will control him like a puppet for the rest of his life, Jordan slumps down as far as he can in his chair and prays for mercy. He concedes that he is thoroughly pussy whipped. His woeful attempt at prayer is soon interrupted, some woman is talking so loud he cannot think straight.

This pretty woman is yammering at Mark as if he owed her money. Apparently also pussy whipped, the Professor humors her and Jordan doesn't know why. Mark never lets anyone talk over him in his own domain. Maybe he likes her sexy British accent.

"Gabrielle," Mark groans as he struggles to get a word in. "If you'll just let me answer…"

Nope, she continues ranting on and on about how British frigates are invincible or some other such nonsense. A bored Jordan can't believe Mark is listening to this dribble.

Both Russians and British air ships are derived from stolen NAU designs. They have nothing to brag about. He stares at the woman for a second. She is shapely, unlike a typical Nuhu stick. Could she be a human? Not likely. She looks rich. Her clothes are cut almost as well as Mark's.

His mind soon wanders back to Jen. There are so many pitfalls about having a relationship with her, be it lunatic sister or lunatic girlfriend. This morning he saw her with Christian Palin…kissing no less, even after their deep conversation. He wonders what if she does like Palin in some way? Blondie is a very handsome guy. Truth is Jordan is a fool for even contemplating a twisted life with Jen as her male concubine.

The puppet, fortunately, finally finds enough presence of mind to focus on Mark's class, especially since Mark's hand is gripping his shoulder tightly. Jordan looks up at his instructor, who frowns back at him, his eyes oozing with pure evil malice. Trying to avoid this awful visage, Jordan averts his eyes. Mark's gaze, it is rumored, can turn students to stone. Fortunately, the professor decides to move on before taking Jordan's miserable life force.

Spared, Jordan's eyes are now free to move around the classroom. The space is large and has a significant lab area. There is a collection of engines: fission, electric, and ruined. God forbid he ever adds a rickety combustion engine. Mark is liable blow everyone up.

Hanging from the ceiling, every conceivable aircraft currently in use are carefully modeled and displayed. On his desk, there is also a small model of his G850 car. What damn show-off, Jordan thinks.

The lecture has been about the workings of the Pentam "Clean" Fission engine. This is the engine that revolutionized modern airship design. Several diagrams of the engine are then projected on wall panels around the room. In the front of the class, a master display shows an animated view of the engine as used in a modern air carrier. These engines are simply huge. Mark points at a cross section of metal rods — Hexium.

Mark explains that Hexium combined with plutonium produces energy with no nuclear waste and it's only true by product is an inert dust that is harmless. As the particles collide, he continues, energy is released and then the Hexium particles immediately recombine the molecules into a new inert matter known as post-accelerated particulates or PAP.

Hexium is a man-made material that is produced in great quantity in Europe and has made many NAU friendly nations wealthy. In total, Hexium is created with six different components. One is a mineral and is extremely rare, hence drawing a king's ransom in price, Boxrite.

Because of this, Pentam engines have remained the exclusive domain of major military vessels. All other vehicles use much less powerful, far cheaper, hydrogen/electric hybrid engines (HOEL engines) or high capacity batteries / turbines (HITU).

These HOEL engines are clumsy and wasteful as far as Mark is concerned. Hydrogen is plentiful, but this class of engine has a severely limited power to weight ratio, not very good for the aerospace industry. Hydrogen is tricky and volatile and not very happy being shot at. HITU fighters can have multiple engines and batteries thus improving their lifespan, and their pilots, on the battlefield.

This quickly leads the class into an argument of whether the costly Pentam powered air carriers are worth their price. A group of Air Corp Officer Trainees take the offensive, firmly defending air carrier strength and flexibility. Mark Whatley is bemused. His interest regained, Jordan starts to pay attention, which is fortunate timing...

"Grant Junior!" Mark says loudly. "You served your entire wretched youth in the Air Corp. What do you think old man?"

After grinding his teeth, Jordan answers up, "I was stationed on the heavy Carrier Spearpoint for a time. It was a slow beast. The Spearpoint is completely dependent on fighters and escorts for its defense. Carriers have little in a way to project force on their own if their fighters are taken down. Power to weight, you can either carry guns or planes, not both."

One of the Officer Trainees cuts in, "Then by default, since the fighters are powerful, the air carrier is powerful. An air carrier is undefeatable."

Knowing better, Jordan cracks a half smile and laughs, "It's an empty shell without the fighters — a toothless lion. Carlton Brummer is rolling in his grave with that comment."

Mark chimes in, "And, the fighters don't have any range without the air carrier. Power cells limit the range of current HITU fighters." Mark rubs his fingers together as he smirks, "What about an air carrier and a battleship then? In the Battle of Seattle, it was Admiral Grant's use of battleships that turned the tide. Not fighters. The Admiral was able to intercept and keep the rebel fleet off-shore, eliminating their ability to back up their ground forces."

"Admiral Grant had several air carriers at his disposal too," the Officer trainee argues back.

"Right, he did, they were also to slow to arrive, but he also had one thing the rebels didn't. They didn't have the heavy artillery," Mark says.

"Those rebel air carriers were vulnerable to attack from the battleship's big guns which proves Jordan's point," the British student interjects. "You busy up the fighters and big guns prove victorious. That's exactly what Admiral Grant did by moving in his faster, light carriers and frigates to engage the rebel carriers. Once their fighters were put down, he moved in with the battleships for the kill."

"That's only one instance," the Officer trainee insists. "Anyways, the battle was really won by a fighter pilot."

A proud Jordan smiles bemused.

"Rubbish. The pilot only saved people. The battle had been won decidedly already by then," Gabrielle points out. "In pure military terms, what the pilot accomplished was insignificant. Politically, the military had their dessert to go with their dinner."

After an awkward silence, Mark clears his throat loudly and moves on, "Modern military strategy discounts the big gun vessels and Admiral Grant used that thinking to his advantage. So we either need fighters with longer range or carriers that can take care of themselves, but Jordan raised an interesting point. Does anyone know who Carlton Brummer is?"

Gabrielle answers, again, "He was a maverick designer. He designed the original air ship and all current ships are still based on his design. That is, before he went bonkers."

"Speaking of crazy, anyone ever hear of the IndiAtlantic?" Mark asks.

"Do you mean the IndiPacific? The first air ship?" one of the students suggests.

"No, the IndiAtlantic was the last ship Brummer built. It was supposed to be revolutionary. The IndiAtlantic was designed with energy shields and radical robotic armor. Armor that was radar controlled and moved to brace the hull at impact points. It was supposed to make the ship lighter and faster, plus with such heavy defense, nearly invulnerable to small aircraft. They installed the biggest Pentam engines ever designed. Those powered a magnetic hovering system so advanced that no one but Brummer could understand it. When it worked, the IndiAtlantic could even hover motionless with minimal power use. Unfortunately, none of it worked reliably, cost a fortune and ruined Carlton Brummer. He died soon after its failure," Mark explains. "I think they took the hull and re-used it as a lowly cargo transport in effort to offset the costs. It is never wise to give one person too much power over a project, or anything else for that matter."

"Some might say the IndiAtlantic failed because of government second-guessing, but who really knows the truth. The idea was brilliant though," Jordan says with a bit of sadness. "A fast, maneuverable, armored battleships with energy shields against almost an attack, not just fighters, would have been a true game changer. Too bad poor Carl didn't have the heart to fight on."

A woman asks, "What about missiles? Would missiles be susceptible to electronic shielding? Electronic fields can only disperse energy weapons right?"

"Good point," Mark replies. "Shields are limited due to the amount of energy required to produce a field. You would need a field generator for about every fifty feet. Every curve or surface variation would need to be addressed. That's why they are not commonly used. They are not currently practical. Most missiles would easily penetrate a shield since the shield is projected only about two to three feet from a surface. The kinetic energy of a missile would still drive it into the target," Mark answers. "On the other hand, missiles cannot get passed most RACE (Radar Controlled Energy) guns. They automatically lock onto a missile and wipe it out. Plus, there are other physical or electronic counter-measures on air carriers and battleships. Most heavy ships have a barrage gun to throw up a ton of flares or flack as a backup. Anyways, you would need a great many of missiles to do any kind of damage without a large warhead. But even a nuclear warhead, if detected, could be countered. A nuke doesn't detonate so easily. So if you destroy the delivery system as with a RACE gun, you reduce it effectiveness. Unless, you're going to strap it on to your back and take it on board that way. Even then, you would still have to bypass the ship's security sensors. So missiles are still just the domain of fighter to fighter combat."

"What about an EMP?" Jordan asks, though he already suspects the answer.

"An electronic magnetic pulse weapon? Ha!" Mark says scornfully. "If we can give credit to Echotech for something, it is their hardwired computer systems. They are well shielded against that kind of attack. It would be easier, though still nearly unthinkable, to disable the flight systems. You would only need to be able to fry about three levels of backups and physically destroy any redundant mechanical systems."

"How about Russian ballistic missiles ships? Those fire non-nuclear warheads and are a big concern to NAU planners," Gabrielle asks. "SAW's are powerful weapons too."

"They pack a wallop if they hit. As you noted, they have either an acoustic or conventional warhead," Mark answers. "But like any projectile, more so in the bigger ones, a computer driven RACE gun would take it out. Those lasers are very good at damaging the delivery system so that they never reach their target. SAW's are relatively large items and not yet useful outside of being heavy ordinance."

"Unless like you said, you take out the flight systems. You could override a ship's command codes," Jordan adds casually. "Take the electronics out of the game...and you've got yourself a shooting gallery."

"Not likely to happen again," Mark says. "Orissa was a onetime affair. The Russians got lucky."

A student asks, "Has shielding technology progressed to be useful since the IndiAtlantic tried it?"

"No, they fried the Pentams on the Indi. We probably won't start seeing shielding units until the next generation of power plant is invented. Speaking about tremendous power, it is the Pentam engine that makes an air carrier stay aloft and gives battleships their punch. The Pentam punch is what still makes a battleship an effective weapon in these times. Those guns can smash into almost any known material."

"Except Exitor," a riled Christian Palin adds.

"Even Exitor would eventually heat and break. Granted any kind of ship made of Exitor would hold together with holes blown all over its structure due to Exitor's tight molecular structure. But if Hexium is expensive, building an entire capital ship out of Exitor would ruin any country."

"Maybe just a fighter then," Jordan casually adds.

"Possibly, with a little magic," Mark says with a wicked fire in his eyes. "But that would still cost too much to produce in any quantity. A synthetic Exitor or Exitor composite would be needed to start the next revolution in military hardware. Wouldn't it Jordan?"

Jordan nods intrigued, "Yes it would."

"Ok boys and girls. That's it for today," Mark yells as he claps his hands.

As the students pile out, Jordan lingers.

"No apples?" Jordan asks, putting his feet on top of a chair, "Maybe too much fantasy for the little tin soldiers today."

"They're kids. You've been around," Mark growls and pushes his feet off the chair. "They've spent their mandatory stateside, not like us, especially not like you," Mark then asks, "Cut them some slack. Hopefully they won't have the same experiences we had."

Agreeing, Jordan sighs, "I can't imagine someone volunteering for extended service anymore."

"Many still believe in the nation. Many believe fanatically," Mark says with reluctance. "Some would say that is a good thing. Some wouldn't."

"When a god rules a nation or the nation becomes a god, people suffer," Jordan says and gets up, picking up Mark's car model. "Nobody knows god's will and no human is a god. The sad fact is humans rule humans — and poorly at that."

"You know Jordan," Mark changes the subjective and slaps Jordan on the back. "Let's get some chow...in the city...my treat."

"Wow. A second free dinner? You're not going to propose are you?"

"Not this time," Mark smiles and flashes his very white teeth. "This is about a job."

"Fantastic, you just made my day," Jordan smiles back, barely holding in his excitement. Could this really be the break he needs? "I'll see you tonight then." He takes off.

Before Mark can even take a seat, Jen comes busting in looking insane and frantic. Beads of sweat are dropping off of her brow and her eyes blood shot.

"Hey Jen, you just missed Jordan," Mark says, but is soon concerned about her sick appearance. "I was just about to clear up my desk and get out of here. You feeling alright?"

"I don't know," Jen says feeling nauseous. "Lately, I just feel like I can't rationalize anything, like my mind runs away from me. I'm always exhausted."

He looks at her closely. Her eyes are dilated wide and are a sickly gray; her face creased with stress.

"I was so excited to have Jordan back and...um...I just keep acting like a total nightmare. It's like every time I want to get close to him, I just say the opposite. I...I...keep pushing...pushing him away. Mark I...I need..." her brain suddenly shuts down and she loses track of what she was saying.

"You OK?"

"Mark," Jen says nervously. "I think I'm sick." She then nearly topples over.

"Are you on something? You look terrible." He runs over and catches her. She is sweaty and her heart is racing.

"I'm fine," she says recovering her balance. Her eyes are once again clear and sharp. "We had to use Unity Movement funds to bail out some people from jail," she says quickly, her hands trembling. "We're running short on money. I need Rina's O.F. passwords. I have a buyer."

Stopped in his tracks, Mark looks up to her and smiles cynically, "You got to be kidding."

"Kidding? No. I'm not," Jen says surprised. She knows she shouldn't be asking him, but for some reason she can't control herself. She feels compelled to get the money...anyway she can.

"Jen stop this," Mark says holding back his anger. He moves to sit down, annoyed that he allowed himself to be caught up in her act. Leaning back on his chair, he snorts, "I'm not going to betray Rina. Not a chance."

"Why not? Ask her about Rain Malone! She is not what she seems." Jen yells. "I need anything, something to sell. Please Mark, help me out. Don't you realize Rina is a double agent?"

Knowing full well that Rina is in fact a double agent, Mark becomes worried about this conversation and decides to cut to the chase. "You protesters are nothing but a joke. The truth is no one important supports you because you just go around breaking things. How is that an alternative to the OverForce? You guys protest but don't educate. Stop yelling and say something. The money will come naturally."

"Forget it," Jen says, trembling with rage. "I'll get it myself." She storms away. "You'll see. Rina will be your downfall."

A puzzled Mark sits in his dark classroom. He begins to wonder about Jen's sudden mood shifts. Concerned, he allows himself to think the worst. She has been his friend for years and he is not about to let her become a mindless pawn of the government. Perhaps Jen is the true double agent…and doesn't even know it.

But how to do you prove what supposedly does not exist? He will need her blood.

THE PATHLESS FOLLOWED

From the busy, but controlled, roadway of the Golden Gate, Jordan can see hues of gold, green, and blue light illuminating the white marble city. There is an occasional flare of a red or white sparkle coming from these manmade canyons. Higher up, polished glass reflects both geometric shapes and the sea in a seamless, undulating live abstract painting. Stretching up from the fog banks, San Francisco is a true Emerald City, except this city sparkles with neon and liquid crystals.

From the bridge, they head down Lombard Street toward Van Ness. Towering buildings, lit like torches, meet them as they enter the City. There are no traffic jams and pedestrians walk freely about as the City watches all like a big, unseen mother.

Mark Whatley likes freedom and drives most of the time by himself, but even he respects the City, allowing its traffic control system to take over operation of his precious vehicle. Jordan and Mark are relegated to mere passengers.

"No override mad genius?" Jordan dares to ask.

"I just don't wanna use it," Mark gloats. "I like to move with the city."

Upon reaching the downtown district of Nob Hill, Mark hits the virtual "dock" button on his car's central display. His G850 gently veers into an opening on the side of a non-descript building with a simple neon sign: "Parking Cortex – Good Rates."

The opening leads to a service tunnel where several cars are lined up on red squares. Each square contains a large, individual metal platform. The G850 is guided to an empty one and comes to a stop. Both men exit the car as a small card reader on the wall blinks its red eye madly, attempting to get their attention. Mark waves his phone over it and it changes to green. Having finished paying, he motions Jordan to follow him.

As the men leave the platform, a wall of red lasers surround the car. In the blink of an eye, it is then quickly taken away, washed, and stored in a vault-like underground garage even before they even exit the structure.

Passing the historic St. Francis hotel and its newer sister hotel, the sail-like New Francis, a light sprinkle of rain starts to fall.

"Stupid phone was supposed to alert me about the weather," Mark growls disapprovingly at his phone. "We'll be alright. T-Nos is around the corner."

"It's just a little rain," Jordan states bravely.

"Well sir, let me get a water hose," Mark snickers back, looking concerned over his jacket. "Bad for the leather."

As they approach the restaurant, Mark elbows Jordan. He is pointing to a row of beauties waiting to get in. They all turn to see the handsome men coming.

"I told you this place is good," Mark says with a wink.

Practically horse whipped, Jordan stops in his tracks as he sees a sign, carved elegantly into brass, on the restaurant's window, "T-Nos is pleased to be a Nuhu only restaurant."

A bouncer moves quickly to block them, "New rules gents. We I.D. Cough them up."

With that, a frustrated Jordan turns, walking over to the other side of street. Mark stares at the sign in disbelief. He then chases after his fast walking friend who is already halfway back to the garage.

Feeling apologetic, Mark says reassuringly, "Come on man. I've been here lots of times. They'll let us in."

"They'll let me in...because of you."

Frustrated and knowing Jordan is right, Mark looks around to make sure no one is within earshot and says, "We're supposed to be faster, stronger and smarter. I've only got you beat on smarter."

"I'm going over there," Jordan argues, pointing to a greasy-spoon chain store named "Happy's" of all things. "That's good enough for me. They don't I.D."

Mark retorts, "Don't compromise. You say so all the time."

Looking back at T-Nos, Jordan starts to get agitated. Small pellets of water are rolling off his hair, as the light sprinkle becomes a shower. Zippering up his jacket, he sighs, "People like things the way they are. Even Jen, she's starting to conform."

"Doesn't make them right," Mark says while gently nudging him to move under an awning. "But do you think being a mass produced product is a good thing?"

"That's a loaded comment," Jordan says and looks at Mark. The professor then leans up against a wall, deep in thought as if trying to make a difficult decision.

"There are things you don't know about how this society operates," Mark admits looking introspective. "True evolution will not be denied by our lame attempts to copy it. The government is not telling us the full story about Nuhu genetics." Mark then says in a near whisper.

A little nervous with Mark's candor out in the open, Jordan looks around for any cops. Fortunately, the street is fairly devoid of people. "You should cool the rhetoric," he advises his short friend.

Insistent, Mark says, "Everything has a cost. Free speech shouldn't be one. There are reasons for every Nuhu to be concerned."

"Don't exaggerate," Jordan corrects, "you only think you are not superior."

"But I'm not free," Mark asserts, "I only have the illusion of freedom. You may not have equality, but you can be truly free. That's why they fear you."

Jordan is silent.

"We need to talk. That is why we're here tonight," Mark says with a sustained uneasy breath. "This is your chance to be a hero again."

"Heroes," Jordan answers with grave finality, "usually die. I've risked my life enough."

"When is the path less followed ever safe?" Mark smiles and points down an empty alleyway. "When good people turn their back, the bad walk in. The bad people are walking all over us."

One last time, Jordan looks back at the T-Nos with its line of perfect, beautiful Nuhu people standing outside. They are the future as planned by the government. Turning away, he looks down the alley, which Mark is heading down — alone. This is the path Mark is offering him, dark and mysterious. He follows Mark like the fool he is.

***

On the other side, Mark exits the alley and comes to a sudden, complete stop. Noise and yelling are coming from across the street. Walking up next to his friend, Jordan sees a swirl of activity. Pointing, Mark directs his attention to a heavily guarded hotel where protestors are pushing up against police lines. Curious, they decide to have a closer look.

Rows of riot police are keeping the crowd of onlookers and protesters back from the hotel. In Jordan's opinion, the RP's are worse than the Over Force. The riot police or RP wear tan armor-plated suits and carry multi-barreled energy guns, Shepherd EBR-11's in fact. It wouldn't take much to start a slaughter with one of those rapid-fire guns.

The OverForce, at least, wears a simple grey uniform, carries a simple handgun and kills secretly and carefully. These RP's have been known to kill more bystanders than the agitators they are supposed to suppress.

The RP's have no faces as their helmets completely cover their heads, leaving them featureless, guiltless. Except for two glowing eye panels, there is little to tell if these guys are alive under all that gear. They remind him of the army's shock troops who wore similar, but more refined armor. No matter what, RP or ST, they're all bad news, all blind killers.

"You don't see that many Zephers every day. Somebody important must be in town," Jordan points out as parade of hovering limos begin to descend from the sky. They are accompanied by some nasty "GunOrbs" which are little more than guns with wings.

The entourage comes to a floating stop by the entrance of a hotel, The Orthodox Palace.

"It's President Eaves. Rina said he's in town to meet with the local big wigs, but most likely Magen…and Quintero," Mark mentions, "and others supposedly long dead."

Jordan's ears pricked up, "Quintero? Is that a man or a beverage?"

"I wish he was a beverage than I could just piss him away," Mark snickers and changes the topic quickly, "Let's get away from this place."

Neither notices Jennifer Grant entering the hotel. She is being escorted in by a familiar, young black woman, who is whispering into her ear.

ROBO SUMO

Next to a pyramid shaped skyscraper, very few things would stand out. Glowing with multicolored lights, the circular "Kobe Building" is one such sight. Jordan immediately relaxes, as he knows he will be welcomed here. The Japanese banned genetic engineering long ago and have no "Nuhu" program. Therefore all makes and models are welcomed in Japanese businesses, though it still doesn't hurt to be Japanese.

The friends walk around the block to the master entrance. Two very pretty teenage girls in formal uniforms greet them as they enter under a crystalline archway. Jordan notices that girls have a discrete tube running up into their pant legs, providing heating and cooling.

"The Kobe" is constructed from different colored glass floors, which uniquely rotate in different directions. And of course, the lobby floor is "floating" on a magnetic field, motionless, if you don't count the spinning ceiling. The ceiling is covered with a semitransparent, flexible plastic loaded with blue lights, giving the appearance of rippling water. No equally fanciful building exists outside of Japan.

Walking toward the hollow center of the building, Mark and Jordan find several tubes of glass elevators zooming up and down the core. Not the most practical of buildings, the Kobe was designed by an eccentric who took pride in artistic achievement over profit per square foot. As luck would have it though, an address at the Kobe is very desirable.

A goofy looking humanoid robot with rotund legs, arms, and a flat head barks out advertisements for the countless entertainment and dining venues available above. They ignore this animated advertisement and head right into an arriving lift. There is humanoid female robot in the rear dressed in a metallic kimono.

She asks, "Yuka kudasai?"

Not missing a step, Mark answers, "100th floor" and the robot bows.

"Jitto shite kudasai," the robot then says.

"Stand still," Mark translates. "This thing really moves," he tells Jordan.

They are soon speeding off to the top floor as Jordan frantically reaches for a safety bar.

In about an eye blink, they reach their level. The elevator doors open and a safety rail that circles the inside perimeter of every floor conveniently dips to allow the passengers to safely step out onto the moving floor.

"Ashimoto ni ki o tsukete kudasai," the robot advises as they walk out.

Ignoring the advice to watch his step, Jordan looks up at the roof. It is completely made of a transparent composite material. If not for the interior lights reflecting on it, Jordan would have assumed they were standing outside in the open.

The entrance to the restaurant is only a few steps to the right and is shaped like a cheesy impression of a Japanese paper-paneled house. A giant, garish neon sign with kanji symbols, "武士の宮殿" meets them as the pair pass under the house's entryway.

"Hello sirs. Welcome to the Samurai's Palace," the overly polite receptionist says in an exaggerated, high-pitched voice.

"Ah, a private table please," Mark says and hands the lady a few bills.

"My pleasure," she says. With a wave of her hand through a beam of light, two giant doors in the guise of an old Japanese palace gate open to the reveal the night sky and stars everywhere.

Walking down a few steps to the restaurant floor, Jordan notices that the floor is made from the same transparent plexisteel, as most of the roof. The view is unprecedented with almost no obstructions as this floor extends out beyond the rest of the Kobe. Jordan feels like he is about to eat on the top of Mount Fuji. The sensation of walking on the nearly transparent floor takes a little getting used to even though several well-placed LED lights within the floor provide a comforting sense of depth.

On their way to a table, they pass an artist's conception of a sumo match apparently being fought by two giant robots. Suddenly, the robots move! Jordan jumps and laughs as the sumo robots come to life, pounding on each other nosily. Their movements are restricted do to all the hydraulic cables and supports required to animate their vast metallic limbs, but it is still an impressive piece.

Several men and women are standing around the bar next to the Sumo arena, hollering it up, intensely interested on each match. Apparently, bets are being placed on each bout. The sumo on the right, with the blue trunks, is the crowd favorite.

Jordan and Mark are asked to remove their shoes before taking a seat at a low-rise table surrounded by immaculately white pillows. The table sits at the very edge of the room on the extreme of the overhang, far from any prying ears. With the floor as transparent as it is, both men feel like they could fall at any minute.

On the other hand, the fall would be a spectacular one. The Coit tower ruins are in the distance, looking quite majestic. The tower was ruined some years ago by an errant Sky Skiff. Beyond that, he could see the upscale island of Alcatraz glowing in the night. The 'Raz, as it is called, is the most exclusive resort in the area, complete with an artificial, heated beach surrounding the entire island. He often hears whispers that the water is still not warm enough.

No sooner does the waitress arrive as does Mark orders sake. Meanwhile, Jordan remains transfixed with the view. She promptly leaves.

"In Japan, they don't have a genetics culture. It is not considered clean or natural," Mark smiles. "I bet you didn't know that."

"I did, actually," Jordan remarks, turning around.

"You must be reading some contra-band. Naughty naughty," Mark says as the sake arrives. A drink is quickly poured for each of them. They toast in Japanese and loudly yell, "Kompai!" taking a shot each.

With a quick flip, Jordan then puts his napkin aside and gets up. "I'll be back."

"One drink and you already need to take a leak?"

"It was a long drive," Jordan complains as he struggles to get his shoes back on. "Where is it?"

"By the neon dude," Mark answers, already pouring another round.

On the far wall by the bar, Jordan sees an animated sign of man jumping up and down while holding his crotch. Obviously, the restroom is back there.

The bar is now even more crowded than before as the red trunk sumo, to the surprise of all, wins, causing a commotion. In a rush of money exchanges, Jordan is pushed down along a side corridor.

This leads to an open-air "smoking" balcony and is empty except for one person. Jordan can see a woman's long black hair flying around like a flag in a windstorm out there. She is very close to the building's edge and no one is aware. Trying to avoid any unnecessary entanglements, Jordan heads back toward the restroom and then veers right outside.

As he opens the door, a strong rush of air hits him making it hard to breathe. He can't imagine why anyone would come out here…unless they're hopeless smokers. The woman, who happens to be not smoking, is a slender wisp, hardly visible against the night sky except to Jordan's superbly sharp eyes.

With the aid of a low flying skiff passes over, the whole area is briefly lit up allowing Jordan to observe the woman in detail. She is wearing a long, beautiful shimmering green dress and is stunning to the utmost degree. Her features are perfect, flawless, mannequin ideal with more of a toned athleticism. This woman must be a Nuhu, but he's never seen a Nuhu so natural. In fact, he can't stop staring.

There is a flash of gold as the skiff departs. The woman is spinning her wedding ring around her finger, pushing it off bit by bit. And then in an instant, she tosses it away over the edge and then begins to push herself over.

Alarmed, Jordan cannot let her do it. He coughs loudly.

Finally becoming aware of someone behind her, she turns suddenly, chastising him in Cantonese, "Sin san, ni ha chun ngo la!"

Fortunately, Jordan knows the language a little. "I'm sorry I scared you," he says calmly.

She easily switches languages too. "I didn't hear you back there," she says with a hint of an English accent, her hand over her rapidly beating heart.

"With all this wind, it would be hard to hear a train crash," Jordan smiles. "You're going to catch a cold. Come in, please."

"Thank you. I mean, in this world, who really cares about anyone anymore?" the woman states, trying to hide her tear soaked dark-green eyes from him.

Green eyes? Must be contacts, he thinks. "Well, I'm not everyone," Jordan says. "I just hate seeing people get colds."

153

With a fast step, she approaches him fast as lightening. Their eyes meet straight on. "You look familiar to me," she says with sudden curiosity.

Humble Jordan jokes, "That's because I'm the devil."

"Unlikely," the woman says ignoring him. "It'll come to me. Military? I think a pilot."

"I am, but not good enough to jump after you," Jordan mentions and begins to motion to the door. "How about you come inside? My lips are turning blue."

She hesitates and looks back at the edge. "Fate brought me here for a reason. You interrupted. Please just turn away."

"From what I've seen, life changes in an instant and fate has little to do with it," Jordan says seriously. "We have the power to overcome. So I say, decide on who you want to be and then be done with it. Don't run away from life, just change it."

"You sound like my father. He is at the same time the most Chinese and the least. He holds fast to traditions, but has no patience for talk of fate. He is soldier, a very good one. Like you."

"What makes you think I'm that I'm a good soldier?" Jordan asks playfully. "Told you I was the devil."

"The best soldiers care about people. You obviously care," she says, smiling for the first time. She then continues, "I disagree with you about fate. I think your sudden appearance will not change much in the long run. You are only prolonging my pain." The woman moves closer to Jordan. She is now much calmer. "My destiny is clear. And, it's not one I want."

"Destiny? Funny you should mention that, I was not supposed to be at this restaurant. In fact, I was supposed to be over at T-Nos. You could say fate put me here. Now on the other hand, I did choose to come out here. I could have ignored you, gone to the restroom and be stuffing my face with raw fish," he counters, "but instead, I'm freezing my ass out here like some nicotine freak."

The woman laughs, "Personally, I like unagi. It's cooked."

"No courage," Jordan states. "That's ok. Sometimes it's better not to take any risks."

"You took a big risk coming out here. I might have been crazy."

"It's a character flaw," Jordan admits. "I'll buy you a warm drink if you come inside. Maybe, I can even introduce you to a fish you might like. Life sucks, but the food can be pretty good."

She laughs, thinks for a second and looks at him warmly. "You win," she says and proceeds to go inside. Jordan follows. She turns to him whip fast and says, "Thank you, I'm fine now."

"Ok then," Jordan grins. "I'll just stay here until you leave." He stands in front of the door.

The woman looks embarrassed. "What's your name?" she asks, her eyes narrow and focused.

"Jordan," he says and offers her his hand. She shakes it firmly. "My father told me it's an old Bible name," he details. "What do they call you? Frosty?"

She looks past him and sees a poster. It is labeled, The Sierras at Dusk. "Sierra," she says without a hint of hesitation, comfortable at being someone else.

"Sierra?" Jordan raises an eyebrow. "Like the poster behind us?"

She grins, "Observant little devil you are."

"Cousin!" yells a worried Lt. Amy Zhu coming down the corridor. "Where you've been Yingtai? Did you see those robots in their underpants? Can we get a drink somewhere else instead of this theme park?"

"Amy?" Jordan says with a happy surprise, recognizing Admiral Grant's energetic helmsman.

"Jordan Grant!" With that, Amy gives him a big bear hug, nearly toppling him over. "Cousin. This is Admiral Grant's son. This idiot should be dead!"

Amy Zhu rambles on and on, but Sierra says nothing. Instead she studies Jordan's eyes as if diamonds. Her gaze is searing, taking him apart and analyzing his very soul. "The famous son of the Admiral, savior of Seattle," Sierra says. "Now you make sense to me. The last knight of the realm."

"Too bad he's human, huh?" Amy mentions. "Otherwise, I'd date him. He's kind of ruggedly cute don't you think!" Amy laughs, rubbing Jordan's arm. "He's been crested though. His father gave him a beautiful silver sword."

Sierra's interest is piqued. "Silver?"

"Oh, I'm being rude," annoying Amy realizes. "Ah, Jordan, I guess you've already met my cousin, Yingtai. She's better known by her English name, Emily Wu. She's from Hong Kong and kind of famous," Amy finishes, never taking a breath.

"She apparently has many names," Jordan says with a big grin.

"Huh? Oh!" Amy says perturbed. "It's not uncommon for people from Hong Kong to have English names too. Bet you didn't know my Chinese name is Xiang. Anyways," Amy hesitates before continuing, "she and her husband own EchoTech." Amy appears to have overstepped, getting a stern look from Sierra.

"I know the company. Their guidance system is on the Sharkhunter," Jordan recalls.

"I programmed that," Sierra remarks. "The Sharkhunter is underestimated machine that can be pushed very hard before it breaks, just like you apparently."

"It broke. I didn't," Jordan comments.

Amy butts in joking, "Two humans that broke the mold in one place. Imagine that!"

"Amy I thought your family was Nuhu?" Jordan injects.

Wanting to do her own talking, Sierra speaks up instead, "The Hong Kong Free Trade Zone is not a genetics state, at least not entirely...*thankfully*."

"Yingtai," Amy mumbles loudly. "It's a privilege to be a Nuhu. Come let's go." She begins to tug at Emily to leave.

Likewise concerned, Jordan looks back at Mark. He is already red with drink...and oblivious.

An always alert Sierra catches his movement and her eyes fall on the Professor. "You're here with Mr. Whatley. Say 'Hi' for me."

"Don't mean to rush," Amy buts in again, "But we are attending a speech by President Eaves later this evening." She is concerned about her cousin's outspoken views in such a crowded place.

"Nice to see you again Amy," Jordan mentions.

"It's too bad heroes can't be everywhere all the time," Sierra notes and gives Jordan a hollow last smile. "Good-bye Jordan Grant."

She seems determined to end her life, Jordan thinks. He then finishes by saying, "We make our own happiness Sierra. No life is beyond redemption."

Storms of Fire

Some invisible barrier in Sierra seems to break and her face takes on a very gentle expression. She takes out her phone, pistol fast, and types on it. Jordan's phone lights up, but he doesn't notice.

"Is everything all right?" Amy asks. "You guys have a strange way of saying good-bye."

"Never good-bye," Sierra smiles giving him a wink.

With that, the two women disappear into the bar crowd.

For someone he knew for only a few minutes, Jordan instantly misses the remarkable green-eyed woman. She is something else. Putting aside false hopes, he starts walking away and then stops for a second. He turns back around and catches a glimpse of Sierra starring back at him. She waves. Jordan then disappears into the bathroom, though he feels a cold shower might be more helpful.

FORBIDDEN TOPIC

Once relieved, Jordan finds his way back to the table. He sits back down as if nothing has happened.

"Was that Emily Wu of EchoTech?" Mark asks slurring his words a bit. He shakes it off. "Were you talking to 'The Demon Queen of China'?"

"Said her name was Sierra," Jordan answers, trying to avoid the question.

"Check your back, there might a knife," Mark grumbles somewhat angrily. "There is no idea EchoTech hasn't stolen or copied. That's why the NAU likes them."

"She also said 'Hi'," Jordan adds.

"Old Demon Queen probably wants something from you," Mark warns while pointing a chopstick at Jordan's face. "She came to visit me once, copied a whole drive of info while I was in the can. That woman moves like lightening."

"Now explain to me, how did she get into your super-secret lab?" Jordan questions bemused, spinning his sake cup like a potential projectile.

Reluctantly, Mark admits, "Malone approved her visit."

"Very pretty though...for a monster" Jordan points out. "Hard to believe she's human."

"Hardly human!" Mark says as he stabs the table with a knife. "That face is removable. I wouldn't be surprised if she is on performance enhancers." His own face becomes rigid and he says quietly, "She kills people Jordan. I know it. Everyone knows it."

"Everyone kills indirectly," Jordan states.

"No you dope, she *is* the assassin," Mark snaps. "She's like the scorpion that the turtle gives a ride to. Even if you help her, she'll bite you."

"I've killed a scorpion or two," Jordan replies with a grin, "and a few turtles."

"I had to deal with her because I couldn't say no. I'd rather shove a slide rule down my throat and up chuck spare parts," Mark says. "Jennifer Grant is an angel compared to that vamp. Stay away."

"Ok. Ok," Jordan relents, beaten.

"You know I'm right, because I'm right," Marks slurs. If Mark's previous comment hadn't been so ludicrous, Jordan might have missed his next statement. "So today is your birthday," Mark exclaims, spiting some sake across the table.

"You drunk. My birthday was in June," Jordan laughs, brushing his spoiled hand off. "You're a few months late and a few too many shots over."

"A few points of advice before we continue with this talk, I am intent on getting drunk till I can't walk. Also concerning women, I don't want to talk about any of them," Mark babbles. "Those are battles mere men can't win."

"Mark you know…" Jordan bemoans. "You suck. You're already drunk. What's with the love talk? First you rag on me for talking to the Demon Queen of China and now…"

"I don't know why she's changed so much," Mark says and smacks the table hard. Jordan has to keep the sake bottle from tipping over.

Assuming he is talking of Jen, Jordan nods his head in agreement, carefully pouring his sake back into the bottle. "There's no magic reason."

"Well let's move," Mark says and raises his drink. "Congratulations to the both of us. I'm leaving for the Malone Design Bureau in the spring and so are you. I got you a job, a great job. That's your birthday present and yes, it's hell of late."

Brightening up, Jordan is speechless, "No joke?" His excitement quickly ebbs. "Is this another favor for you from Malone?"

"Test pilot for a top secret project," Mark says with a grin. "My project, not his."

"The OverForce will never approve my application to work on a sensitive project and…"

"This is totally off the books, off the records and off the planet."

Jordan nearly coughs up all over himself, "Just what are you talking about?"

The waitress comes over and takes their order. Jordan is about to talk when Mark hushes him and orders about every possible sushi combo available in perfect, fluent Japanese.

"You're a pig. If you keep eating that way, you're gonna look like one too," Jordan points out.

"Silence or I'll flunk you," Mark threatens in a fake serious way.

"Why is Malone so interested in me? First with Pac-Tech and now this. Coincidence is a bit much."

With words burning on his tongue, Mark points his finger at Jordan and shakes it numerous times wanting to say something, but doesn't. He looks sullen and then pulls out a black box, looks at it and then put it away. "Good, no one's listening." Mark says with a deathly cold tone, "This is not for the NAU."

Suddenly pale, Jordan looks around as well. Mark is a rebel. "You?"

"Before you get all bent out of shape, you should know that you'd be following your father's footsteps," Mark states, still looking a bit nervous.

"My father?" Jordan repeats. Things are starting to make sense to him now. Taking a deep breath, Jordan demeanor becomes melancholy as he accepts the reality that Mark is truly talking about revolution. "Why?" he asks.

Mark's lips quiver and he says very carefully, "People don't change overnight. We just fought a rebellion where half those people were on our side. Suddenly, seemingly in days, they turned. Explain Admiral Bricker?" Mark looks at Jordan's hands. They are still steady unlike his. "He was your dad's best friend."

"You've got my attention," Jordan says, intrigued and frightened at the same time. "My Dad shot down Bricker's destroyer over Seattle, but every war is filled with such stories of betrayal."

"I don't buy it," Mark says. "The government makes us. That's the real danger and the real reason so many of us are willing to face a civil war. I don't want to wake up someday and be someone else."

"People always try to explain the unknown with a conspiracy," Jordan reminds him. "You're only half Nuhu. Why worry?"

"You know how we Nuhu men are built. All blanks. They need a needle to pull out the good stuff. We're almost like women. Once a month I pee out my monthly supply of sperm." Mark says with disdain. "My parents went to a NUHU certified clinic. That's why I'm still classified as a Nuhu even though my mom is human. Who knows what they really did to me?"

"I know the facts of life already. If I wanted to get a Nuhu chick knocked up, especially the younger models, I know I would need to have it done through a clinic. They remove her egg and I fill a cup. Magic," Jordan says with a smirk. "I don't think the NAU has a self-destruct gene in you somewhere. Why would they do it? Come on Mark."

"A sharpened mind is a terrible weapon, an uncontrollable weapon, especially when controlled by someone else," Mark then says with real fear, "Look at Jennifer's change. Doesn't it make you wonder? Just like Bricker."

Jordan argues back, "Jen is just turning into her mother. Samantha was a free spirit once upon a time. When you're young, it's easy to fight for causes. As you get older, you just want security no matter the cost to your ideals."

"Man, do you think I would be here if that was the case?" Mark adds. "Do you really think I need to teach you biology again? The science doesn't make sense. We found unusual chemical traces in the Pure Nation rebels and in no one else."

Not really wanting to hear this, Jordan is silent and lost in his own thoughts, wondering if this could be the cause of Jen's change. Still unsure, Jordan stares out into the dark night. "A random chemical but no link?"

"Do you think thousands would be involved if there was no threat? This is not about the few, but the many. If you value your father, Rina or me, help us. We are begging you Jordan. Believe in us."

"Mark...you really want me to believe the government would go through all this trouble to control an already content population? Natural humans are dying out all by themselves."

"This is not about logical thinking. This is about emotions. People who are afraid will do anything to survive. They see enemies everywhere. They fear their own creations will rise up against them. Fear drives people to do awful, illogical things," Mark states barely controlling a shiver. "Those in charge are very afraid of something they can't control and they are acting on that fear."

"You mean they fear humans," he says finally.

"Yes," Mark admits, but doesn't reveal that they fear a particular *kind* of human: the aberration. He worries that this particular topic will open a can of worms. "If we don't work together, we're all fucked."

"I'm in."

"Good," Mark sighs relieved. "Now, we can go back to getting drunk."

"I don't get drunk. You know that," Jordan smiles weakly.

"My theory is that if I get a gallon of alcohol into you. You just might," Mark suggests.

"It might also fry my organs."

"Meet me one week from today at my secret lab," Mark commands.

"You never told me where it is hence the secret."

"The old Civil Airport in Novato. Thursday at eight in the morning. We have some preliminary work to do: flight systems checks and software proofing. Mind-numbing crap and such."

"Mark," Jordan says with grave concern and looks sternly at the professor. "If any of this comes to light, it's going to be worse than what happened on that frigate back in Burma. We won't be able to escape this."

The food arrives at that moment and Mark is distracted. Shoveling food into his mouth as if it is his last meal, Mark attempts to talk. "We'em goom too bee bussuzy tuz wozzy."

"I hope that was Japanese," Jordan mentions, disgusted.

Mark swallows, "We are going to be busy to worry."

"By the way, any money involved in this job?" Jordan says hopefully.

"Your starving days are over," Mark replies cheerfully smiling, rice sticking to his teeth.

"That's good," Jordan sighs and looks at his sushi. "I'm tired of you paying for everything."

"Just get ready, the surprises get uglier from here, but I can't freaking think straight anymore," Mark grimaces and starts drinking from the sake bottle.

DEVIOUS INTENT

As the two friends leave the Kobe building, a welcome, cool ocean breeze swirls around them. They make their way back to the garage, not saying much. Mark is walking a little slanted as if his left foot has gone flat.

"Jordan. Walk into the wind like this!" Mark throws his arms out like a plane while making engine noises.

Grabbing him by the back of his jacket, Jordan maneuvers the drunk engineer through the after dinner crowds. He has to pause to allow the man in black to barf into a tree. "Mark, you're embarrassing me," Jordan growls.

Finally reaching the garage, Jordan lets go of Mark. Mark leans up against a wall and doesn't move.

"Mark. Recall the car," Jordan instructs. He makes a swiping motion.

Thoroughly drunk, Mark swipes his empty hand over the scanner. Jordan walks over, finds Mark's phone, and scans it across the plate. One of the metal platforms begins to blink blue. They walk over to it.

"I can't drive. Jordan are you drunk?" Mark asks. "What am I saying, Mister Grant never gets drunk. He's made of Exitor."

"We're both drunk. My blood alcohol is probably through the roof," Jordan moans, "though I do feel fine."

"You shouldn't have disarmed the autopilot then," Mark grunts. "You took my phone. Now the car is dead. Security device."

"What the…never mind," Jordan mumbles.

After a few seconds, the car moves onto the blinking plate. Mark immediately sits in the driver's seat as Jordan shakes his head in disbelief.

"If you're going to sit there, how do I reset the autopilot?" Jordan asks, not amused.

"Click your heels three times and think of home." Mark then waits for a laugh that never comes. "Just kick the front tire a few times. Kick it hard."

A disbelieving Jordan holds still for a second to see if he is still joking, but Mark only waves him on.

163

Going up to the front of the car, Jordan stands next to the huge
metal striped tires. He taps the passenger side one with his foot.

"Harder!" Mark yells.

Following orders, Jordan lays into the tire with three swift kicks.
The car jumps violently and then beeps. A couple other people stare at
him as if he is a raving lunatic.

However, inside the cabin, the computer voice quickly kicks on,
"Autopilot engaged."

"Jordan," Mark laughs, "you're my hero."

***

Down in the lobby of the Orthodox Hotel, people are leaving in
droves after President Eaves' press conference. The Orthodox is an
ostentatious place of white and black marble that draws a clientele that
is more interested in image then comfort. In fact, the beds are rumored
to be made of marble.

Another meeting of sorts is just about to begin.

Her mother would be right at home here, Jen thinks. Her room is
no less busy than rest of the hotel with mirrors everywhere and
furniture that could anchor boats. She walks over to one such gaudy
wall length mirror and exams herself. Her cleavage is almost escaping
her barely-there white dress. She rolls her eyes. She hates this game,
but that's the way it has to be. Her bra is showing and she decides to
remove it all together. A sick feeling wells up inside her and tears fall
freely, ruining her freshly applied make-up. God, she doesn't want to
do this again.

The phone rings and she does not answer. She doesn't have to. It is
the signal that her contact is now free and waiting to see her. Pulling
herself together, she quickly applies another coat of liquid beauty and
leaves.

Taking the elevator down to the lobby, she enters one of the hotel's
lavish bars. The women and men in here are dressed impeccably in
black tie and make an effort to avoid eye contact with each other. This
speak-easy has red silk streamers crossing the ceiling that provide a
buffer to the lights above, casting the whole place with a hot red glow,
but also providing shadowy corners. All the tables are lit from below

and glow warmly white. Sitting alone at a table, she finds her contact, the insidious Thomas Wu hiding in darkness.

"Nuhu women are so picture perfect," Thomas says, eating up the sight of the scantily clad Jennifer, an image of nearly bare sexuality. "Especially you, my beautiful American Venus."

"Thomas you need a new line," Jen groans sitting down in front of him. Yet to her better judgment, she feels herself drawn to this powerful man. There must be something wrong with her. "You used the same one last time."

He laughs, "I'm not a romantic. So what do you have for me today?"

"I broke into the old man's system again. I found some sketchy info on some drone testing out in the desert. The best thing I have for you is a document on the new capabilities of the Mark 3 air carriers. They call them world dominators are something menacing like that. Boring, I didn't read it all," Jen says as she orders a drink from the screen built into the table.

A few seconds later a robotic "waiter" delivers the drink. The robot is just an arm suspended from a track in the ceiling.

"What do you think? Anything good," she asks Thomas.

"The carrier document is worth a fair amount of cash to some of my European friends," Thomas says. "The rest is interesting, but of questionable value. I really want an O.F. access." He sees a slinky Asian woman and shifts in his seat. From another table, the young black woman, who has been watching, waves off Thomas. Fortunately for him, Emily Wu is nowhere to be found.

Quick to notice, Jen says in an insulting tone, "Worried about the wife?"

"My so-called wife could make small work out of us," Thomas warns with a rush of anger. "However, she's supposed to be busy tonight."

"Sounds like a lovely person," Jen mentions. "At least, she's not a Cotillard follower. You have any those creeps in Hong Kong?"

"Useful to have a demon at your command, but I made her into too ferocious of a beast," Thomas answers. "There are Cotillard believers all over. End of the world this. End of the world that. Fuck them all. Just a bunch of noisy crickets."

"They should save us some trouble and just end their own lives," she jokes. "What exactly are they afraid of?"

"Afraid of working," Thomas grins. "Couldn't you push Whatley or Dupont? Seduce one or the other? I'll make it worth your while."

"I'll work on it," Jen sighs, finding the suggestion both disquieting and appealing at the same time. "I need money now though."

"Same terms. I'll give you a loan based on my estimate of the value of the goods. You'll have the money delivered tomorrow. It is very risky for me to keep doing these favors for you. The NAU is giant client of mine. I expect a little more attention for now on…and a bit better articles of sale. Otherwise, I'll find someone else to visit in San Francisco who is bit more…fresh."

As if slipping into a different skin, Jen finishes her drink, "I'll remind you why you like me so much." She slides a finger down the slit of her dress.

Thomas hesitates for a second. "There is something you might be able to provide that would gather a harvest of wealth. Can you obtain your father's command codes for the Arlington?"

"Wow. That's a big request," Jen sneers, nearly floored. "There could be a world of hurt for me if those are traced back. The NAU is real touchy about any code leaks. A couple of thousand dead kind of does that."

"Exactly. If you got me those, my client would pay enough that you wouldn't need to see me for a long time," Thomas smiles, "and I know you don't like seeing me."

"Everything is a transaction with you," Jen snarls. "I didn't know I had a price until I met you."

"Everyone can be bought," Thomas smiles even more. "I like a world of dollars since I have all the dollars."

"My father carries the codes on him personally. A regular person wouldn't know how to read them, but I do. That much is easy," Jen states. "Why do you want the codes? That could seriously compromise my Dad. I don't like him, but…"

"But what?" Thomas says. "Greatness has no fear. All the famous rulers of the ancient world moved aside their parents to ascend the throne. Do you really think he loves you that much? Anyways, I guarantee this will never be traced back to you."

"For a crest, you have a deal," she says coldly.

"Two people in the same family can't have a crest. You know that," Thomas snorts. He writes a number on his phone's touch screen and then proceeds to show it to her. Jen's eyes nearly bulge out. He laughs, "I think that amount of cash should be enough to betray daddy."

"Impressive number," she says. "I could run for office with that." She has second thoughts, but then smiles, "The codes are only for business use. Right?"

"Absolutely. How soon and how regularly can you have the codes?" Thomas asks impatiently.

"I won't see my Dad until Thanksgiving so I won't have a chance until then," she explains.

"Not good enough," Thomas frowns. "I need codes for the spring."

"No problem. He only ups the numbers by one each month," Jen hurriedly reassures him. "Every summer he starts with a fresh set. All his passwords follow the same pattern."

Thomas laughs satisfied, "Good. Let's go upstairs and have a little fun."

Suddenly nauseous, Jen wants to get up and run. Instead, she just follows him. The idea of having sex becomes a non-issue, just like breathing, something that just needs to be done and she doesn't know why. Who is she becoming? The more she tries to think about it, the more her sex-drive goes into overdrive.

SNOW DEVILS OF INDIA

With a sigh of relief, Jordan switches off the auto driver as the car approaches Mark's nondescript track home. Even with Mark's nice salary, the professor can only afford a simple house in pricey Marin.

A sleepy Rina comes out as the Onzo stops in the driveway. As Mark would never park his beloved car outside, she assumes Mark is stinking drunk. When the car stops, her fears are realized. The driver side door opens and Mark rolls out onto the pavement soon after.

"Hey Jordan," Rina says as she opens the garage door. "Pull the car inside. He won't be happy if he finds it outside tomorrow."

With ease, Jordan drags the drunk safely inside and then drives the car into the garage.

"That man cannot handle his liquor," Rina sighs as Jordan exits the car. She quickly closes the garage behind them.

About to crack a joke, Jordan turns to talk to Rina and soon realizes it is a little cold and her nightgown a bit too transparent. Blushing, Jordan rapidly looks away.

"Really now," she says, "are you this shy in the locker room?"

"Not usually, but…I'm gonna call for a taxi," Jordan says and pulls out his phone.

"Don't waste your money. Just knock out on the sofa and I'll drive you home tomorrow," she suggests. "Help me get the rock star into bed first."

A toasty Mark groans as Jordan easily picks him up and drops him in his bed. Rina is in the kitchen preparing coffee and she soon heads out to the lavish living room, complete with a wall sized entertainment screen.

But before Jordan can even reach the couch, Rina hands him a cup of super-heated coffee. "Here, go ahead and warm up," she says, though now safely wearing a robe. A reserved Jordan sits down and she studies him carefully before asking, "Did you take the offer?"

He nods his head. "And you, a rebel OverForce officer, who would have thought it possible?" Jordan states as if the idea is incredible.

"I recruited Mark on the behalf of Martin Malone," Rina admits. "Malone gave me a second chance at life. Once upon a time, I wasn't the nicest person."

Speechless, Jordan feels numb as if the just waking from a dream. Everyone around him is a rebel. Now, he is too.

"You've made the right choice. I've never worked with better people," she says honestly. Rina looks suddenly sad as she states, "You and Mark go back a long way. I think you are closer to him than to that sometimes sister of yours."

Jordan agrees, "At least, he acts like my brother. Jen on the other hand…"

"Say no more," Rina sighs and throws up her arms in disgust, still stung from her day out with Jen. "I still don't see what you see in her. Seems self-centered and controlling."

"Do you really think I would love a women like that?" Jordan shies and nearly looks to break down. He hides his eyes behind his hands while a sympathetic Rina watches.

"Of course not," she replies, but doesn't know what to do. Rina is not used to open emotion and struggles to show that she cares, so she says what she knows instead, "Beautiful women are not like other women. They have a certain power."

"It never went to her head back then," Jordan recalls sadly. "The sad little orphan had a Nuhu princess as his best friend and it looked, for a while, that it was going to be more than that."

"I understand, but power is drug," Rina states from experience. Many times in the OverForce she had used her sexual prowess to exploit the sexual weaknesses in others. And for a time, she relished the power to manipulate, but it is a knife that cuts both ways. "You are handsome man. Don't tell me you never used your looks to get your way."

"I lived in my head for the longest time, in faraway fantasy lands, in the sky. Jen, well, she was in the brightest star in my dreams."

"A flawed diamond in a unreal sky," Rina sighs and thinks about her and Mark, another improbable coupling.

"I thought I knew all her flaws," Jordan recalls with a degree of melancholy. "Then we all went to war and everything changed."

"Mark spent his fifth year of mandatory assigned as an assistant to Malcolm Moore. Right?" Rina inserts, quick to get away from the uncomfortable subject of love. "I remember that about Mark's file. I think he had already earned his PhD by then too."

"Spent his nights studying. That brain of his is always in motion," Jordan confirms. "You know. Moore was OverForce once upon a time."

"You're not supposed to know that," Rina replies coldly taking particular interest in this detail. "Moore's death is a bit of an urban legend in the OverForce ranks. The stories are a bit…sordid."

There is a horrible cry from the bedroom. Rina jumps to her feet. Jordan, on the other hand, remains motionless.

"He always has nightmares," Rina states holding her chest. "There are things he still won't tell me."

"Do you really want to hear this story?" Jordan says, drinking down his coffee. "It's classified, but that's how I know about Moore."

"Must I remind you, you are talking to an O.F. that has turned against her nation," she snickers and then laughs bitterly, "Come on, scare me."

"Region of Orissa, nation of India, better known as the Orissa Conflict. That war cost Mark a lot. He almost got shot once for trying to do the right thing. Second, well, that's an even more unpleasant story. We crashed landed on the Nepal / India border during a mission."

"Nepal?" she says and looks amazed. "That's like the legend I heard. It's about a secret transport that crashed in the Himalayas," Rina recalls. "They say that the nuclear fallout did terrible things to the people of that whole region, causing horrible mutations. The story says that one man after the crash had to fight his way out of the mountains. That he found horrifying things out there, creatures. So horrible, the whole story was suppressed. Was that you? Did that really happen?"

"There is a reason Mark never talks about this." As if seeing dark images in his mind's eye, Jordan takes a deep breath as wishing not to remember. "Mark and I are friends because of a shared childhood. We trust each other because of shared experiences — terrible experiences."

***

1999 - Somewhere above the Himalayas…

Ice is covering the PT-707 Ignis' windshield. Alarms are ringing throughout the cockpit of the large cargo transport as their de-icing system overloads and fails. The wind is thumping against the fuselage, rattling the electronics.

"Jordan," the black woman pilot, Captain Stephanie Griger, yells, "Try to restart engine two. We need to get up over this storm!" She has her hands full as the transport buckles hard to the left. The ship suddenly then is thrown hard to the right.

"What the hell was that?" a young Lieutenant Jordan calls out.

"That's all I need. A rookie co-pilot," Griger growls. "We've flown into a combat zone. We're getting fired on."

Before them, two huge air carrier task forces are engaged in bloody battle. Fighters sizzle past them, even in the blizzard. The shadows of Russian and NAU carriers loom overhead.

"No go on engine two," Jordan yells. "It's a rock." He looks up and sees two frigates opening fire on a Russian carrier.

A tremendous blast sounds from directly above them. Within seconds, a wing section from a Russian IAF-70 Hellbat slices across the cockpit, severing the nose off the transport. Griger screams as shrapnel cuts across her leg. The instrument panel plummets down pulling her seat out into the elements. Luckily, her seat tangles on some cables and holds. Terrible, frigid air blasts her body as she watches ships pass beneath them.

With his instruments still intact and functional, Jordan is forced to take control of the heavily damaged ship. He switches to full manual as ships start to fail. The transport is going down fast. The last engine is damaged and does not have power to push the plane up. They are going to go crash no matter what he does. Craggy mountain peaks come into view and Jordan reacts quickly to avoid them. With a hard turn, the transport lurches to its right side, barely missing the tip of a mountain.

To his luck, he sees a flat plain in the distance. He aims for it, but the ship is dropping too fast and heading for a slope. It hits ground! Hard. The plane begins to slide down the mountain face when it hits a ridge. To his amazement, the plane then bounces back into the sky. Jordan has seconds to redirect the plane and thrusts the engines hard forward before they completely fail. The giant plane glides for a moment and then slams down on the plain. But the heavy craft does not stop; it instead slides across the frozen surface, rushing toward a cliff. The transport hits a rocky outcropping just short of the drop off, stopping with a final thud. The fuselage groans and buckles as it settles. Griger's seat breaks free and dangles over the edge of the cliff. A vast, black emptiness is below her.

As if by levitation, she is pulled away from the ledge. Thankfully, her co-pilot is no weakling.

"I can see why that young Professor Whatley insisted on you," Griger yells over the wind. "Good crash, pilot. Now get me the heck out of this storm!"

"Yes Sir," Jordan smiles. He then rushes to open the access door to the cargo bay, pulling the injured Griger behind him. There is a small passenger cabin directly behind the cockpit. Here Jordan finds Mark holding his head. He has a gouge across his forehead.

"Mark. Is there a medic on this team?" Jordan asks, his face wet from the snow. He sees that many of the other passengers, mostly other engineers, have not survived the crash.

"Maybe in the back with the payload?" Mark warbles. "There is a security detail of NAU regulars back there," Mark says and goes over to an elderly man in the front row and asks. "Malcolm? Are you alright?"

"They guaranteed us a smooth flight," Professor Malcolm Moore says with bubbling anger. "Captain Griger! What the hell happened?"

An angry Griger speaks up from the floor, "This ship was poorly engineered. Engine froze up in the cold. Then, our freakin' nose was cut off by Russian fighter. We're lucky to be alive." She closes her eyes in extreme pain as Jordan wraps a belt around her leg as a tourniquet. Griger is bleeding a pool onto the floor around her. She still manages to keep talking, "Fortunately for all of us, Grant didn't panic. He brought the plane down in one piece."

"Grant? Where were you during all this, Captain Griger?" Moore questions.

"Hanging around," she says. "Jordan, go find that medic. Moore and Whatley, secure the plane. Cover up any openings in the fuselage before it starts to freeze in here."

Not wasting any time, Jordan moves back toward the rear cargo bay, leaving the rest up front. He moves slowly as the Ignis has eviscerated itself with wires and panels thrown all through the fuselage like torn open guts. The cargo bay is isolated by a two folding blast doors, which he cannot open. The electronics have failed and he must manually crank the doors apart. It's a laborious effort. As the bay finally opens, two giant cannons can be seen hanging from the ceiling, dangling gently back and forth, intact and safe. The soldiers, on the other hand, are much less fortunate and not many have survived. A blonde medic is seeing to the wounds of the few survivors.

"Medic. The pilot is badly cut up," Grant says. "I managed to slow the bleeding, but she'll need staples."

"I'll be right there Jordan," a familiar voice answers back. "I've got my hands full."

"Jen?"

"Who else?" she groans. "Our lovely friend Mark said this was going to be a safe little vacation and that we could all hang out in Italy afterwards. Well, Lieutenant, the good news is that those of us, who are still alive, are only a little beat up." Jen finishes patching up her patient. "Done. Let's go upfront."

She follows Jordan back up to Griger, who is now holding a gun. Jen quickly proceeds to remove the shrapnel bits and staples the wound closed. Griger merely flinches, never making a sound, even without any kind of anesthesia.

"Someone needs to go and get help," Moore demands, pacing back and forth. Snow is beating against the windows, which only agitates him more. "We must have some humans on board that can be sacrificed."

"The emergency beacon is functioning," Grant replies, helping Jen move Griger onto a row of seats.

"Cool it with the rhetoric Moore," Griger gripes. "I know all about your past. OverForce means nothing to me right now."

"One once, one always," Moore says. "You are a big strong lad. Mexican right?" he says smiling looking at Jordan. "You're not a real citizen. You're part of the annexation. All you Canadians and Mexicans are lucky to have us take care of you. Show some gratitude to us, hike out and find help like a good lad."

"Shut up already," Griger yells out as Jen administers a shot of morphine. "No one is leaving. We stay together, all of us, until help comes." She charges up the gun and unlocks the safety. "I'm in charge or, if you have a problem, you can talk to my superior." Her weapon points at Moore. "And this is him." She tilts the gun back and forth.

"What if help doesn't come?" Moore argues, standing back. "We need to make alternate plans. Whatley and I must survive. These prototype weapons must survive. They could turn the tide of the war."

"The war is temporarily suspended," Griger says. "Grant, secure all weapons in the gun locker. Take an AEB-7 rifle for yourself in case we have visitors. Move the bodies of the dead and place them outside. The cold will preserve them."

"What about rations?" Moore asks.

"We have a week's supply…for two people," Griger states, now getting woozy from the morphine. "Grant will portion them out."

"Lieutenant Grant," Moore argues back, "you must provide for the Nuhu survivors first."

Jordan does not answer and this alarms Moore. "Just exactly what race are you Grant?" the old man asks.

"I'm not a Nuhu," Jordan says with a hint of disgust.

"Then you cannot be in charge," Moore complains loudly. "Whatley! You said this man was qualified. I trusted you with picking out a first class team." He turns on Mark and grabs him by the collar. "You dishonor your race."

Hearing enough, Griger fires into the ceiling and everyone goes silent. She then says forcefully, "This is a military operation and I am the ranking officer. We all live or die together, that is it. Grant is in charge." She hands Jordan her Gerini AEP-2ST pistol. The Gerini is a fierce handgun and everyone knows. No one makes a move.

Not wasting any time, Jordan quickly proceeds to implement Griger's instructions. As night comes, the ship becomes deathly cold. People group around to keep warm. Luckily, the survival packs contain a few heat sticks. Jordan spreads them out among the survivors, but he can't find Jen.

Reaching the stern of the transport, he sees Jen starring out of a large reinforced, circular window. The window has a huge anti-aircraft gun sticking out of it which is already half covered in snow.

"How long will those sticks last? 12 hours or so? Not enough," Jen says, moving some cargo blanket over herself. "You look tired Jordan. Time to take a break."

"It's cold back here. Come back amidships with everyone else," Jordan suggests. With a sudden tilt, the ship shifts to one side. Feeling a breeze run across the top of his head, Jordan ducks instinctively as the cannons above him swing. The unsettled weapons make angry creaking noises as the ship sinks deeper into the snow. After a particularly loud clank, they both quickly grab hold of each other. "We're OK," Jordan tells her. "Those guns are magnetically latched to the ship."

Looking up, Jen then talks through her nervousness, "Moore likes to take credit, but Mark figured out how to make those things work. Moore is just a well-connected thug." Jen can't help laugh, "Lucky Mark, got pulled out from his mandatory only to end up back in the war."

"Trouble is nothing new to Mark," Jordan remarks. "We almost bit it after the Russian counter-offensive last summer."

"Shh, you don't know if Moore might be listening," Jen says looking around. "Mark told me what happened. You really shouldn't be talking about that," she warns. "Moore will use any excuse to push you aside. Jordan you always make me worry so much."

"Moore can bite my ass," Jordan growls. Ducking under the cargo blankets, he sits next to Jen and puts his arms around her. "If you insist on staying here, so will I," he says.

She quickly takes hold of his hands for warmth. Jordan smiles and hugs her. "I've always liked your smile," Jen says, trembling slightly. "Why is it that you stay so positive?"

"There are things I still want in life," Jordan says with a brilliant smile. "Life started me out with nothing, I'm not going to die that way. One day I'm going to have a family."

"I'll give you that family," Jen says with conviction. "After the war, I'll be ready. There's nothing more that I want. Surprised? I was going to tell you in Italy."

"Jen be serious."

"I've loved you since I was a kid," she admits as her fair complexion turns a bit red. "My feelings have only gotten stronger."

"It's never going to be easy to be a mixed family," Jordan sighs loudly as the fuselage creaks. "We are going to be outsiders."

"Nuhu and human? What stupid titles. I've never believed in any of that shit the government feeds us," she says genuinely angry. "Look

175

at you and Mark, the best two guys I know. Not exactly a glowing advertisement for Nuhu science."

"Jen, you know I've had a crush on you all my life," Jordan says looking a bit far away. "I would like nothing more than to call you my wife."

"Things don't look so good right for us. At least, now you know my true feelings."

"Tonight we're still alive," he says, "and I'm with you. Couldn't ask for anything else."

"I love you," she says quietly. "I will love you till I die."

As they get closer together, her hand slowly begins to unzip his flight suit. He moves to stop her, but Jen puts her finger to her lips and silently instructs Jordan not to resist. In the face of certain death, all problems become small. They make love with no regrets.

A day and night passes with no sign of rescue. Griger is passing between consciousness and unconsciousness. Professor Moore has been secretly giving her double doses of morphine. The snow outside does not relent and the ship is nearly buried on one side, making it more difficult to be spotted from the sky.

Jordan goes to sort out the day's rations and finds the locker already broken into. Their meager food supply is gone. Only an empty container remains.

"Mark," Jordan yells. "Someone raided the MRE's."

"What?" Mark says alarmed and scans the faces of the survivors for guilt.

"Perhaps it wouldn't have happened if Grant was spending his nights with us and not with the pretty young medic in the rear of the plane," Moore growls. "You should have been guarding it."

A horrid animal-like howl echoes from outside. Soon, the survivors can hear several things moving around the outside of the transport…and then scratching against the hatches. There is a loud BANG, BANG as the creatures bash at the circular rear window.

Startled, Jordan moves in a flash and opens the weapons cabinet. He is about to start handing out guns when silence comes again.

As fast as they came, the beasts are soon gone. Only to be replaced by the wailing of Jennifer as she hastily runs through the transport up toward them.

A terrified Jen slams into Jordan's open arms. "There's large animals outside! Some kind of apes."

"The woman thinks she saw as Sasquatch," Moore jokes, but he is shaking with fear.

"Yeti," Jen corrects, swallowing hard, "but this creature didn't have white fur. It was covered in black hair."

There are three loud knocks from the outside. This time though, the banging sounds deliberate. Soon, the three bangs are repeated.

"Mark, guard the weapons," Jordan says. "Let me check it out."

"We're saved!" Moore yells and heads to open a hatch. One of the soldiers stops him before he opens it. "Let go you fool!" the old man barks.

"I didn't hear an aircraft," the soldier warns.

They all stare at each other in silence. They all can hear distant howling again.

A heavily accented voice yells out, "Is there anyone in there?"

Taking no chances, Jordan takes his collapsed James Firearms AEB-7 (Air Corps Assault Energy Bolt Model #7) riffle out and snaps in a 45 round charge. The weapon's barrel expands into the locked position. As the gun charges up, he heads for the hatch and looks through its tiny portal.

A horrifically deformed face smiles back at him and politely says, "Do not be alarmed, I will not hurt you. I am a hunter from the valley below."

Cautiously, Jordan opens the hatch. A rush of cold air swirls into the cargo bay. The man enters. He is tremendously tall, close to seven feet with a face that is covered in large boils. The man wears a tattered collection of coats sewn together to cover his massive frame. For a mutant, he is an impressive sight.

"Forgive my appearance," the man says, putting down his massive bow. "I am child of the nuclear sickness." One of his hands only has four fingers and is gently resting on a giant curved sword, worn by his side. "The dead one's outside must be thrown over the side of the mountain. Terrible things have found you. See for yourselves, but only if you are strong of stomach."

A few dare to go outside. There they find that the dead have been partially eaten. The bodies lay ripped open without regard. Innards spread all over the snow with clear bite marks. Some in the group throw up.

Horrified, but resolute, Jordan approaches the hunter. "Thanks for the warning," he says and then turns to Jen, "Get a detail together and dispose of the bodies."

A green looking Jen, though reluctant, does as instructed for once.

"You people cannot stay here and wait," the hunter warns, pointing around them with his muscular arm. "These mountains are thick with radiation. Your radios will not work. I will take the strongest amongst you and journey to the lower valley and to my village. Be warmed, the path will take many days."

"If this place is laced with radiation, what do you hunt up here?" Moore asks callously. "We can't believe this thing."

"I hunt the same devils that attacked you," the hunter says insulted. "These devils feasted upon my village," the man angrily says. "Evil has been born from our nuclear war. Nature has been disturbed and now seeks retribution."

Pushing Jordan forward, Moore insists, "Grant must go. He is the strongest. There is no denying that. Look at him, he is a brute just like this hunter."

"Absolutely no!" Jen fires back, running outside. "We will pull names and decide fairly. Fuck genetics."

"Moore is right, this time," Jordan states, giving the old man the evil eye. Jordan then grabs Mark and quickly takes him away from the others. "Mark. I'm going to leave you in charge. Don't trust anyone. Things will be getting harsh soon."

"Jordan, you sure you can do this?" Mark asks. "Maybe, Jen or I should go with you. There are enough people to look after the injured. Those things were all over the fuselage and you'll be out in the open with them."

"I'm not like everyone else and you know it," Jordan reminds him with a sly smile. "The lack of food hasn't taken a toll on me. I still feel strong."

Begrudgingly, Mark sighs with agreement, watching as a few of the survivors begin rolling the dead off the side. "Truthfully, do you think there is any hope?" he says.

"Always," Jordan replies as he pulls out the survival suit container out from a storage unit next to the hatch. He starts putting the heavily quilted, white suit on as a concerned Jen watches from a distance.

"Hey a little advice before you go," Mark says. "I think they said it best back in basic training…"

"Just do it and smile," Jordan recalls, shaking his head.

As he leaves with the hunter, Jen and he exchange a long look as if saying good-bye silently. Soon, Jordan is lost to the snowy landscape.

With sharp drop offs and cavernous gullies, the hike down is as treacherous as the hunter had warned. It takes several days through bad weather to make any progress. The mountain seems bottomless, endless and Jordan's hope is tested.

As night falls on the fourth day, the two hikers take shelter in a rock cave. The cave has an odd blue glow.

"This rock is radioactive," Jordan says concerned. "We can't stay here."

"No," the hunter says, cracking a smile. "I know where to walk and where not to. This cave is an old Exitor mine. That is only the spirit of the rock you see. It will protect us. Tomorrow, we will reach my village. From there, you should be able to call for help," the hunter says as he lights a fire.

Taking his gloves off, Jordan's fingers are starting to turn slightly black.
He tries to warm them over the fire, but they hurt terribly. He thinks about Jen and Mark. Are they too showing the first signs of frostbite as well? Thoughts of his friends make Jordan aware of his helplessness. His body is tired, but he must force himself to continue. That's all he can do to help them.

His mind is in knots about Jen. He doesn't know how to feel about her. What they did felt right…at the time. Even though he keeps telling himself that they did nothing wrong, Jordan can't shake a persistent queasiness.

The hunter pulls out his giant silver sword and sharpens it with a raw chunk of black Exitor ore. He slowly passes the rock across the length of the blade.

Settling down, Jordan toys with his radio to occupy his mind. It picks up nothing but static, but soon the hunter's sword attracts his attention. "Is your sword made from this cave rock?" Jordan asks.

"No, not from this cave. This weapon has been in my family for generations. It has killed many evil things," the hunter answers. "If Lakshmi blesses me with courage, hopefully, it will kill many more." He touches a small ivory medallion around his neck.

"These creatures you hunt," Jordan wonders, "they are…"

"Devils," the hunter corrects him. "They attack and kill the young and the weak. They took my youngest and now I am here seeking justice for their cruelty. No other father will know my pain. Even if it costs my life, I swore to my village that these spawn of Raktavija will not spread."

"Raktavija?" Jordan repeats looking puzzled.

"In the texts of the Devi Mahatmyam, there is described a demon named Raktavija whose very blood creates clones of his evil self. These devils have a terrible hunger. They hunger for blood and their tribe is growing. They are breeding, thriving in these hellish peaks."

"You were tracking them when you came across us," Jordan realizes. "I'm sorry. I'm sorry we got in your way. Their trail will be lost."

"Saving lives is not an interruption," the hunter tells him. "I am glad I crossed paths with your ship. All life is sacred."

"Even these beasts you hunt?" Jordan asks.

"Even them. They are only hungry and their hunger has turned them evil. I regret what must be done, but they cannot be healed," he says with a sense of sadness. His eyes suddenly grow big with alarm. There are some strange sounds. He stamps out the fire in the cave and whispers, "They are outside."

Jordan hits the floor of the cave and takes aim at the entrance. He can see only outlines of creatures moving about on all fours. They are large with hair draping off every limb.

"The spirit of the holy metal will protect us," the hunter assures. "They will move on. We will hide here till sunrise and let them pass."

A pained expression is on the hunter's face. Jordan knows where the creatures are going. They are heading back to his village.

"Two hunters having a better chance," Jordan says, "than one."

"You have a responsibility to your friends," the hunter reminds him. "If we die, they have no hope."

Jordan says looking at the horribly deformed man, "I cannot sacrifice your family for my friends…as much as I might live to regret it. We have the opportunity to strike the devils down. If we succeed, both."

"Yes, your plan makes sense," the hunter admits. "Do not be offended, but you are not like the other western soldiers I have met." The hunter stands up and takes his sword. "Let us deliver a quick justice."

***

Even though his legs feel weak, Mark slowly walks the length of the long ship. It is the only thing that keeps his mind off food. Reaching the cargo bay, he examines his nearly frozen canons. There is a layer of crystallization across them. Just a few days ago, they seemed so important. Now, they are nothing more than useless junk, leaking junk. He steps into a pool of liquid. It must be coolant from the canons since it has not yet frozen.

Many have died from the cold since Jordan left. It is too early for starvation to have taken hold, but he is no doctor. He suspects that will come soon enough too.

A stubborn Jen has taken to guarding over Griger. They sit buried under a tent of cargo blankets. Sticking her head out, she waves Mark over. And as soon as Moore disappears, Mark dips down to talk to her. "Hey dummy," Jen says quietly, "why is Moore keeping the dead inside with us? It's ghastly."

"He doesn't want to attract those animals again," Mark assures, brushing frost of his trademark goatee. "Moore said he wants to make sure the bodies get back home to their loved ones in one piece."

"Oh come on. Does he? For real?" Jen groans and motions for Mark to come closer. "I saw him extracting some liquid from the canons. The next day somebody died. Isn't that interesting?"

"Don't start Jen with rumors," Mark utters in disgust. "It's not like there's anything left to fight for. All the rations are gone." Mark trembles as a cold wind travels through the transport. "The ship is starting to crack from the weight of the snow. It won't provide much protection for long."

Standing back up, he begins to pace again. Obvious to him, they are going to starve or freeze to death soon. He thinks it might be better to take a long hike out into the cold. Freezing isn't so bad, he tells himself, the last few minutes of life are filled with delusional warmth. Maybe, it's worth it.

SNOW DEVILS OF INDIA – Part 2

A harsh moonlight is blaring down upon layer upon layer of fresh snow, lighting up the devil's rock shelter as if under a spotlight. The two men struggle not to be seen on this earthbound moonscape. There is a slight snowdrifts blowing ever so gently about them, but not enough to provide cover for their movements. With little choice, Jordan and the hunter are lying flat on against a hill directly above the monsters. A few of the creatures are walking about and Jordan sees them clearly for the first time.

This horrific sight will forever stain his memory. His heart races and terror takes hold of him, unable to comprehend what could have caused this. He looks over at the hunter, but the hunter does not acknowledge his puzzled gaze. The hunter only keeps a steady eye on the clearing.

"Now you know," the tortured man says, speaking softly and deeply, "this is the of truth of human kind. Take away society and law and we become beasts. Just like hungry dogs, people will do anything to survive, even forget their humanity."

The creatures are revealed in the steady cold and moonlight to be human...or at least of human birth. Their teeth are filed to sharp points. Their hands are extended beyond normal, more claws than anything, maybe the result of years of inbreeding.

"They were once like us many years ago," the hunter tells Jordan. "They became deformed and embraced their terrible animal shape. Now, they no longer see us as brothers, but as food. So as with any other dangerous beast, the time has come to put them down." With that, the hunter slides down the snowy hillside.

Charging up his rifle, Jordan follows. Silently, they slip into the midst of the nest. They walk quietly, the thick snow muffling their approach.

Then with a sudden burst, the hunter races into the middle of the devil tribe and fiercely attacks. Limbs fly off in all directions as the hunter unleashes his vengeful sword. Angry and fearful screams fill the night. Racing behind the hunter, Jordan opens up with precise fire, covering the hunter's advance.

The snow hides all sound. A benefit before and now a disadvantage as a creature jumps on Jordan's back. He catches a glimpse of huge fangs coming down toward his face. Dropping the rifle, Jordan reaches back and pulls the large monster over him, sending it tumbling. There is no time to recover the rifle. Taking fist to face, Jordan knocks a few teeth out with his heavy punches. Bloodied, it charges up at him again. This time, Jordan manages to grab the beast by its mangy hair. He flips it onto some rocks, stunning it. This gives Jordan the slightest bit of time. Grabbing his rifle, Jordan swings around and bashes the monster's head in.

Two more of the fiendish things are running toward Jordan at full sprint. He turns and fires precisely, hitting one in the heart. It falls dead. The second jumps out of the way and then charges. Jordan does not flinch and bats the creature's head baseball style and it flops down motionless before him. Furiously, he then opens fire on the rest.

As the hunter's sword has been swift as well, the creatures are soon dead. Jordan walks around examining the devils. He can barely even imagine they had once been human.

"This is the future of mankind," the Hunter says. "If we are not careful, nature will be polluted by our own supposed cleverness. No matter what, we can never control it. It will spiral out of control and turn on us. That is our greatest and most arrogant flaw."

Then to his dismay, Jordan spots a group of huddled children, offspring of these cursed people. He is filled with conflict over what to do with them. Jordan raises his gun, but is reluctant to do what he thinks must be done. He hesitates, but the hunter soon intervenes.

"No," the hunter says, pushing the rifle down. "These young ones know not of the parent's ways. They can be saved. They can be taught a new path."

"They have been surrounded by evil so long. Do you think that's possible?" Jordan asks, but has already powered down his rifle.

The hunter then replies, "Without forgiveness, without mercy, hunted animals will always fight. No, the killing stops here. I will try to help these children. For my own humanity, I must be believe there is still goodness in myself and perhaps…in them."

***

Morning has come again on the transport and so has death. Now only four are still live, Moore, Jen, Griger and Mark. Griger barely makes the list.

A frightened Jen begs Mark for a weapon, but he refuses. He steps away and hides inside a lavatory. The smell in here is wretched, but it is not what he thinks.

The door has been opened and Moore is standing behind him. Moore's breath is the source of the stench. It becomes worse as he speaks, "Whatley, I need to show you something in the stern."

A barely functioning Mark follows Moore back into the rear of the wreckage. There is a huge crack in the fuselage and snow is blowing in. Believing that this is what Moore wants to show him, Mark stashes Griger's Gerini pistol back into his jacket. Having the Gerini makes him feel confident as this medium sized gun packs a wallop, even though it only has a measly ten rounds. The Air Corps likes them for their lightweight and dropping power. Mark likes it because he can't shoot straight and he doesn't have to with this thing.

However, Moore walks past the opening in the roof, he instead moves on to swath of silver. Here in the back transport, Moore has set the dead bodies in a row, covered by silvery survival blankets. A thin layer of fresh snow covers everything here, though some blankets have obvious, recent handprints on them.

"What do you want?" Mark says, barely able to form words he is so hungry and cold, the gun still resting in his hidden hand.

"Jordan is not coming back," Moore says with a mad look in his eyes, "But you and I can survive, I in my brilliance have discovered a solution to our problem."

A small puddle of frozen blood is visible from under one of the disturbed blankets. Mark pushes Moore aside and reaches down, quickly pulling the cover off. He dry heaves, nothing in his stomach to come out. The body has been chewed on extensively.

"Listen to me my friend," Moore begins a mad rant, "don't be a fool. I have survived days on this food. There is no shame. We must do away with the last two survivors. If we have enough food, we can make it down the mountain. There will be enough clothing to pad us...and enough food to survive the descent."

Mark shakes his head 'no' and backs away.

185

"There is no other way!" Moore shouts. "It is either this way or we die! Nobody knows this technology except us. With the advantage of these canons, this bloody war will come to an end. We'll be heroes. All it will take is one small moral sacrifice. You must do it."

For a few excruciating seconds, a few seconds he will always regret, Mark considers Moore's offer seriously, his delirious explanation making sense to him in some way.

"You killed them all?" Mark asks.

"I only speed up the inevitable," Moore answers.

"God damn it, Moore," Mark says with a shudder. He then quietly murmurs to himself, "In the absence of light, we must become the light. In the absence of light, we must become the light."

"What are you saying? Speak up!" Moore growls.

A gun fires in the emptiness.

Smoke comes off the hot barrel of the handgun. Mark has shot Moore straight between the eyes, point blank. The blast is so powerful it caves in Moore's head.

Hearing the commotion, Jen comes running down and screams as she sees Moore's headless corpse. She screams even harder when sees the violated bodies.

Grabbing her, Mark pulls the hysterical Jen back toward the front.

"You need to kill me Mark," Jen begs. "I don't want to become an animal like that. Kill me please."

"Jordan will return," Mark pleads. "He'll never give up. I know him. You know him."

"There's no hope," Jen says pathetically as she deliriously tries to grab his gun, but Mark resists.

"Then we'll freeze," Mark says with solemn determination as a mentally crippled Jen sulks to the floor. There is pulsating sound as the cargo ship begins to vibrate. Something is flying over them.

Both see a shadow pass outside the large circular window at the same time. They reach the door as a rescue ship, a Dragoon troop shuttle, lands carefully next to their crash site. As its side door swings up, Jordan comes out and stops, seeing only the single pair of survivors.

"Just you two?" Jordan asks, stunned.

"Griger is still alive, barely," Jen says her voice shaky and pushes herself inside the shuttle. "I'm done with the military," she cries. "I don't care. I'm done."

Tears fall from Mark's tired eyes and he falls to his knees by the door of the cargo ship. He doesn't come forward.

"Jordan," Jen mutters as the paramedics rush over toward Mark. "Inside the plane...bad things."

"There is one alive in the front cabin," Mark says pained.

A pair of paramedics moves past him to get to Griger.

"Grant," Mark says, his mind nearly broken, "Secure the cannons in the back for me. You have to do it. No one else goes back there."

Jordan nods his head and starts back to the rear of the plane. He soon comes across the horror and surmises what happened. Quickly before anyone sees, he comes back out toward the front.

"Anyone else alive back there?" a paramedic asks Jordan.

"No. Empty. They must have thrown all the dead over the cliff," Jordan lies. "Let's get these survivors out of here. There is a bad refrigerant leak and the canons might be unstable."

Mark mumbles, "I have to stay with the plane. Um, the guns, I need to make sure...they are safe."

The captain of the rescue ship comes out, "Professor Whatley, that won't be necessary. A team is on the way. They'll make sure your cargo will follow you out."

Terror fills Mark's eyes. He looks over at Jordan.

"I'll wait here for the team and show them the damage," Jordan says. "I'll make sure *everyone* remains safe. Okay Mark?"

"Good, that'll be good," Marks sighs relieved and enters the rescue ship. He gives Jordan a knowing nod.

As the shuttle leaves, Jordan moves back into the wreckage, gathers the bodies, and throws them all over the edge.

                                ***

After hearing the story, Rina can barely move.

"That's why the story was buried," Jordan says starring down into the emptiness of his coffee cup. "Mark did the right thing."

The usually strong Rina feels a little sick and heads out to the backyard to get some air. There is a large moon moving slowly across the dark sky. "We think we are so great but who are we kidding."

An emotionless Jordan follows and stands silently against the dark sky.

"I hope those children will be OK," Rina says, but she is really talking about herself.

"Griger put me in for a commendation," Jordan states quickly, glad to talk about flying instead. "For saving those cannons and staying quiet, I was also given choice of assignments. Happiest day of my military career."

With a shadow half engulfing her face, Rina then asks cautiously, "The hunter called those people devils. He called them that because they allowed themselves to be consumed by evil. I feel that's me. Am I the devil?"

Jordan says with little emotion. "Hard to tell good from bad just by looking."

"That's not what I wanted to hear," Rina replies nervously.

"When good and evil look the same," he says with a slight smile, "go by the actions and not the face."

THE SPARK

As a class settles in, Mark slowly walks around chit chatting with the students. One of them is Jennifer. He gives her a quick tap on the shoulder.

"Ouch!" she barks loudly.

"Just being friendly," he says and goes to the front to begin his lecture.

Later on that night, Mark is still in his classroom as an overdressed woman walks in. She tentatively scans the room to make sure no one has seen her come in. Taking out a metal tube, Gabrielle hands it to Mark.

Very carefully, he inserts a small needle containing a sample of Jen's blood. "I hope I'm wrong," Mark sighs. "If they are using the agent outside like this, we have a lot to fear."

Stoic and calm, Gabrielle quickly seals the metal tube and puts in her messenger bag. "I'll have my Grandfather look into it immediately. Frankly, I think she's just a hateful bitch."

***

Believing in the infallibility of his own cleverness, Adrian Simmons and a bunch of would-be rebels dart across a small grassy opening and stop under a dense oak tree. From here, they can see the mansion of the prominent Nuhu scientist, Dr. Lester Magen, the local ghoul or god depending on the point of view. There are several buildings here including one that has no windows and only one door.

Armed with tiny cans of directional paint, they approach the back of the mansion and hide behind its large white garage. They figure, in the epitome of a sophomoric gesture, that this would be a great place to leave their marks.

Painting to their hearts content, they laugh and giggle at their mischief making accomplishment. There are five in Adrian's little assault party and unbeknownst to them, they have been spotted, long ago, by an OverForce security team. From the street where they came in, to the tree where they put on the silly black ski masks, all the way

189

through the clearing in the forest, and finally here, the back of the garage, every step has been charted, even every breath counted.

Curious, Adrian and his buddies walk over to the building with no windows. There is a large sealed refuse container against the back wall of this imposing edifice. While the other take advantage of this blank canvas, Adrian tools around the strange container. He then takes a pair of bolt cutters out of his backpack and snaps off the lock holding the lid down. There is not much in here just a bunch of medical waste, syringes and what not. Fearful for his own health, Adrian quickly closes the lid and moves away. Unfortunately, he has seen more than can be allowed.

As this OverForce unit has been assigned to guard Dr. Magen house and interests, they now need to act. Tonight a statement would be made of these hooligans that there are limits. This, in the OverForce way of thinking, is not a heavy-handed punishment. The doctrine of the NAU is absolute. There is a place for protest, but no place for any kind of spying.

From the trees, the OverForce agents lower themselves quietly toward the ground. Slowly, they walk in near silence to the front of the garage. They can see everything clearly. Their optical night vision makes sure of that. They calmly wait for the "rebel spies" to finish their work and come to them…and they soon do.

Adrian and his gang have been caught red handed. At first, they all act brave, yelling insults at the black suited assault team. That is, until they hear the ominous hiss of energy weapons warming up.

"You can't hurt us. You have to take us in," Adrian yells. "That's the law!"

They do not answer.

A woman, a Nuhu woman, is standing next to Adrian. Noticing this is no longer a game she steps forward. "I am Nuhu. I want to call my parents. You can't treat me like them."

She is right. One of the OverForce members guts her rapidly with a knife. She is dead in seconds. To shut her up for sure, her throat is then slit.

"Anymore race traitors? We will oblige you with a quick death," a voice from the OverForce group echoes. "A quick death for anyone who provides information. Who are the leaders of the rebellion?"

They really don't know. Rina has obviously not shared her knowledge.

Adrian's group remains silent. However, their silence is met with a gun discharge. A boy no older than 13 falls to the ground, his leg has been blow off at the knee. Tears strain down his fearful face, unable to cry such is the pain. He is bleeding quickly to death and none move to help him. Soon, he is also dead.

Unfortunately, this is too much for one of Adrian's cohorts.

"That guy there. He's one of the leaders. His name is..." he shrieks.

"Shut up you idiot," Adrian angrily yells back.

"...is Adrian Simmons. Spare me...please, please, spare me."

Adrian is pulled aside and violently stripped of all his clothes down to just his underpants. He is beaten for a half-hour in front of his gang.

Clinging to life, Adrian is then asked the same question...who are your leaders? He does not answer. Instead, he smiles. The OverForce turns their attention on the last two survivors of his party. They break their legs, but Adrian says nothing.

"Don't be a damn martyr," a girl cries in agony, struggling to pull off her ski mask. "It's not worth it. Tell them what you know Adrian!"

Two ropes are lowered from a tree and placed around the necks of the two injured individuals. Adrian says nothing as they are raised into the air. They are slowly raised and lowered several times, bringing them to the verge of death and then back again. Adrian's lips quiver, but he does not speak.

Finally tiring of their game, the OverForce agents pull the ropes tight one final time. The two gurgle violently for a short while before going quiet, dead quiet. Only the swaying of their corpses makes the faintest of sounds.

Adrian begins to shake as an OverForce officer draws out a killing instrument so vile even a foul stench emanates from it. The serrated edges of this black sword are stained a muddy red from repeated use. It is only known as the Stock #6, Intimidation Tool.

The blow comes quickly and accurately. Adrian's bowels hang loosely from him, his stomach expertly cut open. He wants to drop to the ground, but they hold him up by his arms. Adrian sees his guts dangling slightly above the ground. He is unbelievable still alive as an unholy pain fills him. Screaming, they covered his mouth. They are masters of the art of torture even their gloves are lined to cope with bites.

"Tell us the names of the real leaders. Only then will this interrogation end. What were you looking for in the container? What do the rebels know of Dr. Magen's research? Answer now!"

His mind flashes to a vision of Jennifer, but he knows telling them of her would do no good. They are not looking for her anyways. They think there is some greater rebellion. Is there? If there is, he has to protect it.

"They don't know anything. That's why they sent us," he whimpers. "I've never meet the leader. All my orders come by some faceless drone."

Strength comes from deep inside of him and he accepts death. He will die defying the OverForce and their master, the NAU. This is what he always wanted...to defy them...to deny them. All humans will know his name. He keeps telling himself that. It is a wonderful story, even as a rope is tied around both his wrists.

"Tonight I become a hero," Adrian spits out. "I am free."

"You will all just disappear," an OverForce officer says coolly. "We do this all the time."

Adrian's heart is broken as his body is pulled up next to his friends. He is dangling several feet above the ground. His arms dislocate in the process. Unable to swallow, he wishes for water as the hours pass. The thirst is worse than the pain.

After a few hours, the sun rises from the east. Still alive, Adrian smiles. The sunrise is a beautiful thing. With that, he closes his eyes and waits for a desired death. Finally, his body gives out sometime around noon. He and his friends are allowed to crisp in the sun till evening. They are then pulled down and taken away for disposal under the cover of darkness.

MRS. FATE CALLS

"Attention!" Mark yells just as Jordan answers the phone.

Still half asleep and half naked, Jordan simply grunts in response, his eyes lids locked closed. He pulls the covers over his head, trying to hide from the morning sun and cancels the video call option.

"Wake. I command you. It's Saturday and time to have some fun," Mark says with no joy in his gravelly voice of wickedness.

"We just went out Thursday," Jordan says, pulling himself up. "I had three classes yesterday. Go play with yourself." The sun hits him right in the eyes and he groans like an unearthed vampire.

"Mountain soiree tonight. You in or out?"

"Fine whatever," Jordan replies, still not awake.

"Bring someone," Mark orders. "Your muscles alone should be able to scare someone up."

"There is Carmen at the registration office, but she thought I was a Nuhu," Jordan recalls and jettisons a bunch of books from his bed.

"Lie then," Mark suggests. "Just don't get her pregnant." The dark man then says as he hangs up, "Not that you can."

"You jerk," Jordan says to no one and gets out of bed. Mrs. Grant is staring at him crossly from across the lawn. He quickly darkens the windows to hide his horrible human form. Not so long ago, the question of who to take on date was a no brainer. Once again, the ghost of Jennifer past haunts his thoughts to his utter dismay.

Stumbling across his disheveled house, the sluggish pilot mopes, eyes half closed, until he reaches the fridge. Just when he is about to grab some OJ, his phone chirps loudly causing him to spill juice down his bare chest. He shivers with annoyance and frustration, nearly crushing the glass in his hand.

Going back to the bed to retrieve the phone, he sees that a text message has arrived. He opens and reads, "Answer the phone." As he finishes, the phone rings and he almost drops it. He hesitates a bit, but then answers.

"Hello," Jordan says, a bit annoyed.

"Did you enjoy your raw fish the other night?" the voice asks.

"Sierra?" Jordan blurts out with surprise. He assumes correctly that she imaged his phone.

"You know Sierra is not my real name, but I like it," she says with an invisible laugh. "How are you doing?"

"Fine…um…uh…I think," Jordan replies awkwardly. It is not every day the most beguiling woman you ever meet calls you out of the blue. "Eh…How are you?"

"You're tongue tied. I'm charmed," Sierra laughs loudly this time. "Listen, an unexpected business meeting came up. I'm here through the weekend. Do you have any ideas what a girl can do?"

A devious Jordan thinks the unthinkable.

"You still there?"

Mark did tell him to get a date for the night. "Sierra. Would you like to go out with me?" he asks and then thinks that Mark is going to have a fit when he sees Sierra. He loves the idea.

"I'm a married woman," Sierra replies, "maybe we shouldn't…"

"I didn't see a ring on your finger Peter Pan," Jordan says playfully.

There is a long pause and finally…"When and where?"

***

6 PM and Sierra is waiting for Jordan at Pac-Tech's transport hub. She is over dressed, way over dressed and getting hungry stares from all who pass. It's nothing that a middle finger doesn't fix.

"Going to the Christmas ball?" Jordan pronounces, smiling as he walks up as she finishes giving the bird to a crew of jocks. "Making friends?"

"I'm not a piece of meat," she remarks. The sun is just starting to go down over the hills in the distance. This makes Sierra look even more alluring despite her antics.

Actually, Jordan doesn't look half bad either. "Any models die in the making of that dress?"

She bites her lip, "A few." Her skin-tight skirt is all the way down to her ankles. "My so-called husband had to fly to New York at the last minute and I had to give his presentation."

"You look like you're going to a job interview," Jordan jokes.

"I do the hiring," she answers firmly and pokes him in his rock-hard chest. She is momentarily impressed.

"Can you even sit down?"

194

"Now that you mention it," Sierra shuffles around. "No. How about you carry me." She waddles over toward him.

"I'll do what I must," Jordan says and pretends to try to lift her. She shrieks and laughs, pushing him away.

"Bad!" she says with a crooked smile. "I know all about bad men."

"I'm not so bad," he rebukes.

"We'll see about that," she jokes and leans up next to him.

Jordan quickly replies, "Don't worry, you're in charge. My bad self is secured."

"Promise?"

"Absolutely," Jordan grins. For a moment, their eyes examine each other. It is a tiny moment, but telling. They already have a natural attraction to each other.

At that moment, Mark and Rina pull up in the Onzo. Jordan can vaguely hear Mark swearing as he opens the door and steps out.

"Hello Mr. Whatley," Sierra says regaining her icy composure. She offers her hand and Mark shakes it lightly, barely wanting to touch it.

"The infamous Mrs. Wu. Buyer and seller of illicit goods. Evil sorceress of the technical world. Aye ya ya," Mark growls with little regard for insult. "Any luck with that drive you stole?"

"No. Lucky you," Emily says smiling. "Your encoding is very impressive." She had already broken his code though. However like the best of honest thieves, she didn't like what she found and erased it, well, mostly; she did provide a few sectors to her client, Martin Malone to satisfy him.

"Seems you are keeping better company these days," Mark groans as he gives his idiot friend, Jordan, a stern look. "Since you're *his* guest, come on in."

Sierra, seeing Rina for the first time, says, "Hello Ms. Dupont. How is Martin these days?"

Not wanting to answer, Rina averts her gaze.

"She is off duty," Mark mutters.

"Congratulations," Sierra remarks robotically. "So…shall we go?

The head up a long winding road up into Mt. Tamalpais. In their trouble filled youth, Mark and Jordan would go up here and explore the forests and back roads, made more interesting by the fact that the whole mountain top was off limits due to a surveillance station situated near the peak. That didn't stop them then and doesn't stop them now.

Hiding along the roadway to the peak, the four wait as the forest guards go home. Now, the path is safe.

"They don't monitor this road?" Rina inquires.

"We wouldn't be here if they did," Mark says proudly. "They only watch the main road."

With beer, polish sausages, jumbo shrimp, and even a telescope in tow, they drive up further on the old fire road until reaching an area over grown with flora and fauna.

Being sneaky and having too much time, Mark has cut away enough brush over the years to hide his car from the curious. From this hidey hole, the trek to the very top of the mountain is easy, even in heels for someone, and they are soon met with the best views in the land.

Tonight, a gentle breeze is blowing across the peak, but it is warm enough for a fall evening. The sky is amazingly clear with a dark blue fringe around the horizon.

The four troublemakers can see the various lights of the cities below and the massive glowing crystal ball that is San Francisco in the distance. Diamond-like sparkles bounce off the rippling surface of the bay, but that is nothing compared to the stars of the wide-open night sky.

Mark and Rina are gently getting buzzed, sitting warmly around the dim glow of a smokeless, electric BBQ. After a quiet dinner, the couples split. Already in their own little world, Rina and Mark laugh quietly and kiss under a knotted tree.

Sober and much less touchy, Jordan and Sierra are standing a bit away. Now that they are alone, she is feeling awkward and Jordan picks up on this. He quickly sets up the telescope that Mark brought. Sierra peers humbly at the endless shapes of the heavens, a happy smile soon spreads across her face as she relaxes.

Tonight, all pretenses have fallen away. There is no secret police officer, no corporate big wig, no genius and no hero on the roof of the world, but just two couples finding life away from titles and labels.

"There was a time," Sierra says with barely controlled excitement, "when I dreamed about visiting the moon. I use to dream about a lot of silly things only to find that world is about…"

"Compromises?" Jordan says, finishing her statement. He is standing next to her starring out into the sky, being carefully not intrude on her space. Though, he wants to give her a big hug.

"Yes," she says feeling like she needs a hug, but hoping he doesn't feel so inclined. After all, she is supposed to be tough-as-nails.

A pensive Jordan thinks about his own problems with compromise before asking, "What kind of compromise would drive a person with so much wealth and power to want to dive off the Kobe?"

As her toughness melts, Sierra's thoughts seem to be eating her; "So you think money and happiness go together?" She then tells him how it is, "Let me explain, money provides security, nothing more. The twist is that the cost of security is happiness itself." Sierra then backs away from the telescope, her smile gone. "You should look. It's beautiful…faraway and impossible."

Kneeling down, Jordan takes a quick peak. The moon is perfectly focused. However, her intent seems to have been to distract him.

A hopeless Sierra stands off to the side, looking at the ground, her hand quickly wiping something away from her eyes.

"Bad topic?" he asks.

"Hard for me to know why I need to live. No real friends, nothing." Sierra then points to Mark and Rina. "You're two up on me. Wealthy man."

"Stop exaggerating," Jordan counters and approaches her. She turns to block him from getting too close.

She then laughs coldly. "Oh I have plenty of business acquaintances. They only want what I can provide," Sierra answers. "Trust is difficult amongst us villains."

"Villain?" Jordan repeats, a bit intrigued and a lot concerned.

"I have a black sword," she says very seriously, staring him straight in the eyes. "And who am I with, my opposite, a man with a priceless silver sword from Lopez & Sons."

"Black sword? Black heart too?" Jordan questions.

"You tell me," Sierra answers, snapping a twig between her fingers. "Most people would say the heart has gone bad too." She sees a tiny flower on a bush and crushes it.

"And crushing flowers proves it?" he says.

"Everything is meaningless," she says and brushes her long hair back. Sierra comes up close to him, her face hovering next to his. "I have no idea why I'm here. How about you tell me?"

"Beats me," Jordan says and playfully bumps her away.

"Liar," Sierra replies, bumping him back, "The things you said to me at the Kobe. They got to me."

With a perceptible shudder, Jordan admits, "My life has seen too many dark episodes for me to turn away from others who are suffering."

Upon hearing this, Sierra then seems to get angry and gripes, "Everyone I care about has forgotten me. You just want something from me. Don't you?" She starts to walk back toward the path to car. "Tell Whatley he can get his revenge some other way than tempting me with you." She points at him accusingly with her hand.

"You're right," Jordan says surprised at Sierra's reaction as he follows her along the trail ridge. "All I want is to screw you. Let me get my tools."

"Not funny," she says stopping, nearly toppling into him. "Good people are easy to read. They don't have hidden agendas."

"You just said I was using you," Jordan reminds her, crookedly smiling.

"You made me feel weak," she says and continues to storm away from him, but abruptly heads back up the hill. "Jordan don't follow me." Obviously distracted, she trips hard on a root, but with unimaginable agility, gracefully recovers. It is a near impossible feat, but it goes unnoticed.

A polite Jordan quickly gives her hand.

"What are you going to do? Carry me the rest of your life?" she argues, pushing him away.

"No, but I can carry you back to a nice blanket and you can take those heels off," he suggests. "After that, you can do all the exploring you want."

"I don't need you," she groans and heads back on her own. Finding the blanket, Sierra tries to sit down. She has to roll over on her side to get down, her tight skirt fighting her.

Jordan reaches down to help her again and she slaps his hand.

"Remember, you said I'm in charge," she growls. "I told you I don't need you."

"OK boss, how about a job then?" Jordan laughs as he watches her struggle with the dress.

Finally down, Sierra waves him to sit next to her and he does. She scoots in close to him and says, "I would never hire you."

"Ouch," Jordan complains.

"Bad fit for EchoTech. You have a problem with honesty. You are. A problem with kindness. You practice it. And, a penchant for heroics. Documented. My husband is the opposite of all those things and therefore a billionaire," Sierra states as their faces float close together. "I can't divorce him, but..."

"I'm not interested in an affair," Jordan says looking a bit peeved, pulling away from her. He is such a romantic dolt.

"That's not what I meant. I meant we could be friends," Sierra says softly and then asks, "Did Whatley tell you about me?"

Embarrassed, Jordan nervously scratches his scalp and fails to reply.

Shaking her head, Sierra sighs, "Someone like me does not deserve any kind of love." She slouches down, big time. "My real job is not business."

"Assassin," Jordan states flatly.

"Yes," Sierra confirms coldly and without any hesitation, feeling ashamed of herself and her true purpose.

Even though not expecting such an honesty replay, Jordan doesn't flinch. In fact, he puts his hand on hers.

"Why doesn't that scare you?" she asks.

Jordan doesn't answer, but stands up and walks over to the ridgeline again. He sits on large rock overlooking the bay. Sierra, intrigued, follows him, after hiking her skirt over her knees and dragging the blanket with her. Several lights can be seen bobbing around the Golden Gate from here. Jordan points to them as she sits down.

"Sky Skiffs," he forces a laugh. "Never fly straight in a breeze."

"I am a killer," she says sincerely. "You're not. You are what people want to be. Do you even realize that? I, Emily Wu, rich woman, wishes to be like you. I covet the title of hero. I really do."

"I don't even know how many people I've killed," Jordan admits to her. "From the sky, you don't see the damage. The pain is far away."

"My father was a general once," she confides. "Soldiers don't always have the option of a conscious. Theirs is to do and die. My father disagreed with that idea. He said you must only fight the good battles. Otherwise, you might as well turn the gun on yourself before someone else does."

Unsure, Jordan replies wearily, "I want to tell you something, because I feel that you might understand."

"Then you are being stupid," Sierra scoffs and thinks about all the people she has double-crossed in her corrupt career. Then again, they were all scum. "Trusting me of all people."

Jordan sits silently.

She taps him. "Well go on," Sierra says. "You're my only friend. Who am I going to tell?"

His mood darkening, Jordan takes a deep breath and quickly looks to see where Mark and Rina are. Noticing his expression, Sierra's ears prick up. "Mark and I were in the service together. We saw lots of horrific battles, but nothing as bloody as India."

"The Orissa Offensive? The Russian surprise attack?" Sierra tries to clarify.

"The NAU operates with the belief that they are the dominant force in the world. They didn't know that the Russians had stolen our air ship designs. Even though India is a radioactive mess, there's lots of valuable raw material both sides still wanted. The Russians managed to hack our computers and lock us out," Jordan elaborates. "All ships had the same codes at the time. It was arrogant thinking. Now, they say it's different."

"I know. I helped redesign the software. You saw the worst of it. Didn't you?" Sierra says softly, moved by his faith in her.

A haunted Jordan seems to be reliving the battle in his head. "Bodies were falling from the sky on fire over Burma. Russian chemical missiles exploded inside ships, burning everyone. We were already beaten when the orders to retreat came in," Jordan recounts. "Our casualties, to put it mildly, were unimaginable. Mark and I found ourselves on a serviceable frigate. I was at the comm. and Mark was at tactical as they had lost half their bridge crew. When we were flying out, our commanding officer ordered Mark to bomb the capitol city of Rangoon, wanting to leave nothing to the Russians. These were innocent people, people who patched us up, so Mark wouldn't do it. The Captain then put a gun to his head. And stubborn Mark, he still wouldn't do it." Jordan pauses for a long time, he then says, almost chocking on the words, "So I did."

"You? You bombed innocent people?" Sierra says alarmed. "To save your friend?"

"I shot the Captain," Jordan corrects with no emotion.

Unintentionally, Sierra laughs. "So that's why you call yourself a killer?" she says a bit amused. "You're right. We are the same. I'd kill him too."

"What I did was an act of mutiny," Jordan says. "I don't compromise my morals so easily, but I did that day."

"I compromise all the time," Sierra says. She looks over at Jordan and studies his face. "The world economy is a war dominated by the NAU. To survive, to compete, an international company must employ all kinds of tactics."

"Do you ever regret it?" Jordan asks and stares back at her.

"Of course," she says with a glazed look in her eyes. "My husband needed a monster. So I became that to make him rich, not that I wanted to."

"What kind of marriage is that?" Jordan states as wayward Sky Skiff flies overhead. It lights up the area for a bit and then vanishes into a cloud.

Sierra admits, "I was in a bad way and he exploited it. Sadly, I tried to love him. A hundred girlfriends later, I gave up."

"You tried to love him?"

Nodding, Sierra then says sadly. "After I crossed into my thirties, he lost interest in me."

"You don't look thirty," Jordan interjects.

"How about thirty-two?" she smiles.

"Your husband must be blind."

She gently touches his face and remarks, "You look old. Too much worry. True killers have no regrets. You do and so do I. So what are we?" Sierra looks away from him and down at her hands.

"It's not impossible to turn back," Jordan says with understanding. Master Kenji refuses to reveal his last name for fear of his past, a past where he also carried a black sword. "My master's sword used to be black too, but not anymore."

"Master Kenji has no family, no ties," Sierra protests. "Tell me you regret saving me at the Kobe. Tell me I should have jumped. Tell me I deserve to die," Sierra says frustrated.

"This world only has the meaning you give it," Jordan states. "Make it what you want and stop making excuses to leave."

Humbled, Sierra is silent and stares hard at Jordan. He looks back at her unflinching.

"You know who people really hate? Not you," he says with resentment. "They admire you. They want your power and prestige. People hate me. People don't believe in saints anymore, unless the sinners become the saints. That is why I have hope for you. If you can change, the world can too. That's what people want to see. That's what they need to see."

Sierra is taken aback. The tears begin to fall freely from her eyes. She collapses helplessly into his arms. He holds her tight. "Jordan," she pleads. "Don't make me think this way."

"I'll stop," he says and strokes her hair.

"You're going to laugh at me when I say this." Sierra then says, cheering up. "I'm going to tell you about a dream."

"Go on."

"There was an island with nobody there: empty and alone, no cities or anything," she says.

"An island of monkeys?" Jordan jokes and arches his arms like an ape.

"You're the monkey," Sierra frowns and pokes his belly.
"It was an empty place and I was there alone. And then I realized that I had left my old life behind and I could begin again. It was a good dream," she says.

"A lady once told me that hope is the fuel of dreams. It is what makes them fly," Jordan says, trying to hide a smile.

She takes a tissue and dries her eyes and leans her head on his. "Our dreams will just be added to the pile of the broken."

The wind is picking up and Jordan wraps the blanket around them. The lights of the bay are glittering in the distance. He really likes her and doesn't want this night to end. For a moment, he thinks about Jennifer. A long time ago, he felt the same way for her.

"It's a pretty view," Jordan states. "Isn't it?"

"I said you can't change me," Sierra tells him again.

He points out toward an island in the bay named Angel Island. "Maybe that's your island out there."

"Jordan that's enough," Sierra frowns, looking peeved. "Who was the lady that told you that fantasy about hope?"

"Her name was Sophia," Jordan answers cryptically, "kind of a mom figure, I guess, but gone now."

"I had a professor in England named Sophia too. We were like sisters," Sierra recalls. "I was at Oxford for a while before the money troubles hit us. I bet you she's asking, 'Where did the damn Yingtai go? She had promise,'" Sierra forces a laugh. "I had my reasons for leaving. It happens."

"My memories of Sophia are fuzzy now," Jordan recalls. "Maybe, one day I will say the same thing about you."

"Did you love her?" Sierra questions.

"I did," he admits.

"Do you want to love me?" she asks quizzically. "I am not for you."

Jordan goes quiet. This is not what he wants to hear.

"I made the decision long ago to give up on myself, to simply become a tool of my husband, Thomas," Sierra states. "Fate is cruel to have us meet so late."

"We make our own choices. We fight our own fears. We stand against the tide," Jordan remarks. "You chose to come here tonight. No mysterious force made you."

"Others make our choices. We run from our fears. We fall and never stand," Sierra replies. "I wanted to live a night of fantasy and I have. In the morning, I'm still the villain and you are still the hero. Destiny has made its choice. I just don't have to be your villain."

Disheartened, Jordan stands up frustrated.

"Don't go." She grabs his hand.

"For a person who claims to be liar and a witch, you are the most direct, honest person I know," Jordan says examining her hand. It is soft for someone who handles weapons so often. Her grip is tight and she is not letting go. He squeezes back. "Do you know what the big lie is?" he asks her.

"What could you possibly know about lying?"

"Just one thing," Jordan says coming down, looking right into her green eyes. "They tell kids that monsters live in the dark, which is true. What they don't tell you...is the lie. That hope is also in the darkness, hidden," he says. "I don't want you to love me. I don't want you to be my friend. I want you to find that hope in the darkness. I did. I was drowning, nearly dead. And there at the end, I found hope. It was always inside me just like it's in you."

Sierra is stunned and cannot answer. He's right. For the first time in her life, she feels real love building in her black heart.

***

The trip back home is a brisk one. They had spent most of the night on the mountain. When Mark drops them off, the time is close to 4 am. As his G850 drives off, Jordan walks with Sierra toward his house.

"Did you call a taxi?" Jordan inquires.

"Should be here any minute," Sierra says, now carrying her shoes in her hand. "Is that your place? The little glass house?" She points to the glass roof peaking over the hedges.

"Come on. Have a look at the property," Jordan suggests.

Sierra looks at her phone. The taxi prompt shows an ETA of ten minutes.

"Quickly," she says grinning.

They walk through the gap in the hedges and end up next to Jordan's glass house. Here they stop and look at each other. Her nylons are torn to shreds and her dress looks like it was washed in mud. Jordan, in contrast, looks immaculate.

"It's nice," Sierra states breaking the silence. She moves over next to him and leans over. Her body heat a comforting sensation in the chilly morning air for Jordan. "Should say 'Bachelor Pad' right over the door."

"Sure," Jordan agrees, "The chlorine smell from the pool is a natural aphrodisiac." He slowly puts his arm around her waist. She doesn't flinch at all, but instead lets her hand find its way to his firm butt. It is Jordan who flinches at this unexpected touch.

The lights of the taxi can be seen glowing in the distance. Sierra looks back toward the street. Turning quickly, she cannot resist him anymore. She hovers over his face and their breaths mingle. Slowly, her lips fall closer and closer to his. He pulls in and she kisses him.

Jordan's first reaction is to pull away, but there is something genuine and intoxicating about her. Her emotions feel so real, so true. He kisses her back gently. Every kiss becomes longer and longer as their passions finally break free.

He spins her around and braces her up against the glass house. The kissing gets more physical and a potted plant is sent flying. The shattering pot makes a terrible pop. A light soon goes on in the main house, but neither notices.

"Sierra," Jordan says trying to catch his breath, but she puts a finger to his lips.

"You're the only one who knows the real me," the unimaginable whispers back.

They both smile and kiss again, taking solace in each other's passionate embrace, hoping for a chance to move inside.

A horn sounds as the taxi stops outside the hedgerows.

"Stay," Jordan asks as he cradles her face with his immense hands.

Shaking her head, she then runs off, blushing like some thirty-something year-old schoolgirl. And with that, Sierra is gone.

Alone again, Jordan is left with an empty heart. Then again, what was he expecting? He leans up against the cold glass building, letting it cool his passions.

"Who was that?" Jennifer asks coming around the pool with a flashlight. She sees that he is flush even though her own breath proves the chillness of the air.

"Garden gnome," Jordan states with a sad expression, his feelings still exposed. He really wishes Jen would just sink into the ground at this moment. The last thing he needs is a dose of guilt to add to his emotional confusion.

"Really?" Jennifer pries and tries to peer into the cab as it leaves. She is suddenly full of yearning for her old love. Reaching out for him, Jordan pulls away. He has never not wanted her touch.

"Not really and you know it," Jordan snaps back as he stares at his former love. It is an awkward place to be. These two women haunt him. And like ghosts, they merely appear only to disappear shortly thereafter.

"Who was she?" Jen inquires not so innocently, not liking the idea of competition. Her true feeling rushing to the forefront, pushing any idea to the contrary aside.

"An older, married, extraordinarily beautiful garden gnome."

Jen frowns, "I don't approve, not at all."

"I don't think I approve either," Jordan sighs deeply.

"I thought we were going to try to…oh…" Jen looks confused, but fights through it, "…um…you know, try to make up. Is this how you make up? Forget about the conditions, let's just not throw everything away."

Flabbergasted, Jordan looks pale and confused. A raw Jen looks at him with earnest hope. His confusion strikes a new high as he tries to digest the impossible words that just came out of her mouth. He desperately wants her back, regardless of all the tough talk. Suddenly for the first time in his life, he hesitates to respond to her. Sierra, to his disbelief, has planted a seed that is furiously growing.

At that moment, Jennifer's phone rings. Having moved on from her butterfly phone, she pulls out her keys and looks at a small colorful triangle. A woman's picture is displayed on it. She is screaming in mute. Jordan recognizes her as one of Jennifer's "protest" friends. The picture glows red. Whatever she is calling about, it must be urgent.

"I have to take this call," Jen says and turns her back to him, answering the call. She talks quietly, but seems to be getting very worried.

Jordan catches the last sentence, as her voice gets louder.

"What do you mean missing since yesterday? I've been busy. OK. I'll go look for him. No, I don't know what Adrian was up to. No. I didn't tell him to do anything. Yes. Right now. I'm coming down,"

Jennifer finishes her call and turns to Jordan. "I have to go to the University."

"It's late. I'll go with you," he suggests, even though he is dead tired.

"No, since it looks like I've been replaced," she says with real sadness and quickly walks away toward the garage.

Feeling like shit, Jordan bangs his head against the glass house. At that moment, dread fills him and he doesn't know why. It is a feeling that has lingered with him. Something evil is in the air, something not so far away now.

METALLURGICAL MERLIN

Thursday morning and the skies have opened up. Sheets of rains are falling on him as if he were Noah on the ark. The whole week has been overcast and foggy, but never rainy till today, the one day Jordan has to wait for a bus. Several protestors are roaming around behind him, oblivious to the cold and wet. Jen must be pushing them hard as their numbers have steadily increased. He hopes they don't scare away his ride.

God anything for a car, he prays. Even a 70 HP Korean four-wheel solar death trap would be acceptable…but they are illegal in the Union. Ah hell. He just wants anything mobile with a roof so this new job cannot start out soon enough.

His mood soon goes from foul to murderous.

As the rain really starts to swirl, the bus finally shows up. Jordan is relieved to see it and stands up. But at that exact moment, some protestors run across the street forcing the bus into the gutter, splashing Jordan with enough water to float a boat.

Soaked through to his skin, Jordan hurriedly climbs onto the bus. He tosses himself on one of the back seats and stares out of the window dazed. A puddle forms below him as green trees soon start to rush by. The bus is soon free of in town roads and is zooming north along the MagWay.

The silhouette of Mt. Tamalpais shrinks away and signs announcing the city of Novato loom quickly ahead. Here at the edge of Marin, Mark's refuge emerges, a little abandoned airport.

This sad strip of aviation wonderment is situated on an expanse of smelly, brownish blue marshland. But the marsh is doomed to extinction as Jordan can see new developments going up in the distance. The bus slows quickly, only stopping long enough to drop him off. The airport is a way off and he has to follow a rutted road that does a good job of scaring the locals away.

Risking a possible broken limb down this pothole-filled road, Jordan carefully maneuvers over muddy pools filled with oily blackness. These are the tell-tale signs of large trucks and big deliveries. The ruts that are carved deep into road are many and long. Something of scale is going on here, but you could hardly tell by the activity alone. There isn't any. There is only a lone, sleep-deprived guard who looks like a disciple of the uberphine gods. Jordan approaches the small booth at the base of road.

"Yes?" the guard says, with a crushing grip on his coffee mug stained mug. The mug bears the EchoTech logo of all things.

"I'm starting work here today."

The guard taps on a pad on his wrist and reads, "Grant, Junior."

"Jordan," Grant Junior corrects.

"Finger print here please," he pushes out the pad to Jordan. After tapping it with his thumb, the guard hands Jordan a blank badge.

"Make sure you keep that on you at all times. There are A.I. perimeter guns hidden across the property so be careful. If you forget the badge, the gun will try to confirm your identity by voiceprint. They're not that good, especially if you have a cold. So otherwise, don't move till we come and disarm the bot," the guard instructs as if deadly robots are the order of day. "If you decide to break the bot so that they don't bother you anymore, they cost about a half million…each. Don't do it."

Upon setting foot on the abandoned airport, the rain finally lets up and Jordan can see the lay of the land clearly. There is only one pristine new building — some kind of domed hanger. Otherwise all the buildings look like they would be happier lying down instead of standing. He's heads for the hanger only to be proven wrong.

A light is coming from inside a ratty warehouse and this light appears to be emitting from a plasma welder. Plasma welder must equal Mark, he thinks, and beelines for the sparks instead.

As he steps forward, the sun weakly peeks through the heavy rain clouds. A few pinpoints of light descend across the wetlands causing transparent rainbows to form over the marsh. This provides a satisfying break in the grey sky with color. For a second, Jordan forgets about the job and stares out across the scene. Mark, shrouded in bulky work overalls, comes up behind him.

"Storm is breaking up," Mark says. "I've never really understood your love of flying." He pulls a set of heavy wielding glasses off his head. "Flying is just a mode of transportation through an atmosphere. It's where it takes you that I find interesting."

"In the sky, I'm an ace," Jordan answers and kneels down, picking up some soil and rolls it in his hands. "Down here, I'm no better than this dirt."

"Everything grows from dirt. Dirt is fair. Everything starts the same. Everything ends the same," Mark says, looking glum.

"I'd rather tumble into the unknown then rot in the ground," Jordan replies and drops the dirt.

"That's why you're perfect for this job," Mark notes and motions Jordan to follow him.

Large steel beams hold up the artifice that is the outside of the warehouse. In actuality, the inside of Mark's design lab is surprisingly modern considering the dilapidated surroundings. A lot of money has been spent supporting whatever mad project he is working on. Most of the lab is automated with robotic arms and cranes that are at his beck and call. None of these sophisticated machines are currently operating, leaving the lab silent and still. A small "trash bin style" robot comes up to them, so named for its simple circular shape. Mark places his gloves and glasses upon its flat head and takes a beer out from a slot. He offers one to Jordan, but he shakes his head no. The bot then beeps and rolls away.

"One second while I finish some work," Mark says taking a sip of his drink. Putting it down, he moves in front of an advanced data panel, a large slab of wall-sized glass. It is both an electronic chalkboard and computer.

Engineering panels are unique tools. The user stands or sits in front of it and uses the "world" engineering language of "Jobbs." Jobbs speak is made entirely of number combinations and function words that allow for quick entry of formulas and programming with minimal manual input from the user. Jordan ignores the verbal noise and the abrupt movements Mark makes for a few minutes, as every engineer has their own variation. A complex diagram briefly appears on the screen before being replaced by columns and columns of numbers. Mark selects a section and begins to edit.

Jordan only catches the final part of the edit.

Mark spits out in rapid succession, "Command begin. 0011 1100 0000 break 2124. Connect 12 and 14 sub programs. Complete. Save to Ventus file." He taps on the screen which promptly goes dark.

As the sun comes in through warehouse's overhead windows, a sparkling material catches Jordan's eye and he walks over. There before him is a sheet of a beautiful sheet of reflective metal. Then he realizes what he is looking at, it is a sheet of pure Exitor. A prize not even equaled by gold or diamonds. Jordan is about to reach down and touch it when Mark stops him.

"It's extremely sharp, even flat. I haven't entirely worked out that problem yet. Sometimes flat. Sometimes not," Mark warns and sighs, "Pretty though. Shiny thing Exitor composite."

"Exitor composite? That's impossible."

"Welcome to the chocolate factory Charlie," Mark says with a fanciful laugh. "Exitor molecular bonds cannot be broken without ruining the tensile strength of the material. If you believe it's alive, like some do, you kill it that way. It becomes brittle."

"This can't be real. You're kidding me," Jordan says shocked. "Artificial Exitor?"

"Not exactly, the stuff hates being broken apart. But, the inherent strength of those bonds allowed me to find a way to stretch it. I simply filled in the gaps. So you get a sheet of Exitor composite from an inch of the real stuff. One-tenth the cost, not as strong, but still stronger than any material on the market. No joke."

Jordan stands their dumb founded. He is staring at the holy grail of modern metallurgy. "Documented?" he asks.

"1/4 to 1/2 strength depending on the blend components and the stretch," Mark answers and looks up at the ceiling. "Arm 6, bring over a scope."

Arm 6 then scoots away at speed and soon returns with a new attachment to its lower appendage. It rotates the scope and lowers the eyepiece in front of the two men.

"One problem," Mark says as he adjusts the scope, "Exitor, for a lack of a better term, is prickly. The new structure is like a million miniature razor blades. Somehow, it is capable of being either sharp or flat at will. Kind of like water can be solid or liquid. We really don't understand Exitor that well. I don't really understand Exitor that well and I'm an expert. You can see the roughness under the scope and that's my main problem for mass production, no consistency."

Looking into the scope's monocles, Jordan, without thinking, rests his hand on the Exitor plate. Panicked, Mark pulls him away and immediately checks his hand, but Jordan is unharmed.

"What the hell?" Mark barks. "You should be diced like a tomato." Looking into the scope, Mark moves Jordan's hand closer and farther to the Exitor. "The beastie likes you," Mark remarks calmly, but his face tells a different story. He's smiling. Jordan has some sway over the Exitor. This is something Mark has never observed and Jordan then seems to read his mind.

"Do you think it knows I was touching it and not you?"

"It's not alive yet it acts alive. Some people take a very spiritual view about Exitor. Faith has no place in this modern world though," Mark mentions enthralled. "But maybe we should be open to what we call a life form. How we treat things."

"Master Kenji noticed that Exitor acts differently around me. That's when he agreed to teach me as a kid. He says a true master of Exitor could communicate with it." Jordan says.

"Kenji claims to communicate with it?" Mark asks intrigued.

"Yes."

Somehow Mark is not overly perplexed by this answer. He respects life. For an atheist, Mark had a strong sense of right and wrong.

Mark then says, "Kenji-san has faith in the unseen. I have to see to believe. Perhaps, that's why I can't get this stuff to behave."

"Understandable, you're a man of science. I'm just not convinced whether it's good or evil. Maybe, like a wild animal, it's neither."

"A metal with an agenda," Mark states and stares at the Exitor plate a long time. He then slowly allows his hand to hover over the plate of Exitor.

"You'll never fully understand if you don't trust in the unknown," Jordan encourages.

"It's not your hand."

"No, but I don't like it when I'm treated like I'm not alive either," Jordan admits. "Respect it and you'll be respected back. Lesson one from Master Kenji."

Taking a deep, deep breath, Mark places his hand on the plate. The Exitor sparkles. His hand is fine.

"Much left to learn," Mark says perplexed. He pushes the scope away. "You are a contradiction Jordan. If life had treated me as awful as it has you, I'd have no faith of any kind, not even in science." Mark says and looks over at Jordan. "You have too much respect for the unknown. Blind trust is unsafe."

"That's why I have a scientist as my best friend," Jordan says.

"Ah balance," Mark says.

"Anymore magical items around here?" Jordan says and they both laugh.

"Let's go meet the wizard and find out."

"You are the wizard," says Jordan.

"If that's the case, just follow me then," Mark suggests and leads him outside. They tromp across a muddy field and head to the doors of the domed hanger. A giant A.I gun sits right over these doors and it moves down to scan them. Mark and Jordan wave their badge and the gun recoils back up to its safe position.

"What do you keep in here?" Jordan laughs. "The Kraken?"

"Charlie, in here is the chocolate factory," Mark warns slyly. "Last chance to turn around and forget all about changing the world crap and other such nonsense."

To Mark's dismay, Jordan does hesitate.

The dark man then says quietly, "I am the product of an industrial nation. I want to believe I am more than that...but it's not true. I am an inventor. I control the things I make...and I myself am an invention. I myself am controlled, but don't wish to be," Mark's voice shakes, "This whole country is seeking freedom, but they don't realize it yet. You are the good knight. And I as your Merlin, I will give you the strongest steed to ride into battle. Believe that I am really a wizard and that we fight for right."

Jordan simply responds, "Show me the chocolate factory."

With an elegant move, Mark keys in a code and opens the vast hanger doors. An amorphous covered lump, about the size of a large car, sits in the center of the cavernous room.

"This is our future," Mark tells him. "We must have smarter people, better technology to succeed. A new nation needs to be both strong and smart."

Looking beyond the doors, Jordan notices that this is unlike any hanger he has ever seen. The hanger is round inside and has an odd red dirt floor. Around the perimeter of this strange space, multiple opaque windows allow light in. The whole place has the red glow of a warm engine, the light reflecting from the red floor. He then realizes it is rust from the charred walls.

"What happened in here?" Jordan asks. "Just how many times did this thing blow up?"

"Broke a few eggs that's all," Mark says and makes his way to the center of the room. Grabbing the edge of the canvas tarp, he makes ready to pull. "Are you ready Aladdin?"

Not very big, whatever it is, Jordan thinks. If this is what all the mystery is about, he hopes it is more than just another modified car. "Let's see this rug of yours."

Mark pulls the tarp off. It is only a plane...a little plane at that. It has the shape of the letter "A" and has several dimples all over its wings. The thing is barely big enough for one adult, or two packed tight. Its engine is huge and takes up the entire back end.

"Nice toy. Cute. Does it do tricks?" Jordan snickers. "The fake Exitor was more impressive."

"This is made from the composite Exitor. The one batch that didn't try to cut me open," Mark smirks and opens the latch to the cockpit. The large transparent canopy slowly pushes upwards then forward revealing a single seat with room for instrument packs behind it. He hits a combination of switches and pulls the throttle slightly. The plane's engine hums softly, appliance like, and then the plane jumps about a foot up and hovers...effortlessly.

Jordan is intrigued. He could see some dust being blown around under the craft. Something of this ship's size would require an immense amount of power to hover and should be blowing up a dust storm. He tries to push it. The plane does not move, not even an inch. The darn thing seems to be actually compensating against his force.

"It ain't gonna move," Mark snickers with a proud smile. "Meet the Ventus A, technology test vehicle." Pushing out his chest, he then says proudly, "Air particle fusion drive system with..."

"Air fusion?" Jordan stammers. "What the hell is that? Hold that...how the hell is that?"

"Let me finish," Mark chuckles. "Look here, the flight surfaces are perforated with 1mm holes which allow for maximum surface lift and optimal direction control. Power can therefore be directed to almost any surface. Being made of the Exitor composite, these holes do not compromise the strength of the outer skin. The Ventus A uses up to 60% of its surface area for maneuvering control. You can loop this thing inside this hanger. Oh yeah, there also the two vectored nozzles on the back for tremendous, nearly unlimited, forward thrust. You see there's no gas tank."

"That's amazing. You made a mechanical humming bird. So birdman, what is up with this air fusion nonsense?"

"Alright, air fusion. You got a taste of that in the car."

"That's right," Jordan remembers, "the odd intake on the Onzo."

"On that day, the engine burned zero fuel after I engaged the air fusion engine, AFE for short. All the power was supplied by the tiny waste particles suspended in the air around us."

"That explains the necessity of the ugly gigantic ice cream scoop on your otherwise beautiful car," Jordan states, walking around the vehicle. He finds an engine air inlet on either side.

"Ugly? Each to their own," Mark scoffs. "Same concept here on the Ventus A. Those scoops you are looking at feed the engine air. It burns the particles to produce energy. High capacity batteries store the energy for start-up, the intake fans, and electronics. It may even work underwater or in zero G, if you carry or collect some kind of matter for fuel. In the drink, I suppose it could run on particulates in the water as long as the aqua is being pushed into the intakes, but I didn't design the intakes with that in mind. Curios to try it out though, but I don't want to lose it to Poseidon just yet. Totally opens the world and beyond to exploration...limitless exploration."

"The only other fusion engine I know of is the size of a warehouse and can only power a LED light. Now, you show me one that can be squeezed into a car and runs on dust?" Jordan mentions bemused.

"Don't get your hopes up about space exploration. We'll probably be dead before that."

Jordan's comments seem to piss Mark off. He admonishes him loudly, "This government doesn't want people to reach out of their defined roles. They want us to be happy with the status quo. People who think like you and I, and there are many, can't live in a zoo. I can't, I won't, live by some else's design. I'm too curious."

Jordan agrees.

Mark adds, "This will be our advantage. When the time comes, and it will come, we'll be ready for a fight. Here is the engine to carry our dreams Jordan. It can help us win this fight and then take us forward to a future of unbelievable discovery."

"So this is the glass elevator," Jordan says.

"Take your seat for the ride of your life." With that, Mark moves aside and motions Jordan to enter the cockpit. Jordan sits down and feels immediately comfortable in the surroundings. It is good to be back in the office again.

He hears a voice, a female voice. The voice is speaking to him directly, "Hello. I am the Whatley/Malone Ventus-A. You have been recognized, pilot Jordan Grant, access granted. Command?"

Jordan thinks, "Flight Screen."

The screens on the main panel above his legs blink on as the plane's avionics controls and flight systems are displayed.

Mark looks alarmed.

Again, Jordan thinks, "Scroll all screens. Descriptive narration please."

The screens start displaying various pages of info as the female computer voice briefly explains the major functions of each.

"Sorry about that Jordan," Mark growls frustrated. He begins to open up panel after panel. "Must be some glitch...the Ventus shouldn't be doing this. I haven't made any inputs."

"Everything is fine," Jordan says transfixed on the screens. "I did."

"You haven't said a word," Mark mentions and looks at Jordan for signs of a joke. "How are you communicating with the Ventus?"

"Exitor composite huh?" Jordan turns and asks. "It hears my thoughts."

"No comment," Mark growls.

BUSINESS WOMAN

Shanghai, China

At the North China district office of EchoTech, a bored Emily Wu sits at the head of beautiful glossy oak conference table wishing to be with a certain someone. She taps the table with her fingers, poking her own reflection in the eye. The calculating Mrs. Wu doesn't mind wood, but actually prefers solid materials like marble and granite. Those materials make an object hard to modify. From a security point of view, it also makes it difficult to conceal things, but this is *her* table.

Fine wine is being passed around and the atmosphere seems jovial. Just when the deal seems to be closed, an overdressed man in a dark suit and dark aviator glasses pushes his wine glass away.

"French wine not to your liking?" Sierra asks, her slender figure rising up from a slouch. "You do know they don't even make it anymore. Sad really and very, very expensive."

The overdressed man, Mr. Chu of the Western Triad, then knocks over his glass to the gasps of all those in attendance.

Discouraged, Emily keeps smiling anyways as the rest of the table goes deadly quiet. She was hoping to avoid the dry cleaners this trip, but she never gets her wish.

"Don't try to pressure me little Mrs. Wu," Mr. Chu warns. "After all women are physically weak. You came here unescorted."

"You are so right, well played. I'm at disadvantage. So feel free to speak your mind, but remember you are still in my office, my house," Sierra states, slowly sipping her wine. "Our corporate alley, Han Medical, has agreed to pay you a handsome fee for safe passage through your territory of Zhejiang Provence."

Several armed men barge into the meeting room. They focus their guns all the seated individuals. Some begin to whimper and cry, but Emily still looks unconcerned.

"EchoTech brokered this deal, not us. We want Han Medical to use our local trucking businesses," Mr. Chu demands. "Otherwise, tell Mr. Wu to screw himself."

"This is not a sign of respect," cracking her knuckles under the table, Sierra sighs loudly. "I will have to talk to security about this."

"I own your security people," Mr. Chu states. "Mrs. Wu this may be your house, but this is my territory."

"No changes to the contract," Emily says sternly, looking increasingly mad. "Your trucking companies can't deliver a carton of milk and your prices are comical. EchoTech requires Han Medical to remain profitable. That's our only interest here, profit. We either can share the wealth the way it has been decided or..."

"We all know," Mr. Chu interrupts, now standing, "that you have no love of the triads, especially us of the Western Triad. Remember, you are in Shanghai now, not Hong Kong. This is our place and your tower of glass is ours to violate."

"I admit I have no love of your trade in human flesh. Mr. Wu does not share my dislike, but he is not here," Sierra's hands slowly move up to the edge of the table. An opening under her right hand slowly pops open. "As a woman, I do take offense."

"Women are things to be sold and bought," Mr. Chu snickers. "Especially the ones that think they are better than men." He looks up at his thugs. "Take her out of here. I want to deal with Han Medial alone." His fat middle finger wags at the business people seated around the table. "And if they won't deal..." With a cackle, he then runs a finger across his throat.

"We won't be cut out," Sierra states sternly.

"You seem to desire a harsh end," Mr. Chu replies calmly, standing up. "If you don't shut up, a thousand men will molest you. Then, I'll send Mr. Wu ten whores to replace you."

Sierra warns, "I don't appreciate empty threats."

"Take this cunt from my sight!" Mr. Chu insultingly orders, especially considering there are other women at the table. "Unless you plan to lick me, you have no more use here."

"EchoTech has substantial ties with the Hebei Triad," Sierra states as the thugs begin to close around her. "Their trucks run on time and I would have no issue handing them your territory." Her muscles begin to tighten up. She has already decided whom to kill first and how. "This is your call."

"You don't scare me demon queen. You're just a skinny little trophy for a great man," Mr. Chu says, trying to control his laughter.

His men join in the joke and are distracted. He sits back down and that is his final mistake.

"I am no one's trophy," Sierra growls and pulls her sword out from its hiding place inside the desk. She is superhuman fast, so fast her movement is a blur. Before the thugs can even react, she jumps on the table, swivels on her knees, and cuts the jugular out of one thug with a flick of her sword.

A gun is pulled, but she is on to it. Her sword flies across the table, skewering the man to a wall. Before his dying body releases the gun, Sierra is already holding it to Mr. Chu's head. The other thugs back away. Sierra has drop lets of blood running down her face as her bodyguards storm the room.

"I...I...agree to the terms," Mr. Chu says.

An emotionless Sierra sneers, "Contract terminated." She fires and Mr. Chu's head explodes into a thousand juicy pieces. Sierra hardly blinks.

***

Hong Kong, China

Her own personal desk is made of pure granite, pure perfectly dark solid granite. A sword sits motionless on this desk, black as ink, almost lost amongst so much darkness. One drip of blood glides effortlessly across the blade, just as buckets of it did the night before.

Sierra rubs the paper cut with her thumb. It is nothing. She can make herself feel little pain when necessary. With her manicured fingernail, she rubs the wound again, somewhat liking the ting of it. Her deep green eyes follow closely as another drop rolls across the blade. There is the slight noise of air moving, her eyes dart over to the double glass doors that guard her immense office.

Juno, Sierra's assistant, enters and presses a button next to the door. The shades keeping the room nearly in complete darkness roll back. A smog-filtered amount of orange sun breaks in, illuminating Juno's short blonde cropped hair. The indistinct Scandinavian beauty gathers up some of Sierra's papers scattered across a meeting table. Suddenly aware of a presence in the room, Juno jumps startled.

"I'm sorry Mrs. Wu, I didn't know you are in today," Juno says and then stops, her eyes becoming transfixed on Sierra's assassin's sword. "What a thing of beauty. Powerful, even still like that."

Sulking, Sierra says nothing, simply rubbing the blood off with her fingers. Her lips barely move as she speaks up, "Swords have a profound history. They are often symbols for nations…for women…and men. Profound thing a dark sword, stained by the blood of many lives."

Not listening and still transfixed on the black sword as if a jewel, Juno asks, "So Emily, did you have a nice trip to San Francisco?"

"Yes, actually, met a man with a silver sword," she says and remembers her night on the mountain. A small smile cracks across her face, but it soon vanishes.

"Did he meet an interesting end like Mr. Chu?" Juno asks, smirking.

Choosing to ignore Juno's heartless question, Sierra looks at herself in a mirror. A woman of unbelievable beauty looks back. She is tall for a Chinese woman, her features strong. She has the typical almond shape to her eyes, but her nose is long and straight. With a face far from flat or round, but pointed and sharp, exotic is too soft a word for her looks. This blended appearance is heightened by her unusual eye color. When she was younger, she would even wear contacts to hide the green shade.

But in time, these looks made her a prize. Fortunately, her father kept her focused, introducing her to the way of the sword and the discipline it demands. She took to the martial arts with extreme dedication and soon became proficient and perfect. Her father was proud of her back then, as Sierra had promise to be more than just a flower. His hopes were soon soured.

With a slap, Sierra puts the mirror down. "I wish I had seen it. A silver sword is rare, almost unheard of," she says, not mentioning her own ruined blade.

"I prefer the black ones myself. Symbols of a rich life," Juno replies, studiously organizing papers.

"I am not surprised," Sierra says with a frown. "Juno all you love is money."

"There is no shame in that," Juno replies a little affronted. "For those of us not lucky enough to win the genetic lottery, we must do with what we have. After all, I don't have the benefit of your remarkable beauty, not many do."

Frowning, Sierra looks at Juno with displeasure. The skinny assistant takes a step back, a feeling of dread building in her, knowing she has said too much.

"I'm sorry Mrs. Wu. I spoke out of line," Juno says with a shiver. Sierra is a dangerous person to anger. "Your husband sent over a classified file for you to examine. It's a hard copy file from the NAU. Should I go get it?"

"Go," Sierra answers with no interest.

"Yes Madame," Juno barely manages to whisper and whisks herself away. She soon returns with a metal encased file and hands it to Sierra. Sierra wipes a finger across a plastic security strip and the file opens. Juno carefully spreads out the contents for her boss. This mostly consists of several prints of battleship schematics.

"Did Mr. Wu tell you what he wants me to look at?" Sierra asks perturbed. "I've seen these before. This is the wiring diagram for the third gen navi-system going into the Shiloh and others."

"There's been a change," Juno states. "He didn't elaborate. Should I conference him in? He only said he wants you to re-approve these designs. Apparently, the NAU wants to install our new software in all their capitol ships. I think that's amazing. What a windfall!"

"I know…but things are not always as they seem. We are very good at secrets here and sometimes that overrides good sense," Sierra comments as she sees a very odd change to the design. The system's wiring has been relocated to run along the HVAC lines…no big deal, but why? She shoves the papers aside to be dealt with later.

"Mr. Wu also asked if you by chance copied the contents of the drive you obtained from Professor Whatley. Apparently, there is some outside interest in the research," Juno says.

"The contents were encrypted and unreadable," Sierra lies having broken Whatley's code. "The client accepted the data as-is, but it was useless."

The technology she saw on the drive troubled her. It was radical. Last thing she wants is another Orissa on her burdened conscious.

However, her and her client, Martin Malone discussed the implications and agreed to limit the use. She provided him enough data to build his new drone. Drones don't require pilots so she figures that is one less person having to face death.

A file is poking from underneath the pile of paper. Sierra pulls it out. It is an adoption form for a girl in France.

"Juno, what's this?" she asks.

"Nothing important," Juno says taking it from Sierra's hands. "The publicity department thought it would make you and Mr. Wu look more socially responsible as many of these kids are being radicalized by the Cotillard movement. A great many wealthy families are adopting French children on a whim, anything to keep them from that awful faith."

"Adopting a child for fun?" Sierra sighs loudly. "I don't have time to properly raise a child. Take it away."

"French authorities don't allow the children to leave the country. It's just an adoption in name only, simply a funding method," Juno says and heads for the shredder. "Mr. Wu already declined the request. However, the publicity director wanted you to have a look too."

Her interest rekindled Sierra smiles devilishly. She likes the idea of side stepping Thomas. Taking the papers, she signs them. "It'll be good for EchoTech."

"Yes, ma'am."

Satisfied in her act of rebellion, Sierra then picks up her sword and is about to put it away when...

"I've heard," Juno says, "that a black sword is a sign of power. Also, I've heard that a sliver sword merely means that you are pure of heart...silly thing." Juno scoffs.

"Silver means you have purity of spirit, clarity of purpose. Black means a loss of purpose, failure of the spirit," Sierra explains and swallows hard.

Juno retorts, "Only weak people would say that."

"My father was...is not a weak man," Sierra says with restraint. "Thank you Juno. I don't need you right now." Normally, Juno and she would have a good laugh gossiping about Hong Kong high society, but today Juno is far from amusing.

"Yes Madame," Juno says and turns quickly, leaving like a blur.

With sword in hand, the great assassin walks to the window. She allows the sword to hang loosely beside her. Sierra's mind is racing at the speed of light. Her thoughts cannot be focused and she sighs frustrated. Reaching up, Sierra clicks the face of a panel.

"Yes Emily," Juno answers.

"Juno have my driver bring a car."

"Immediately Mrs. Wu," Juno's voices rings out in a ghostly manner from the wall nearest to Sierra.

***

Immensely over built, Hong Kong is city of forests, forests of high rise buildings. Hong Kong easily dwarfs any NAU city in its audacious constructions and garish opulence. Money flows through the streets to anyone with technology for sale. It is a city built on the trade of secrets.

From her floating limo, Sierra stares numbly out the window as bronze-gilded buildings glide by. The world outside is rush of glittering, hazy images and the same could be said of her thoughts. Dropping rapidly, the limo switches to "land mode" and skims above the street. Bridges and walkways are strung from building to building in this neighborhood, making flying a treacherous endeavor.

Her limo soon pulls up to a run down, but safe looking apartment building on Lai Chi Kok Road. This is definitely a working class part of town as her ride draws many stares. Her bodyguard and driver, a heavily built Australian, quickly opens the door and follows her out.

"I'm fine Carson, wait here," Sierra orders and walks in. Carson stands by the limo, his heavy handgun barely hidden inside his coat.

Walking up a flight of stairs, Sierra bursts into a small apartment. Her fat, lazy brother, a small time public servant, snores loudly as he comfortably sleeps on a couch. Her mom is cooking in the kitchen and ignores the rude entrance of Sierra.

"Where's Dad?" the dishonored daughter asks.

"Why do you need him?" her Mom demands, refusing to look away from the stovetop.

"He cashes the checks easily enough," Sierra says angrily, "that should buy at least a few moments with him."

"Upstairs, working on the public garden," her Mom states and walks away. Sierra stares at the freshly cooked food in the kitchen. She misses her Mom's cooking.

After climbing a stairway narrow enough for a submarine, she emerges on the roof. A small garden has been started here in a variety of wood boxes. Only a sliver of sunlight hits the roof as the apartment building is surrounded by even taller edifices.

The once again overdressed Sierra finds her Dad working diligently in a planter box full of vegetables. He is a frail looking older man with a cane resting by his side, yet there is still something distinguished about him. She knows he has heard her coming up. Little escapes her father's attention.

"First you leave the house I bought you. Now, you're out here growing food," she says shaking her head. "What are you doing with my money? Giving it away?"

"Exactly, this city has many poor that go ignored," her Dad says proudly. "I feed them."

"Ha," Sierra laughs, "I'm the one feeding them."

"Your brother owns this wreck of a building and at least his money has no connection to Thomas Wu," he says, turning to face her with a broad smile, "I prefer it better this way. I got tired of Thomas asking me for unsavory favors."

"I can't believe the government treats you like this," Sierra says and kneels next to him, angrily digging at the dirt. "They should at least pretend in public to respect you."

"My usefulness is over to them," he says with no regret. "I was a servant of the people and I still am…in a way."

"Drop the honorable solider act Dad, I can't stand it." She holds a plant as he covers its roots. "They still blame you for failing. That will never change."

"One day your bribes to the security council will not be enough," he admits. "They will take revenge for my supposed failure. I know what you think. You think that your sacrifice will spare me. They will use you just the same as Thomas uses you."

She doesn't answer.

"What is bothering you?" her dad asks. "Must be something pressing for you to come here, Emily Wu."

"Don't call me that," Sierra barks out and then lets out a deep sigh, "You taught me the art of the sword, the way of the honorable warrior. How to be true and virtuous. I thought it was all nonsense...no one could be that way...not even you." She looks at her dirt-covered hands. "What is the real meaning of a silver sword? Is there any truth to those tales you told me? What could it mean for a man with a silver sword to like...like me?"

"Those were just silly childhood stories," her dad responds and keeps working. "Go back to your Thomas and your chosen fate."

"That's what I thought," Sierra says and gets up to leave.

Her Dad notices the missing wedding ring. "Yingtai," he says quickly and grabs her hand. "Where's your wedding ring?"

"I threw it off a building," Sierra says. "That's when I met him. The man with the silver sword."

"Was he attracted to your beauty or to something you were about to do?" he asks forcefully. "People with silver swords care not for beauty. You must have been in trouble."

"What does it matter what I was doing?" she says and pulls her hand away.

"A sword only reflects and does not define. The man you meet is a man of virtue," her father says and smiles. "This man with the sword. He likes you? Despite your history?"

"Yes."

"He sees something in you," her father says with a deep, low sigh. "Leave Thomas and follow your heart. Life is calling you back. Answer it."

Sierra looks to the busy sky above. It is full of small, single seat flying craft buzzing around. "You know I can't."

"Damn the consequences" the great General Sheng Zhu says, standing up tall and proud. "Daughter ask yourself...am I who I want to be?" her Dad finishes his statement and returns quietly to his work. "Don't use fate as an excuse for not being able to make a difficult decision. As you know now, happiness is not about wealth. Happiness is internal. Do you have that?" he asks, looking up at her one last time. "Let me die happy, Yingtai. Let me die knowing you are free from evil."

SPIRIT OF THE BLADE

Coughing hard, Master Kenji lingers by a tall redwood tree, haunted by an old nemesis—cancer. There is a pleasant breeze tonight slowly passing across the forest behind his house and that helps calm him. He has never known surrender and pulls himself up tall, fighting the pain. Recovering, Kenji moves with a quick step toward a small temple, hoping his guests did not witness his struggle.

Fortunately, the temple sits unattended and silent.

Rolling out a straw mat, the old master sits and meditates in the darkness of the evergreen forest. His sword, placed before him, begins to slowly glow. An ethereal blue light imbues the area, flickering every now and then, foreshadowing the fading of his own life. The sounds of nature soon seem to seep away except for the rolling trickle of a small stream near-by.

Kneeling next to him, a woman in brilliant flowing white robes appears. Her face is covered by an emotionless sliver mask. It only has two slots from which two impossibly topaz colored eyes peer out.

"I fear that bringing Jordan here was not in his best interest," Kenji sighs, his body otherwise motionless. "There is a sinister element at work here."

"I have noticed," the Silver Mask says, herself the image of stillness. Her hair flutters ever so slightly providing proof that she is real and not imaginary. "Magen was one of the original deviations. His ability to be ruthless in the pursuit of Quintero's goals is infinite. Jennifer Grant is being converted, but to what end?"

"I should have killed him when I had the chance," Kenji recalls, looking up at the Silver Mask for the first time. "At the time, I choose to work for him. Now, I am too old to right the sins of my past." His sword dims. "Can anything be done to help the sister? Admiral Grant has already sacrificed much."

"Your concern is misplaced," she reminds him, her mirror mask reflecting Kenji's gaze back at him. "It is his son who many fear."

Unconvinced, Kenji smiles and then laughs, "Good, he will show them all how stupid they are." He touches his silver blade gently and it sparkles. "I do not believe in the prophecy. I believe in actions."

"The sister will become a prisoner of her own body," the Silver Mask says with a grim truth. She looks down at her hands as if they were covered in blood. "I have no cure for her. Nuhu are meant to be disposable."

"I remember her as a little girl, struggling to keep up with Jordan. Always trying to best him, sometimes succeeding. She will fight her way back," Kenji states with the faith of a long time teacher. "I cannot see the Nuhu as just empty vessels. They are people."

"Perhaps but what can we expect from a creature with two souls in one body."

"Only one soul. The Other is not real," an unearthly voice sounds out across the forest. With a rush of wind, every tree becomes still. Leaves begin to float up, defying gravity. The blue hue becomes overwhelming, lighting up everything in an electric shower of sparks. A woman of impossible thinness floats across the spaces between the woods. She is translucent, angel-like, and beautiful in a way that no human could be.

"Spirit of the blade?" Kenji says shocked. He has never seen a blade spirit in a physical form. He looks over at the equally stunned Silver Mask. They both quickly bow.

"Even artificial being are made from that of the Earth," the delicate-looking creature says. "The Nuhu must be saved or our world will not survive. The deviants have created a wave of darkness that will crash upon all of us." She looks over at the Silver Mask. "You. Deviant. You alone amongst your kind has survived. Repair what you have done while you still can. Help the Nuhu."

Just as the spectral vision had started, it ends in the blink of an eye. Kenji simply looks back at the ground, saying nothing.

"How does one person face a monstrous wave and not be consumed by it?" the Silver Mask says with little emotion. "They are many and I am just one."

"Who am I to guess the will of the spirits?" Kenji speaks quietly. "You are the one who has lived many of my lifetimes."

"And I have made the mistakes of the multiples of your lifetime."

"There is an answer," he says and begins to stand up. The pain is coming back and he holds his side as if struck by a blade. Turning away, Kenji hides his pain from the Silver Mask. His sword shimmers as if sharing in his agony.

"Tell me then. What do you know?" the Silver Mask sighs, showing a glimpse of sadness at her assigned task. She stands with little effort as if blown up by a breeze. With a ghostly movement, she comes over to Kenji.

"You must become an unmovable object, a force of nature itself. You must become the shore upon which the waves break."

"I am many things, but a force of nature…no," she states and lowers her head. She begins to walk away from Kenji.

"If you cannot, prepare the one who can," he says to her back. "Jordan is ready."

She stop and seems to dim in the low light. Looking back at Kenji, she removes her mask, safe that only he can see. Fear is all over her face. "I will not sacrifice him," she whispers.

***

For the last couple of years, Jen has been incapable of sleeping well. She takes a couple of pills from a container, stuff her mom takes to sleep. They don't seem to help much as the dreams have become more and more disturbing.

As she drifts away, her subconscious becomes alive, slowly moving into reality. A dark shadow moves within her very own mind, breaking through barriers that nature never intended to broken.

Jen wakes up, cold and alone. Her clothes are tattered and wet. She is surrounded by metal bars. No matter how hard she tries, no matter how many times she escapes, she always ends up back in the cell. Each time more frail and weak.

An image of herself can be seen in a mirror across the room. This image is not of her current state. In the mirror, she looks utterly perfect, Nuhu perfect. This other woman begins to move and approaches. It is no reflection, at least, not anymore.

"You are a fighter," the Other says. "Though I have tolerated it, you have become too much of a distraction from my orders."

A distraught Jen cries out, "Don't take my life from me. Please, I'm in love. If you do this to me, I'll never have a family. We'll never have a family. Don't."

"You let me out with every pill you took. You can't trust anyone, can you? Not even our own mother," the Other states and looks at her with sadness. "Sometimes, I wish you did have the resolve to stop. I don't like the things I'm asked to do."

"Don't make it sound so one sided, you were always there pushing me on," Jen fights back and then snarls. "I know you feel for him too. No matter what, you are still a part of me and I know you love him."

The Other turns away and hides her face. She is deathly silent for a while before answering, "He refuses to comply with Nuhu law. I must adhere to my duty no matter what I feel for him."

"Why?" Jen pleads, rattling the bars on her cell. Her hands rubbing bare against the corroded metal. "Why must we be so loyal? You will destroy everything that is good in our life."

"I don't have the ability to choose. I only have the ability to follow," the Other says with a bit of sadness. She turns to look at Jen. "I must destroy you. It doesn't make sense to me to do these things, but I must."

"My friends will save me," Jen says resolutely. "Jordan will never abandon me."

"We'll be dead soon enough and so will he," the Other sighs. "My instructions are clear and the events are already set in motion. Long live the NAU and the Nuhu race. I will see to it that it will be a reign of a thousand years even if we are not part of it."

"I will never let you harm him," Jen says with a fierce convection. Suddenly, the Other falls to her knees and flies up against the cage wall as if by a magic lasso. Choking her Other self, the true Jen growls, "Never." But before she can destroy the Other, she wakes up and begins to cry uncontrollably. The fit of crying goes on and on. Jen doesn't understand why she is so sad, so mad. There is no memory of her dream, only disconnected feelings and a sense of betrayal.

***

A shivering Gabrielle walks through the hallways of the Koborn estate. Her Grandfather likes to collect old weapons and there are various swords of different ages and different states of decay all around the mansion. This gives the house a somewhat medieval feel and it always gives her the shivers.

Entering her Grandfather's office, she is meet with the warmth of the colorful tapestries and flags of her country, England. She immediately feels better and walks over to him.

He is starring out across a vast forest. This is easy since an entire wall is made of glass panels. Though he hears her come in, Koborn is unusually subdued and stirs a cup of tea endlessly.

"Dupont is here for the results," she says, now also starring out into the grayness of the morning.

"Difficult decision whether or not tell your friends the truth," he says and puts down his now cold tea. He spins his wheel chair to face Gabrielle. "Jennifer Grant has tested positive."

"Can she be healed?"

"Even if we could, should we?" Koborn says knowing he is about to throw Admiral Grant's daughter under the bus. The Admiral has been a longtime friend. "When you cannot save everyone, you must save who you can. Jordan and Mark must be spared this news."

A calculating Gabrielle then says with little remorse, "Once they are converted, we should not consider them alive anymore." She waits a bit and follows with the even more callous statement, "In fact, can we really trust any Nuhu?"

"I wish to hope," Koborn says with reluctance. "I need to ask you to lie for me. Can you do that?"

"I would prefer not to, but I will do what I must."

He turns away from her, "Tell Dupont...tell her that the test is negative."

RINA'S FALL

Colorless and barren like the face of a sunbaked skull, the OverForce's offices on campus are not at all welcoming. A sizable crowd of students are seated in the reception area waiting to be interrogated for one offense or another. A nervous Jen is escorted through the building by the burly, but somehow still female, receptionist. She is taken to an office and ordered to wait. A loud, solid thud rings as a heavy bolt locks behind her.

Looking around this staid space, Jen finds little to see and an even less to prove an actual living person works here. There are a few merit awards and some ominous looking certificates hanging on the walls. They all share the same black frame making them indistinguishable from each other. Interestingly, no cameras. Obviously they don't want to record what happens in these offices. Her eyes fall upon a picture of Mark, placed under a plastic desk protector. That's all that identifies this room as Rina Dupont's office.

A voice sounds from behind Jen and she jumps, startled.

"Jennifer Grant, what can I do for you? We're very busy today with all your damn protestor friends," Rina asks impatiently as she darts into the room having just returned from the Koborn estate. She takes a seat behind the desk and stares narrow-eyed at the blonde witch. "People assume you're in trouble if you come here. Are you?"

With her feathers a bit ruffled, Jen notices that Rina is dressed in her full O.F. regalia. Her posture is perfect and her manner direct. This is not the casual Rina that hangs out with Mark. Uneasy, Jen second guesses her motives, but the uncontrollable drive that has possessed her of late won't stop pushing her on. Jen then mentions with rehearsed precision, "My friend, Adrian, has disappeared. Do you…"

Instantly on guard, Rina cuts in, "Is this really the conversation you want to have? If so, the police office is down by the stadium. They handle missing people." Rina's tone has a touch of warning laced in it. "You shouldn't be here."

"I used my friend's fake ID." Fearful, Jen gets nervous and begins to tap her hand against her chair's metal arm. She notices this and stops.

"What kind of friends do you have that can get you a fake ID that passes an O.F. scan?" Rina points out.

"Police don't make people go missing," Jen fires out hoping to get off the topic of fake ID's.

"This is a game you should not be playing. As far as I know, Adrian Simmons was relocated to a security camp for his own protection. Satisfied?"

Jen nods, "Can you review his file?"

"Let it go," Rina warns and leans forward.

"I just want to make sure he is OK," Jen lies.

Annoyed, Rina logs onto her system with a sigh. Within a second, Rina's face goes rigid and her eyes slightly wince. Whatever she is looking at is horrible. "Like I said, relocated."

Jen flares up, "Where? To France? When is he coming back?"

Sounding agitated, Rina replies, "He will not be coming back." She hunches down on her chair. Her face is beginning to show the strain of a job she never cared to have.

Overreacting a bit, Jen demands in a high shrill voice, "I want to file a formal request for a disclosure of Adrian's location."

Shaking her head, Rina laughs in disbelief.

"He was young. He made a mistake. That's not reason enough to send him to France."

A worried Rina then politely suggests. "Any inquiries are required to be investigated. They don't care if you ask a question, but they do care why."

"Process the request," Jen counters, unable to change her mind.

"I am required to warn you that a request for a formal investigation will be noted to your permanent security file. This is not a good thing."

Jen laughs nervously, "I am well within my rights as Nuhu citizen. My brother, like his father before him, is an Officer of the State."

"Now he's your brother. For a while, I thought there was a reason for your behavior, but I was wrong," Rina growls while gnashing her teeth together. "If you do this, I'll have to investigate your relationship to Adrian."

"Then arrest me," Jen insists. "See how much Jordan will like you after that."

Ignoring her, Rina continues, "It'll only take one person to point the finger at you to give the O.F. the authority to detain you for questioning. If you refuse to answer or your answers are suspect, you will be put on permanent observation. Worse, if they find that you are actively conspiring against the government, you will be considered a dissident, a race traitor with links to the human equality movement."

"Protests are not against the law."

"The OverForce enforces the unwritten laws," Rina states coldly. "We have authority over racial matters. Period."

Unresponsive, Jen does not answer. She can't.

"Jen, Jen, Jen. I'll have to swipe your I.D. card to begin the query. Your *real* identity card," Rina huffs, somewhat bewildered. "This will guarantee an end to your days as a rebel. Do you really want to add another failure to your resume?"

"I can always fuck my way back on top," Jen laughs hauntingly. Cautiously, she reaches in her purse and pulls out her I.D., handing the card to Rina. A reluctant Rina moves to swipe it across her monitor's built-in scanner. "Officer Dupont," Jen interrupts and then loudly commands, "I want the request certified. I just don't trust you."

"So that's the way it's going to be. Isn't it?" Rina says disheartened. She's been more than open with Jen.

"I know that you would try to protect Mark and Jordan at any cost. They'll just have to deal with the consequences of my latest crusade," Jen states. "We're going to pressure the government until they tell us what happened."

Annoyed, Rina walks around her desk and sits on the lip. She stares down the haughty Jen before saying in a near growl, "I'll have to get the receptionist up front to certify your request. You've just made your life a living nightmare."

"Take your time, Officer Dupont," Jen says casually as Rina steps away.

As soon as the redhead is out of sight, Jen immediately races to the other side of desk. The terminal is locked, but Jen has the answer. She snaps a thumb drive into an open data port. Programmed to steal, the little data leech immediately attempts to break the password. It fails. The encryption is too strong. The computer then flashes a warning…password nullified.

"Shit!" Jen howls in frustration.

She then finally notices that on the monitor are thumbnails of Adrian's execution. Jen is stunned by the sheer brutality of the images and the O.F.'s clinical coverage of the event. After a second, the screen goes dark. Distracted, Jen doesn't notice the gun coming to rest on her temple.

"I am within my rights to terminate you," Rina informs her with little keeping her anger in check.

Trembling wildly, Jen notices that the gun tip is warm. It has been charged and is ready to be fired. Jen is aware that Rina is not kidding around.

"Go on," Jen challenges, though she is terrified, leaning into the gun. "You're good Dupont. I never even heard you come back in."

"If I didn't mean to spare you, you'd already be dead," Rina states never flinching. Her finger locked against the trigger. "Mark told me you were out to steal my password." Rina pulls the memory stick out from the computer. "I was waiting."

"You don't have the courage to kill someone of my status," Jen says ready to pee her pants as Dupont presses the gun harder against her skull.

In disbelief of Jen's arrogance, Rina then laughs cynically, "You wouldn't be the first princess I've killed."

"So the murder of students is OK with you?" Jen argues back unsteadily. Rina still has not lowered the gun. "Adrian was a simple, harmless dreamer. I gave him a gun once and he had someone throw it away. Can you put that down now?" Jen pleads, starting to shake violently, nearly ready to beg.

Unflinching, Rina's face takes on a sickened look as her phone rings. She answers it, "Yes. I'm aware of the breach. No, I wasn't in my office. Yes, whoever it was is gone." She hangs up and exports the pictures to the memory stick. "Get out of here, Miss Grant," she orders, lowering her gun finally. Rina takes the memory stick and throws it at her. "Let the people see what really goes on."

A nervous Jen stands up slowly and heads for the locked door, never taking her eyes off the armed officer.

"Hope you can really do some good with those images," Rina states, taking her seat calmly.

"What's all this going to cost me?" Jen asks holding the door handle tightly. It doesn't budge.

Shaking her head in disbelief, Rina says, "It's gonna cost me." Rina looks down at the picture of Mark. She strokes her fingers across his face.

Conflicted, Jen says nothing, feeling a bit ashamed, but not regretful. "You never processed my request. Did you?" Jen insinuates.

"I was going to protect you against yourself," Rina says with her distaste for Jen clearly showing. "After they pick me up for my re-education, I won't be able to mitigate the consequences. Be prepared. People are going to be hurt if you handle this the wrong way. Let the pictures speak for themselves."

"They will," Jen says.

"Now you know we're not all bad."

"You want to fit in, but you never will; you're a wolf in a herd of sheep. One day the shepherd will shot you," Jen says as the door opens.

"You're not the shepherd, Jen," Rina warns. "You're just one of the sheep."

THE SHEPHERD

In the late afternoon, a text message on his phone makes Jordan break into a cold sweat. Jennifer's message simply says, "Trouble. Need you." He slides the credit card sized phone back into the outside pocket of his shabby wallet. For a few minutes, Jordan considers whether to bring his sword or not. Best to be an Officer of the State today, he figures.

***

Angrily worded placards and banners litter the Pac-Tech campus. There are rowdy bands of people running around making a raucous noise. Countering them, a large group of NAU officer trainees and crested students, swords and all, are chanting the national anthem by the library. It is a madhouse.

Down by the Quad, several hundred protestors are centered about a half-circle shaped concrete monument with the NAU's black and red flag at its center. This concrete moon, moss covered and old, is the focus of the lawn. Above it, the two twenty foot iron statues of "model students" stare down. They are robed and appear stern and obedient, perfect examples of future NAU citizens, unlike the surly bunch below them currently.

Here of all places, the protestors have setup their makeshift stage. A burning man of paper is hanging from a pole, obviously meant to be President Eaves. A student throws an NAU flag up onto the fire causing howls from the crested students. There are people here has not seen at the before, some much older people then should be a student rally. What's worse…the size of the crowd seems to be doubling every minute.

On the ground next to him, Jordan finds one of the placards. There is a picture of a mutilated body displayed prominently on the sign with the words, "OverForce Justice?" Jordan recognizes the dead man as Adrian Simmons and must control himself from retching. It's a stunningly vile image. Mark's words echo in his head. He said the NAU government would not tolerate change. He appears to be right.

236

Up on the roofs of the university buildings, police snipers are taking posts. They are electrically camouflaged, but their suits do not work well in direct sunlight. Jordan can pick them out having used this kind of camouflage himself. He knows to look for an obvious shimmer caused by the suit's optical-reflective skin trying to project its surroundings. And when those surroundings include bright sun, previously dark roofs have an unnatural glow. They are better in the dark, but so is a garbage bag.

Only the police still used these awful "fake skins." They are prone to electrocute the wearer if hit by any kind of Electromagnetic Pulse Weapon (EMP). The military banned the damn things after a few too many soldiers became burnt marshmallows.

As Jordan makes his way through the busy university, people keep their distance from him. They all think he's a government supporter. After all, he is lugging around a sword. He frowns at this idea and makes his way toward the Student Union.

He is stopped by police, but soon let go after identifying himself as an Officer of the State. They tell him that he is expected to provide back up if things get ugly. Jordan shrugs. No wonder they aren't confiscating swords.

The Student Union is a bustle of activity. Several security guards are trying to pull down a large banner printed with the letters, "FU NAU." Jordan can't help but chuckle. Pushing his way through this chaotic environment, he looks for his wayward sibling. He spots her near the Union offices.

"What do you want here? Government prick!" a short, scared but determined woman howls at him, getting in his way.

"Jennifer called me," Jordan says and tries to side step around the woman. A disappearing Jennifer walks into a glass walled area. She is the focus of some attention and is soon swallowed up by a group of people.

"Back off or I'll bite your face off!" the woman growls and smacks Jordan on the chest.

"Who are you anyways?" Jordan asks frustrated, not used to being treated like a child anymore.

"Why? You gonna report me!" She yells right into his face. "I'm a human and I'm proud of it you fascist!"

237

"I'm no fascist…listen."

"Only the Officers of the State carry swords and they all suck dicks!" she screams at full volume and kicks him in the chins. "Bunch of assholes!"

"Aye!" Jordan yelps. Trying to move again, he finds the short, stocky woman always in front of him again. This time she jumps up on his neck and hangs off his back.

"No one sees Jennifer Grant. No one. Especially not you creep!" she roars into his ear.

Pushing her off as gently as he can, a beaten Jordan looks down at this 5-foot 1 inch woman. He could chop her head off and be done with it, but that might attract too much attention. In lieu of flying body parts, Jordan starts waving his arms madly trying to get Jennifer's attention. He yells, "Jen! A little help!"

She sees him finally and laughs, coming out to where they are. The little woman now has Jordan pinned up against a wall, her head thrust into his gut.

An amused Jen orders her to cease and desist, "Annie. He's fine. That's my Dad's pet."

"Oh?" Annie says quizzically. "Are you a full service pet?"

"No," Jordan growls and pushes Annie aside, causing a loud crash. "Thanks Jen," Jordan groans.

"Come on," Jen says hushed. "Things are edgy around here. Why did you bring the sword? Don't you have a gun or something?"

"Gun?" Jordan repeats, looking a bit pale at the suggestion.

After rescuing him from Annie, Jennifer escorts Jordan into an empty, private office. Here on a table are the scattered, original prints of Adrian's murder. Jordan doesn't need to see these again and focuses on Jen. Her eyes are wild with excitement as if planning for a big party.

"Who's your pit bull Jen?" Jordan asks, steadying her shaking hands.

"Everyone is little scared," she explains, quickly pulling her hands away. "Annie is over protective of me. Her parents vanished one night three years ago. Made her a little paranoid."

"That would make anyone paranoid," Jordan says, moving his sword away as it pokes him on the side of the head.

Jen produces a picture of a group of corpses. "They killed Adrian and four others. The official story is that they are at a re-education camp. I've never seen this kind of treatment for vandalism. Sick…some of them were Nuhu."

Alarmed, Jordan picks up the pictures and notices a series of lines across the bottom. He recognizes the coding immediately. It is distinct.

"You shouldn't have these," Jordan observes. "Jen. These are OverForce."

"Yes. I know."

His breathing becomes tense. "Did you steal these from Rina? These are traceable."

"I think you got this all wrong," Jen replies back stunned. "They were given to me." She hesitates a second and then admits, "At least, Rina was good for something."

Scared, Jordan sighs, "What was she thinking?"

But Jen is not hearing him, she looks up and dreams, "Tonight this whole damn university will burn with a thousand storms of fire. And from this fire storm, a new power will be born."

With horrible sinking feeling, Jordan sees some students with knives and bats. "Burn the campus?" he asks with a shiver.

"I'm going out on that stage and we are going to demand justice in one unified voice. Then I'll set them loose. It'll be glorious."

"Do you even listen to yourself? This reaction is way out of line. Where did they take him down?" Jordan says, more worried by the second.

"Magen's house on vandalism raid."

"The old witch doctor? Are you kidding me? What did they see to be killed like this?"

"Listen to me, Magen's harmless. I know," Jen insists. "He's practically a grandfather to me."

"You hated Magen growing up. Jesus, Jen does your mom get your pills from Magen?"

"Why are worried about this now?" Jen angrily yells and throws an empty pill container at him. "My mom stopped giving me those weeks ago. Satisfied?"

"You stopped?"

"Are you going to go out there with me or not? Did you see the size of the crowd out there? I've mobilized thousands of students from hundreds of schools! This is my time," she says impatiently. She shakes his arm impatiently. "This princess needs her knight!"

A text from Mark appears on Jordan's phone. It reads, "Rina is in trouble. She is worried about students getting hurt." Jordan shows her the message.

Rolling her eyes, Jen simply turns away.

"I think you made your point. You've embarrassed the government. Send these people home," Jordan pleads. "You've got all kinds of radicals out there. Radicals the government might not want to let leave."

"Call it off?" Jen scoffs and then reassures him, "People are coming to our side. They are coming down here to rise up. This is the beginning of something great and you don't want to be a part of it?"

"That's naïve and stupid," Jordan says loudly. "You got the attention you wanted. Stop before you get attention you don't want."

But Jennifer Grant can't stop. She must stick to her pre-programmed plan.

"Good enough?" Jen shouts, her eyes wide with disbelief, filled with sudden anger. "Go console your precious Rina. But I'll remember this Jordan, you lied. I'll remember this as the day you weren't here for me." She is trembling with rage and spite, all directed at him.

Without warning, he grabs her by the waist and lifts her over his shoulder. Even with her kicking and screaming, he begins to take her out of the room to the shock of all around her. People rush to help, but Jordan is determined. He pushes people away as if they were mild irritants. "Everyone go home," he orders. But before he can get out of the student union, Jen bangs the back of his head with the handle of his sword. In pain, he drops her like a sack of potatoes.

"What do you think you're doing?" she demands as she struggles to stand.

"You're fucking sick," Jordan screams, blood trickling from the back of his head. "I don't know what they did to you, but I'm going to find out."

Without warning, she bashes him across the face with the wooden handle of a near-by protest sign. He tries to protect himself, but she is relentless until the stick finally breaks. "I hate you," she says and runs off.

All the people around the area begin to laugh at him.

Stunned and near tears, Jordan shakes his head and storms away, his face bloodied and his resolve broken.

***

Empty and desolate, the area around Mark's lab is quietly unnerving. The hallways are eerily devoid of students and the low sun is casting deep shadows throughout the building. At the lab, Jordan reaches for the door, but it's locked. He knocks on the door, but there is no answer, only silence greets him.

"It's me, Jordan," he says, wiping away the blood away from his face.

There is a hiss as the electronic lock releases and lets Jordan in. Inside this dark space, only illuminated by a single lamp, he finds Mark sitting at his desk, head down in his hands. A squinting Jordan can barely see Rina leaning up against a wall. She looks over at him. Her face is stained from tears and immediately moves to embrace Jordan.

"What happened to you?" she asks.

"Nothing," a sympathetic Jordan answers and hugs her back. "It's anarchy out there. You need to go break it up."

"It's already beyond my control," Rina replies. "The O.F. already know the pictures came from me."

"How could you trust Jennifer?" Mark growls, staring down at her like some ominous priest. "Look at what she is doing out there?"

"The blood tests were negative," Rina cries back. "I thought it would make a difference this time."

"Stupid woman," Mark howls. "Always trying to make up for the past."

Jordan snaps back at him, "Hey let's keep our cool here. What blood tests?"

"I had Jen's blood tested," Mark snarls, baring his fists at invisible opponent. "I thought…"

"So you were wrong about her?" Jordan points out, feeling that he was lead on. If Jen's decisions have been her own, he has been nursing a false hope. "I believed you. I just tried to kidnap her because I thought she was sick. What a jerk I am."

"Nobody really knows what to believe," Rina sighs, tossing her hands in the air in mock surrender. "It just means Jen wasn't affected."

"Listen to you two talk, how pathetic," Mark roars. "Jen betrayed us as people…and worse as friends. Let her die."

Tired of Mark's attitude, Jordan focuses on Rina. "A lot of influential people send their kids to Pac-Tech because it is a safe. Why would the university regents allow students to be murdered?"

"We didn't," Rina explains, her mind erratic. But in a moment of clarity, she realizes, "But Adrian wasn't killed on school grounds. Secret police, secret orders. It must have been another team…a security detail."

"No one is going to blame Magen for any of this!" Mark states with building rage, his face rigid. "Just those kids out there and my stupid OverForce girlfriend!"

"You're right Mark…like always," Rina concurs. "Don't worry, I like being whipped and raped. That was my childhood."

"No fucking way," Mark says alarmed and stumbles over a desk. "That's not going to happen. We run."

A disheartened Rina sits down in a chair. "I'm staying," she says quietly, but defiantly. Distressed, Mark then looks back at Rina with an expression as if somebody has just died, but she is not deterred and states stoically, "Maybe they didn't turn Jen, but they have turned others. I know it. I made a promise to myself that no other child would have to live my life."

"How long before the other regents come for you?" Jordan asks, watching the door for any movement.

"Anytime now." Rina holds herself upright. "No OverForce officer has ever been found guilty of betrayal. They just get retrained." She pretends to laugh. "God I fucked up."

"God damn this country," Mark yells. Getting up, he tosses his G850 model at a wall, smashing it. The wheels bounce off in all different directions. "You know what this about! It's about us. They're trying to flush out the rebellion and that selfish piece of shit Jen is helping them. I should have seen. I should have seen long ago."

Both Jordan and Rina look down at the ground. They know he is right.

Mark rants on, "Trust me, part of me wanted that result to positive. That girl, I treated her like a sister," Mark bangs on his desk. "Peaceful change. Total crap."

Jordan speaks up, "I don't think you're right about that."

"Adrian was not a violent guy," Rina adds. "Those images could have brought the OverForce to its knees. Jen is pissing on his legacy."

"You tell that to the animals out there. They got snipers pointing guns at everyone. They want to send a message that no one is safe," Mark bellows. "Those are my students and I put them in danger."

"I have my own Adrian Simons to make up for," Rina tries to touch Mark, but he pulls away.

"Just don't say anymore," Mark says through gritted teeth. "Rain and Jen are not the same."

"Yes they are," she breaks down and looks over at Jordan, "I was ordered to kill my best friend and I did it because I was scared. Her death caused the riot back then...now...I've caused this one again."

"You were only sixteen," Mark says in her defense.

"I've spent my adult life trying to erase that memory," Rina admits, sulking against the wall. This is not something she likes to talk about as her whole posture changes. The proud officer is reduced to a regretful child wishing to be forgiven. "I was just born to do evil."

Mark suddenly softens and comes over to her as if she said something she isn't supposed to and holds her tightly. "It was not your choice to join them. It was not your choice to kill Rain Malone. Who you are now, that's the real Rina." Mark comforts her, caressing her hair. "Jen made the choice to abuse what you gave her. That's not your fault."

"Can anyone really be innocent in this society?" Jordan interjects. "I killed when I was 13."

"Stop it both of you," Mark states loudly, having heard enough. "Evil people twist the truth. Tell us that selfish things are justified, making it sound convincing, practical, so that we never try to do anything to change that. We are not going let that happen to us."

"The best lies are told to the very young." Rina walks over to the broken Onzo model and starts to pick it up. She holds the pieces in her hands and recalls, "A few years ago, I went to Martin Malone and confessed to murdering his daughter. I asked him to kill me."

"You never told me that," Mark says stunned.

Tears roll down Rina's face. "He forgave me and asked me to help change things so that it could never happen again." She struggles to put the model back together. "If there is a god, why won't he help me? I'm trying so hard."

Finally calming down, Mark takes the model pieces out of her hands and puts them down on his desk. He looks into her eyes and says, "Rina, they have all the advantages. We have to be smarter than this. If we are not united, they'll destroy us."

"Compliancy is not acceptable," Rina says fighting away the tears, her inner strength beginning to pull her through. "We are the soldiers, not those kids out there. How can we not act?"

Jordan notices she has the rosary in her hand again. She is furiously running the beads through her fingers. With a final sigh, Rina puts them down on Mark's desk.

"Cotillard believes that world is ending," Rina says quietly. "She teaches that we should prepare ourselves, to clean up our live as best we can so that we have few regrets. She teaches to accept and not to fight because no matter what the devil is here amongst us...that we are all dead already." Both Mark and Jordan stay quiet, not knowing where she is heading with this. "I used to want to believe that. That nothing changes. And if it does, it only changes for the worse. None of it is true. I'd rather make a thousand mistakes then not try to be better...to be good." She looks at Jordan. "Jordan stop Jen. You can do it still."

"How?" Jordan replies quietly.

"Swallow your pride and go to Samantha Grant," Rina pleads. "She'll do anything to protect Jen. She's friends with Magen and President Eaves. Make the call."

There is a knock on the door and all stare at each other in utter silence. Rina slowly moves to open the door. Several OverForce officers are standing outside waiting to take her away.

A SHARPENED MIND

Mentally neutered by the quickness of recent events, Mark and Jordan both sit quietly in the dark lab for a few minutes. Rina is gone and neither is feeling very good as her fate is uncertain. The feeling of helplessness is tangible.

Putting away his pride as requested, Jordan finally gets up.

"What do you think you're doing?" Mark questions.

"Pissing Jen off forever," Jordan answers, reaching for his phone in his back pocket. "Samantha will find a way to make the government back off and this whole crappy day will be over."

The room shakes violently, causing the hanging models to sway into each other. This is no earthquake though, but a low flying vehicle passing over the building. The noise of the machine echoes back and forth between the walls.

A disbelieving Jordan is unnerved. The sound of the machine is augmented by sounds of cracking glass and yelling. He knows what has started.

Moving out into the hallway, both peer carefully out a window. What they see is not good and neither has to say a word. This is the worst of all possible outcomes.

Several bon fires, consisting of stacks of garbage, are burning. Plumes of smoke rise into the dark evening sky. Rioters are running around, taunting the police. The police, hundreds of them, are in full riot gear. They are closing off all exits from Pac-Tech.

Jordan sees the cause of the tremble. A GunOrb is circling the area. In the distance, he can see a second one quickly approaching.

GunOrbs are complex flying globes and are hardly ever called by their true name, the Fort Hawks Oracle AP-6. Their spheres are magnetically suspended in place between two arms, which in turn reach back into a beefy airframe. Not very fast and not needing to be, the GunOrbs can turn their "sphere turret" in almost any direction and rain down death. They are the perfect weapon for crowd control…or crowd removal.

"Go down to the server farm," Jordan orders.

"Why?"

"Go there and call security. They know you are a person of value and will come for you," Jordan instructs, his tone know radically different as if a different side to him is emerging. "It's blast proof and you'll be safe."

"Yeah right," Mark says and continues to look out the window. "I think I'll stick around and watch the show," Mark answers sarcastically.

Angrily, Jordan drags him away from the window. "You don't get it. Do you? They are blocking the exits. You were right. The time of tolerance is over." His expression changes, getting cold and serious. "Today the government reveals its true face."

"They can't really make this a military action?" Mark looks stunned at his friend. He has heard this tone in his voice before. "In the service, you could always sense a battle, but I hope you're wrong."

"This whole thing is a set-up. There is no way they could have gathered all these resources so quickly," Jordan says and backs off. He fingers the sword strapped to his back and decides on a dangerous course of action. "The government wants to send a message. I'm going to change that message."

His mind focusing, Mark realizes Jordan's intention. Mark grabs him strongly by the arm. "You can't fight them alone."

"My fight started when I was born," Jordan says with clear resolve, "and I was born alone."

"You have always been incapable of giving up on lost cause. If anyone has ever overcome all the shit in life, it's been you," Mark says. "This time I'll fight with you. You said all heroes die. This will be a good day to die."

"Not this time," Jordan smiles at his friend's devotion. He partially draws out his silver sword. "Make the eyes in the sky blind for me."

"You can't beat them all by yourself," Mark states strongly, grabbing him by his arm. "You don't need to die for those people out there. They want me."

"The government told me who to kill for years and I was the perfect citizen," Jordan replies with the fires of hate and battle brewing in the window behind him. "What can be more an act of rebellion, of freedom, then to save those who don't matter from those who think they do?"

Nodding his head, Mark reluctantly steps back. He looks at Jordan as if seeing him for the last time.

"Today is my day, not yours," Jordan says, his eyes narrowing. "They won't kill me. I'm going to kill them."

***

On every battlefield, Jordan always thought about the peace of home. This time, the battle has come home.

Red hot ash and blinding smoke fly across Jordan's face as he walks outside. The horizon glows a dark red as the sun goes down, light from various bonfires now more dominant against the growing darkness. From the transportation hub and back, thousands of people crowd the Quad, centering on the makeshift stage. Both Nuhu and humans are filled in here. Who is who and who is on what side is nearly impossible to tell. His mind flashes to crazy Jennifer; she is supposed to be in the middle of this ticking bomb. Fortunately, even with his eagle eyes, he doesn't see her. Maybe, hopefully, she has changed her mind, though he thinks that is impossible.

As Jordan cautiously walks out into the Quad, he finds himself looked upon with hateful eyes and suspicion by the students. Some in the crowd are carrying knives, flashing them at him half-heartedly, lamely warning him to away. Knives, he thinks, that is the best they could do?

No less frazzled, the police are also jittery. After all, these are not professional peacekeepers…just well paid brutes with guns. They are setting up positions at every exit point. The police are equipped with scanners that can detect weapons and they must know weapons are in the crowd — a perfect excuse to open fire, but they can't tell exactly who has them. Jordan fears that once the firing starts everyone will become a target, armed or not. His sword seems a silly choice against so many, but he still needs to find a way to break a whole in this fish tank.

A cry, cold and harrowing, hits Jordan's ears.

Screams ring out and bodies suddenly fall as flashes of hot white light up the night. Shots pierce flesh and bone of those around him. Blood splatters on his clothes.

Who fired first nobody knows, except someone did and brought down hell on earth. Red rivers began to steam across the pavement. A cloud of crimson fog stains the sky as blood vaporizes from the impact of the electronic weapons.

Running desperately for all sides, the crowd howls in terror. As Jordan feared, the police begin firing arbitrarily. Even students trying to escape are shot without a second thought. But this gives Jordan an excuse to fight; he is being fired upon too.

Trying not to kill, but to harm, Jordan attacks quickly. The police are not expecting an Officer of the State to turn on them. He catches two off guard and they cannot react. Jordan notices the squad of hidden soldiers too late.

All eight soldiers come gunning for Jordan. Unfortunately for them, this is close-quarters combat. He moves instinctively and limbs begin flying. Anticipating their firing patterns, the former flyer manages to deftly avoid getting shot. Before he knows what he has done, eight corpses lie on the ground missing heads, arms and legs. It is a disgusting sight but Jordan is too effective a killer with a sword. Though an easy victory, Jordan knows that if there is one squad there must be many, many more stationed around campus.

With a clear channel of escape for the beleaguered students, Jordan is shocked when none comes forward. Frowning, he realizes he looks like the enemy. The other Officers are having a good time hacking away at people, unaware that some of their own ranks have been killed in the melee.

With little warning, a nearly out of her mind Carmen runs into Jordan. She screams upon seeing the carnage around her. "Don't hurt me!" she pleads.

"Carmen. It's me. Grant," Jordan yells loudly, trying to get through to her. "You're safe with me."

A policeman rushes toward them with his PD-2 gun drawn. Without a flinch, Jordan defends himself, bashing the attacker across his helmet. The helmet nearly flies off with the head included.

"Jordan!" Carmen screams, finally recognizing him. She then suddenly realizes he is fighting *against* the police and soldiers. "Let's get out of here."

"Carmen," Jordan instructs calmly, "Call the other students this way. It's the only way out. They'll listen to you. They think I'm one of them."

"Who cares?" she laments.

"And who cares about you?"

The realization dawns on Carmen. She waves her arms wildly, "This way! It's open. This way!" With that, she runs off. But it is enough, as waves upon waves of students start pouring toward the open path. Jordan briefly smiles and is about to make his own retreat when...he sees *her*.

Not moving, Jennifer is lying flat on the stage. He can't tell if she's hurt...or dead. Inside, a key turns unleashing an unholy, primal power. His eyes narrow, focusing on her, willing her to be alive. Deep inside, his love fires up again. For all their history, for all their past, he cannot let her die. Like a rocket, Jordan ignites and he is off at full sprint toward her. No matter what, he will not be stopped.

The firing becomes frighteningly indiscriminate. Bodies fall around him like a cascade of dominos in a Rube Goldberg machine. Jordan loses his footing and trips over a fallen Officer of the State. The Officer lies with his black sword still tightly in his dead hand. He has been shot in the head by an errant sniper round. No one is safe.

His mind jumps into gear, scanning the area, dissecting the dangers, forcing him into survival mode. He is aware of the storm of deadly gunfire that encircles him. Where is it coming from? Every one of his senses combines to create a 3-D picture in his head.

As long energy bolts spark by his face, his vision sharpens. In his head, the scene has lost all its gore. All the people become objects and lines, technical things to be managed. Spotting the police, they glow red in his head and became shapes to be avoided. Their PD-2's fire short, weak bursts. Calculating the trajectory of fire and crowd responses, he locates the sniper positions and anticipates their possible attacks. Their Hammer SF-8 sniper rifles have a long, precise energy bolt, but they cannot repeat fire quickly. With shocking precision and speed, the path to Jennifer becomes clear to him in his head.

Dodging bodies and limbs as so many hurdles on a track, he runs halfway to the stage as if on fire himself. He brutally strikes down any police officer who gets in his way.

To his relief, Jennifer starts to move.

The police are closing in on the crowd. A pitch battle is going on over by his opening. Students are pushing and punching desperately to escape. There is a loud explosion. A grenade? Smoke comes from the one last exit. His opening has been shut. Fury boils in Jordan as bodies continue to drop around him at a relentless pace. It is becoming a turkey shoot. There is no end to the hunger for murder today.

One particularly vicious police officer has cornered several protestors. He's got a James IEB-7 assault rifle. It shoots fast and hard. The students are vainly attempting to surrender to him. Jordan is studying his movements and his read is not good. Everything is happening in only milliseconds as the officer snaps a fresh energy clip into his rifle. He prepares to fire on the unarmed group. They cry for mercy, but adrenaline is pumping freely. There is a burst of fire. One protestor falls dead as his guts turn to vapor.

Deeply locked away notions of justice blow open in his mind; Jordan cannot let this happen again. Before he knows what he is doing, his sword swings out and slams into the policeman.

Armor or no armor, the policeman never sees it coming. Something passes by him, gentle like a feather in the wind, touching him. With an excess of gore, his chest rips opens and his innards pour out. Jordan does not even skip a step as the bloodthirsty cop splits in half.

His little noble act has been noticed. Jordan is being tracked by a sniper.

Even though Jordan has noticed the gun tracking him, he is not faster than light. There is no cover. Turning, he barely sees the long bolt racing toward him. It is on a course for his chest. He reacts, moving the sword in front of him; desperately hoping it will minimize the blow.

The bolt bounces off Novo as if a rubber band and disperses into the air. This is pure luck as this is obviously *not* a known property of Exitor. Soon, he is overtaken by a fleeing crowd of students, causing the sniper to lose track of him.

"Tell us what to do!" Some of them yell, having noticed his filleting of the policeman. "Tell them we're not all armed!"

Jordan looks around. All the exits out of the courtyard have been locked down tight. He sees several policemen rushing toward the forest…hoping to secure it. The way into the forest is still open and porous. "Make for the woods and keep running," Jordan suggests. "Don't stop and watch. Run! Run hard."

He pulls away from the crowd and sees the edge of the stage. Parts of it are engulfed in flames. The two statues of the perfect students stare sternly looking down at the Quad as if pleased.

There is a policeman firing upon the bodies on the stage, making sure they are all dead. No longer worried about sparing their lives, Jordan comes out from the smoke unnoticed. He takes the policeman's life in quick flick to the neck.

Finally reaching Jen, Jordan pulls the mutilated body of another girl off of her.

Dazed, Jen can barely open her eyes. There in the midst of hell unleashed, Jordan is standing over her. He did as he promised. He came for her even after everything that has gone wrong between them. Her heart nearly leaps out of her chest as old feelings surge through her. But before she can let love carry her away, the reality of situation hits her.

As Jordan struggles to get Jen to her feet, his hands slippery with blood and guts, she sees the destruction around her.

"Move it Jen!" Jordan orders, feeling sick to his soul. The smell of burning flesh is all around.

"I can't leave! I led these people here," Jen says hazily, trying to find her footing. She is shaking uncontrollably and rushes over to the mutilated girl upon seeing her.

Jordan is momentarily motionless. He recognizes the girl.

"Get her out. Please," Annie speaks softly to Jordan. It is her blood on his hands.

Unable to look at her, he turns and scans the area for trouble. This should never happen again, he thinks over and over. With every thought, anger builds. He pushes the feeling away. He has to stay clear minded.

"Jordan help me save her," Jennifer pleads.

But he knows there is no hope; Jordan has seen fatal injuries like this before. He makes a vain effort to pick up Annie none-the-less.

With her body broken, the fallen protestor howls in agony, "Get Jen out. She needs to keep the fight alive." Her eyes then roll up into her head. Annie is dead.

"She pushed me out of the way and saved my life," Jennifer cries softly as Jordan puts the brave girl down. A huge chunk of flesh is missing off her back where several energy blasts, probably intended for Jen, had hit. A disgusted Jordan looks around the stage. It is as if a hurricane had blasted through a meat locker.

A despondent Jen reaches for her dead friend again, "Annie! Annie!"

Knowing they are now on borrowed time, Jordan has to get them out of the kill zone. Picking her up by the waist, he drags the reluctant Jen off the stage.

At that instant, Jordan hears a familiar, terrible sound. He pulls her behind the stage and ducks. Above, a GunOrb is circling, a hovering dark demon fresh from Hades.

A flurry of energy rounds fly down around them. Bodies lying on the ground light up like candles of flesh and fat ready to burn. Slowly, the cries of the masses fall silent as all animated objects cease to live. The GunOrbs are have been unleased and there will be no mercy.

Struggling, Jordan manages to pull the dumbfounded Jennifer toward the heavily wooded hills behind the school. She slips again and again on the incline. Once again, Jen is over dressed for the situation in her pricey strappy sandals. He drags her up the hills by the pure brute force of his muscles.

Somebody screams seeing Jordan's sword. He diverts and heads away from a gaggle of women hidden inside a dead tree.

Several other students are hiding amongst the trees too watching the bloodshed unfold below.

"You can't stay here. They'll come," Jordan yells at them. "Run as deep into the forest as you can. Don't show yourselves till morning." Not many listen.

Focused on escape, Jordan turns and starts running hard over protests from Jennifer and her feet. But soon she goes quiet; Riot Police, in full armor no less, are coming up the hill. Grapples fire into the trees next to them. These thugs are pulling themselves up at an alarming speed. Jordan pushes Jen harder to run. Rustling noises and lights flash from above, Dragoon troop ships are coming down. Terrible cries come from all directions around them.

"I told them to run," Jordan grumbles. "We need a distraction."

"Why should they run?" Jen warbles. "Why would they do this us? Why?"

"They can always make more of you," Jordan states with cold honestly.

A Riot Police Officer quickly rappels down barely ten feet in front of them. Jennifer gasps. Jordan does not hesitate. His blade flies across the space between them.

Not having had enough time for a full swing, the sword does not penetrate the agent's thick armor. The dumbstruck thug still ends up flying onto his back. But Jordan is merciless; he quickly rushes over and repeatedly hammers the sword through the armor. The agent gurgles up blood and finally dies. Jordan recovers his sword and sheathes it. He sees the man's gun and picks it up. His damn IEB-7 assault rifle is damaged and fizzles on activation. There is a huge gash in the metal casing from where the sword brushed it. Jordan then notices a Shepherd CV-76 pistol in the agent's belt holster, but an odd rush of wind soon distracts him.

"The pistol! Grab it," Jordan orders Jen as the trees rustle in unison. She acts fast and picks up the hand canon. The horrible, unmistakable sound of a GunOrb passing by can be heard. Not so close yet, but close enough. Pulling Jen away from the noise and deeper into the woods, things get uncomfortably quiet.

Abruptly stopping, Jordan then tucks both of them behind a tree. He covers her mouth and motions for her not to move. There is a dark figure hidden amongst the evergreens, slowly surveying the forest. This figure looks more machine than man. Jordan has seen these shock troops before, but has never seen one in action from the opposing side.

They wear armor that covers their bodies head to toe. Square and large, these armor plates make them look massive and muscular. A Shock Trooper's ruthlessness is legendary. A single glass visor, the enhanced vision visor, is the only non-armored section. Worse, they carry the legendary James PB-16 combat canon which they can aim using their visor alone. The weapon is a wide dispersion energy canon, EMP generator and rifle all in one. It also weighs a ton and then some.

A young man runs by and right into the trooper's line of sight.

Firing the huge cannon, the Shock Trooper rocks the whole forest. Jordan pushes Jennifer to the ground as wood splinters blow past. Pieces of ground beef fall around them and they do not have to guess where it came from. There is nothing-recognizable left of the kid.

Grabbing the powerful Shepherd pistol from Jen, Jordan dives out into the open. The Shock Troop is marching toward them and takes aim, but slowed by the heavy armor. Jordan is far quicker and fires a strong blast into the shock troop's visor. The beam simply appears to disperse. Then howling louder than a wounded animal, the trooper stumbles around blinded, dropping his massive weapon behind him.

This is all the time Jordan needs. In a flash, Jordan draws his sword and rushes his opponent. But the trooper recovers as Jordan's sword sparks against the man's shielded forearms. Jordan swings the sword around and hits the trooper's left arm, pushing it away. The trooper staggers, his arm instantly broken.

Lifting the sword fast above his head, Jordan thrusts down hard, driving the sword precisely through the transparent eye slot and out the back of the head.

Unnerved, Jennifer looks down at the defeated shock trooper, convulsing on the ground. This is the best soldier the NAU has and Jordan has killed it like some irritable insect. Jordan is already retrieving his sword when Jennifer feels her voice come back.

"What are you Jordan?" she says in a broken voice, disturbed by his ability to be ruthless.

"Do you think I lived this long by hesitating," Jordan says as he finishes pulling the sword out of the eye slot with a sickening grate. "I knew I could blind with the gun. This is how you survive. Deal with it."

Hearing the growl of the GunOrb again, Jordan pauses for a second and picks up the trooper's gigantic gun. He quickly checks the PB-16 combat canon. It seems to be undamaged.

"This is a P.I.G.," Jordan says to Jen. Flipping a switch, the riffle hums again and Jordan smiles, "Time for some payback."

A resistant Jen whines. "Let's go. I don't want to see anymore."

"Your friends deserve a chance," Jordan says and anchors himself.

"There is no hope for anyone," she says, pulling at him. "Please."

"There never is till you make some," Jordan says with spite. His face remains unfazed and focused. Starring intently at the gun scope, he aims the gun up into the trees. A strange wind is blowing across the canopy, heading right at them.

A GunOrb is closing in on their position. The tree leaves are rustling in a mad manner and Jordan tracks with it.

With a display of light and swirling dust, the GunOrb appears in a gap amongst the treetops, Jordan quickly hits the safety. The pile driver muzzle glows blue and opens up wide.

A petrified Jennifer wonders why Jordan doesn't fire. The GunOrb is pointing away from them. Slowly though, the machine begins to turn right toward them. She wants to run, but he is still motionless. What is he waiting for?

With an effortless move, the GunOrb spins around toward them and begins to move its horrible weapon to fire. Jennifer stands entranced by the sparks of the two energy beams that holds the globe suspended. There is certain beauty to it.

Jordan hits the trigger. A single EMP burst spirals out. The burst flies straight and true, but does not hit the GunOrb. He misses! No, he hasn't. Instead, the shot passes through the suspension beam and disrupts it. As the beam fails, the globe topples over on one side. Unable to support the whole mass, the second beam overloads and releases. Crashing, the globe plummets to the ground and explodes. The airframe spins madly about in the sky, out of control, and disappears, crashing in the distance.

A satisfied Jordan smiles, but soon his face-hardens.

"That'll attract every soldier toward us!" Jen howls.

"I know. They'll spend hours chasing us in here," he says with the utmost resolve. "Two lives for many." Down the forest about a hundred yards from them, Jordan sees a whole patrol of Shock Troops approaching. And behind them, what seems appears to be a whole army. Dropping the heavy gun, Jordan takes hold of Jennifer and begins to run again. "Let's go," he yells. "My plan worked too well."

"You can't leave the canon!" she yells back.

"Then you try running with it."

A blue light comes up from behind them engulfing the forest. Bursting apart, several trees explode around them. There is so much firepower projected in their direction that the whole forest seems to be entirely engulfed by flames. Fires burst out amongst the trees producing an instant inferno.

The good news, what little there happens to be, is that fire provides a wall between them and the Shock Troops. The bad news is that a fire is racing after them, chasing them down. All the trees are as dry as timber, bursting like firecrackers. They are soon cornered and pushed up against the lip of a wide chasm.

Looking around, Jordan cannot see any escape. The gap is close to twenty feet across and at least sixty feet down with roots and rocks strewn all over the sides. There is no chance of surviving a jump to the bottom.

Thinking fast, Jordan looks at the source of many of the roots. A huge ancient redwood is next to them, teetering at the chasm's edge. The tree's base is the size of a boat. Jordan feels a ping of guilt for what he is about to do. Brandishing his sword, Jordan looks at the skinny piece of metal against the enormous tree.

"You idiot, you should've kept the gun," Jennifer cries out, now near hysterical. "Good luck with that mister lumber jack."

"It would have blown the tree apart," answers Jordan and then mumbles. He turns on the tree and begins to hack. Nothing, a few bark chips fly off.

Running out of time, Jordan feels the heat of the forest fire on his back. He looks across at the gorge and his hope fades. A faint white light is upon him. Novo is glowing. An intense heat is coming off the blade. Jordan is momentarily impressed. He has never seen a blade act this way. The heat intensifies, but the grip remains cool. He realizes the Exitor is reacting to him again. It's trying to help him.

Turning fast, Jordan unleashes a ferocious blow against the tree. With a horrible shudder, a rip appears across the base. The sword has gone through the tree as if a blowtorch. A red line of fire continues burning deeper and deeper, finally splitting the base. A mighty moan sounds as the redwood topples over followed by a horrible cracking as hundreds of branches are sheared off. Lurching out from the chasm, a cloud of dust fills the air as the tree settles.

Struggling, the pair clambers up and onto the topside of the tree and head across. The fire is now lapping at their makeshift redwood bridge. The tree lurches to one side. It is unstable, rocking side to side as they try to get across. Sparks are falling upon the tail of the tree. Jen stumbles, ravaged by fear, and begins to slowly crawl. Other fire engulfed trees are falling around them, sending streams of embers down their way.

No longer having the luxury to wait, Jordan lifts Jen up into a fireman's carry. The tree begins to roll and Jordan jumps for the opposite edge, dropping Jen. She falls hard onto the ground, but safe. Jordan's legs are dangling over the gap's edge and he scrambles away as the huge redwood begins slip down into the now fiery abyss.

Once away from the damn gorge, the woods become dense and green, resisting to burn. It is enough of a break to allow the two to escape from the firestorm.

Making their way down into a small town, they find themselves on a street with several businesses. The shops are all closed and the lights of emergency vehicles can be seen in the distance. No one is around as the fire department has apparently evacuated the area. In the sky above, unmanned fire skiffs are flying overhead and toward the forest fire.

Relentless, Jordan makes his way to one of the shops and forces the door open. Tentatively looking inside, he pushes an exhausted and numb Jen in before him. He notices it some sort of fine glass workshop, filled with vases and glass plates. Judging by the dust on the items, this particular shop has been derelict for a long time.

After locking the door, Jordan checks the backroom. It is less visible and has opaque windows. He motions Jennifer to move back there. She drops to the floor and cries quietly as he quickly goes to a window and cracks it open. He peers out into the street and keeps watch for any movement.

"Let's hope the fire fighters are not using infrared to scan the area," Jen whimpers.

A calm and collected Jordan replies quietly, "Don't worry. All eyes are on the University."

"Do you really think something is wrong with me?" she asks, angrily wiping tears off her face. "Jordan, I, I, never meant for any of this to happen."

"What's done is done," he says with his tired eyes now closed. Taking off his blood splattered jacket, Jordan finally allows himself to slump to the floor.

"I shouldn't have hit you earlier," Jen says, moving over next to him, though her body tells her to turn away. She pushes through the mental barrier and says, "Thanks for coming after me."

"I kept my promise," Jordan sighs and looks at her with immense sadness, his love for her more of an anchor to pain then comfort.

"And you suffered for it," Jen says remorsefully, putting a hand on his arm. "Why do you still love me?"

A pained Jordan strokes her face.

"Is there still something about me worth saving?"

A barely conscious Jordan smiles weakly and looks into her eyes. He kisses her on the check lightly.

"I just feel dirty inside all the time. Maybe we should go, just like you wanted. Ever since I came home, I haven't felt like myself," she whispers to him.

He doesn't answer.

"I have changed. Haven't I? That's why you don't answer," she says as if knowing the Other may emerge at any time. "Though I want to be the woman you knew, I know I can't anymore. So before I hurt you, I want you to get far away from here…from me. There is evil here Jordan. It infects everything."

"Then leave with me," Jordan suggest, pulling her toward him. "We can go to Japan."

"I want to," Jen says fighting against herself, "but…" She tries to tell him about the Other though no words come out.

"You can't let go, can you?"

"No," the Other speaks out, silencing Jen. "I can't go."

A disappointed Jordan sighs loudly, frustrated. He tries to roll away from her.

Fighting the voices in her head, Jen thrusts her hand on his chest, pulling him back toward her. A diminishing Jen has to fight to keep the Other quiet. "Don't think. Just don't think."

They kiss, but she soon passes out, exhausted, once again denied her deepest wishes.

Unable to sleep himself, Jordan stares out into the workshop, his focus blurry, not looking at anything specific, but aware of everything. He holds tightly onto Jen, afraid of what the morning will bring. A troubling feeling stirs in him. In a way, he knows this is the last time he will hold her this way.

FADING

A bitter and alone Jennifer enters her parent's house. The wrath of her mother is waiting for her. As she crosses the marble threshold, she is meet with a melee of questions.

"Where the hell were you all night? I was so worried. What were you doing?" Samantha shrieks. "The police have been over five times already with the OverForce in tow no less."

"Sleeping around," she says coldly.

"This is no time to joke. First you go off your meds, now this."

"The police are looking for me?" Jen says, tired and not really caring. "So what? Can't you make them go away? I thought you were somebody."

"I saw Jordan with that sword yesterday. I wondered what he was up too," Samantha is nearly snarling with rage. "He is not a pure breed but we have to deal with him."

"He's never done anything to you. Has he?" Jen shouts back, finally losing her temper. "He saved me again last night and maybe hundreds, maybe thousands of others. That's why I'm angry. I am the broken one, not him! You did this to me. You did with all those fucking pills."

"Jennifer!"

"No it's true," Jen yells. "One day you'll know. You'll know."

A bewildered Samantha looks outside, "Oh God. The police are back." She grabs Jen by the arm. "Why did Jordan have to come save you?"

No longer able to control her emotions, Jen is flush with fear and rage. She is the one who stood on that stage. The University is covered with cameras. She takes a deep breath but cannot force herself to go outside. Suddenly, Jen feels like she wants to kill someone. Trembling with hate for all inferior beings, she looks at her mother, her pathetic mother and wishes her dead.

Two police units pull into the driveway. Several policemen get out along with two OverForce agents. They don't get very far before Jordan is in their way, sword drawn. The police pull their weapons, but appear nervous. Jordan is calm and confident. Police Lieutenant Anthony Strum comes forward and tries to calm all parties.

"Cool down Sir. We all recognize the honor of the crested, but this does not involve you. You may challenge this investigation, but I assure that is all it is. We need to question Jennifer Grant," the Lieutenant explains. "She is believed to be one of the organizers of the riot last night."

"Strum? You were on the Carrier Texas back in the war," Jordan says and then lowers his sword. "You are looking for *Jennifer*?"

"That's right," Strum responds. "Some witnesses claim to have seen Jennifer on the protest stage. These O.F.'s want to take her in for some routine questioning."

"Let's not waste time with the human," an OverForce officer remarks.

"Grant," Strum says. "It is your privilege to kill these OverForce agents."

The OverForce agents back off.

"Do I have your word as Air Corp's officer she will not be harmed," Jordan asks Strum.

"You do," Sturm says with a deep sigh. He waves for the OverForce agents to stand-back.

At that moment, Jennifer comes busting out of the house, finally mustering some courage.

"Jordan enough! Stupid human animal!" Jennifer pushes him away. The OverForce officers laugh. Sturm and the police remain quiet. She looks at Strum, "I accept the terms set by Jordan. We can go." Jordan looks at Jen concerned. She says to him, *"We'll* be fine."

The OverForce agents move to take Jen. Strum moves in front of them. Strum says. "I will take her. She's my responsibility."

An unnerved Samantha walks out and sees Jordan with the sword. She immediately butts in, "Jordan. I know you mean well for my daughter." She pushes Jordan back like some wayward guard dog. "That sword provides you some protection, but we must admire our security forces for their restraint." Looking over at Strum, Samantha sizes him up. He is a fairly short man, overshadowed by Jen, looks middle-aged but isn't. "Mr. Strum," Samantha says, "Please see my daughter is taken care of."

"Yes ma'am," he answers. "That is my intent."

Giving her mother a disgusted look, Jennifer allows herself to be taken into custody and is quickly placed in the back of a police cruiser. She is driven away.

"This is not good," Jordan growls, putting away his sword.

"Was she involved with the bloodshed last night?" Samantha asks. "I need to know so that I can work my contacts."

"I hold the responsibility and honor of the Grant name whether you like it or not. It is my sworn responsibility to protect this house, even if this house does include you," Jordan spitefully says. "It's been your constant interference in her life that's made her this way. Always pushing her to climb. Yes, she was involved and I had to kill to save her...again," he says and begins to walk away.

"Jordan," Samantha fights to say. "Thank you."

"Don't you ever thank me," Jordan says angrily. "You are no mother to either of us."

***

Coming around a hill, she can see the building, the Marin Civic Center. It is a majestic structure with a long curving blue roof and ornate circular windows. This is the center of county operations and police headquarters are located right below it, underground.

The entrance is a plain, concrete abatement with an oversized metal door. This makes it even more intimidating. There is clack of metal locks releasing and then the unmistakable hiss of hydraulic pistons as the door opens to allow the cars to enter. The tunnel down is illuminated only by a few fixtures on the walls. Cold and sickening fluorescents then flood light on everything as they come to a stop in a large empty room. A single set of stairs leads down further. She is escorted out of the car by Lt. Strum.

"What's down there?" Jen asks.

"Interview rooms," Strum says. "Better if you stay quiet."

A ghostly pale Jennifer is directed toward a small, dimly lit room. She passes a large cell on the way with a group of terrified looking students hand cuffed to a ceiling beam.

"The prophecy will come true and you all will face the fury of the righteous," a crazed woman yells. Jen recognizes her from the University. She is the same loon who ran up to Mark and Rina that one

262

day. The woman screams at the top of her lungs, "You hear me! I believe and no one will take that from me. My soul is divine and not from a machine. God will save me." Guards push her into what looks like a dentist's chair and then proceed to close the door.

Hurriedly, Jennifer is then taken down a hall to an empty cell. The room has no windows or furniture, only four metal reinforced walls and a heavy steel door. There is blunt nail on the floor, not much use as a weapon, but someone used it as a pen. Scratched into the wall, Jen sees a message. She reads it:

"To the righteous who follow in my steps. Know that a human boy will be born to dead parents. He will be blessed by nature with strength and courage beyond all others. His fury will bring closure to the Earth. For in time, we will all fall silent. Fear the revenant. Fear the destroyer of worlds. His time has come. So says the prophet."

The inscription is signed with a symbol: two silver vertical ovals with crosses inside them.

Though feeling a slight shiver, Jen has little time to think about the prophecy's meaning. She is soon pulled into a large interrogation chamber. Unlike the OverForce offices at school, this place is lined with cameras.

Inside the room, there are several police officers waiting for her. Strum directs her to a perforated metal chair, bolted to the floor. Jen notes that a convenient drain is located right under the chair.

The same two OverForce agents who arrested her walk in and stand in back of the room. A panel lowers from the roof with several projects on it. The projection starts on the floor as a simulated overhead view. Slowly, the image builds around them to convey a 3D rendering of the University environment, but sometimes the image would suddenly go flat. This made the projection hard to watch and a bit nausea inducing. Jennifer feels herself turning green.

Interestingly, the entire projection is a blur. None of the people imaged have any detail…then Jen realizes the police have no details. Someone, most likely Mark, must have sabotaged the school's security footage. But why would Mark put himself in danger for her? Then it dawns on her, he did it to protect Jordan. Mark must have known Jordan's intentions.

"Miss Grant. Question. Do you know what may have caused this distortion of the security feeds?" Strum asks. "Even satellite imagery was blurred."

"I have no idea. I'm not technically inclined," Jen says truthfully. "Sun flare? My major is general studies, but you probably already know that."

"Do you know who did it?" Strum follows up.

Jen hesitates slightly, "It is a technical university, could have been anyone."

The OverForce agents stir.

"Miss Grant. You are known to relate with certain radical elements at the University. We have witnesses who report that you were on stage yesterday," an OverForce agent quietly asks. "Why would you be on that stage if you were not involved?"

"If I had been there, I wouldn't be alive. I don't deny that I was part of the demonstration, but I ran when the shooting started," Jen says calmly. "There is no law against attending a demonstration."

"No," the agent agrees, but the tone is icy. "Is it possible the protestors were helped by an outside source...an opposition group? A group with military connections who would have access to such technology?"

"I don't know. I ran. I found my friend's car open and hid in there for the night. I must say, even as a Nuhu, that I do not understand the heavy handed nature of the response," Jen says defiantly. "I believe a great deal of the blame falls upon the police and the OverForce."

The people in the room mumble angrily.

"Weapons were discharged from the crowd," an agent explains. "Officers came under fire and responded accordingly. The response had nothing to do with the demonstration itself," the agent replies. "An attempt was made to lock down the school for the safety of the students, but failed. Several of the protestors fought back and broke out. Containment was achieved at great cost. However, most of the agitators escaped."

Starting to agree with them, Jen rages inside, battling with herself, but doesn't let it show. She has a strong desire to turn in Jordan, her feelings of love turning to outright hate. But even in her hate, she can betray the man who saved her. The word "never" keeps ringing in her ears over and over again. "Perhaps I was mistaken. You had to protect the public after all."

"It is all an unfortunate set of incidents," Strum adds. "The situation is regrettable, but the actions taken were deemed appropriate at the time." He looks sadly at Jen. "It is the worst kind of lesson...for everyone."

"Do you know what Jordan Grant and Mark Whatley are working on out in the old Marin Airport?" a female OverForce agent asks. Jen did not notice her enter the room. She remains in shadow and Jen can only see her hands. The agent is a young black woman, but that's all the detail she can make out.

Jennifer replies, "I didn't know he was working on anything. I didn't even know he had a job."

"Jordan Grant never told you he is employee of Martin Malone," the female OverForce agent snickers. "Interesting."

"No. He didn't. Anyways if it is a Malone project, a government project, it's none of my business. Shouldn't you ask Jordan these questions?" Jennifer retorts.

The people laugh.

"Jordan Grant is an Officer of the State, a decorated war veteran and his friends include one of our agents, unlike you," the O.F. lady points out. "Rina Dupont may have gotten in trouble for mishandling some information, but she has a solid record. Her files state implicitly that Jordan is loyal to the NAU."

"If he is so beyond reproach, why the questions?" she asks.

"Jordan doesn't put a lot of confidence in you, does he? If that's so, why should we?" the female O.F. agent asserts. "All we have are rumors from unreliable sources for the events that occurred. Phones were found, but several EMP's set off that night made waste of their memory chips. As you can see, these recordings gave us no clues. I know you were involved in detail with the protestors. Who covered up for you? Who provided you access to Dupont's computer?"

"President Eaves," Jen admits.

There is some muffled laughter.

"Dupont's computer was hacked by someone using a Chinese data worm. A very expensive device not many could afford," the female O.F. agent says. "We found wounds commiserate with a sword, though someone may have picked one up from an unfortunate dead Officers of the State. However, there are many skilled foreign operatives who are both masters at hi-tech theft and murder. You have the financial resources…"

"Too bad Jordan is not here, he wouldn't tolerate this language. He could kill everyone in this office and no one could do anything about it," Jen threatens. "Isn't that right? Lt. Strum?"

"Essentially, yes. But I think you know that already," Strum answers, looking peeved. "Acts of treason are never taken kindly, regardless of rank."

"If I was treasonous, show me the proof," Jen demands.

"We have enough evidence to sequester you for a while," the female O.F. agent states.

"Then file the charges," Jen challenges, "and I'll call Jordan."

"That won't be necessary," the female O.F. Officer says with obvious spite. "We make it our business to know as much as possible. Perhaps I wanted to see if you would tell me restricted information, had access to restricted information, or are capable of obtaining restricted information." The female OverForce agent then says slyly, "This whole incident was caused by an unfortunate breach. However, the true criminal has not been found. The criminal who distributed the data to the students, that person is the one we want. The one that broke our security safeguards."

"Trust me, I didn't do it," Jen scoffs.

"I don't trust anyone," the female agent responds. "Nuhu or human, everyone lies. You touted your Nuhu heritage more times than I can count. You may not be the leak, but you are a liar."

"Who told you I associate with bad elements anyways?" Jen argues back.

"Your boyfriend, Christian Palin, filled us in on your activities," the female agent says to the laughs of the gathered. "He even said that Jordan never participated in any events…even after you begged. No Jennifer, we only hear stories about you. He said you were a close friend of Adrian Simmons. How does it make you feel what happened to him? That someone cut him open. That someone let him slowly bleed to death in the sun."

Battling with herself to the point of exhaustion, Jen struggles to carefully say, "He was my classmate and kind to me. That's why I attended the event. I am angry that he died the way he did. No one deserves that."

"Interesting friends you have, radicals and law breakers. Perhaps Christian should look elsewhere for his entertainment," the female agent jokes. "We hope, now that Adrian and his supporters are either dead or frightened, that there will be no more protests. We hope that a peace will fall upon the school. We hope that the student movement is over. Do you understand us, Miss Grant?"

"I hope for those things too," Jen answers, unwilling to hear anymore-veiled threats.

"Good lessons all around then," the female agent says. "We've heard that you are very good with a sword. Are you going to compete again in the ICE competition this year? Hope you make us proud like a good citizen."

Jen's blood runs cold. They might think she did the fighting last night…did all the killing last night…herself. For a brief second, she thinks about turning in Jordan again, but deep her love blocks the Other.

"Yes. It's a great sport. I'm sure my points will help propel the team to victory. Though, I would really like an individual medal this year. As you know, Doctor Magen is a great supporter. He is helping the team with our physical training," Jen says, hoping it will be enough to slide past. "Why do you ask?"

"Miss Grant, I think we are done here, since our hands tied from more complete…investigation techniques," the female agent says nonchalantly. "Be a good little girl out there, we'll be watching you…of course…for your own safety." The agent closes a brief case and leaves while the room is still dark. Jen catches the initials "R.M." on the case, but is too angry to make the connection.

\

WAVES UPON THE SHORE

With the campus closed after the incident, Jordan finds himself running mindless errands for Mark. He thinks that all this busy work is to keep him from thinking about the battle. So far, it has not done much good.

As for Mark, he seems to have buried himself in his lab never to be seen again, only reaching for the phone to annoy Jordan. The fact is neither is doing very well. As for Jen, she seems catatonic lately and spends a lot of her time locked up at home.

The only positive for Jordan is that he gets to drive around in Mark's beloved car, though it doesn't handle so well up San Francisco's many hills. The car either refuses to speed up gradually and lurches madly ahead, or crawls about in safe mode, unable to balance its massive power to do traffic grunt work.

Just as he is about to go home, Jordan receives a text message from Mark. Here we go again, Jordan thinks. Yup, it's another mindless errand.

Pulling up to the posh Mark Hopkins Hotel, Jordan valets the car and smiles. He'll make good old Mark pay for it. Whatever the heck an engineer needs from a hotel beats him. Coming to the front desk, he is greeted by the desk clerk.

"Hello Sir. How may I help you today?"

"The name is Grant. I'm here to pick up package for Mark Whatley," Jordan replies.

"Upstairs in our bar, The Top of the Mark," the clerk explains and points to an elevator.

As Jordan rides up the ornate elevator, he nearly breaks down. He doesn't really feel good after the fight at the University. Could he have done more to stop it? And now, Jen is avoiding him too.

However, he can't fight the irony that Mark would have him pick up something at a hotel called Mark and at a bar called The Top of the Mark. That boy has some serious ego issues. Very likely, all this probably just for a bottle of fancy booze…or a box of seriously pampered machine parts.

Upon entering the bar, the hostess is already waiting for him. She points him toward a table. A very attractive…and very familiar Asian lady is waiting for him.

"You don't look like a box of parts," Jordan says, sitting down next Emily Wu.

"I hope not," Sierra laughs and smiles back coyly.

"You like tricking me," he says.

Sierra ignores his comment. "Heard about the bad things that happened at Pac-Tech. As much as I knew I shouldn't, I needed to come to see you."

"Could have called," Jordan points out.

Taking his hand, she says looking into his eyes, "Not the same."

Jordan recalling the horror in his head, holds her hand even tighter. "It's going to be hard to go back to the University and pretend like nothing happened."

"Would you like something to drink? Might help," she offers, still holding him tight. "I was going to have some lunch, but nothing here really interests me. Sorry, I'm sure that sounds rather elitist," Sierra says, fiddling with a menu. "Please, pick whatever you would like." She looks at her watch.

"How about we go find something we both really want to eat. Frankly, I don't want to eat alone," Jordan mentions. "But if you have to go, I understand."

She does need to go to a meeting, but can't refuse him. "How about salty chicken," she answers. "It's a favorite of mine from when I was a kid. Haven't had it forever."

"Traditional salty chicken. Sounds good to me," Jordan stands up. "Let's go to Chinatown."

Reaching the intersection Bush and Grant, the contrasting pair walk under the fancy gateway that symbolizes the entrance to Chinatown.

Coming across a restaurant with the desired white chickens hanging in a window display, the pair enters the restaurant. Sierra's demeanor suddenly changes. Her face is relaxed and the smile returns. The new smile is gentle and real, not forced or painted on like before. She is a completely different person around him.

Tea comes to the table and she quickly pours him a glass. The restaurant is low rent, but busy. It seems to fit them well though. They are quickly swallowed up in the crowd.

"My Dad and I used to always eat in places like this," Sierra recalls, happily sipping tea. "Those were good times. I miss them."

"I know a little about your father. Master Kenji speaks highly about him. Apparently, they had it out a few times when Kenji was a different kind of man."

"Sometimes the best of friends start out as enemies," Sierra says. "As we go through life, our needs change and so do our morals."

Unwilling to accept this statement, Jordan looks across the bay toward Marin County...and Jen. It seems she is never far from his thoughts.

"You can never trust any Nuhu...and you can never trust any humans. It's not for a genetic difference. It's just how human-kind operates. There is nothing *kind* about us," Sierra explains. She has only ever seen the worse of people and it comes out in her views, but Jordan obviously feels differently, she can tell by his silence. How someone can hold onto to hope so feverously, she doesn't understand. "How did you save all those kids at the university?"

"Me?"

"Who else?" she says confidently. "Better question...why? Why do you care?"

"Someone has to stand when others run," he admits, looking distant. "To stop a wave, you must become the rock." He remembers Kenji saying the same thing many times.

"And when you're gone, there'll be no one," she says sadly knowing that he will eventually be claimed by his actions.

"If I die, I hope that two will replace me," he replies quietly.

She looks at him mesmerized and giggles nervously. The feelings he is bringing out in her have long been dormant. No wanting to feel love, she just continues to giggle hoping the feeling will go away, but there is no denying the truth.

"You ever tried the crispy sesame balls with the taro paste inside," he says trying to break-up the tension.

"Red bean is better."

"Those are good too," Jordan laughs happily.

"Let's order both."

After a meal rich in rice, congee, and chicken, Jordan and Sierra take a walk through the streets of Chinatown. They linger in shops, not really looking at anything in particular, but having a good time just the same.

"Why are you here?" Jordan inquires as they stop by store filled with antique replicas. "Not that I want to complain. It's just the real person doesn't fit the notorious description. Who really are you Emily?"

Sierra is standing next to a grumpy-looking dragon that she uses as an armrest. "I'm someone different around you," she admits. "It's a nice feeling that is addictive. Silly, I know."

"Just don't act like a rich girl and ask me to be your lover," Jordan sighs as he thinks about his past relationships.

"I really don't know where this is going. Maybe nowhere. But right now, I just want to be your friend and only that," Sierra says and takes him by the arm. "A close friend."

"You make no sense," Jordan laughs.

"I know," she kisses him on the cheek, "but I won't lie to you. You'll always know what I think." Distracted, Sierra stops in front of a store full of candy. There are a lot of kids looking inside. She remembers being poor. Sierra then announces, "I'm buying! Anything you guys want!"

The kids rush inside, pulling their bewildered parents with them. Sierra dumps a wad of cash at the register and watches as happy pandemonium ensues.

"You do this all the time?" Jordan jokes.

"Only lately," she laughs as throngs of children hug her long legs.

With a devilish look in his eyes, Jordan laughs back at her and then asks, "Hey, you ever been down Fisherman's Wharf? They have excellent seafood."

"Food again! We must be crazy," Sierra jokes as she pulls herself away from the clutches of the lovelorn children.

"We'll get you some practical shoes and walk down there. Burn off lunch," Jordan recommends.

Just then, Sierra's phone rings. She has a text message. Apparently, she is late for her meeting. Quickly replying, Sierra excuses herself. Lucky for some sleaze balls today, they get to live a little longer.

She is silently selective about who she assassinates. They have to be dirty. Otherwise, she just gives them a good scare, letting her reputation do most of the work. Today, she is not interested in Emily's affairs, only Sierra's.

"Everything OK?" Jordan inquires.

"Emily's problems, not mine," Sierra replies whimsically. "Let's go find those shoes."

"Sounds good," Jordan says, problems can indeed wait. Unfortunately, they don't go away.

As day gives away to night, they walk around the beautiful city. Occasionally, they stop and look at the Golden Gate Bridge, silently reflecting in the bay waters. They don't talk very much. They don't have to. Life has given them a small break and they have seized it, enjoying each other's company for as long as they can.

Late at night, they stop by a quiet bar with a view of Marin County across the bay. They sit at a small outside table.

"Day's over," Jordan says with regret. "Makes me wish tomorrow wouldn't come."

"There is no easy way to wash away our identities," Sierra says. "No matter what, tomorrow will come and we will back in reality's grip. And please, don't tell me it doesn't have to be that way."

"It doesn't," Jordan blurts out. "Too bad you can't be Sierra all the time." He is really starting to feel strongly about her, but he pushes the feeling away, still wounded by Jen.

"A true relationship requires a true commitment. If I could do that for you, I would. As it is, I'd rather disappoint you in a small way than a large way," she sighs, secretly breaking inside too. "At least, you will always have the best version of me."

"I know," Jordan grins.

Sierra reaches out and holds his hands tight. "Living life as an illusion can be a beautiful thing. Let's make tonight last as long as it can. Talk to me please. Talk about anything that is not important. Talk about the sky, the moon, or the sea. Anything faraway."

"You've ever been to Alaska?" Jordan asks.

"Never."

"They have this glacier in Juno. You can almost walk up to it. The glacier looks blue, but as the ice breaks away, you can see the ice is perfectly clear, like crystal."

"That clear?" she says, longing to see it with him.

"Impossibly clear. Beautiful thing...nature."

"Yes it is," Sierra says with smile. She is a million miles away in her thoughts. And in that far away land, she can still hear his voice. For a few hours, she is truly happy.

As they end up back at her hotel, both refuse to let go of each other.

In the end, they ignore the obvious truth. Regardless of wealth and fame, they are both just humans, with simple human needs. Needs that their regular lives do not fulfill, but neither is willing to face that fact. As they enter her room, they kiss with mad abandon. For the night, they will live in a dream. A dream that could be reality.

San Francisco knows lovers better than they know themselves. It is a mischievous matchmaker, but even this city's magic doesn't always work. Love doesn't often give second chances...there is always someone new. And speaking about forbidden loves...

About two in the morning, Mark starts to wonder about the whereabouts of his beloved car.

RISING SUN

An austere beauty, the mysterious creature that is Rain Malone enters the room with Dr. Magen. Magen, who like usual, is hidden behind an opaque curtain. She moves and sits down on the chair, just like Samantha Grant before her. "Officer Malone here to present findings as ordered."

"Please begin your report," Magen says, his voice harsh, cold and devoid of compassion.

"The test subject shows signs of confusion and anger. Though the programming seems to mostly have taken control, there is still a dangerous amount of the original personality surfacing," Rain tells him as she looks through her papers. "The oral version of the trigger drug is not as successful as we would have hoped. The amount required to allow the immergence of the security control has to be unusually high in order to defeat the brain's natural resistance."

Magen agrees, "So the data sampling is correct. Whether or not the serum 5 is introduced in one dosage or several, it is becoming ineffective."

"Unfortunately, the Jennifer Grant case study confirms the Pure Nation data sample. The slow introduction of the control creates the same interim state. This interim state is toxic, causing a personality split. The mind cannot handle having multiple commands and begins to break down causing mild to major psychosis," Rain states mechanically. "Fast or slow, serum number 5 is no longer viable."

"Understood. I had hoped that on a small scale the results would be less destructive than it had been in the past with serum 4. Something has changed in the Nuhu population. A Nuhu should not be able to fight the serum. We'll need to keep working we achieve a final solution," Magen says with the utmost disappointment. "Did the secondary objective produce any result? Did the rebel force reveal itself?"

"We estimate by the level of our casualties that they must have had a sizable task force at the school. The witnesses report a scene of utter chaos. Even under threat and with the use of truth agents, nothing was revealed. We must assume that the rebels have immense resources and loyalty in the area as they vanished without any evidence. There was widespread tampering with surveillance instruments. The assumption must be made that they have military supporters."

"This will not sit well with Quintero. If a rebellion is being nurtured secretly here in the shadow of the Western Capital, he will assume they are everywhere. Frankly, I do not relish the idea of a population of schizophrenic puppets on the loose again. Pure Nation was the result of Quintero fearing a rebellion within the Air Corps. We had never used serum 5 on such a scale. Those were my creations, my children which later had to be put down. Issue the edict to find a new subject for serum number 6 – the aerosol. There must be instant emergence of the Other with no fear of reversion or psychosis. Test and test again."

"Yes sir," she says looking dour.

"What of this human Officer of the State? He intrigues me. What can you tell me?"

"From what I understand, he has some liberal qualities, but is seen as an ideal citizen and with unquestionable loyalty to the NAU."

"What does it say about our society when the best and brightest is a human? It shames Nuhu science."

Having no answer, Rain simply goes on with her report, "What should we do about Mark Whatley's mystery project? Do we risk offending Malone?"

"Teach them that there is no autonomy," Magen growls angrily. "Thank you Clone 15. Proceed with your assigned duties."

***

In the early morning, Sierra prepares to leave her hotel room. Jordan awakes to the sound of the door closing. He sits up in the darkened room and stares blankly at the wall - alone.

Within seconds, the door re-opens and Sierra steps back in, refusing to look at him in the face. "I'm sorry," she says with that unmistakably melancholy tone that doctors have when they pronounce someone dead.

Jordan nods, accepting the facts as they are. With that, she exits, leaving a blooming relationship in disarray. Like so many other things lately, Jordan is forced to accept a reality he doesn't like and can't seem to change. With no reason to stay, he quickly dresses and begins to drive home.

With the pre-dawn light just barely illuminating the shape of the Grant house, Jen wakes up with a start. She is sick to her stomach, but her mind is momentarily her own. For some reason the last couple of weeks, she feels like an outsider in her own body. Ever since the University incident, she has been blacking out over and over again. Yesterday she even found herself in bed with Christian Palin! A man she has loathed since she was child. Struggling to keep calm amidst the realization she is losing her mind, Jen stares down at the little glass house from her room. She then sees Jordan coming from the driveway and her decision is made. With her father arriving home soon, she will beg Jordan to take her to see him immediately for a full medical evaluation… and not to stop until they reach him.

A frustrated Jordan storms into his little glass house. He has an awful feeling of defeat bubbling up in him and regrets letting things go so far with Sierra. No matter what, she never would have stayed. After being abandoned so many times in the past, he should have known better then to get his hopes up.

Drowning in anxiety, he pulls out his sword and begins to clean the immaculate blade over and over again till his fingers go numb. His thoughts soon go to Jen, he knows something is wrong even if the tests proved otherwise. It's been weeks and they haven't talked. With a nervous breath, he looks at his reflection in the sword's perfect mirror skin.

The blade glows blue changing the ambience of the room. Jordan looks around in awe. On the blade, words once again appear:

"Her path is not her own."

Freaked out, Jordan drops the sword and backs away. He thinks he is imagining things but the words soon disappear and the blue glow fades, returning normalcy to the room. He hates when the sword acts up.

Jordan reaches down to recover the sword. It flashes these words:

"In justice for all you will find strength."

Then, it barks at him in a female voice, "Jordan."

He yowls loudly, dropping the sword. Shaking, Jordan turns and sees Jennifer in the doorway.

"A little nervous aren't you?" Jennifer mentions, kicking the sword out of her way. Novo slides across the floor and hides under the bed, seemingly of its own will. "I…um…I want you to…I want you to…" she then suddenly goes quiet. "Oh god, what did I come here for?" Tears come quickly, but she has no idea why she is crying. If anything, she's furious.

"Are you OK?" Jordan asks concerned.

"You know why they aren't after you? You are invisible. Just some ghost on static laced video," Jen laughs strangely with a quiet anger. "They think you are some saint."

"Why haven't you come by? I've tried to call you, but you just ignore me."

"How do you tell someone that you don't want to see them again?" Jen sighs.

At a loss for words, Jordan just stands there.

"Over at the Civic Center, my name is now on some record as a potential enemy combatant."

"I warned you that this could backfire," Jordan replies. "So now what? You want me to go turn myself in?"

"No, it's just that every time, you always come out ahead."

"What happened at the University? You call that getting ahead?" Jordan fires back. He moves toward her and she pulls back, almost afraid of his potential touch.

"What are you working on with Mark?" Jen retorts. "A project so black even the OverForce is asking about it?"

Jordan doesn't answer. He can't.

"So we're gonna have secrets between us now?" Jen cries out. "Are you kidding me? You damn loser!"

"You already know there are secrets between us."

"Let me tell you this, since you love your sword so much. A weapon cannot lead. It cannot teach. It cannot feel," Jen admonishes him. "When are you going to realize I am the real leader?"

"You're no leader," Jordan states flatly.

"You really are the Admiral's heir…you think I'm nothing," Jennifer says trembling. "You weren't born from him. His rotten blood runs in my veins."

"You have more genes in common with my pocket calculator than him."

"Jordan stop fighting me," Jen says, her eyes going wide. She is now trembling with rage. "It's easy to stand up to me now. One day it won't be and you will regret that day. I promise."

"So now you are true Nuhu princess? Aren't you?" Jordan says, struggling to calm down. "You said you didn't want to give up on us. That we had a history worth keeping. Why Jen? Why give up now?"

"I try to tell myself that I can love you, but it doesn't work. It makes me sad that I am this way, but there is no ignoring the truth. You are not worth the risk."

"For the last time…" Jordan offers, struggling to keep his anger under control, "…come with…"

"Fuck you Jordan," she snarls, punching a glass panel with her bare hand.

"Good-bye Jen," he says with reluctance. "I hope you find your happiness."

This statement seems to melt her rage for a second. "I will *never* hurt you," she promises, "no matter what, but don't expect any more from me."

"I love you," Jordan admits. "I think I always will."

"I know, but this time you can't catch me," she says sadly as her ability to speak fades away, her true self falling away into darkness. In an instant, the real Jen is gone.

Slowly, what has become the new Jennifer leaves. There is a vague, far away felling to apologize to Jordan and run into his arms, but this nonsensical idea soon fades away. She decides to go see Christian instead. He will understand her better. Suddenly, everything becomes so clear, whatever past she had with the human can be forgotten. She then finds herself smiling blissfully.

***

Feeling that he has no home, Jordan takes Mark's car and drives up into the headlands, looking for any kind of solace. Driving like a manic, he screams his head off as he cuts corners and throttles the very dangerous car. Any slip-up and he could end up in the bay…after a plunge of a few hundred feet. Reaching a dead end, he slams on the brakes, spinning the car. It stops short of a cliff.

He finds himself walking on that same windy bluff like so many times before. There is no wind this morning, just the pale purple glow of the rising sun against the ocean. There is also no Jennifer anymore. He worries that life will take everyone away.

The feeling of desperate loneliness that has always haunted him is now greater than ever. Perhaps it's just an orphan's guilt, but no, he made a mistake coming home. A man like him has no business thinking about family and love.

"Why God! Why?" he screams, his inner pain finally pouring out. "I loved her."

He stands on the cliff, looking out at the darkness as it pulls back to reveal the vastness of the sea. Just like a sunrise, happiness is a moment soon gone. God is strange, Jordan thinks, giving only tastes of heaven and mouthfuls of hell.

The old anger begins to swell in him. The old hate begins to churn. Why should he suffer when those who cause the pain smile? The images, the smells of the University attack are fierce and acid in his mind. He truly is an anachronism. He just wants to lash out at someone, something or anything to drown the pain within him.

He wants to kill.

Why then not let the hate out? Why not follow Jennifer's path? Perhaps everything would be better in ruin. Everyone would be happier in the equality of famine and destitution. War, his true companion. War the friend whom he has turned his back to. War the eraser of dreams and love.

But he has seen the face of war, a face with wide-open soulless eyes, a mouth full of decay and the skin of a long dead animal. A face that no one should see.

This is why he hates it.

Hate.

That word never seems to leave him, but he vows to fight against it. For true freedom to exist, there can be no blind devotion to flags or races. Perhaps, that is what his father was trying to tell him.

Rina's industrial-looking white car appears and parks behind him. An evil looking, darkly dressed man gets out it. He heads over to Jordan.

"Jen said I would find you out here," Mark says, looking like a man who has been living under a rock. "I guess you guys are done."

"You ever wonder why we even bother living? We pretend nothing is important while we hate ourselves on the inside," Jordan says, barely controlling his anger. A light wind blows across the grass as if trying to temper the fire within him. "A few years ago, I couldn't have imagined a world without Jen. Now what do I have left?"

An understanding Mark sits down next to his friend. He hands him a small bottle of chocolate milk, of all things. In the past, this always made Jordan feel better. Having no better resource, he stopped to buy one.

Smiling like a little kid, Jordan takes the sad little beverage and takes a sip. This seems to let the steam out of him a bit.

"I never understood why you loved that stuff so much," Mark says, studying the dark outline of the horizon. "Now that I'm older, I know. You were never allowed to have it. The funny thing is…today you can."

"So what?" Jordan sighs. "It's just a stupid little thing."

"Take away the little things and eventually the big will follow. The world I dream of is of big ideas. Big ideas start small. When you were a kid, did you ever think you could have one of those?"

"No."

"Then here's to the little victories. Small or large, you didn't lose. What you did at the University made a difference," Brushing himself off, Mark stands up and looks at the sunrise. "One day that sun will rise for you. So let's go see tomorrow. Better worlds have to be made and no one can do it alone, not even me."

As the sun light brings Jordan out from shadow, he stands up. Nothing is going to change with him sitting on his ass. Maybe a better world is waiting, somewhere under a sun that has not yet risen. And for Jordan, that is a little idea worth fighting for.

WAR DAWN

With the flash of plasma cutter lighting up the room, Mark is a man of focused intensity as he expertly divides up a piece of Exitor-composite. His abandoned airport hideout has become a retreat for the emotionally wounded engineer. Seeing Jordan enter the lab, Mark shuts down the ferociously powerful machine and removes his safety mask.

"Took your sweet time," he crows.

"That thing would make a nice little canon for the Ventus," Jordan says and points to the cutter. He puts down a couple of coffees and a bag of pastries next to it.

"Yup let me latch a big heavy tub of goo to the back of the ship," Mark howls knowing that the weight of the glamorous torch would be something grotesque. "Precision cutting is not required of a weapon."

"How are you doing about Rina?" Jordan asks bluntly. "I've been trying not to ask, but you never leave this place."

"About as good as you with Jen without the histrionics," Mark replies and takes a seat in singed and ripped old sofa. "I think about what they are doing her and it just…" He looks out across his state of the art lab but finds nothing of beauty to replace what he has lost. "It makes me feel angry that I can't do anything about it. Hateful at everything."

"Understandable," Jordan sighs and goes to look at an open instrumentation panel. He wonders if Mark has pulled all the controls out of the Ventus again, but before he can ask Mark speaks up.

"How does your dad feel about Jen…about what happened at the University?"

"Don't know. He's been very quiet," Jordan says with a shrug. "The Arlington just arrived today for maneuvers off the coast. I'm supposed to meet him later today."

"Should be a fun conversation," Mark sniffs and rams a donut into his mouth.

***

Rushing past people to her first class flight to Hong Kong, the always elegant looking Emily Wu is annoyed by the non-stop chiming of her phone…which she had been ignoring. Like some nocturnal spider, she pines for the comfort of her dark, isolated office, especially after having acted inappropriately. This is especially true after taking someone's life...today its true for vastly different reason. Knowing the calling won't stop, she walks over to a quiet section and takes the call from her assistant, Juno.

"What is it?" Emily says coldly, frustrated over her indecision with Jordan. Instead of embracing her feelings, she is running from them. A few weeks ago she wanted to end her life and now she is rushing to get back to it.

"Mr. Wu requests that you delay your flight," Juno says with an obvious hint of fear. "Um...the OverForce will apparently have some new equipment they want you to analyze and inspect."

"Why can't they get their own people? I just want to go home," she sniffs as she thinks back to the hotel room. She really shouldn't have run off on Jordan like that. Men like him, much like her, don't take kindly to being treated like pieces of meat.

"They are going to seize Mark Whatley's..."

"Tell Mr. Wu no. I'm tired," Emily says in a huff and hangs up. A look of panic takes hold over her face. She begins to rush to the top of San Francisco Main Transportation Hub and scrolls up Jordan's contact info. Again, she hesitates. Does she really want to get involved? Her fingers provide the answer as they tap the call icon.

"Sierra?" Jordan answers as he chews on a bran muffin.

"Are you with Mark?"

"Yes. So what?" Jordan replies. "About this morning..."

"The OverForce is on its way. Get out of there."

"Oh shit," Jordan growls. "Mark is not going to leave."

"Don't do anything rash. I'll call Malone," she says and hangs up as she boards a Sky Skiff heading for Marin.

***

With the shape of a heavy weight boxer, Martin Malone is no push-over and does not look like your typical nerd. He fills a room and dominates any conversation just with his mere presence. As he stands at a design table with his engineering team, he takes a second to look out at his vast ship yards spread about before him. Several titanic warships are in various stages of assembly. His phone rings and seeing the caller, he quickly excuses himself and goes into an empty office.

282

"Emily, I'm busy," he says in what could be a joking tone or not.

"The OverForce is going to raid Whatley's lab," she says with clear desperation in her voice. "Just got the call from my office."

"Since when do you care about Whatley?"

There is no answer.

"I see...not the professor...perhaps the assistant," Malone says with a slight laugh. "I will send good people to help *them*."

"Send people? Fight?" she repeats stunned. This is not the answer she was expecting.

"The time for playing nice with the secret police is over," he states and hangs up. "Not everyone is a pushover."

***

As he disparately looks for weapons, Jordan's phone suddenly goes dead as one final message comes through, "Martin sending help." He grabs a surprised Mark as he comes out of the toilet, pulling him toward a window. There is no one outside...yet. "The OverForce is coming," Jordan warns, "and we don't even have a shotgun in the place."

"Bring them on," Mark says looking more excited than scared. "We have full autonomy here. Fuck them." He moves away from the window and grabs a device from his desk. "This is a military installation and they are not welcome."

Jordan jumps as an alarm blares to life.

"Code 101. Security Override. Code 101," an electronic voice warns as the perimeter guns go down. A row of dozens of bland white vehicles begins to descend down into the little airport. It's a massive show of force for an agency that likes to operate discretely.

"Lovely 101, the government backdoor access code," Mark tells Jordan as he strums the little remote. "The OverForce think they are cutting me out, but I have a few surprises for them."

"It's not worth dying over a plane," Jordan states, grabbing him by the arm. "Whatever you are planning, don't. Let Malone fix this."

"I do have my orders. I stay no matter what," Mark says with a cold determination. His eyes are twitching with adrenaline. He wants this fight to happen. "You probably already know that. Malone knows that too."

The two young men go out to meet the ominous convey of government cars. These are not just regular cars, their armored.

Bristling with weapons, a few OverForce agents come toward them. All of their faces hidden behind black helmets. One stands forward from the rest.

"I have a warrant to secure all technology at this location," the faceless lead officer states as his comrades take positions behind the vehicles as if anticipating a fight. "You're co-operation is expected. If you oppose, you may file a complaint with our regional commander."

"The OverForce is a civilian agency," Mark yells loudly and steps forward bravely. "This installation is working on highly classified Air Corps research. You'll have to go through the Pacific Command Admiralty to get any kind of warrant that isn't a pile of pig shit."

The officer moves closer and pulls out a pistol, holding it by his side. "Are you declining to co-operate?"

Knowing what is coming, Jordan looks at Mark and hopes he has some truly spectacular trick up his sleeve. All they have is a sword between them, no cover and no element of surprise. Having just been through a hellish battle a few weeks earlier, he decides to speak up, "I'm an Officer of the State. You cannot just..."

"Two people can be erased. We do it all the time," the lead O.F. says coolly as the sound of energy weapons being charged up fills the icy air. There must be at least forty agents. "Stand aside or be put down."

Mark smiles. He was hoping they would say that. He hits a remote in his hand and the perimeter guns suddenly lurch back to life, spraying a hell fire down upon the OverForce. Several of the Officers in front are ripped to shreds as Mark and Jordan split up. Mark dives for the main lab as Jordan races back toward the hanger. The guns fire endlessly, ripping up the OverForce vehicles as if they were mere soda cans.

Getting smart, the surviving OverForce agents fire a rocket at the closest perimeter gun and proceed to knock out the others in quick succession. With their numbers only cut by a few, they rush after the two men with no fear. They should be afraid.

The main lab is quiet and motionless as the OverForce spreads out. Suddenly, two robotic arms lift two plates of Exitor composite up creating a wall. Firing at will, the OverForce's bolts fling off the metal as if no more than spit balls. Having exhausted their energy clips, they must reload. This is Mark's cue and he makes quite an entrance.

Decked out in his plasma safety gear, he swings out the heavy cutting device. A warning is flashing on its control screen "safety features have been overridden!" He taps a button and opens fire. The hot plasma streaks across the lab passing through all obstructions as if they were all made from cardboard. The hapless agents have no defense against the sizzling attack. Some have gaps on their bodies the size of bowling balls. Mark yells out in defiance, "Come on! Come get some you assholes!"

Outside, Jordan is cornered and cannot make it to the safety of the hanger. He is pinned down and cannot fight at long distance with just Novo. One of the armored cars darts by him and stops by the hanger doors. The OverForce agents quickly attach explosives to the doors. The massive blast reveals the small plane hidden inside. In retrospect, Jordan is happy he was not in the hanger as debris rains down around him.

But then out of the explosion's smoke, two warriors emerge and attack the OverForce by surprise. Jordan recognize Master Kenji, but the second is a mystery. His old master cuts through the agents as if slicing a row of celery sticks in half. Kenji is so swift and silent that they O.F.'s are totally non-responsive. But it does not take them long to regroup, they begin to charge the sword master, firing at will. He flings his sword out and to Jordan's amazement it boomerangs around the group as if on remote control, clearing the space around him in a shower of blood. He's never seen a sword used like that...then again he's never seen a sword *fly*. It's scientifically impossible, but he doesn't have time to dwell on physics.

The second warrior then sweeps in to cover Kenji. She is a delicate, thin woman with two brilliantly silver swords and an equally silver mask. Her technique is more refined than even Kenji and she is twice as fast at cutting through OverForce armor. In fact, she is inhumanly fast and this makes up for her lack of size. Between the two, they open a hole for Jordan to escape.

Pointing, Kenji signals for his student to head for the hanger. The young pilot dives into the melee and fights his way toward the Ventus. To his misfortune, the bulk of the OverForce agents have made their way here. Jordan finds himself being nearly surrounded. He begins to butcher them mercilessly, but they do not retreat.

There is the sudden hiss of a sword to his back. He turns to defend himself but finds a bloody mound of the OverForce bodies instead. The heavy smoke is making seeing difficult. Jordan can only make out that his silent guardian is brandishing a black sword and there is no doubt in his mind who this is. Between the two of them, they clear out the hanger.

Wrapped in black from head to toe, the mysterious warrior soon runs off toward the main lab. Her black sword leaving a trail of blood from her surgical attacks.

To Jordan's horror, Mark *has* disassembled the cockpit of the Ventus. All the flight controls are missing rendering it seemingly immobile. But before he can think, Jordan sees the dark shape of a Gun-Orb descending toward the entrance of the hanger. It arms its weapons and takes aim at the Ventus. If the OverForce can't have it, they are going to destroy it. He has no choice and dives for cover.

Without thinking, Jordan looks over at the Ventus wishing it would move. As the Gun-Orb fires, the Ventus moves aside. Jordan catches on and orders the Ventus to escape under the Gun-Orb.

The little plane zooms away and flies under the garish death machine, though is too crippled to fly properly and skids into the near-by marsh. The Gun-Orb turns to follow it.

With a tremendous shudder, the whole building shakes. Jordan thinks he knows what it is, but can only hope to be right. A huge shadow descends across the whole airport as an ear piercing howl rolls over them.

Stumbling outside, Jordan does not see what he expected. Instead, he is greeted to the sights of OverForce reinforcements. A line of Gun-Orbs and transports fills the horizon. However, he is only concerned about one of them. Taking aim at the Ventus, the first Gun-Orb then suddenly explodes as it is hit by a cannon blast.

A stunned Jordan is knocked on his butt by the blast. Then to his astonishment, he looks behind him and sees his father's battleship, the Arlington, descending. The sight of this massive warship over this quiet San Francisco suburb is a sight to say the least.

The Arlington takes up a protective position over the airport and aims its mighty guns at the OverForce reinforcements who show no sign of retreat.

"Lt. Colony, get me the OverForce regional commander on a channel immediately," an angry Admiral Grant orders. "Lt. Zhu, keep those ships in our sights. If they try to pass us, blow them out of the sky."

A stodgy looking man appears on one of the Arlington's display screens. He seems sweaty and nervous. "Admiral Grant! You have no right to fire upon my people!"

"It's obvious you have no control over your dogs and wild dogs need to be put down," Admiral Grant fires back. "Your team infiltrated a secure Air Corps base. This is a closed facility and the any trespasser, government or not, is to be shot on sight."

"That's not acceptable," the OverForce commander barks back. "Pull back. We are landing."

"Full broadside now!" Admiral Grant orders and instantly the sky is turned yellow and orange with gun fire. In a second, the OverForce reinforcements are vaporized. He then turns back to the stunned OverForce commander. "Unless you have an answer to that and want to provide my staff with more target practice, you are done here."

"This will not be the end Admiral Grant!" the OverForce commander screams and cuts off communications.

"Lt. Zhu engage a patrol pattern until the facility is re-secured," Admiral Grant quietly instructs. "Ready my shuttle and a security detail."

"Maybe the OverForce will think twice next time," Lt. Colony snickers as he looks at smoldering remains of the OverForce task force fall from the sky. "One day of justice for thousands of crimes. Still doesn't add up."

Admiral Grants nods in agreement, but then says, "They won't let this go unchallenged. They won't forget."

Below in the battle damaged airport, Jordan and Mark walk amongst the bodies of the slain OverForce officers. Unlike himself, Jordan seems distant and distressed. "It never ends," he says quietly standing over a ripped open body. "They kill. We kill."

A vengeance filled Mark ignores him and orders, "We'd better get the Ventus under covers before the whole county shows up to take a look. God. We could use Rina right now." He moves toward his invention which is half-stuck in mud. "Trying to keep this quiet is not going to be easy."

"Who's the lady in the mask?" Jordan asks as the Silver Mask goes about making sure all the OverForce agents are dead. Kenji is by her side keeping watch. "She's deadly."

Mark says, not really knowing her that well, "She's been with Malone as long as I know. You should be happy that you weren't alone this time." He begins to examine his ship and looks deeply upset. "This is a nightmare. How the hell did you get it out here?"

Not feeling victorious, Jordan steps away from Mark and wanders the decimated airport. He's seen fights like this before and this is the aspect he finds the most troubling. Within his sightline, he can see homes only a few miles away. People he knows live there. The smoldering ruins of the OverForce task force dropping down upon them. No, there is no escape for him, for anyone, from what is coming. As strong as he may be, he cannot stop the wave of war from crashing upon the nation. He can only oppose it and he will…with all his heart. Jordan looks up to the sky as his father's ship. He feels a momentary rush of pride as he sees his father's shuttle landing, but it is soon gone.

A melancholy Sierra is standing in the distance, but she does not approach. They are share a knowing look, but no more. She waves good-by at him and then disappears behind a cloud of lingering smoke. As always, she only stokes the fires in his heart for a moment before leaving him cold.

War is here and he can't believe it, though for now it's just a small vicious affair. Staring at the bodies of the fallen, Jordan feels as if a huge weight has been put on his shoulders. There will be more blood and he cannot escape. "Little victories," Jordan says with a hint of sadness as he talks to his sword, "won't be enough to stop the violence that is coming."

The sword sparkles, revealing the words:

"There are no little victories."

A concerned Admiral Grant comes walking up to him and stands quietly next to his adopted son. Jordan looks tired and drained by the battle. The Admiral then says to him, "The cat's out of the bag. Soon, there will be no hiding."

An angry Jordan responds, "The rebels didn't lift a finger for the students at the University, but to defend a weapon they send a battleship?" He struggles to keep his temper under control. "I don't see this like you all do. Dad, this is home."

A patient Admiral Grant hides his internal struggle too. He knows that Jen has been converted…just like his wife so many years ago. He's been living a lie to keep his true family…his son…safe. Now, he can no longer protect Jordan. Today might have about protecting a weapon for most, but not for him. He understands Jordan's frustration though. "We fight to show a hidden monster," he says mournfully. "People will get hurt. It's inevitable. Some of those people will be people we love."

Not accepting that answer, Jordan admonishes, "Monsters are everywhere. Around us, next to us, even inside of us. Who are the real monsters? Are we not monsters too?"

"You pick the side that is the least of evils. You compromise. You follow orders. That's how I've always lived my life."

With Jordan's sword shining brightly in the morning sunlight, he looks back at his father with a fierce convection and says, "Then I'm not a good solider anymore, I can't do that."

"Son if you can figure out what true evil is without becoming corrupt yourself, that is indeed a miracle," Admiral Grant sighs as his soldiers fan out, securing the airfield. "I only know one thing; truly evil people have no regrets. I have plenty. One regret is that I wish I had fought harder for things I cared for, but I didn't. I'm not a monster nor a monster killer…not by a long shot."

Jordan says, looking alone and distant even though surrounded by a flood of activity, "What matters to me are the people around me." He sees Mark struggling with the Ventus. "Why fight for things that cannot die?"

Admiral Grant starts to laugh, "You are starting to know what really matters. Better now at the start then at the end." He points to Jordan's sword. "Lopez said that your sword is not a weapon. He said one day you would understand. Today, it's good enough that you know you are not a soldier…that you're just a human. A better one than even me."

"Human?" Jordan says, finally cracking a smile. His father says the word "human" as if a compliment. Maybe it is. In fact, he thinks, there are no humans and no Nuhu…only good and evil. "Maybe your time has passed, but mine hasn't. I will not have your regrets." He looks at his father directly in the eyes with understanding and care. "You know…a lady once said that I am the last knight of the realm."

"Why would she say that?" the Admiral asks with curiosity.

"Because there is one thing I'm really good at," Jordan states and sheathes his sword, "killing monsters."

Made in the USA
Charleston, SC
23 November 2014